PRAISE FOR

A Place Called Winter

"In this delicious novel of illicit love and bold reinvention, Patrick Gale takes us on a great Northern American Adventure with all the fleet-footed grace of his much-loved British family sagas." —Armistead Maupin

"Absorbing, moving, and beautifully written, with echoes of E. M. Forster which I found especially enjoyable." —Amanda Craig

"[A] fascinating novel...A PLACE CALLED WINTER does not offer resolution, but it does offer hope that emotional truth and loyalty to that truth may be a way forward." —Helen Dunmore, *Guardian* (UK)

"A mesmerising storyteller; this novel is written with intelligence and warmth." —*The Times* (UK)

"A tender tale of loss and love...Neatly constructed and written in a prose of beautiful lucidity, Gale's novel offers up an absorbing and often moving story." —*Sunday Times* (UK)

"This is an intensely personal book. Gale was inspired by a true tale from his own family history, and the depth of feeling shows. It's one gay man reaching out to another across a century of social change, and his most powerfully moving novel yet." —*Independent* (UK)

"A dramatic and affecting portrayal of dislocation, extreme environments, and the traumatic effects of enforced secrecy."

—*Observer* (UK)

"What Gale does so well is to delineate the unpremeditated consequences of actions...The final chapter left me with a lump in my throat." —*Guardian* (UK)

"Gale is not a sentimental writer; he's vividly aware of hardship and despair, but the overwhelming emotion in this fine book is one of tender, life-affirming joy." —*Sun* (UK)

"His best book yet." —*Country Life* (UK)

"This is a convincing and fascinating portrait of daily life over a century ago in a far away place. The mixture of adventure, historical saga and romance is utterly heartwrenching."

—*Sunday Mirror* (UK)

"Gale employs his gift as a writer to will such pockets of tolerance retrospectively into existence—for the sake of his relative, as well, perhaps, as for all of us. Humanity does not look quite so wretched through Patrick Gale's eyes." —*Spectator* (UK)

"A novel that gets under your skin." —*Irish Times* (UK)

"Lightness of touch, one of Gale's characters observes, is desirable in a novelist, and it is one of Gale's virtues...Rich in atmosphere and period detail...this enjoyable tale is both witty and poignant." —*Daily Mail* (UK)

A
PLACE
CALLED
WINTER

P̶ATRICK G̶ALE

GRAND CENTRAL
PUBLISHING

New York   Boston

Copyright © 2015 by Patrick Gale
Reading Group Guide copyright © 2016 by Hachette Book Group, Inc.

Originally published in the U.K. by Tinder Press, an imprint of Headline Publishing Group, March 2015

Grand Central Publishing
Hachette Book Group
1290 Avenue of the Americas
New York, NY 10104

www.HachetteBookGroup.com

Printed in the United States of America

First U.S. edition: March 2016

Grand Central Publishing is a division of Hachette Book Group, Inc.
The Grand Central Publishing name and logo are trademarks of Hachette Book Group, Inc.

The Hachette Speakers Bureau provides a wide range of authors for speaking events. To find out more, go to www.hachettespeakersbureau.com or call (866) 376-6591.

The publisher is not responsible for websites (or their content) that are not owned by the publisher.

ISBN: 978-1-4555-9408-5
LCCN: 2015955178

For Aidan Hicks

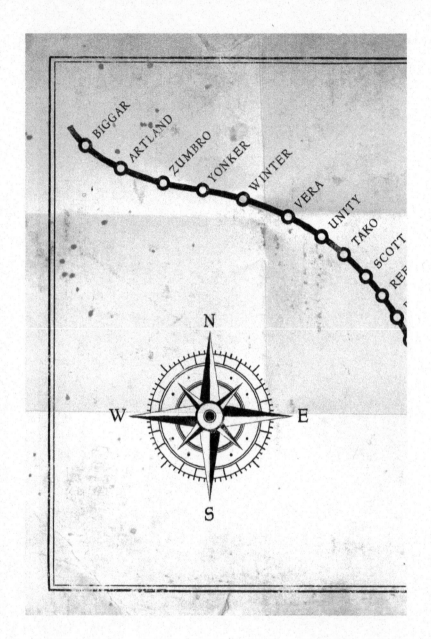

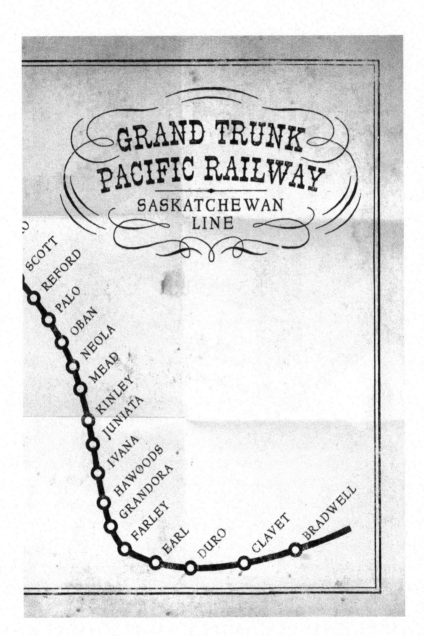

BETHEL

A violent and excited patient is forcibly taken
by his legs and plunged head foremost into an
ordinary swimming bath. He is not permitted
the use of his limbs when in the water, but is
detained there, or taken out and plunged again
in the bath, until the required effect of
tranquility is produced.

L. Forbes Winslow, *The Turkish Bath in
Mental Disorders* (1896)

Chapter One

The attendants came for him as a pair, as always. Some of them were kind and meant well. Some were frightened and, like first-timers at a steer branding, hid their fear in swearing and brutality. But this pair was of the most unsettling kind, the sort that ignored him. They were talking to one another as they came for him and continued to talk to one another as they fastened the muff on his wrists and led him along the corridor to the treatment room.

He was the first in that day, so the echoing room, where even ordinary speech was magnified to a shout, was quiet except for the sound of filling baths. There were eight baths in a row, only three feet apart. From a distance they looked like ordinary baths. Close to, they were revealed as having a kind of hammock slung in the water.

"I don't need the hammock," he told them. "Or the muff. If you want me to climb into a bath and lie there, I'll do it. I don't need the hammock. Please?"

Ignoring him, the attendants broke off from their mumbled conversation. One unbuttoned Harry's pajama jacket. The other undid the cord on his pajama trousers so that they dropped to the floor.

"This is to calm you," one said, as though reading out an official notice. "You've been excitable and this is to calm you down." He tweaked Harry's jacket off his shoulders. "In you get."

"I'd much rather have an ordinary bath. Please, not the belts."

In a practiced movement, one of them seized his ankles while the other took his shoulders and they tipped him and lowered him into the nearest bath so that he was held in the hot water by the hammock. The temperature was high but not unpleasant. It was the loss of control that was unpleasant. One attendant held Harry's wrists in place near his waist while the other buckled a thick leather belt across his chest. They held his legs in place with a second belt, then they tugged up a thick tarpaulin cover, like a sort of tent, to enclose the bath entirely. There was an opening in this which they brought up around his shoulders and secured about his neck with straps so that as little steam as possible would escape. He was now held, immobile, in the flow of hot water with only his head on view.

"Please," he said. "Don't leave me."

The attendants wandered away, still talking. They passed two more attendants bringing in someone else who was shouting that they were trying to murder him. When the new man was undressed, he pissed on the attendant crouching in front of him and the ensuing fuss gave him the opportunity to run away. There were curses and yells from the corridor and whistles were blown, then came the muffled sounds of someone being kicked and sat upon.

The man's silence, when they brought him back in and secured him in the bath immediately next to Harry's, was worse than any shouting. And when they left him alone in the running water, he twisted his head so as to stare at Harry, which was more disturbing yet. Harry gazed through the clouds of steam at the taps and the sea-green tiles, and tried to pretend he wasn't really there.

"I know you," the man said, quietly but insistently. "I know you I know you I—"

He woke with a convulsion and sensed his own shout had roused him. He wasn't in the dormitory. The dormitory had so many bedsteads crammed into it that some, including Harry's, were in the middle of the room. The bedstead here was iron and painted white, but there the resemblance ended. He was in a small, wood-lined room, painted a calm sky blue and with thick white curtains across the little window. It was simply furnished. There was a rag rug beside the bed and a bedside table with a lamp and matches on it. His boots were on the floor and his coat on a hook above them. A suit that wasn't his hung on a hanger on the next peg along. On a plain wooden chair was a neat stack of underwear, shirts and socks he knew were not his either.

Wide awake now, he found water on the washstand in a jug and washed. He stared at his face in the little spotted mirror hanging there. A gaunt stranger stared back at him. He did not remember growing a beard, but, of course, where he had come from there were no razors and no looking glasses either: nothing to wound or inflame.

Dressing in the spotlessly clean clothes, which fitted him so well he might have been measured for them as he slept, he made an effort to be calm. *Breathe*, he told himself. *Remember to breathe*. And he remembered another man's voice telling him that very thing and had to sit abruptly on the little bed to compose himself, so acute and ambivalent was the memory stirred.

Venturing out into dazzling morning light, he would have thought he had woken in a kind of heaven, were it not for the lingering sense that hell was flickering just out of sight, whichever way he turned his gaze. He knew he had been in hell. He had livid marks on his wrists and ankles where restraints had cut and bruised his flesh, and when he moved his back, it still ached from blows and kicks that had rained upon it.

Earlier than that, before hell, his memories were more damaged still. These memories lay in rooms he couldn't enter. In the quiet moments of lucidity between baths, he had approached them closely enough to sense they were wrapped in a grief so powerful that even to put his hand on the doorknobs would fry his skin.

Now he was in a river valley with lush grass cropped by sheep and a couple of languid cows, running down to a broad, brown river on whose powerful current he had already seen several fallen trees sail past from left to right. Great ranges of blue iced mountains lay to either side, their lower slopes thickly forested. A church bell rang somewhere off to the left. The beauty of it, the intensity of the colors and the relative silence, overwhelmed him for a moment and he sat on a little bench to recover.

He was not insane, although he felt sure the experience of being treated as though he were would soon have deprived him of his wits had it continued much longer. He looked up, attention snagged by a buzzard's cry. *I know a hawk from a handsaw*, he thought. It was an asylum, not a prison, where he had been, but he had been deprived of liberty, and, so far as he knew, without trial.

The attendants had come for him as usual, after breakfast, and he had assumed that the endless, soul-eroding process of pacifying him by water treatments was to continue. He marginally preferred the cold wrap to the continuous bath, if only because it was administered in a smaller room where he had precious peace and quiet, provided he didn't begin to shout out in a panic. If anything, though, it was even more constraining than the bath, involving as it did being tightly wrapped in a sheet dipped in cold water, around which were wound two more sheets, a rubber mat and then a blanket, before he was left secured to a wire bed frame, sometimes for three hours, quietly dripping first with water, then with sweat.

Today, however, he wasn't to have a treatment.

"You're going on a journey," one of them told him. "Young Mr. Ormshaw has picked you to help with his research, so we need you nice and quiet."

They rolled up his sleeve and administered an injection that was clearly a powerful sedative, for by the time they had given him socks to wear and handed him back his old boots and overcoat, he was so foggy in the head that he couldn't have spoken any of the questions that crowded his mind.

His little cabin had a shaded terrace on one side of it. It was one of several such, clearly built from identical kits, arranged in a half-circle before a large log-framed house that resembled some fanciful idea of a Tyrolean chalet and on to whose veranda he half expected chorus girls to emerge in dirndls, holding hoops of paper flowers and singing of love and springtime.

For it was springtime, which was presumably why the river was so mightily in spate. The greening woods behind him were full of birdsong and, sitting on his terrace, he watched birds, chipmunks and squirrels darting back and forth on the grass, going about the exhausting spring business of putting on fat and finding a mate.

He had no sense of where he was or how far he and the silent attendant with him had traveled. Being expected to board a train had stirred up in him such violent misgivings that they had been obliged to administer a second dose of the sedative, so he had slept like a drunkard for much of the journey. The latter part of the voyage, by road, was undertaken in darkness. All he registered as he tumbled into a bed whose linen had been chilled by sharp mountain air, was relief that his bed was on its own, and that he could hear only his own sighs and breathing, not the shouts and weeping of others.

A gong sounded from the main house. Harry flinched, prepared for the idyll to be broken by orderlies or nurses, but glanced across and saw only a simply uniformed maid standing by an open door. Noticing him, she raised a hand in greeting, tapped the gong a few more times as though for his benefit, then slipped inside again. The door of the next cabin along opened and there emerged a slender blonde woman wearing respectable but antique clothes.

"Good morning," she said in a high voice, and he rose to meet her. As she offered him a small, lace-fringed hand, he saw she was considerably older than her figure suggested.

"How do you do," he said.

"Are you going to breakfast?"

"I...I imagine so."

"You must be hungry after your journey," she said. She had one of those little-girl voices which so often seemed to mask an aggressive nature. "We heard you arrive but were under strict instructions to leave you in peace. I'm Mabel. We use no surnames or titles here. The good doctor is Quakerish in his leanings." She laughed, skittishly.

"I'm Harry," he told her.

"Delighted. Harry, let me take you to breakfast."

"Is this a hospital?" he began, and she laughed again.

"Another forbidden word. You're quite the rebel, I can see! It's a *community*. A therapeutic community. Now, here's Bruno."

A mannish woman in a boxily tailored outfit, a sort of suit, had emerged from a third cabin. She shook Harry's hand and fired off a series of questions about his journey he felt quite unable to answer, not having been aware even of where he had come from. She was gently rebuked by Mabel, which she took in good part, and they proceeded toward the house. Other doors had opened, and all told, some eight of them were now walking that way. Apart from the two ladies he had met, all were men. One of them, a black man Harry assumed was someone's servant, stood back respectfully and, naturally, unacknowledged, until the rest of them had passed.

As they neared it, the door to the cabin closest to the house opened. A tall Indian woman had emerged, dressed in quietly elegant Western clothes. She ducked her head as he looked at her, showing off the black hair she wore in a thick cascade. Mabel gave a little cough, drawing his attention back to herself.

There were two rooms at their disposal, both overlooking the river. One was the snug library, into which he merely glanced; the other the dining room, in which their host bade them all a general good morning before singling Harry out for greeting.

Harry recognized him as one of the doctors who had occasionally questioned him at the asylum—a tall, dark-haired young man with a thick mustache that emphasized his sad, moist eyes. Instinctively Harry stiffened.

"It's all right, Harry. You're among friends now," the doctor said and shook his hand emphatically in both of his. "Did you manage to sleep in the deafening quiet?"

"Yes, thank you, Doctor. Mr. Ormshaw."

"I'm Gideon, here, Harry. Now, let's see..." He glanced at his pocket watch. "At ten o'clock please come to my study."

Breakfast was spread out on the sideboard in a sequence of steaming dishes. "No meat or alcohol here," Mabel told him in a murmur. "Gideon believes they are destabilizing."

"Thank God for coffee," Bruno added. She noticed that Harry was standing, staring. "Are you all right?" she asked.

"Do...do..."

She watched kindly as he stammered. "Take your time," she murmured.

"Do we help ourselves?" he asked at last.

"Yes."

"And...where are the attendants?"

"Bless you, there are no attendants here."

They were informal to the extent of serving themselves and sitting where they chose. To his surprise, the Indian woman and the Negro had joined them. Unsurprisingly, they each ate alone. One of the men was a nervous giggler. Mabel was a person who chatted even when no one was talking to her. It made him wonder what she was like when there was no company to animate her. Bruno hung on her every word, clearly an abject slave, but was constantly passed over by Mabel, who seemed to regard mere female attention as cheap currency.

With their tidy spring suits and small touches of elegance, a silk handkerchief here, a pocket watch there, the men clustered at one end of a table reminded him of something. It was only as he watched them roll their napkins at breakfast's end that he realized it was the gentlemen of the Gaiety chorus. In London. A lifetime ago.

Each resident was assigned a napkin ring of a different design. Harry's had a pattern of ivy leaves. Feeling the heavy white damask between his fingers, he struggled to remember the last time he had used a napkin.

"A far cry from the snakepit, isn't it?" one of the men said, watching him, and was shushed by Mabel.

"We don't speak of such places here," she said, then turned a kind face on Harry. "Gideon believes in the healing power of civilized touches," she said.

Both black man and Indian had left the room without his

noticing. Emerging on to the terrace, after hot breakfast rolls as soft and pale as infancy, he saw that the man was at work in the garden already, tidying the path edges with a spade and tossing the trimmings into a barrow. Perhaps Mr. Ormshaw was a socialist as well as a Quaker, to have patients dine with his servants.

A small macaw had been set out on a perch to enjoy the sun. It was discreetly shackled to its post, he saw. It waved its wings in greeting as he emerged, displaying feathers so bright they scorched the eye, before picking a nut from its little bowl and falling to preening. For the second time since waking, Harry was overwhelmed by the clarity and beauty of it all and felt he might cry.

"Look but don't touch," Bruno said behind him. "Gideon took him on when he bit a girl's finger clean in two. We all have our unspeakable pasts here..." And she made him a kind of salute with her fingertips before striding down the steps and off through the grounds with the air of one taking a constitutional.

There was a piercing whistle from across the valley and he saw the steam from a train making its way through the trees and caught a flash of its paintwork. The sight sent a painful shudder through him which he felt briefly distort his face. A cuckoo clock, surely chosen in irony, was chirping ten in the hall as their host stepped out to find him.

"This way, Harry," he said.

For all the informality, Gideon had not eaten breakfast with them. Perhaps, despite his socialism, he found the maintenance of a certain distance useful? He led the way through the library, where several residents were reading or writing, out into a sort of conservatory and into his consulting room on the far side, which stuck out from one corner of the house so as to command a fine view of the river.

He stood with Harry admiring the swirling waters for a minute.

"The mighty Athabasca," he said.

"Does it ever flood?" Harry asked.

"Oh, yes. I lost my dog to it last winter."

"How upsetting."

"There was a hole in the ice and the silly thing was fascinated by the way the water repeatedly splashed out of it. He wouldn't stop going over there, so I kept him tied up. But then some kind person let him off and he fell through and drowned before we could cut him out."

"Have you forgiven them yet?"

The doctor smiled. "Not yet," he said. "I forgave the resident right away—she was so upset. Forgiving the river may take a while longer."

They sat on either side of his mahogany desk, on which he had an open file.

"So, Harry. Welcome to Bethel. How was breakfast?"

"Delicious, thank you."

"Good. This isn't an asylum, although everyone here is what my colleagues at Essondale—where you were—would call mentally ill. All of you have displayed behavior or declared opinions that have caused people to want you put out of the way.

"I happen to be making some of those behaviors my particular study. I depart from my colleagues in regarding them not as pathological but as intrinsic to a personality type. And I have won the state's trust sufficiently to have been allowed to bring some of you here to help me with my research. You are not under lock and key. You are at liberty to walk in the gardens, to follow the trails in the woods and even to go into Hinton, should you wish. All I ask is that nobody leave the immediate grounds unaccompanied and that you always let me know your whereabouts by signing yourselves out in the register on the hall table.

"I also ask that you respect one another's privacy; we all have stories but I prefer those stories to emerge voluntarily, not through interrogation.

"I ask that you respect one another's differences, too. You may already have seen—you almost certainly will see—behavior you might regard as odd or even wrong. But remember that, in the eyes of the attendants at Essondale, or wherever, your behavior has been odd or wrong as well.

"Here endeth the homily. Do you have any questions, Harry?"

"Only..." Harry began. "It's so different here. Like a private house."

"It is a private house." Gideon smiled. "It's my house."

"Do we pay fees?"

"You are all here as my guests. When you leave, if you choose to send a donation for the furthering of my work, I won't stop you. I inherited a certain amount from my father and it pleases me to spend it this way."

Harry sensed the good doctor and his father had not been in sympathy.

"So. I need to ask you a few things before we start..."

He rattled off a series of questions. What was Harry's name and birth date, where did he live, who was the king, who was the prime minister, how would he react to a slug beneath his shoe, a cat being tormented by small boys, a naked woman in a public place. Harry avoided crushing the slug, chased off the boys and covered the woman with a blanket.

"So," Gideon said. "In the crudest terms, we have established that you are not insane or dangerous. You are, however, suffering from a trauma, a trauma not unlike that which we've seen in all too many men returning from Flanders with battle scars to the mind. Harry, I plan to use hypnosis to help your mind open the doors it is so desperately holding closed. Has anyone ever hypnotized you before?"

"No."

"No need to look apprehensive. You will be aware throughout, and if I find you are becoming upset, I will bring the procedure to an end. Agreed?"

Harry nodded.

"Hard to take your eyes off the river, isn't it?"

"Yes."

"That's good. I want you to sit over here in the armchair. That's it. Sit back. Take a few deep breaths. Relax. Why do you laugh?"

"Sorry. You just reminded me of someone I used to know."

"Happy memories, I hope."

"Yes," Harry told him, surprised by a memory of lying on a narrow bed, listening to the sounds of a Jermyn Street afternoon through an open window. "From this distance, I believe they are."

"So. Deep breaths. That's it. Relax. And keep your eyes on the river. Find a point in its middle, where the current is strong. Imagine the current is flowing through you. It's sweeping through your mind, sweeping all thoughts away. Your mind is just a chamber. An empty chamber, quite white, utterly peaceful. There are no rules here. You can speak your thoughts and nobody will know. Nobody will judge you. Do you understand?"

"Yes."

"Good. Harry?"

"Yes?"

"Tell me who you love."

STRAWBERRY VALE

England has always been disinclined to accept
human nature.

E. M. Forster, *Maurice*

Chapter Two

Harry Cane's father had died of boredom. The medical diagnosis had been apoplexy, its unofficial translation a surfeit of rich foods and alcohol. The root cause, though, Harry felt sure, was leisure, and the boredom it engendered. Harry's father had in the past lived for work and had not known how to fill his time from the moment he sold his business and stepped sideways into the dubious luxury of idleness.

For most of his twenty-eight years, Harry's life had been largely, complacently male. And he had the good fortune not to have to work for a living. His father had done very well setting up one of the first horse-drawn omnibus services south of the river, which he had expanded to a small empire serving four busy routes, before he was one of the wily ones, along with Tilley's and Widow Birch, to sell out late to the LGOC.

Rich, and no longer tainted by direct contact with horse sweat and the streets, Cane Senior married for love, but wisely too. Her family's money was older, rinsed by time. They had met, before he was quite so wealthy, because it was dung purchased cheaply but in great quantity from Cane's stables in Greenwich, Brixton and Sydenham that enriched her father's fields and orchards in Kent. Her family disapproved, but not so very hard—she was the youngest of six and had both a stutter and a heart defect. When she died—of the heart—being delivered of Harry's younger brother Jack, it was found she had left her own money to Harry so that he might be raised a gentleman.

Some widowers took consolation in their children, but Harry and Jack's father discovered he could not bear to look upon his; they only reminded him of what he had won and lost. Jack was still a baby, of course, but at four, Harry was already his mother's child, with the same high brow and candid curiosity of expression. Neither child had a weak heart but Harry stuttered when nervous, just as his mother had, and, like all the men in her family, pronounced his Rs as Ws, which made it particularly irritating that he had not been christened Thomas or William.

Mr. Cane entrusted the boys to a wet nurse and nursery maid respectively and, as each turned five, to a bracing preparatory school on the Kent coast, where they boarded in the holidays as well as term time. He, meanwhile, pursued discreet consolation on the Continent. He was an assiduous, if stern, letter-writer and he sent presents at intervals: cricket bats, penknives and such.

Once Jack joined Harry at school, the brothers were devoted to one another, and protective. They were in effect a family of two, and were by no means objects of pity. Each had classmates whose parents had sent them "home" from brief, idyllically filthy infancies in India or Africa for the indefinite future, concern that they should grow up English trumping any weak parental pangs.

In time, the boys were moved on to Harrow. The school had been picked by their late mother, apparently, because it was smart without being overly intellectual. It would, she believed, make them useful metropolitan contacts while lying reassuringly beyond the reach of their father's former bus routes. Word of how their bills were paid leaked out, however, perhaps via some spiteful teacher, perhaps from Jack's unguarded, trusting chatter.

Although he was the younger, and thus fell naturally under Harry's protection, Jack had always been the stronger and more confident of the two. He faced the world openly, with a sunny faith in others that won everyone's favor in turn. His most habitual phrase was "It's simple." Life for him was as straightforward as a boys' adventure story: people were either good or bad, the right course of action was clear, and good would always triumph. God, being English, meant everything for the best, and the life He gave us was full of rewards if only we buckled under and did our bit. Jack was handsome, good at games, decent, and thus a constant source of worry to Harry, who was sure that at any moment something would happen to shatter his cheerful outlook.

Perhaps because he had been old enough at their mother's death to suffer by it, to have known the pillowy welcome of the boudoir from which he was abruptly banished ever after, Harry was as unlike Jack as their mother had been to their father: wary, fearful, given to brooding. He was not proud, but teasing left him with a horror of humiliation on the playing field and elsewhere, so his defense was to withdraw. He was not a scholar—his brain seemed too sluggish or too dreamy to grasp the things demanded of it—but he was never happier than when left alone among books, and would spend hours turning the pages of atlases, novels or tales from history, alive to the alternative versions of himself they seemed to proffer. He lacked the knack of forging easy friendships but grew habituated to benefiting from the ones Jack was forever striking up.

Jack would never accept defeat in the face of his brother's shyness; it was so alien to his nature that he could not understand it, could not imagine how shyness might feel. As they grew into young men, the younger became as solicitous of the older as the older had been of him when they were boys, so that it was a reflex in him to make room for Harry in any social engagement, in any pleasure or outing. As often as not, his friends would have a retiring sibling in their turn, and so Harry would form not-quite friendships, friendships at one remove, which remained dependent on the generous impulses of his brother. When Jack joined the Harrow cadet force, as was expected of them all, Harry took to terrible fantasies that his brother would sign up for some distant war and be lost to him.

Their mother had left enough money to educate them through university, but Harry could not see the point. The only future he dreamed of—born of visits to friends of Jack's or relatives of their mother—was to live somewhere surrounded by his own land, to have an estate or just a farm.

Jack, by contrast, knew exactly what he wanted. Ironically, he had always been obsessed with horses. He drew them with increasing expertise and knowledge in the margins of his exercise books, read about them, and, like Harry, rose early every morning to ride. They both loved riding, but when they accompanied their father to his cavernous south London stables, it was Jack who reached out to horses, talked to them, and asked questions of the grooms. He swiftly ascertained that horses needed vets and that vets made money, good money. He studied hard and so intently—compared to Harry, who studied with no end in view—that he soon won a place to study at the Royal Veterinary College.

Jack joined Harry at his bachelor lodgings in town. While Jack pursued his course, and came home bright-eyed with the excitement of it all, bringing the faint scent of formaldehyde with him and occasionally a rowdy gang of friends, Harry slipped into a daily pattern of gentlemanly idleness that might have lasted for years. A brisk routine with Indian clubs, a shave at his barber's, a vigorous walk around a park, a visit to the club in which their grandfather had enrolled him—involving the newspapers, a quiet lunch, a digestive read in the library—and then a call on the London and Provincial Turkish baths in Jermyn Street for a bath and massage. Then he would call back to his club for tea before walking back to their lodgings, where he would dine with Jack.

Unless Jack had other plans, their evenings were quiet, so Jack could study, and their nights early. Their lives were careful, temperate and, on Harry's part, quite chaste, in marked contrast to those of their neighbors. The apartment they rented was in a fashionable building of bachelor lodgings to the north of Piccadilly. The wholesome routine of their habits was overseen by Mrs. Allardyce, the same respectable housekeeper their father had first taken on as their nursery maid, who traveled in from Lambeth every day to cook and clean for them.

Their absentee father's death, announced by a visit from the family solicitor, who in turn had been contacted by a lawyer in Nice, was more troubling to Harry than to Jack. Jack had never really known the man, except through his formulaic and unrevealing letters (*I am glad to hear of your excellent exam results...I approve your choice of lodgings...*), so the death felt no more a cause for grief than the news of failure in a distant mine in which one had briefly considered investing. Naturally Jack looked to Harry for his cue as to how he should feel and behave. They adopted black suits for a year, of course, but Harry would not hear of Jack falling behind in his studies for the observance of form, although they did have a week away to attend their father's burial in Nice's English cemetery.

The funeral was a strange, chilly affair. (It was a revelation to Harry that the South of France had bad weather.) Besides the two of them and the local Church of England parson, the weather-beaten consul was in attendance, as were two plump

Frenchwomen in veils, one of whom had to support the other
when grief overcame her at the graveside. They melted away
into the drizzle before Harry could introduce himself, and the
consul was either discreet or genuinely at a loss as to who they
were.

Harry could not pretend to be grief-stricken. If he mourned
anything, it was the lack of anything to mourn. His memories
of his father were so scant and so distant that they had become
rigid to the point where he could no longer trust them. He remembered, or thought he remembered, walking alongside him
on a shingle beach, but it was the difficulty of walking on shingle while holding an adult's hand that informed the memory,
not any paternal warmth. He remembered a luxuriant beard a
little like the king's, and a tang of limes and something sweeter
from some manly preparation or other, a beard oil or a shaving
water. He had absolutely no memory of his voice, and realized
that he had come, with time, to supply a voice, as he read his
father's letters, that belonged to a disliked master at Harrow
and not to his father at all. His principal feeling on losing this
second parent was to miss his mother with something like fresh
grief and to feel a powerful yearning for nothing more complicated than feminine company.

They had no women in their life beyond Mrs. Allardyce, and
she was not precisely *in* it, and was better at sustaining a pie
crust than a conversation. Their building was designed to ac-
commodate only bachelors, but neighbors upstairs and down
would entertain more or less respectable women by day and
occasionally Harry would coincide with these visitors on the
stairs or in the entrance hall. Feminine conversation, exotic in
the building's habitual quiet, would peter out as he opened a
door or rounded a staircase corner. He would lift his hat in
greeting and be met with a greeting in return, or demurely

downcast eyes, and then the conversation would start up again behind his back, leaving him with torn rags of sentences and no less tantalizing wafts of violets, perfume or soap.

In the theaters, or in shops, or on his daily walks, Harry observed women as one did wild birds, noted the elegance or occasional strangeness of their fashions and the way their behaviors changed depending on whether they were alone or in company, with a man or with other women. But there was no woman he counted as a friend, none he could truly say he knew. He had known Mrs. Allardyce all his life, but she was the soul of decorum and released personal information so rarely that on the occasions when she let slip that there had been a Mr. Allardyce but that he had died fighting the Boers, or that she shared a house in Lambeth with her four unmarried brothers so was *quite used to the ways of men*, he found himself chewing over the gobbets of information days later in a way that hardly seemed decent.

Had they a sister or mother still living, or even friends with sisters, none of this would have been so and women might have become normal, even uninteresting to him. Their mother's parents used to make a point of inviting them to visit in the country every summer and, now they were adults, would surely have set about making suitable introductions. The boys' grandfather had long since died, however, and his widow become senile, and their uncles and cousins, who had always regarded their existence as a piece of social awkwardness, had let all communication wither.

Harry looked around him, especially at his club or in the Jermyn Street hammam, at the men who had never married— one seemed to gather by osmosis which they were—and thought their lives did not seem so very disastrous. Provided one had a Mrs. Allardyce to keep one fed and clean, and the services of a tailor and a barber to keep one presentable, the single manly life was apparently not so bad. He noticed that these men reached a point, perhaps over some tacitly understood age limit, when they began to be called *confirmed bachelors*, which implied they had passed (or failed) some test, or even, kindly, that their single state was of their own choosing and not a cruelty of fate.

After their father's death, Harry was made aware of where the money that had always materialized so reassuringly in his bank account came from. Apparently under the impression that he was a species of cosseted imbecile, the family solicitor talked him through it with such pedantic slowness that his brain did indeed begin to feel barely able to retain all the facts. Most of his father's estate was tied up in property—terraces in Brixton and, indeed, Mrs. Allardyce's Lambeth, whose rent was raised by agents. As part of the bargain struck when he sold off the omnibus company, he had acquired stock in the LGOC and a portfolio of shares in affiliated railway companies. At some point—presumably during his sojourn on the Continent—he had obtained a considerable interest in a German armament company, which had performed extremely well, and in a ballet company, which was on the verge of bankruptcy. The residue of Harry's mother's legacy had been used to buy a row of houses in Kensington.

A property in Nice was to be left to a Madame Grassert. Harry remembered the woman at the graveside, how her veil had become caught in her mouth, how firmly her little black-gloved hands had grasped at her friend's arm. Had she, he wondered, been led to expect more?

The solicitor carefully avoided Harry's eye but, staring at the Frenchwoman's name on the paper before him, said, "Your father's French bank account was frozen at the time of his death, naturally, once his notary had settled all outstanding accounts.

It might be possible, if you like, to have him pursue the matter to see if any, er, substantial sums had been transferred to... another French account, but I fear these could not be recovered. Should you wish to contest this bequest, however, we could certainly—"

"No, no," Harry insisted. "Let the matter rest." Such gifts were not made without forethought and planning. If she had made his father's latter years happier, she had earned the roof over her head at least. Nice was, he felt sure, not a place he would ever visit again.

The thought of suddenly being responsible for so much property worried him, and he was relieved to hear that once he had signed a few bits of paper, he could leave everything exactly as it was and his now considerably larger income would continue to come in as before. It was brought home to him that, left nothing, Jack now depended directly on him for everything. His immediate instinct was simply to split the inheritance in two, but apparently this would not do. Because of fees, his holdings generated more income for them both if left intact.

"Besides, you're now in a position to marry," the solicitor reminded him, "and a wife and household will draw on your resources far more than your current circumstances do." The solicitor then actually produced an illustration of annual average household costs for a husband, wife, two children and staff of four. Harry had so little sense of what anything cost that he could not tell if the figures were supposed to make him wince or offer a pleasant surprise, so he looked at them blankly, which the lawyer evidently took for risky sangfroid. Apologizing for his forwardness, and saying he was aware that Harry had no father or mother to advise him on such matters, he added that he assumed Harry naturally had little experience of such realities and warned him to be on his guard because he had now become what was vulgarly termed *a catch*.

Harry pondered this in the hours that followed, as he walked the length of Piccadilly and Knightsbridge to soothe his thoughts in a visit to the museums. The idea was so strange. It was not as though his actual worth were suddenly more visible; not even his own dear brother knew it. He knew there were guides to the peerage and the landed gentry; he had looked his mother's family up in the latter in an idle hour in the club library. Perhaps financial information was published somewhere as well, in a husband-hunting equivalent to one of Jack's beloved stud books, and even now some unscrupulous mother was poring over it and placing a little question mark beside his name with her ivory pencil?

He decided to be not secretive, exactly, but discreet with Jack. Jack was more in the world than he, and was naturally trusting and open, so would never suspect people's motives or think to hold things back from them if he thought they liked him. He was one of Nature's friends, not her privy counselors, and had always found the keeping of secrets an intolerable burden.

Harry resolved that ushering Jack through his training and seeing him somehow settled would, in any case, be his first priority. The fending off, or not, of potential mothers-in-law could come later. Even had it not been so important for Jack to concentrate on his studies, the observance of full mourning gave Harry a convenient year in which to remain socially aloof and take stock.

Jack was athletic and good-looking and, without being a peacock, took a natural pride in his appearance and a keen interest in what he wore. He chafed at having to don mourning all year and itched, Harry was sure, to cut a dash again in his rowing club blazer or a suit other than his black one. Harry, by contrast, found he relished the excuse mourning gave for withdrawal. His life had hardly been a social whirl before, but for twelve months he was spared even having to make idle conversation. Strangers and acquaintance alike now treated him with a welcome reserve. It reminded him of the legend he had read as a boy of Perseus granted invisibility by a magic cap. Other boys in the class had bragged of the mischief it would let them work, the people they would spy on or banks they would raid, but he had dreamed only of the way it would let him be entirely alone, unpestered, unprovoked. Ironically, he found himself observing other people in mourning, now that he was one of them, and noting the slight differences in their approaches to the discipline of dressing like a crow.

Chapter Three

Months after black had become second nature, to the point where Harry could imagine wearing it forever, like a handsome doorman's uniform, and weeks after his brother had graduated as a vet and begun applying for positions, Jack burst in on Harry's morning exercises excitedly waving a card. He was dressed like springtime itself in a gaudy blazer.

The card had been left by the mother of a girl he had met at a recent rowing gala. Jack's eight won a cup, and he had fallen into conversation with the young woman when queuing up to enter the marquee to collect it.

"What did you talk about?"

"Well I don't remember. Nothing probably. But she's awfully nice. It was a hot day, so the marquee was like a furnace, and nobody much wanted to be in there. I think I said something stupid about Lady Whatever deserving a cup of her own for standing in there in full fig to make speeches and hand out little bits of silver. She's got about ten sisters apparently. Miss Wells, that is, not Lady Thingummy. Oh don't look like that, Harry. It'll be fun. And our year ended last week so we don't have to dress like undertakers."

"Can't you go on your own?"

"I'm shy."

"Piffle."

"Please, Harry. We never go anywhere and it'd be jolly.

Besides, you're the eldest, so you're the one they'll really want to meet. You're my passport. And it'll do you good, you know."

So Harry agreed, because he could refuse Jack nothing and because he was slightly ashamed that he had not even noticed that they had emerged from their year of mourning. He kept to his usual routine, but did so in a summer suit and blue tie, whose pale colors made him feel conspicuous as he walked around Green Park and St. James's.

He lunched at his club earlier than usual so as to meet Jack in good time. Mrs. Wells lived far out to the west, on the Thames near Twickenham, so they had to catch a train from Waterloo, which felt quite like an excursion, and a holiday mood stole over Harry. As Jack told him all he knew about the people they were visiting, it dawned on him that this brother who he'd always thought of himself as guarding might actually be feeling protective toward him. To Jack, he realized, he must seem a faintly pathetic figure, a sort of hermit.

Mrs. Wells was a solicitor's widow of independent means with three adult sons and a tribe of six daughters. The eldest two boys had followed their father into law, the next was a district commissioner in Africa. The daughter Jack had met was Georgina, the second girl.

"And you intend me for the eldest, I suppose? The one with ginger hair and whiskers?"

"Don't be silly," Jack told him, glancing out of the window at the blackened backs of houses they were passing. "I'm reliably informed she has no hair whatsoever."

Arriving at the small station in Strawberry Hill felt like visiting the country. There were trees, birdsong, hardly any traffic. Consulting his Boot's District Guide, Jack led them down from the platform, over a level crossing and past a sequence of decorative villas to Mrs. Wells's road, which had the preposterously pretty name of Strawberry Vale.

"Didn't Pope live near here?" Harry asked as he glimpsed the river between trees.

"Who?"

"You remember. Poetry. School."

Ma Touraine was a handsome house, older than the smaller ones that had sprung up to either side of it. It was set back from the road behind neatly clipped hedges. It had some small stables to one side, which Jack glanced into instinctively only to pronounce them unused. There was a giggle and Harry saw that three children were observing them from an open window on the second floor. He raised his hat, which provoked more giggling, then a woman's distant rebuke, at which the three heads were withdrawn.

Somehow one expected the matriarch of such a gang to be tall and imperious, but Mrs. Wells was tiny, a little under five feet tall. She was elegantly dressed in a dark violet silk that rustled as she rose from her tea table to offer them each her hand. She wore no widow's weeds, but the striking silver streak in the chestnut hair piled up on her head like a little crown conferred a certain dignity, as did the keys and chatelaine dangling from her waist on a length of jet beads.

She introduced them to a visiting neighbor, who chatted to them about the warm weather and the delightful way the house's gardens ran down to the river and a little landing stage, while Mrs. Wells slipped across the hall to summon The Girls.

A muffled exchange from another room revealed a sterner note to Mrs. Wells's voice. The neighbor took her leave almost at once on their hostess's return, as if on cue, saying, "Oh I only live two streets away and Estervana and I see each other all the time."

Mrs. Wells poured tea, offered little cakes and explained that her eldest daughters would join them shortly but that Winifred was shy.

"So am I," Harry told her.

"Oh," she said, startled by his candor. "That's nice. So few men will admit to that. I fear my late husband was a terrible bully when he was at home, which left some of the children rather cowed. Me too!" She laughed shortly. "Georgina was the only one who stood up to him, so of course she was his favorite. Winifred is more like me. Only artistic."

There was a clattering on the staircase, as of a dropped toy, and much giggling.

"Forgive me," Mrs. Wells murmured and returned to the hall. Jack caught Harry's eye and winked—one of the many tricks Harry had never mastered. "Madame Vance?" Mrs. Wells called up, just a hint of steel showing through her gentle tone. "Would you, er, s'il vous plaît?"

There was a quick handclap, a sharp French command and a thunder of little feet retreating back upstairs.

"I'm sorry." Mrs. Wells returned to her station. "My youngest three. Curious to lay eyes on visitors. With so many charges, Madame Vance cannot always keep control. We are thinking of sending the middle two away to Belgium to be finished by the nuns."

"Are you Roman Catholics?"

"Heavens no, but the Sisters are so good at conferring a certain je ne sais quoi. And, well, I fear one of the troubles with growing up in so large a family can be that one gets lax from sheer exhaustion and the youngest ones are allowed to become..."

"Unruly?" Jack suggested with a smile.

"Overconfident. Ah! Te voici, Georgette. You have already

met Mr. Jack Cane, of course. This is his older brother, Harry. And here, at last, is my Winifred."

Like the principal and secondary couples in a comedy, Harry thought, they were two matching pairs, one blonde, one dark. Only, to his surprise, it was the dark one Jack had chosen for himself, the one who was handsome rather than pretty. But she shared his confidence and easy charm.

"Sorry we took such an age," Georgina said, smiling. "I made Winnie change her dress twice, then she found a grass stain on mine, so then I had to change too. I'm sure you've both had more than enough of Mother's tea by now. Why don't you let us show you the garden?"

"That's a lovely idea," Mrs. Wells said. "But if you go in one of the boats, dear, do let the gentlemen take the oars." She touched a little hand on Harry's arm. "Her brothers encouraged George to be athletic and I fear it can sometimes make her a little headstrong."

"She means bossy," Winifred said quietly and dipped her head.

"So you don't row?" Harry asked her as he stood aside to let her through the French windows before him as the other pair strode ahead.

"Oh not remotely. I mean, I've tried, but I end by going in circles, which makes people laugh at me."

He winced. "It's horrible being laughed at," he said. "People say you should be a good sport and get used to it, but the laughter never seems friendly and one never gets used to it. Or I don't."

"Don't you row either?" she asked.

"I don't really do anything much. I ride. I walk. I like walking."

"So do I."

So they walked very slowly around the pretty waterside

garden while Jack and George, with much laughter, took one of several rowing boats moored to the landing stage and struck out across the water toward a nearby reedy island. Strictly speaking, he supposed, they should all have stayed at least within listening distance, but the scented almost-rusticity of the setting seemed to dispense with the rigid protocol of a Mayfair drawing room. And in any case, Mrs. Wells had followed them out on to the terrace, where she sat in the shade of a little blue awning that hung from the house's rear, and made a show of tidying nearby roses with a pair of secateurs.

"What a lovely spot," he said. "Have you always lived here?"

"All my life," Winifred told him. "I think it suited Father to have us out of the way. My brother Barry—Barrington—calls it the Nunnery."

"Yet you don't want to escape?"

"I beg your pardon?"

"Nuns. One always assumes they resent being locked up and want to escape."

"Really? I envy them the peace." She saw his questioning glance. "It's not always so quiet here," she said. "The boys are all at work and the girls are being sat on by Madame Vance in the schoolroom. There are times when I think the privacy of a nun's cell could be wonderful."

"Oh dear," he said, mock serious, and she smiled, if something so grave could be called smiling.

They reached a wrought-iron bench in the shifting golden shade of a weeping willow, which seemed like a destination, so they sat. Winifred watched George row Jack, which gave Harry the opportunity to watch her. She was, he decided, quite lovely, with fair hair piled upon her head in the kind of relaxed arrangement he was sure had taken a good hour to achieve, and china-blue eyes and a creamy complexion. She was extraordinarily solemn, sad even, yet with a suggestion of irony, of the kind of weary humor he liked best.

"I'm afraid I'm not very good company," he said at last, because he had noticed Mrs. Wells glancing anxiously their way.

"No, no," Winifred protested, turning back to face him. "You're...I'm a hopeless conversationalist. I'd always rather listen."

"Me too. Do you worry about your sister? On the water, I mean."

"George? No. Not really. She's an excellent swimmer. When we were little, it amused Father to throw sticks for her to fetch, as though she were a dog."

"Your mother said she stood up to him."

"Oh yes. She's quite fearless."

"Was he so fearful?"

"Yes. When we heard his key in the lock, we would run upstairs."

"Like nuns."

"Quite. Only I'm not sure nuns are allowed to run. He made poor Mother so nervous she would get palpitations."

"Yet their marriage was a happy one."

"Not really. Just...fruitful. He only took her out once in all their years together."

"No!"

"Truthfully. He liked her to repeat the story, as it made him laugh. Just once he took her into town for the evening in her best finery. They went to the theater and then for lobster and champagne and then, when they came out on to the pavement, there was a tremendous glow in the sky to the west. I suppose it was a sunset but he pointed it out to her and said, 'Look, my dear. That might be our cherubs burning in their beds!' And she was so horrified, she insisted he call a cab for her to go home at once while he went on to his club to meet his friends. It was by way of a lesson, I suppose, and he never took her out again and she never suggested he take her. She used to say he was her street angel—so charming and amusing to his friends and clients and a perfect tyrant in the home."

"How dreadful for you."

"Oh, it wasn't so bad. We lived here, after all, in comfort. And he never beat us or shouted. He simply had a cruel tongue. Well, he beat my brothers sometimes."

"Why do you suppose he married, if it pleased him so little?"

"But it did please him, I think; it magnified him. And he married for love. Mother was extremely pretty once. He wanted sons, of course, to take on the partnership one day, and he enjoyed having us all walk to church behind him. He liked the fact that we filled two pews."

"He was a patriarch."

She nodded sadly. "That's the word."

"Are any of your brothers like him?"

"Bob," she said, without a moment's hesitation, so that Harry immediately worried that Bob might be about to appear. She stood suddenly. "We should fetch George back," she said. "It's quite sunny and she's gone out without her hat and will be getting a labourer's tan."

Jack and George were enjoying themselves too much, however. Jack had resumed rowing duties and George was trailing a hand in the water. She said something that made Jack laugh so hard he had to stop rowing briefly. The two of them looked like an illustration for Modern Happiness, unguarded, relaxed, entirely themselves, in a way that made Harry feel he belonged to the old century. Perhaps it wasn't beauty, ultimately, that won men to women or vice versa, but an ability to make one laugh?

Harry made a gesture as of putting on a hat and pointed to George, but Jack willfully misunderstood, making ever more complicated hand gestures back to make George laugh in turn.

"Does he ever do as he's told?" Winifred asked, in a tone that made Harry wonder if she wouldn't rather be in the little boat instead of her sister.

"Not often," he admitted, and she gave one of her grave half-smiles.

"It's not easy being the eldest," she said.

"George bears it pretty lightly."

"Don't be gallant," she fired back. "It doesn't suit you."

"Sorry. Your mother said you were shy, but you don't seem—"

"I'm shy in groups. I'm hopeless in groups, and that's what a family like ours tends to be. All the time."

"Well I'm shy even on my own. There are days when I hardly speak."

"How wonderful!"

"It's surprising how few words you need once you put your mind to it."

"Do you ever dream about invisibility?" she asked him.

"Often. To be left entirely alone!"

"That's it!" She clapped. "Some people would immediately rob a jeweler's or an art gallery if no one could see them, but I think I would simply stay quietly in my room with a novel."

He was struck by how closely she had voiced his own instincts, and having established that each preferred silence, they walked wordlessly away from their happy siblings and around the rest of the garden, pausing to watch a bumblebee lumbering around the bells of a foxglove and a song thrush savaging a worm.

Mrs. Wells greeted their return with a tray of lemonade and

cake, as though it were the most normal thing in the world to have entrusted a pretty daughter to a complete stranger for half an hour. "Pattie expressed a wish to come down and sing to you all. Pattie is my next youngest girl, Mr. Cane. She fancies herself an artiste. Don't fret," she went on in response to Winnie's heavy sigh. "I told her perhaps another time. Encouragement of talent is all very well, but it doesn't do to go too far. Ah. And here come the athletes!"

Jack had a young boy's instinct for sniffing out sweet things. "If I'm not hungry," he told them, "I'm either ill or asleep."

He had encouraged his companion to replace her hat so as to avoid a scolding. Shaded by its straw brim and blue ribbons, she looked almost demure.

"It's been a delightful afternoon," Harry told Mrs. Wells.

"Well I hope you'll come again," she said, offering him a dry little hand. "Perhaps next time you'll come for dinner, so you can meet my boys?" She pulled a comical face. "Though we'll all have to be on our best behavior for Robert."

"That would be splendid," Jack said.

Harry tried to catch Winifred's eye but she had dropped her glance to the crumbs on the cake plates. He supposed that, being shy, she regarded dinners as a necessary evil.

"Miss Wells," he said.

She looked up, gave one of her sad little smiles and offered him her hand. "Mr. Cane," she said.

George mocked their formality by dropping Jack a deep curtsey, at which everyone laughed.

Chapter Four

A second invitation came from Mrs. Wells, summoning them both to dinner, where they met two of the three brothers.

Robert, the eldest, who was possibly good-looking behind a fulsome beard, suffered from the pompous, hectoring manner of a stupid man who believed himself clever.

Frank, his younger by some six years, had successfully insisted on being made senior partner on their father's death. He was softly spoken, observant, utterly lacking in social skills and really rather frightening. Winifred had already warned Harry he was very clever. Certainly he seemed to regard the family he had been born into with scornful dismay. Harry was glad to be screened from him at table by a parson's amiable wife.

On his other hand, his left, he had Mrs. Wells, who was full of kind curiosity about his mother's family and evidently a little alarmed by the subject of his father. By oversight or mischief, she had placed Winifred so he could admire but could not speak to her. Mrs. Wells was, he began to realize, something of a manipulator.

"You come from a small family, Mrs. Wells was telling me," said the parson's wife.

"Yes," he said. "It's just my brother and myself."

"I was an only," she said. "The functioning of large families remains a mystery to people like us. There are currents and influences we cannot always read correctly. And then, of course, we have to beware of clinging too tightly."

"To what?"

"Why, to those we love! People from large families crave freedom and privacy above all else. I know; my Benedict's father was a Mr. Quiverful."

"I'm sorry?"

"A character from Trollope with a great many children. I tease Benedict that he should have joined a silent order and he teases me back that he might just yet. Oh! We're off already and I've barely begun to scratch your interesting surface!"

Taking her cue from their hostess, she stood, as of course did he, and she made him a little smiling bob and followed the ladies from the room. The five gentlemen were left briefly speechless, as feminine laughter and conversation flared in the hall, then were enclosed in the drawing room. Harry thought cigars tasted of something meaty and long dead, and port invariably gave him a headache because nerves and politeness made him drink it like water. Not for the first time in his life, he felt a craven impulse to create a sensation by hurrying out in the ladies' wake.

He found the courage to wave aside the cigar Robert offered him and was about to pour, as a lesser evil, a small glass of port, thinking he might simply not then touch it and so avoid drinking too much, when Frank said, "Or perhaps you'll join me in a Scotch? Port always gives me filthy headaches. Evil drink, I say. Like drinking wine gone bad. You know where you stand with whisky."

"Yes," said Harry. "I will. Thanks," managing not to stammer on the W in his relief, and he passed the port on to Robert, who snorted disapproval. Perhaps whisky was more expensive? Harry had no idea.

"It's good to meet the famous Brothers Cane finally," Robert said. "The girls have talked of little else."

"How very dull for you all," Harry said. At least, he began to, but Robert was putting him in mind of a particularly cruel Harrow bully he had managed, until then, to forget, so all that came out was "How-how-how..."

Well trained, Jack came to his rescue. "How very relieved you must be to find us both so ordinary. Excellent cigar," he added. "Are they Cuban? Harry won't let me smoke them at home." He knew that playing on Harry's compulsion to correct an unjust or inaccurate statement was one of the surest ways of helping him out.

"Only because, on a student vet's income, you have no business buying such luxuries," Harry said, with no trace of a stammer.

"It's touching that you look to your younger brother's welfare so," the parson said. He had accepted both port and cigar with alacrity but seemed to be saving his cigar for later. "Jack has been telling me you've been like a father to him."

"Well, sir, as I'm sure our host can attest, the eldest has certain responsibilities."

"Huh," Robert Wells said.

"Forgive me, but I'm always intrigued by cases like yours. My wife says I should have made a novelist but I fear I lack the necessary lightness. If you were so busy keeping Jack out of scrapes as you were growing up, who looked after you?"

Harry liked the parson, as he had liked his wife; there was nothing of the prefect about him and he had a kind, plain face. "Why, Jack, of course," he told him, at which they both laughed.

"Harry takes quite some looking after," Jack added.

Robert Wells was one of those men who could not leave a question unanswered, or a subject abandoned. "They're from Africa," he abruptly told Jack. "Our brother Barrington sends them. Taste like Cuban but a fraction of the cost and Empire-grown."

Harry became uncomfortably aware that Frank was about to say something personal.

"Have you always stuttered like that?" Frank asked quietly.

"Absolutely," said Harry, instinctively avoiding an answer that began with a consonant. "It comes and it goes. Unfortunately it's worse with strangers." He could imagine Frank tormenting caged birds in a spirit of scientific enquiry.

"Funny. Winnie didn't mention it."

"She didn't make me nervous," Harry said, which made Robert guffaw.

"He got you there, Frank. She probably didn't say how rude her brothers were either, eh?" Someone began to play a piano across the hall and Robert sighed weightily. "I fear that's our cue for further delights."

"Can't miss my god-daughter," said the parson, folding his napkin as he rose. "I made a solemn vow."

"Is Winifred your god-daughter?" Harry asked.

"No, no. Patricia is. I believe she asked to be allowed downstairs especially to entertain us."

"She needs no encouragement," Frank said as cigars were regretfully tapped out and they all stood.

"I don't think we've met Patricia," Harry said.

"Oh, everyone meets Pattie before too long," Robert told him. "What is it Mam'zelle Vance says?"

"Mees Pattie av a powerfool pairsonality," Frank said.

As they crossed the hall, there was the clatter of plates being stacked in the distant kitchen and the familiar sound of giggling from the shadows on the landing above. Harry saw Robert glare up, mock furious, but then grin and pretend to fire a gun toward his hidden sisters. To find oneself head of such a household in

one's late twenties, or however old he had been when Robert
Wells Senior died, was enough to make a premature ogre of
any man. Pomposity. Severity. Snobbery. They were all masks
for various sorts of fear. And to find himself supplanted by a
younger, cleverer brother in the powerfully symbolic role of senior partner could not have been easy. Harry resolved to judge
him less harshly in future.

After the relative sobriety of the dining room, with its ex-
panses of polished mahogany, dark walls, and impenetrably
varnished paintings, the drawing room seemed as frothily feminine as a gown beside a tailcoat—all lace, flowers and looking
glasses. Mrs. Wells was nose to nose with the parson's wife on
one sofa. George was picking through sheet music on another.
A plump-shouldered girl with dark hair cascading down her
back sat playing at the piano. Harry noticed, as he had not
on their previous visit, a long line of little framed children's
portraits along the white marble mantelshelf: a gallery of Mrs.
Wells's fecundity. A tenth infant portrait, he saw, had a black
velvet bow looped through its frame.

Winifred had apparently been watching for them from the
veranda, where she had perhaps been cooling herself, for
the room had become as hot and airless as a palm house.
She came back inside as they entered and unsmilingly served
them coffee in pretty little cups. Jack joined George on her
sofa, the parson went to admire his god-daughter at the
piano and the Wells boys, apparently now relieved of any responsibility to entertain, headed out to the veranda, where
they soon relit their cigars.

Harry remained standing by Winifred, who was indeed a little flushed but smelling deliciously of roses.

"Are you going to sing for us?" he asked. The piano playing
had come to an end and there was some conference about songs.

"Oh no. I'm quite unmusical. Pattie is the performer. Ssh. Here she goes."

He turned to see that George had moved to the piano stool and the girl whose back had been turned to him as he came in had moved to lean in the piano's curving hip, with one arm artfully stretched along the instrument's side.

Where George was handsome and Winifred was pretty, Pattie, he saw at once, was spectacular, with huge green eyes, lips the color of lush fruit and a figure that, in a hungrier family, might have been used to sell anything from corsets to soap. He forgot the song, some nonsense about convent walls and soft footfalls, but, for its duration, could hardly bring himself even to glance elsewhere in the room.

She had a tremendous magnetic quality, like a panther's. When she was old enough to wear her hair up, which would surely be in mere months, she would carry herself like a queen. It was quite understandable that her childless godfather was so besotted and her mother so anxious to pack her off to the nuns.

When the song had finished and they had all applauded and she had curtseyed and gone to sit obediently on a footstool at her mother's knee, he turned back to Winifred and surprised a look of undisguised sorrow on her kind face. She brushed it swiftly aside, as a maid might a cobweb, but he resolved there and then to do everything in his power to make her happy.

Chapter Five

Breakfast was one of his favorite things about their little house in Herne Bay. There was a conservatory on one side of the house with a view directly over the sea. Winnie had placed a few ferns and palms in there and, half jokingly, called it the Winter Garden. Even in the colder months it was a delightful place from which to greet the day, so they had a table set up for breakfast in there every morning. Winnie was bad-tempered on waking, although she would never admit it. This suited him, however, because he had acquired the habit of early-morning silence. (One of several ways in which they had discovered they were well suited was their ability to keep one another company without either taking offence that the other wasn't talking, or misinterpreting their wordlessness as pique.)

Like all keen letter-writers, she received a great deal of post in return. She would read this over breakfast, having methodically opened each envelope first with a knife not yet buttery, and would retire to her little desk for an hour or two after breakfast to reply while her answering thoughts were still fresh in her mind.

He, too, had taken to writing, but only to Jack. The two brothers, however, could hardly generate more than a letter a week in either direction. So usually all the housemaid set out at Harry's side of the table was his newspaper.

This morning Winnie was down before him, which surprised

him, as there had been some commotion in the night on account of the baby's refusal to sleep again once woken by teething pains, and he had assumed she would grant herself an extra hour in bed and even send for her breakfast up there.

"Morning, darling," he said, and kissed the hand she held up in greeting as she read the latest letter from Pattie in Liège.

There was a letter for him on top of his paper, addressed in a hand he didn't recognize. He opened it as the housemaid brought his kipper and toast. It was from Winnie's brother, Frank the Bloodless, as Jack had christened him behind his back, scandalizing George, who, despite herself, was rather in awe of Frank's brain. Frank had written on Chambers notepaper and the contents were as startling as they were terse.

I must speak with you on a matter of urgency. I will arrive at Herne Bay soon after eleven this morning. Not a word to Winifred, please. I shall return to town immediately afterward.

Harry slid the letter beneath his newspaper but Winifred had already seen the handwriting.

"Is Frank well?" she asked.

"Oh. You know. Frank never says. Boring money stuff."

Winifred's relief at passing from a household where most of the tension arose from money being constantly on everybody's mind, but forbidden as a topic of conversation, to one where the subject simply never arose was still strong, so he knew he could count on her flinching away from it now. She merely said, "Oh," and reached for another piece of toast, with which she prettily covered her mouth as she suppressed a little yawn. Seeing he had caught her in the gesture, she wrinkled her eyes at him with amusement.

"Poor darling," he said. "That was quite a night you had of it."

"All my fault," she said. "I should let Nurse see to her—

that's what she's there for—but once I'm awake and I can hear
her crying, I have to go to her. Later Nurse can take her out for
a nice tiring outing along the front."

Winifred had wanted to live by the sea, which was convenient
as it was far cheaper than the center of town. After several ex-
cursions with one or another sister or her mother in tow to
advise, they settled on Herne Bay, where they took a house.
There followed what felt like an orgy of shopping. Money
might have been something one never discussed, but he seemed
never to have thought about it so much as he did now that it
was leaving his hands so swiftly.

They had been married in Twickenham by the parson he had
met at that first of many supper parties. Winnie insisted on
making her own wedding dress, for she was, it emerged, an amateur dressmaker of exquisite taste and ability and made most
of her own and her sisters' clothes.

They had spent their honeymoon in Venice, where they
made assiduous use of their Baedeker guide and saw more
churches and paintings in three weeks than in both their
lives to date. But they did much sitting, too, for she was a
studious watercolorist. The place was so preposterously, exotically beautiful, the natives so attractive, so frankly sensuous,
that it should, by rights, have proved the perfect setting for a
feast of love.

From the moment Winnie's family waved them noisily off on
the boat train from Victoria, however, Jack running alongside
their window shouting cheeky encouragement, and they found
themselves finally entirely alone together, there was a tension
between them. Whenever he reached for her, she shrank in on
herself, accepting his kisses but so clearly dying within that he
was discouraged, assuming he revolted her in some way. He

hated to see her unhappy, and hated even more to feel himself the cause of it.

Outside, in the piazzas, on the bridges, along the winding alleys, she slipped her arm through his or even held his hand. She leaned her head on his shoulder as they had their photograph taken among the pigeons outside St. Mark's. Out and about she seemed quite contented; it was when they were alone that the dark cloud descended on her and he felt obscurely to blame.

Then they had a particularly good day. It was the first one when they dared to do no sightseeing whatsoever. The breeze had dropped and the temperature became too sultry for walking, so they spent the entire day beside their hotel on the Lido, bathing, reading, observing the couples and family groups around them, talking quietly about nothing dramatic and being brought regular little treats by their avuncular waiter. She drank more than her usual single glass of wine at supper and suddenly came out with it.

Put simply, she was in love with another man: Tom Whitacre. He was a school friend of Robert and Frank's and had been a regular caller at the house as she was growing up, almost a brother really. Only not. And she had been forbidden from marrying him. The brothers didn't think him good enough. His money came from a department store bearing his name, making him too nakedly in trade.

"But my money's from trade," Harry insisted, hardly crediting they were having this conversation in a hotel dining room with people chatting and laughing on every side. "How does a horse-drawn bus differ from a department store? I'd have thought it was worse."

It was quite different, apparently, because Harry's father was dead and the buses, unlike the shop, did not have the family name on them. Besides, the perceived taint on the man's money was only a pretext, she had come to understand; the real ban had come from her mother, who, while content enough to be amused by Tom Whitacre on a sofa, knew enough of the *scrapes* from which her sons had repeatedly rescued him to see that he was rather too like her late husband—a tyrant in the making and possibly a gambling philanderer as well.

"And now I've ruined everything by telling you," said Winnie, almost laughing in her relief at finally unburdening her conscience. "You can pack me off home on the first train tomorrow morning and be grateful for what you've been spared."

"Don't you love me at all?" he asked, after the waiter had brought them each a little sorbet in a hollowed-out lemon skin.

"Of course," she said, visibly shocked. "I love you very much. It's just that I...I loved him first and, well, differently."

"More?"

"No."

"But?"

"Yes," she said. "But. Aren't you furious? Most men would be furious. I was told never, ever to tell you."

But Harry examined his feelings and found he wasn't furious, simply sorry for her, sorry that she had been thus constrained, and darkly amused that her upstanding family had, in effect, so practiced upon him.

She gave herself to him that night at last, a little drunk, perhaps, but relieved too at having been honest with him. He was utterly inexperienced, unlike Jack, he suspected, and certainly unlike his mysteriously potent rival, Tom Whitacre, but he found it easier than he had been fearing. Clumsy at first, they went to it with something like abandon in the days that followed. Baedeker was left out on the balcony and not retrieved. He doubted he succeeded in erasing all thoughts of

Tom Whitacre, who would surely forever hold the appeal of forbidden fruit, but he made her blush and gasp and giggle, and found she was smiling without quite the sadness he had so naively taken as her natural expression when they were courting.

Before they set out for home, he bought her a choker of pearls, and felt far more married to her fastening them about her pretty neck in private than he had done sliding a ring on her finger before witnesses. She was expecting by the time their train returned to Victoria, and told him the happy news once their new doctor in Herne Bay had confirmed it.

Winifred thrived in a home of her own, unoppressed by noise and constant company. She loved the sea. She read. She walked. She painted. They lived fairly simply, with only the housemaid and nursery maid living in. The cook came in each day, as did a girl *to do the rough*. They were befriended by the doctor and his wife, who taught them bridge. They went to church, though not to excess.

Harry created a version of his bachelor life in the brisk, new setting, reading, walking, visiting the library and taking long rides. The one lack was the Jermyn Street baths. He had visited the local spa baths, where similar services were on offer, but the sound of women's chatter carried constantly from the female half of the building, and it lacked the London establishment's exotic charm and shadowy glamour.

On his rides—which were often for as long as three hours, heading a considerable distance inland—he came to know the local farms and found he was developing his agricultural fantasy. The fresh-air routines and simple obligations of farming appealed intensely, but he had no idea how to begin. He assumed one had to be born to it. His maternal grandfather was born to land, of course, but born *to* it, not on it; he had done nothing to maintain his acres, trusting that to managers, agents and tenants.

Harry began to feel useless. Walking up and down the small town's promenades, to the clock tower or out along the pier, however smartly, he fancied the passing glances of men and women skated over him as if he were some kind of invalid. Herne Bay was peculiarly popular for the raising of children, to the point where it was jokingly referred to as Baby Bay, and his passage along South Parade by day was always through a crowd of nannies and nursery maids pushing prams or over-seeing the unsteady walking of small persons in their charge. The cries of children at play on the shingled shore below often seemed to carry an edge of mockery. *There goes the idle man! The useless one!*

He sat in the conservatory, methodically reading the newspa-per, while Winnie retreated to her desk and the maid cleared away breakfast, then he walked briskly from one end of the seafront to the other before making his way to the station. He was early, as was his habit. As he waited for the London train to pull in, he realized it was with something like brotherly af-fection.

He had never warmed to Robert, and had yet to meet the mysterious Barrington, but over the months he had surprised himself by becoming almost fond of Frank. Frank the Blood-less. Frank would have been mortified to know it, but Harry felt sorry for him. Being surrounded by people so much less clever than he was, he must have felt like a member of a differ-ent race, a different species even. What Harry had first taken for coldness, he had come to see was an odd mixture of pa-tience, incomprehension and extreme discomfort. Frank could decline any number of Greek verbs and rattle off a sequence of prime numbers, but he could never anticipate the illogical choices of ordinary humans so was forever being made to feel odd by comparison, a situation little aided by his inability to dissemble when politeness required it, or to talk of unimportant matters simply to put others at their ease. Harry was shy but Frank was awkward, which Harry considered gave them a kind of kinship.

Frank would seem to have recognized this, and warmed to Harry in turn. In his odd, prickly way. A couple of weeks into his engagement to Winnie, Harry had been summoned to Frank's chambers, ostensibly for lunch without Robert, who was off visiting clients in the country, but actually for a bewilderingly candid discussion about money.

Tipped off by a friend in the City, Frank had details of a company about to be floated that he knew for a fact was a sure thing. He was investing a parcel of Mrs. Wells's less lively savings in it and did not want Harry to miss out. Harry didn't feel he could sell any of his property holdings, but much of his capital was invested in bonds and shares he could easily trade in. At Frank's urging he did just that, sinking a third of his capital in the new share issue.

"You won't be sorry," Frank told him. "If I had half your money, I'd do the same. Within six months you'll have doubled your investment and you can take half out again and reinvest if you're feeling cautious."

Frank did not need to do this. It was a kindness, coolly delivered but a kindness nonetheless. The shares had performed just as well as promised.

With the candor that being married enabled, he and Winnie had often discussed her brothers' marriage prospects. Robert, they both suspected, modeled himself on his late father, and probably the King, and had a weakness for actresses. Barrington was a mystery, although it was an open secret that morals and manners were more relaxed in the remoter outposts of empire, so it was quite possible he had come to some unofficial, even tribal, arrangement that could never be acknowledged at home. But Frank was the greatest challenge.

His sisters, rather meanly, had confected the ideal girl for him, who was an utterly humorless suffragette type called Elfine. They would amuse themselves at parties by competing as to who could first spot a girl in glasses—the thicker-lensed the better—and cry, "Oh do look. It's Elfine!"

Harry feared the truth would be sadder and involve a misalliance. The Franks of this world rarely had the sense or self-knowledge to choose themselves an Elfine, but would impulsively throw their heart at a conventional beauty, some Dulcie or Clarabel, whose prettiness would pall almost as swiftly as her girlish lack of education would madden. He had discreetly taken to looking around for Elfines for his brother-in-law.

Frank's train was late, and this seemed to fluster him out of all proportion. Harry assured him, lying, that he hadn't been waiting long.

"I must catch the eleven forty-five back to town, which means we now have barely thirty minutes," Frank said.

"Follow me. There's a perfectly good hotel nearby. You seem upset, Frank."

"I'll explain once we're sitting," Frank said shortly. He looked more than usually wan, the more so for being in such holiday surroundings.

Harry ran through all the possible bad news that couldn't have been put into a letter, and could only think of sudden death—one of the girls drowned in a silly boating accident or

Robert crushed by a tram—but he couldn't see why Frank, least of all Frank, should think to spare Winnie's feelings by secrecy in such a case. By the time they were seated in a corner of the hotel's palm court—where, mercifully, the usually tireless little band had yet to start playing—Harry was every bit as jumpy as Frank.

It was awkwardly early for them to know quite what to order. A waitress brought them two glasses of lemonade and a little pink plate of biscuits. Frank ate two biscuits in rapid succession and drank most of his lemonade. He was sweating, and not from heat.

"Frank, for pity's sake, what is it?"

"The sure thing," Frank said.

"The Wakefields shares."

"Yes. They've plummeted. Haven't you been keeping tabs on them?" The brow furrowed on Frank's feminine, rather nun-like face. If ever he had children, they would find his disappointment hard to bear.

"Well I did at first, but then they did so wonderfully well."

"And you didn't cash them in the way I said you should?"

"I... You only said I could, Frank, not that I should."

"Damn and blast. You're not a child!"

Frank never swore.

"Down to virtually ha'pence a share since yesterday," Frank said. "I checked on my friend, the one who told us all to buy them, and it seems he's fled the country, having neatly dumped all his holdings on the market while the price was at its peak. Harry... I'm so very sorry."

"Not your fault," Harry assured him. "Anyway, they'll come up again. Shares always do."

"Not this time."

"Yes, but—"

"Just how much of your capital had you sunk in it?"

Harry told him, and he swore again.

"I'm a bloody solicitor," he said. "Not a stockbroker. Why were you taking my stupid advice?"

"It was good advice. Very good advice. My fault for not having got out last week. How about your mother?"

"No better than you."

"Does she know?"

"She trusts me. I'll have to tell her."

"She'll have Pattie married to money in a jiffy. Just you wait."

"How can you joke at a time like this?"

"Sorry. It...it just doesn't feel very real."

"It will when you next have bills to pay." Frank glanced at his watch and sighed. "I leave it to you how you tell Winnie. The most obvious solution will be for you to give up the lease here and move in to Ma Touraine. I can move in to Barry's room and that leaves you Winnie's old room and mine. Or there's a sort of coachman's cottage over the stable. Far nicer than it sounds; at least there you'd have an element of privacy. I know how Winnie will miss that. But the move would save you any domestic expenses until...until things improve."

"Yes. Of course. Well. Thank you. We'll see, eh?"

"I must go."

Harry threw down some coins for their lemonade, thinking as he did so how unreal money had always seemed to him, like counters in a game. The relentless little band had arrived and were tuning up as he hurried out after Frank.

He insisted on shaking Frank's hand as he saw him off.

"Kind of you to come down to tell me in person," he said.

"The least I could do. Is Winnie well?"

"Yes. And the baby."

"Phyllis."

"That's right."

"You'll consider what I said?"

"Of course."

And Frank turned away with entirely characteristic abruptness.

Heading back through the ticket barrier, Harry was lightly bumped by a serious young woman running for the same train, book in hand, glasses like bottle bottoms. *Elfine!* he thought, with a little surge of affection for the prickly young man who had just taken such trouble to break bad news.

Since boyhood, probably since his mother's death, he had periodically indulged in fantasies of being liberated by catastrophe. War would descend around him, or revolution, plague, earthquake, tidal wave, something elemental and huge that would shatter all certainty and stability and leave him suddenly, dizzyingly free.

Since becoming a husband and father, he had noted how the fantasies had shifted to become brutally local and specific. He would return from a night away to find Winnie and Phyllis— and the maids, naturally—dead from an overnight gas leak. Or turn the corner on to handsome South Parade, as he did now, to find a mayhem of shouting crowds and firemen and a smoking crater where their house had stood. The images that came to him were appalling. He assured himself they were a symptom of love, no different from a mother's fearful imaginings when her children were out of sight, but he kept them to himself.

Winnie was standing in the conservatory, dandling the baby in her arms to show her the view of the sea. She laughed and waved Phyllis's chubby little arm to him as he came up the path.

Since her confession on their honeymoon, he had decided he owed it to her always to be equally honest in return. He would tell her over lunch.

Chapter Six

Telegraph boys in London were a common enough sight. Smartly uniformed, often with the cheek to go with it, in Harry's mind they belonged, nonetheless, to that less tidy class of laboring men, of grooms, navvies, gardeners and builders. Theirs was an urban tribe whose busy physicality, as he strolled by, could leave him feeling rebuked in his idleness, even as it drew his gaze. This was perhaps particularly the case with the telegraph boys, since Harry led a life quite without urgency, so had never received a telegram and thought it unlikely he ever would.

In the soft nursery scenes of Herne Bay, where it seemed no communication was so insistent it could not be made by letter, telegraph boys were a rarity. Seeing one bicycling swiftly along the front, Harry assumed he could only be bringing exceptionally bad news—of tragedy or financial ruin—to some unlucky neighbor, so was shocked to see him lean his bicycle against his own garden railings and march up the garden path.

The telegram came from Mrs. Wells and said simply: *Please come at once.* Assuming there must have been a family death, although there was no black border, he replied that they would catch the next train they could, then hurried upstairs to the nursery to alert Winnie.

Winnie had inherited her mother's tendency to worry. All the way from Herne Bay to Victoria, she rehearsed out loud the possible scenarios before them: a boating accident, although their father had seen to it that they all could swim; a heart attack—their mother had long suffered from palpitations; Barry slaughtered by savages in Basutoland. Or perhaps, which was harder for her to put into words, Frank or Robert had done something wrong at work and now faced professional ruin or even arrest!

Harry soon gave up trying to reason with her, as it only made her the more fretful; he had learned that at such times, although she would often voice her worries as questions, she was actually talking to herself, so that anything he said was in effect an interruption and thus an irritant. By the time they were on the branch line out to Strawberry Hill, Winnie had made herself so tense that she had stopped talking entirely, and they traveled in silence.

As they waited on the front doorstep, he could hear Kitty and May's voices through an open window overhead, reciting some lesson for Madame Vance. Harry thought it might be capitals of the world. They sounded like their usual bouncy selves—geography was a favored subject, perhaps because it suggested routes of escape from their Twickenham schoolroom—not like girls in a house oppressed by death.

When the maid opened the door, Mrs. Wells was hovering in wait a yard behind her and swept them into the sitting room at once.

"Oh my dears," she told them, drawing Winnie down on to a sofa beside her and holding out a hand to Harry, as though she needed the support of both of them to cope. "Thank God you've come. The strain! I've told nobody yet. I only found out with the breakfast post, and the boys had already left for work, of course. And I could hardly tell Julie and the little ones."

"What is it?" Winnie asked. "Who?"

Mrs. Wells looked her firmly in the face and released Harry's hand so as to take both Winnie's in hers.

"It's George," she said.

Winnie let out a stifled cry. Of all her siblings, her favorite was the only one for whom she had imagined no awful fate that morning. George was so healthy and fearless; nothing bad could possibly happen to George!

Harry recalled that George had been invited to be a bridesmaid at a smart friend's wedding, which meant traveling all the way to Gloucester for the last three nights. There had been much associated fuss in the preceding weeks, first over Winnie's discreet remaking and fitting of the dress the bride's mother had sent from some country dressmaker, and then over the vexed question of whether it was appropriate for George to travel so far unaccompanied. The wedding had been on Saturday. After spending Sunday in some splendor as the family's guest, George was due back at Ma Touraine that evening.

He sank into a nearby armchair and pictured, in the instant, George's happy face as she teased Winnie on the veranda that first afternoon of their acquaintance, and thought of Jack, so far from them in Chester and so isolated socially. Jack would be devastated.

Since Harry and Winnie's marriage, nothing but inconvenience had come in the way of Jack and George continuing their friendship. Although Jack had moved away to take up his new work in Chester, it was understood that there was a keen sympathy between the young people, and Jack had confided in Harry that he planned to ask her to marry him as soon as he was in a position to offer her a home. He did not say as much, and Harry did not press him, but Harry assumed they were harmlessly writing to one another all the while.

The fond couple had been briefly reunited a month ago,

when Jack came to Herne Bay for the baby's christening. (With a touch of loving artfulness, Winnie had invited both him and George to be godparents.) Although doubly chaperoned— Phyllis's adoring grandmother had come to stay, too—they had spent hours in each other's company and would have exchanged all manner of confidences.

Harry looked at the tears glistening on his wife's kind face and had decided he must travel to Chester in person, to break the news that very day, when Mrs. Wells said,

"I don't know whether to cry or laugh. I've spent the morning doing both. I'm quite drained."

"But..." Winnie started.

"She's eloped," Mrs. Wells told her. "The little goose is married." She glanced at Harry with a hint of flirtation. "We now have two Mrs. Canes in the family. Here. You must read for yourselves. I've read them so often, and they're such very sweet letters, I shall be overcome all over again if I try to read them aloud."

While Winnie, he could see, was mastering her irritation that she had been so upset for no reason, her mother fumbled behind a tapestry cushion beside her to bring out an envelope from which she extracted two letters, one suggestively wrapped about the other, and handed one to each of them. They read in silence, as the chanting of the girls' lesson continued to reach them from overhead, then exchanged them with a smile.

In one, Jack apologized for the shock but explained that George and he were deeply in love, impatient to be man and wife, and loath to put their families to any fuss or expenditure. Banns had been duly read in his parish church in Chester, over preceding Sundays. Yesterday George had joined him at the church, where they had been married, with friends as happily startled witnesses, and Mrs. Jack Cane had moved into her new home. In the other, shorter letter, George assured her family that she loved them all but was unable to contain her love for her dear Jack and was now the happiest woman alive.

Giddy with relief at having finally shared the news, and apparently also reassured by Winnie and Harry's happy reactions that it was unreservedly good, and not a cause for worry or shame, Mrs. Wells insisted on opening a bottle of champagne forthwith, and summoned Julie, Kitty, May and Madame Vance to enlighten them, allowing them a glassful each in celebration.

She was predictably nervous of Robert's response to what was, after all, a subversion of his authority, but her fears proved groundless. Leaving Winnie *en famille* for a couple of hours, Harry took the letters to Lincoln's Inn and set them before the brothers. Just as he'd expected, Robert preserved his dignity by harrumphing a little at the young people's cheeky subterfuge but was swift to admit that they were very well suited, that Jack was plainly a hard worker with good prospects and that, at a time when the household needed to reduce its outgoings, he was delighted to have married a sister off sensibly at such minimal cost.

Hands were shaken and Frank cracked a joke that perhaps the next two should be enrolled in a ladies' rowing club at the first opportunity.

Harry left the letters with the brothers and walked the short distance to his own lawyer. There he gave instructions that the deeds to a pair of their father's houses be made over to Jack by way of a wedding present. The rental income was improving, was steady, and would help cushion Jack against the inevitable extra expense involved in keeping a wife.

It was one of his lawyer's juniors who took his instructions, but as Harry was preparing to leave, the older man emerged to greet him and take him into his office for a quiet word. Harry's financial affairs, he was told, had indeed suffered from his misguided investment in Frank's sure thing. Was he certain he wanted to reduce his income yet further in this way? Harry insisted. He had a duty to his brother, but with marriage he felt Jack truly became independent, and he wanted to mark that transition with a significant settlement. In which case, the lawyer said, economies would need to be made elsewhere. With which he opened a gloomy file of figures and forecasts.

Traveling back out to Strawberry Hill to retrieve Winnie for the journey home, Harry wrote several drafts of a letter congratulating Jack, forgiving him the understandable secrecy, presenting the gift of property and welcoming George to the sparse tribe of Cane. The pair must visit, he insisted, as soon as was convenient. Either that, or prepare to receive visitors immediately.

Now that I can leave off any pretense that being your older brother has conferred anything on me approaching wisdom, he confessed, *your marriage seems at once romantic and surefooted compared to the one you both so kindly nudged me into. I have always been the more conventional and cautious of us two, and now am left feeling somehow the less manly. You are making your way in the world, Jack, standing in no man's shadow, while I feel myself incomplete, barely formed, left behind you in an unappealing larval stage.*

He scratched all this last paragraph out. Then he crumpled and threw the draft impatiently out of the carriage window and began afresh and in an unambiguously happy tone.

His confession drew to mind something similar he had hinted at to Dr. Fiennes on one of their bridge evenings in Herne Bay, while they waited for the ladies to return to the card table.

"I'm fifty next year," the doctor admitted. "I've brought countless souls into the world and ushered a good few out of it. I've saved lives and shattered them and still a part of me feels as though I'm not long out of short trousers. I cheer myself with the conviction that most men are pretending to a maturity they do not feel. They swagger and pose and grow beards to hide behind, but they spend most of their lives secretly afraid and ill-equipped, as scared of women as they are of one another."

Chapter Seven

"Look!" Winnie whispered, tapping his knee to distract him from his attempt to find anything of interest in the program.

In the pit, the orchestra had struck up the tune of an especially irritating song that seemed to be everywhere that season, and from the gallery above arose an entirely male murmur and several drunken cheers. The Gaiety Girls were coming!

Harry glanced at Mrs. Wells beside him. The little woman was sitting very upright and forward in her seat, at once straining to see through her mother-of-pearl opera glasses and trying to appear calm. She looked more than ever like a well-dressed partridge.

Musical comedies were Harry's idea of hell. He disliked their forced sentiment and cheeriness, their wildly improbable plots—which so often seemed to involve shop girls elevated to the ermine, or sugar-coated Mittel-European princelings disguised as servants—and the tension induced in him by knowing that at any moment a character would burst into song. He liked plays, proper plays, in which you could lose yourself and believe that real things, important things, were happening. He liked bold plays by Shaw, Pinero or Ibsen. He liked his audiences silent and his theaters small. Musical comedies tended to play in theaters of cathedral proportions in which he suffered vertigo and felt oppressed by the noisy enthusiasm of people crowding in on every side. He had already lost track of the plot of tonight's farrago. The scene was vaguely Tyrolean—wooden

chalets, fringed with artificial red geraniums and with a cyclo-
rama of snow-capped mountains and even a distant lake with
a paddle steamer botheringly immobile in its middle. Into it
skipped the famously beautiful chorus of girls, inexplicably all
dressed as postmen, only in racily short navy-blue skirts instead
of trousers. They sang the entirely unrelated popular song as
they skipped and danced and posted love letters through letter
boxes in the scenery.

Pattie was the last on, her voluptuous figure instantly recognizable. She sang with less abandon than the others and was
often slightly behind in matching her steps to theirs. Perhaps
she was nervous. But this was not the ballet; devotees attended
the Gaiety not for impeccable footwork but for a flesh-and-
blood catalogue of youth and beauty.

How Pattie had made such a swift transition from being
polished by Belgian nuns to showing off her charms on a
West End stage was a story whose barely coherent details were
rapidly being recast into palatable legend. Obliged to return
home by an increasing downturn in Mrs. Wells's income, Pattie found her financial embarrassment all the more acute when
she discovered, too late, that she had left her pocketbook behind in the station café in Liège and had boarded the train
with neither ticket nor means to buy its replacement. Reduced
to pleading in less than immaculate French with the ticket inspector, who was threatening to put her off the train before
they even reached the coast, she was rescued by an extremely
elegant young woman who insisted on paying her fare for her
and buying her lunch.

This turned out to be none other than the young wife of
a composer whose latest show was scheduled for the Gaiety.
Picking up on Pattie's enthusiasm, she encouraged her to come
along for an audition, which Pattie managed to do in secret,

only releasing the news when her excitement at being offered a trial could not be contained.

Her mother cried and her brothers forbade, of course, but Pattie displayed considerable mettle, withstanding them all and pointing out that Gaiety Girls were famously ladylike and stood a much better chance of marrying to advantage than young women immured in villas in Twickenham. She stormed every bit as fiercely as Robert—nobody had suspected before that she had such a temper—and ended by simply going her own way.

Rehearsals happened during the day, while Frank and Robert were off at work, and Winnie acted as chaperone, at least at first, accompanying her to the theater, meeting and being thoroughly won over by her colleagues. Indeed, some expert emergency assistance she lent to the leading lady's wardrobe led to her receiving a flurry of dressmaking commissions, including one from the chorus's acknowledged star, Gladys Cooper.

Winnie and Harry had been obliged to move to Ma Touraine in the end. They had taken the little flat over the stable block, where they were really very cozy. Though nominally independent, they ate most of their meals with the others. Of all the economies he had made in the process of leaving Herne Bay, it was the loss of daily riding that Harry felt especially deeply. When entering a cab, or sometimes when simply crossing a busy street, he would catch the patient eye of a waiting groom or smell the familiar scents of sweat, leather and hay-sweet dung and be unsettled by a violent yearning.

He found that he liked, however, the novelty of life *en famille*. While Winnie busied herself with her dressmaking, he would spend time with Mrs. Wells, simply chatting, playing cards with her friends or wheeling Phyllis around the garden

in her pram. Winnie had never liked his spending too much
time with the child. Often he would be firmly told that Nurse
had taken Phyllis out, or that she was sleeping or on the point
of being fed. Babies needed routines, he was told, in which
his presence would constitute a damaging interference. But the
move back to Strawberry Hill had in some way demoted Winnie from wife to daughter, and she seemed happy to relinquish
the care of the child to others.

Mrs. Wells seemed amused at the novelty of a father showing
an interest in an infant, and sometimes encouraged him to walk
ahead, pushing the pram around the adjoining riverside park,
so that she could follow a few yards to the rear and enjoy the
expressions of surprise or curiosity on the faces of the people
strolling there.

Now that he was their brother-in-law, the youngest girls,
Julie, Kitty and May, were no longer hidden from him in the
nursery but would co-opt him into games and play-readings
and even their lessons. Madame Vance had, perforce, been let
go as part of the economies Mrs. Wells was obliged to embrace.
It amused Harry, and made him feel a little wise and useful, to
quiz them on their geography and French. He even attempted
to teach them some elementary Latin.

They certainly had no good example from Pattie, who had
barely begun rehearsals at the Gaiety (where she soon persuaded Winnie that a chaperone was quite unnecessary, and
even mortifying) when she started disappearing for mysterious
weekends away. One of her friends, who was engaged to an
American financier, had a cottage, or had been *set up in a cottage*, as Winnie said darkly, near Pangbourne, where the fiancé
threw parties. Here, Pattie acquired an aristocratic admirer. He
was a third son, rather cruelly nicknamed Notty, which was
short for Not Quite, as in not quite an earl.

Beside herself with excitement, Mrs. Wells had looked up his family in *Burke's Peerage*. They were known to be immensely wealthy, owning coal mines and a steelworks as well as large tracts of central London. Third son or no, Notty was a *catch*. And yet the manner of his knowing Pattie was irregular, having been overseen by neither Pattie's mother nor his. Having encountered her first as an actress rather than as somebody's precious daughter, he had inevitably engendered a fear—barely voiced in Ma Touraine—that his intentions were less than honorable.

This had been exacerbated when Pattie swanned home wearing a dazzlingly pretty French gold pocket watch he had given her. She was told she must return it at once, since they were not engaged, but in the course of the furious row she revealed that she couldn't possibly, as poor Notty would be too hurt since it had been his grandmother's. Mistresses, or mistresses-by-intent, were not as a rule given family jewels, so this in turn had cranked up Mrs. Wells's anticipation, as had her receiving a letter from the generous gentleman, inviting her and her family to join him in his box for the opening performance of the new show, and afterward for supper.

Even when teased, Pattie would reveal nothing about Notty other than that he was *sweet*, which had led Winnie to guess they should expect someone a little like the King. "Considerably older, rounder and with a beard," she suggested. The image, offered in bed, had taken root, so it had been a shock to arrive at the box to be welcomed by a diffident, sandy-haired young man who was indeed neatly bearded but not much older than Harry. Far from resembling some worldly seducer, he gave off an air of candid innocence and enthusiasm that had Harry thinking him not terribly bright and that perhaps it was he who needed protection from Miss Pattie and not the other way around.

As the ladies of the chorus finished their song and dance, Notty was far louder in his applause than Pattie's kith and kin, and shouted out, "Splendid! Splendid!" so enthusiastically that Harry felt Winnie shrink back in her chair.

Pattie made more appearances, each time in a new costume. Her contribution was neither notable nor risible. That unnerving magnetism she could display in a drawing room, however, was quite lost upon a cavernous stage and amidst practiced competitors. The more verbally supportive her Notty became, the surer it seemed that there was no risk of her ever stepping out of the chorus to become a celebrated promoter of cold cream or toilet water.

Perhaps this was the reason the members of this particular chorus were noted for their advantageous marriages: for all their beauty, their theatrical skills were not alarmingly professional. As Mrs. Wells received compliments and a further glass of champagne in the first interval, and flattered their host by pretending she needed his help to understand the wafer-thin plot, there was in her manner an unmistakable air of relief. Had Pattie stepped forward to the footlights to dance a spectacular solo or comedy turn, had she been called upon, as another girl was, to swing on a garlanded trapeze over the orchestra while the chorus pelted her with silk peonies, her chances of passing from this eccentric adventure to something more respectable would have been drastically diminished.

The Honorable Notty had booked a large private dining room above a nearby restaurant and had encouraged Pattie to bring along several of her new friends from the company. This was a relief, as their host's enthusiasm sat awkwardly with Robert's haughtiness (which, Harry had noted, grew far worse when he was made to feel middle class) and Frank's inability to varnish the truth. Indeed, Frank had just announced that true talent was one thing, he supposed, but his sister was cheapening herself and the family to no discernible purpose, when the party of performers arrived and everyone else burst into nervous laughter and applause.

Harry embraced Pattie—who was wearing Notty's watch, he noted—and she presented him to Gladys Cooper, who dropped him a laughing curtsey to show off the gown Winnie had made her, which was enjoying its first outing. Then there was a little flurry of awkwardness.

The usual questions of precedence were hardly going to arise in a restaurant, and at a round table. They were to sit where they liked, Notty announced unhelpfully—though he naturally would have Mrs. Wells on his right and Pattie on his left—so long as no men sat drearily beside their wives. In her exuberance, and evidently at ease with her admirer's largesse, Pattie had swept up with her more members of the company than could fit round the table. Harry ensured that Winnie had a seat between her brothers, then found himself at a secondary table the staff had hastily swathed in white linen.

He shook the hand of Cora Lane, an actress of a certain age who had sung a comedy song. She looked like minor royalty but turned out to speak a form of Cockney thinly larded with arch touches of elegance she had surely acquired from play scripts. She declared herself charmed, made him a funny little bow when he said, quite truthfully, how amusing he had found her song, and introduced him to the others at the table over which she had effortlessly assumed rule.

There was one other woman—a young, feathered wisp of a thing so shy and wordless it was hard to credit she had ever found the courage to pass through a stage door, much less attend an audition. She was introduced simply as Vera, as though the name told one all one need know, then not addressed again all evening.

"And these are Messrs Pryde, Hawkey and Gosling, whose footwork I'm sure you admired every bit as much as my little ditty."

"Gentlemen."

Harry was unsurprised to find the dancers' handshakes repellently limp. They were of a type he recognized from walks along the Strand or from his visits to the Jermyn Street baths: slim-hipped, ostentatiously flexible creatures who inexplicably chose to ape girls rather than exploit as men the advantages fate had awarded them. One assumed they had parents and siblings somewhere, in some rarely visited country village possibly, but they gave every impression of having emerged, fully formed, from eggs, as brittle as the waxy shells they had discarded.

"And this is Mr. Browning."

Mr. Browning had not come clucking and pecking from an egg; his handshake made Harry wonder whether his own had been sufficiently firm. He was taller than Harry, black-haired and serious.

They sat, Harry finding himself between solemn Mr. Browning and Mr. Pryde. Mr. Pryde insisted on clinking champagne flutes with Harry, simpering, "Cheers, m'dear," then immediately turned aside to pay court not to the resolutely silent Vera, who was on his other side, but to the empress of their little table, who had launched on some anecdote.

"You're stuck with me," Mr. Browning said, and allowed himself a small, self-deprecating smile, which emphasized the interesting cleft in his chin.

"On the contrary," Harry told him. He said it, as he often said things when shy, without thinking. Then he worried that the rejoinder sounded wrong, or misleading, so added, "You're rather a relief." Something in the close way Mr. Browning's deep-set eyes, with their lingering traces of stage make-up, were watching him caused him to stammer on *relief.*

It was one of his rare bad stammers, which seemed impossibly long and loud. Mr. Pryde turned to look at him with passing curiosity and he fancied Cora Lane momentarily paused in her performance to frown at the interruption.

"I'm so sorry," he managed at last. "You're rather a relief," he repeated, to show he could. "It only happens when I'm frightened."

"Well I'm not remotely frightening," Mr. Browning said. "I'm only an actor. Those two on either side of your pretty wife, with the beards, now they'd make any man stutter."

Harry glanced at Winnie, who noticed and narrowed her eyes slightly, privately amused as Robert held forth about something that seemed to involve salt, pepper and both his forks. "My brothers-in-law," he said.

"Ah," Mr. Browning said but did not apologize. "I could probably help you, if you came to me. I do a little voice instruction on the side, when not pursuing my glorious career."

"Oh," Harry began, then remembered to fill his lungs before he started. "I'm not sure I could—"

"I wouldn't charge." Again that discreet, interested little smile.

Food arrived, and because their table was an afterthought and was rather crushed into a corner, they had to shift slightly in their seats to allow the waiters to serve them. In shifting, Mr. Browning ended up sitting with his knee against Harry's within the damask tent of tablecloth. Because he was drunk on Notty's excellent champagne, Harry took a moment or two to register the warm pressure of another man's leg against his

own and a moment or two more to remember that the appropriate response, as practiced in crowded railway carriages and
omnibuses across the capital, was to say nothing that might
embarrass the other party but simply to move his leg aside.

Mr. Browning looked at him directly as Harry lifted a forkful
of crabmeat to his mouth, smiled and, still looking at him,
pressed his knee into his again. "You have nothing to fear," he
said. He scarcely needed to lower his voice because the others
were now making so much noise.

The waiters had not long before filled their glasses, but
Harry felt as though he had just drained his in a single, head-
spinning draft. A rush of warmth mounted to his cheeks. He
was not remotely delicate, but had he stood suddenly, he would
surely have fainted. He was taken with a strong urge to laugh
out loud, but instead managed to say, "I'm afraid of nothing,"
which was so untrue—he had always been a coward and was
demonstrably not of the heroic type—that he then did laugh, as
at some uproarious witticism, at which Mr. Browning watched
him with a kind expression, like someone waiting for another
to finish choking.

Then he briefly cupped a hand on Harry's knee and said,
in what felt like a shout but was probably no more than a
murmur, "My name is Hector, and when you undress tonight,
you'll find my card is in your trouser pocket," adding, by way
of explanation, "My father was a prestidigitator."

Harry had never been given to nightmares, or even to remembering his dreams much, although for a year after his mother's
death he had often cried himself to sleep, as much from a new
fear that he would die in his slumber as from the unremitting
sorrow at her loss. Around the confusing onset of puberty,
when the dire but unspecific warnings of the Harrow chaplain

and the filthy jokes and teasing of the older boys began to make a kind of sense, he had one dream so repeatedly and memorably that it came to resemble a recollection rather than a product of his sleeping imagination.

He was in a group in a classroom or gymnasium under the instruction of some teacher or other when a smartly uniformed man strode in unannounced with a letter. Evidently deferring to some far greater authority, the teacher hastily opened the letter and read it, and then he and the visitor searched through the class. The other boys stepped aside, as if knowing they weren't the ones sought, but Harry just stood there, waiting, knowing, once he had experienced the dream already, how it would end. As the man in uniform grew nearer, he became aware that he was extravagantly handsome, like a prince from a legend or the young Lord Kitchener, yet also dangerous, a man who could have one killed with a flick of his gloved hand. The other boys parted like a treacherous sea, leaving him exposed, yet the sea wasn't precisely treacherous, since he wanted to be found.

The moment that invariably woke him, when the teacher pointed him out and the uniformed man's eyes finally met his own, was as thrilling as it was heart-stopping.

Chapter Eight

The next day was given over to a flutter of packing and preparation. Harry and Winnie and Phyllis and the nursery maid were traveling to Chester for the christening of Jack and George's firstborn.

Jack, as ever, acted upon Harry as north upon a compass. His seemingly uncomplicated happiness, his delight in George, in fatherhood, in having little Phyllis ride on his back while he played pony, were a kind-eyed corrective and made Harry sharply aware how close to the brink he had strayed. And yet, throughout the visit, its busy pleasures, the inspections of improvements to the house and practice, the christening and lunch party after it, a walk around the old city walls, a day at the races and even a morning's excellent riding from a stud near Tattenhall where Jack had the care of a mare and new foal, a voice was speaking to him that said nothing of family or wholesomeness.

On the long train ride home he sought to silence it by taking an interest in Winnie, but she was preoccupied on her own account, sad at parting from George, who was such a favorite of hers, and she soon let the conversation die so that she could read her novel or stare wanly out of their compartment window.

"We could always move, you know," he told her. "Find a house in Chester. Jack assures me the cost of living is far lower there. Then you could see George every week instead of twice a year."

"It's a nice idea," she told him wearily, "but Mother wouldn't hear of it. I fear she has rather come to depend on us. The boys are either severe to her or mocking and the girls give her nothing but worry." When he made no rejoinder, she briefly laid a hand on his arm and said, "But it's a kind thought. Thank you," then returned to *The Queen's Necklace* and left him failing to read Kipling, a prey to thoughts he would much rather not entertain.

On their first day back in town, he found he was persistently shivery, perhaps through having gotten so wet on the ride with Jack, so headed to Jermyn Street after lunch, thinking a Turkish bath would warm his bones a little. He found he had passed the entrance to the baths, however, and made for another doorway entirely, which stood between two shopfronts. He had burned Mr. Browning's card in the grate when he found it in his trouser pocket the morning after the trip to the Gaiety, but apparently the handwritten address on its back had scorched itself on his consciousness first.

It was a flat, he imagined. There were many such small roosts for bachelors. Thrice in ten minutes he saw women enter or leave by a door that wasn't a shop's. He had several times heard it said that no lady would ever be seen in the neighborhood. He saw well-dressed women buying cheese in Paxton and Whitfield, and soap and such in Floris, but perhaps they did so with a grim, breath-holding air before slipping back up to the relative respectability of Piccadilly.

Mr. Browning's building had no knocker or doorbell, only a front door in need of paint, propped open with an umbrella stand. There was a dim glimpse of a hall with a battered table where post could be left. Presumably bell pulls or knockers were on each flat's door further up. But what if they weren't and Harry entered to find himself an intruder in Hector Browning's

house, or worse, if he had mistaken the address, that of an indignant stranger?

He stood on the other side of the street and started to examine the faces of the women passing by. Some were maids
or cooks, to judge from the relative simplicity of their clothes
or cheapness of their hats, but the others were harder to read.
Smart. Smooth. Polished. Very occasionally daring. Were they
blameless or scarlet?

Of course it was in the nature of respectability to reveal or
imply nothing but itself. Any signs were likely to be small: the
discreet callus left by a removed wedding ring, a tugged curl escaping from an otherwise immaculate chignon, perhaps only a
minutely torn hem betraying the violence of a passion recently
sated. And what would be the male equivalents? A hectic flush
to the cheeks, perhaps. Fingernail marks to the back of the
neck. Perhaps only the suggestive seaside smell he had caught
off neighbors in the baths sometimes, a smell in which something was added to the usual musk of a man not yet clean.

Mr. Browning was standing in the doorway. He was at once
shorter and more handsome than Harry had remembered. He
was in shirtsleeves and no collar, his cuffs neatly turned up,
and he was relishing a cigarette and the sunshine and watching
Harry with some amusement. He appeared oblivious to the
throng of human traffic about them, and his attention had the
effect of seeming to block it out for Harry too, so that he crossed
the street without looking, causing a cabby to curse at him.

"Mr. Cane. What a pleasant surprise." Mr. Browning held
out a hand.

"I wasn't sure I had remembered the address," Harry said,
only he stuttered badly on the W.

Mr. Browning didn't wince, or look away, or finish his sentence for him the way people often did, but watched with

interest. "Forgive my dishabille," he said. "You had no appointment."

"Er, no. No, I hadn't."

"But I'm sure we can fit you in." He trod out his cigarette neatly on the pavement, then headed upstairs.

Heart racing, Harry followed him, taking in a length of worn red stair-carpet and hunting prints. He imagined the talk of appointments was for the benefit of passers-by, so was perplexed when, businesslike, Mr. Browning showed him into a consulting room hung with diagrams of the lungs, mouth and tongue and illustrations of the various arrangements of lips and tongue. Among them, not especially apropos, were hung engravings of ancient Greek sculpture: charioteers, discoboloi, wrestlers.

"Never mind the rhotacism or the stutter for now," Mr. Browning said. "We need to get you to breathe properly. At the moment your speech is air-starved, like a bird in a box. Take off your jacket, please, and your waistcoat, so I can see what's going on. That's right. I'll hang them here for you. Now. Feet apart. A little further. Now breathe."

"I am breathing."

"No you're not. Breathe in. Fill your lungs. Keep breathing in. All the way. Now breathe out. There. Too quick. Too starved! Stop being so afraid."

"I'm not."

"Trust me. You're terrified. Breathe in again, and this time say a nice long *ah* as you breathe out."

Harry did as he was told, while Browning watched him critically.

"Again," Browning said. "Don't flinch. I need to touch you to feel what's happening." He stepped up behind Harry and placed the flat of one hand on his solar plexus. "Ah," he said.

"Nice slow one. Louder. Louder! That's better. I want you always to think of your breaths when you speak. Always be
aware that you are using air to form the words and that you
need plenty of it. Breathing is natural but it's incredible how
bad most people are at doing it. They breathe with barely a
third of their lung capacity and their speech is starved and hob-
bles as a result. Were you often scared as a boy?"

"Usually."

"Of a man?"

"Usually."

"Hmm. Now. I need to touch you in two places at once."
He kept one hand in the middle of Harry's chest but placed
his other a hand's span lower, on his belly. "Good," he said, so
close now that Harry felt his words on the nape of his neck and
could smell the citrus tang of his shaving preparation. "You
have some muscle there. Now I want you to use it. Breathe
in and say a long *ah* again. Don't be so self-conscious. All my
neighbors are out at work, and anyway, nobody could care less.
But this time, as you're exhaling, I want to feel you pressing
out on my other hand down here as hard as you can. I'll press
in but I need you to resist me."

Feeling absurd and giddy all at once, Harry did as he said,
pressing out on the grasp that was burning into him, feeling
sweat break out on his chest and back, and the *ah* he produced
seemed like a shout, like no noise he normally made.

"Good," Browning said, hands still in place. "Now breathe
normally and say, *I wasn't sure of the address.*"

"I wasn't sure," Harry began, with no hesitation, no stutter,
then broke off as he felt Hector Browning plant a firm kiss on
the nape of his neck.

For a minute or two they stood there, Browning's lips and
nose pressing from one side and his hands from the other, and

then, very, very hesitantly, Harry brought his hands up to rest on top of the other man's, at which Browning kissed him again and brought one of his legs forward so that it nestled between Harry's.

"I hav—" Harry began, and stuttered.

"Stop," Browning murmured. "Breathe in. Now tell me."

"I have absolutely no idea what to do," Harry said, without stuttering.

"I know exactly what to do. Turn round."

Harry turned to find Browning's handsome face inches from his own. Browning smiled, then kissed him on the lips.

There was a small bedroom off the consulting room, and a minute bathroom with a view of drainpipes.

Some forty minutes later, as they lay panting and naked across the bed, which was so narrow that one or other of them had always to be beneath the other, Browning murmured, "Most of my students come in the late mornings. I am always free between half past two and four o'clock. My door won't be locked. If I'm out when you arrive, just get in the bed and wait for me."

They were lovers for over a year. Animal instinct told Harry that the only way to stay sane during such an undertaking was not to analyze it. But of course he did analyze it, because he was moderately intelligent, sensitive and underoccupied, and because there were usually a hundred and sixty-four hours of each week's hundred and sixty-eight when they were not together. He was soon an expert at the risk he was taking. The notorious trials of the 1890s had left their mark. If caught, they risked imprisonment with hard labor as well as a lifetime of disgrace.

"But we won't be caught," Browning insisted. (It was an oddity of their intimacy that Harry could never quite think of him as Hector and never called him anything.) "The ones who are caught are the fools who stray beyond their class or age group."

Harry was thinking that they weren't of quite the same class, then remembered that his sister-in-law was now a chorus girl, which had rather blurred such distinctions.

"Besides," Browning went on, "you come to me for speech lessons, of which you speak to no one because you're so terribly ashamed."

He meticulously wrote Harry a cash receipt for a lesson after their every meeting, although no money changed hands, of course. Harry filed the receipts in his desk at home, then decided that was ridiculous, so took to burning them once they were a week or so old.

Terror of discovery would steal up on him now in idle moments, usually amidst family. In a crowded, overheated scene, it was like an icy draft only he could detect. Or he would wake in the night and not be able to sleep for the compulsion to imagine the worst. And yet, paradoxically, this terror seemed to form an intrinsic part of the excitement his meetings with Browning brought him.

He had never had a job, so until then his life had enjoyed a smooth interconnectedness, like that of a young woman. But now, like any working man's, it acquired compartments. He did not stop loving Winnie and Phyllis. If anything, he began to love Phyllis all the more, the moment he began to risk losing her forever. Winnie had quietly ceased visiting his bed not long after their move to Ma Touraine—a thing he accepted with guilty relief, even though he never tired of her private company and conversation. He regarded his wife with new understanding, knowing now the strain it must have cost her to keep her unquenched feelings for Whitacre in one box of her heart, her love for her child in a second and her respectable wish to survive in yet a third. Secrecy, he began to see, was corrosive, less of his intimate relationships than of his self-respect. He had never felt so unmanly or immature.

His afternoon visits to Browning's brass bed exposed his clothed life for a sham, even as they awoke in him a whorish shamelessness he recognized as his buried essence.

It was a part of the thrill he felt in the little room, as Browning played him and ploughed him, that his lover forced the admission from his lips. "You like this, don't you?" he would ask. "You want this, don't you?" and Harry never once stammered when he answered yes and found he could even laugh at the recognition of himself the confirmation brought.

There was a mirror over the little room's overflowing chest of drawers angled precisely to reflect them on the bed. Harry rarely looked at himself below the neck at home, unless fully dressed and about to leave the house, and was aghast at first, then fascinated, at the sight of himself, so pale, yet flushed with lust, on all fours before a handsome, hairy-bodied man.

It was inevitable, perhaps, that he became eaten up with jealousy.

"Do you see other men?" he began to ask, or something like it, and Browning would invariably smile and kiss him and answer in some variation of "You will never know," which was worse than any flat denial. It was inevitable, too, perhaps, that the ecstasies Browning drove him to would eventually drive him to say he loved him.

"Don't be silly," Browning would say. "Don't let's ask for the impossible," or "Let's just enjoy what we have," or, worst of all, a smiling but unreciprocating "I know."

Harry didn't love him with his brain. He knew Browning's wit was cruel and his thinking shallow. He knew that Browning,

though understandably vain, was taken up, to the point of te-
diousness, with the tiny world in which he worked.

And yet, had Browning produced two tickets to the Paris
boat train and said, "Come live with me where we can be
ourselves," Harry knew he would have had no hesitation in de-
serting everything and everybody to go with him.

Had Browning reciprocated, been sentimental or even clinging, Harry might have pulled away or lost interest, but the
strictness and control the other exercised over him had the re-
verse effect. He had no souvenirs or keepsakes, beyond what
scent of his lover lingered beneath his fingernails for a few precious hours after each meeting. Letter-writing was of course
impossible.

He did put pen to paper, however. Browning was out one afternoon when he let himself in. Tipsy from a good lunch with
Winnie, who had come into town with him to drop off a dress
for a client then been waved off on the train on the pretext that
he was visiting his broker, Harry had soon bored of lolling, half
naked, on Browning's dirty bed, so had written him a rather
saucy, unsigned billet-doux in an autograph book on the bedside
table. They hadn't discussed it in the heat of Browning's arrival
but he was fairly certain he had read it. He wrote more in the
same little book on other occasions when he was kept waiting.
He allowed the writing to become anything but romantic, as he
sensed Browning would dislike that, making his short effusions
flatteringly pornographic, using words he still could not speak
aloud even in the button-breaking heights of passion.

He often remembered now a chilling little exchange he had
overheard between his cousins, the country ones who had so
little to do with him. One had spoken with disgust of the way a
neighboring landowner beat his dog, and the other had sighed,
"Yes, the man's a brute, but it's an outlet, I suppose…"

Chapter Nine

Harry had been at the theater again. Under cover of supporting Pattie's less than glorious but nonetheless continuing career at the Gaiety, he attended her first show there, and its replacements, assiduously, until he knew every banal song and facile dance step off by heart. The latest offering was the usual drivel and froth, no more profound than its predecessor, but the gentlemen of the chorus, fronted by Browning, had a rather daring number in swimming costumes. (Browning said these were damnably hot and itchy to dance in.)

Tonight, at short notice, Pattie had stepped forward to sing a solo for an actress who was ill. Harry had gone on his own because Winnie had a wedding dress to complete, and had rather enjoyed himself even though, to his consternation, Browning was nowhere to be seen. He called at the stage door afterward to pass on his congratulations to Pattie. He sent up his card to her and couldn't help noticing that several of the departing actors, including Cora Lane, seemed surprised to see him waiting there in the yellowish light.

The doorkeeper's runner, a youth with angry spots, returned, handed him back his card and said he was sorry but Miss Wells was "suddenly indisposed." Harry thought little of this: Notty was probably with her, and he had no doubt that by now, Notty had become her lover. Pattie, he suspected, was too much the sensualist, too little the tactician, and had misplayed her cards and found herself with a gold watch and a lover instead of a plump engagement diamond, a stable future and the remote possibility of a title. She now often *stayed with friends in town* rather than come home after a performance, behavior that nobody challenged or questioned, perhaps for fear of what it might drive her to confirm. Mrs. Wells and Winnie had taken to sighing when she was spoken of, and referring to her, as often as not, as *poor Pattie*. Notty still came to Sunday lunches occasionally, but any hope of marriage was a pallid, sickly thing.

Life in Strawberry Hill had become more comfortable in the last year, since both Robert and Frank had married. Robert had wooed and won a client's wealthy widow and was living in pompous splendour in Richmond. Frank had found his Elfine quite unassisted, a bosomless bluestocking with no sense of humor, who matched him so perfectly she might have been bred for the purpose. They had taken on and restored a house Mrs. Wells had inherited from her mother in distant Camden.

So not only did they all now have more space, but Harry was growing used to acting as head of the otherwise female household. There were times now, after a good lunch perhaps, and playing badminton with the girls on the lawn, when he felt his life richer than Browning's, in his suite of bachelor cells, where the nearest grass was a public park and the nearest loved ones heaven knew where.

There was one room left lit when he came home. He thought nothing of this since it was a household custom always to leave a lamp burning in the sitting room at the front of the house to welcome anyone out late. When he had bolted the front door behind him and hung up his coat and hat, he stepped into the sitting room, thinking to put out the lamp, and found Robert in there, waiting in an armchair with a book.

"Robert, hello. What a nice surprise," he said, though it wasn't entirely.

Robert had jumped up as he entered, evidently nervous. From the smell of him, the glass of whisky he was drinking was not his first. "Please sit down," he said, not shaking the hand Harry automatically offered, but covering the awkwardness of not doing so by patting at his jacket pockets. He had not dressed for dinner.

"Robert, is something wrong? Is it Winnie? Have you eaten?"

"Do shut up and sit down," Robert said, his voice uneven.

Harry sat.

Robert remained standing, swaying slightly. Harry had rarely seen him drunk before and, being sober himself, was peculiarly sensitive to the older man's tension.

"Just answer me this," Robert said. "This one thing." He reached into the breast pocket of his jacket and drew out a small, silk-covered notebook that Harry did not immediately recognize, as it was appearing so much out of its usual context. "Is this handwriting yours?" He fumbled the little book open to a page where Harry immediately identified one of his pornographic messages to Browning.

Harry hesitated, wondering by what grotesque accident such a thing had traveled from the obscure Jermyn Street flat to his brother-in-law's sweaty possession. He was glad he had drunk so little earlier; even so, he needed to choose his words with a care he was not sure he could muster. The fear that had been rumbling in the background of his thoughts all year was threatening to make his hands shake. He discreetly clasped them to his knees, picturing policemen at the door of Ma Touraine, imagining the fuss, Mrs. Wells nervously charming them and saying they must have made a mistake. It was not oakum picking or hard labor in a quarry he dreaded, he realized, nor exposure in a courtroom, but the unstoppable process by which his wife's family and his brother would pass from bafflement to revulsion.

"Who else knows?" he asked, somehow managing not to stutter.

"Is it your handwriting, man? Because if it isn't, I must involve the police in a case of attempted blackmail."

Harry nodded. "It's mine." And now he stuttered. "I...I mean the bit you showed me is."

There was no fire in the grate, simply one of the pretty paper fans Winnie made. Robert crouched down, tugged the fan aside so clumsily it would never sit right again and tore the little book apart. He lit a taper and set fire to the first pages, then dropped section after section to burn on top of them. The brief flare was merry and the lamplight seemed much dimmer when it had died down.

"There," Robert said, returning to his armchair. "I never saw it and neither did you. The bloody thing never existed."

For a giddy moment Harry thought that was an end to the matter, that some sort of gentlemen's agreement had been arrived upon. But then he thought again about the strangeness of the book having reached Robert and knew that couldn't be the case.

"Pattie knows," Robert said at last, taking another swig of whisky. "And Notty, and a fellow gentleman of the company by the name of Pryde."

"I...I don't understand."

"Your partner in sodomy, clearly unaware of what you had written in there, took it along to the theater in the hope of getting a departing autograph from the lady whose engagement is soon to elevate her out of the theater to the ranks of the outer peerage. I believe Winnie has made several gowns for her but I forget her name."

"Sylvia Storey."

"That's the one. But before it could be handed over—and this was possibly the one blessing in a revolting business—Mr. Pryde stole it from your Mr. Browning's dressing room and presented it to poor Pattie, demanding money for his silence."

"But Pryde is..."

"One of your sort? I've no doubt. Which is why his instincts are so readily criminal."

"Did she pay him?"

"Of course not. But Notty did. What were you thinking, man?" His tone was almost kind.

Harry took a breath before he spoke, remembering Browning's lessons. "I don't suppose I *was* thinking."

They sat in silence. The clock in the hall struck one.

"What will you do?" Harry asked at last.

"Oh I shall do nothing," Robert said. "I've done my bit. You, however, will be removing yourself from this family at the first opportunity. I suggest you leave the country and don't think of coming back. We shall look after Winnie and Phyllis. If you make over your remaining property to Winnie, she will at least have an income. You must tell her you have lost so much money through..." here he paused minutely, "another bad investment that you have no option but to flee the country to seek your fortune. The Cape. Australia. New Zealand. There are plenty of places you could strike out for...if you were man enough. Where you actually go need not concern us."

"What if Winnie wants to come with me?"

"She's not the pioneer type, especially not encumbered with a child. But you must dissuade her. If you don't, I shall have no option, as Phyllis's godfather and guardian of her spiritual welfare, but to tell Winifred what I know so that the child can be protected. The same would go for Georgina and your brother. Provided you go, they need know nothing but that you have left to seek your fortune. Your...second fortune. I expect you to be gone within the week, although I would be far happier if you were to leave tonight."

Although Harry and Winnie had not shared a bed for a while, he had her photograph and Phyllis's beside his bed. They were paired in a little leather traveling frame she had given him the previous Christmas, although he was the least traveled man she knew. He held it in his hands a while, staring at the two sweet faces as men once did at little icons of their favored saints, and knowing he was gone already, as far from them in outlook and prospects as he would soon be in location.

He did not sleep but found that the moment his head touched the pillows an unusual clarity of thought descended on him, and with it, an unexpected surge of gratitude to his unattractive brother-in-law, with all his second-hand thoughts and pompous, third-hand turns of phrase. Robert had been placed in an impossible position. To go to the police was to stain his family's name and possibly risk his professional reputation. Not to go, to destroy evidence as he had done, and so let one blackmailer and two buggers escape justice, would always weigh heavily upon his lawyerly heart.

Harry knew what he was escaping. Since meeting Browning, he had become peculiarly attuned to the fate of those Robert would call *his kind* and whom he had heard Frank refer to as *Wildebeasts*. Five years with hard labor. And everyone knew that the dire effects of working on a treadmill or in a quarry on the health of a man unhardened were such that even a year's sentence was a shortening of lifespan. Since the furore over the

Wilde trial, in his school days, court cases were scantly, if ever, reported, as though not to name a thing were not to grant it a reality, but they happened all the time. Browning had heard about them through what he called the *Nellygraph*, and had passed on horror stories with a grim kind of glee. With equal relish he would pore over reports of suicide—by drowning, razor or lye—convinced there were often clues that the wretches involved had been caught out but been granted a merciful interval in which to avoid a greater shame.

Harry was under no illusion that Robert intended mercy to anyone but Winnie and Phyllis, but he was grateful nonetheless. He was also excited by, and frightened of, all the possibilities suddenly before him, and felt again the old tyranny of choice he had thought marriage had put behind him.

Phyllis would forget him soon enough, as he had forgotten his mother except for a strictly symbolic bedside shadow. She would be protected by a phalanx of grandmother, uncles and aunts.

Chapter Ten

Harry breakfasted with the younger girls, telling them how wonderfully their sister had sung on stage the night before, and how Notty and other admirers had hurled bouquets. (In fact her voice had sounded reedy and nervous, the applause had been scant and Notty's bouquet the only one, but he wanted them to picture something happier.) Then he forestalled the maid and carried up Winnie's breakfast tray himself.

To her he gave a more honest account of Pattie's performance, knowing she would see through anything else. He asked about her evening.

"Robert came unexpectedly," she said. "He wanted to see you and I'm afraid we were all so tired we left him alone sitting up for you. Was he still here when you got back?"

"Yes. Money worries."

"Not again."

"Worse this time, darling."

She threw him a worried glance and bit a corner off her toast.

"I need to go away for a bit to, you know, make some money."

"Why on earth?"

"Well, there's no need to sound so incredulous!"

"But what could you do?"

"All sorts of things, if I can travel light and cheaply. Mine companies need clerks. I could even try my hand at tea planting. Or rubber. Or sheep in New Zealand."

"Are you quite well?"

"I'm serious, Winnie. I'm heading into town now to ask around. See what I can find out."

She smiled sadly and shook her head, and he realized with a spark of irritation that she scarcely thought of him as a man at all. "Sorry," she said. "I'm not sneering. Just a bit surprised. Oh, be an angel and look in on the nursery. Nurse may have forgotten that Phyllis has a doctor's appointment this morning at ten thirty."

The front door in Jermyn Street was propped open as usual. Harry slipped upstairs but heard the unmistakable sounds of a bona fide elocution lesson in progress—a woman enunciating, *She stood upon the balcony inexplicably mimicking him hiccuping*, in a way that sounded neither like a duchess nor a guttersnipe, merely artificial and actressy. He found a hard little chair on the next landing up and perched on it until the lesson ended and he heard Browning seeing the pupil out.

"Have you a moment?" he called out and Browning jumped.

"Quickly," he said, retreating into his flat and holding open the door. "You can't be here," he added. "Someone could be watching."

"No one's watching," Harry told him.

"How do you know?"

"My brother-in-law burned the evidence. There'll be no further consequences."

"Other than two of us losing our jobs..."

"I'm so sorry, Browning."

Browning stopped looking quite so stern and planted a quick kiss on his forehead. "It could have been much, much worse."

"I'm so sorry. I thought you'd read what I'd written."

"I had no idea you'd ever written anything. Was it witty?"

"It was absolutely filthy."

Browning laughed. "Oh, I'll survive. I think I'll try my luck in New York. I've got friends there and they say a *genoowine* English accent goes down a storm."

"Ah. Good. Could I..."

"Breathe, Harry. Deeper. Now. Let it out."

"Could I come with you?"

"Whatever for?"

"Well, I...I had been thinking of Paris, originally."

"I can't speak French. I'd find no work except as a dancer, and I'm getting a bit old for that..."

"I could support us. If we lived simply."

"I dislike simplicity. It's rarely comfortable and usually cold."

"So let me come to New York with you. I'll get a job. We could find a flat. Like this but a bit bigger."

"America's laws are no different to England's. Possibly worse."

"We could be careful, then. Two flats side by side."

Browning laughed.

"I love you," Harry said.

Browning stopped laughing.

"I want to be with you," Harry went on, and all at once, now that this seemed possible and not just a married man's pathetic fantasy, it was the truth and he wanted it with all his heart.

Browning turned aside to flick at a pile of papers. "What color are my eyes?" he asked.

"Brown."

"They're green. When's my birthday?"

"How should I know? You've never told me."

"How old am I?"

"Twenty-five? Thirty? I don't know. Does it matter?"

"You don't know me, Harry, any more than I know you."

"We can find out about each other, now we've time. A long boat trip..."

"Christ, Harry! Listen to yourself. You're not attractive when you plead. I preferred you married and unobtainable. In fact that's how I prefer all my men. Men can't live together like a married couple. It's grotesque and whatever would be the point, even if they could? It's not as though they're going to start a family."

There was a knock at the door and this time it was Harry who jumped.

"That's my eleven o'clock," Browning said. "Go."

"Browning, I—"

"Go, Harry. Live long. Be happy. I can't see you again."

"But—"

"I'm opening the door now, so for God's sake dry your eyes."

From Jermyn Street Harry wandered down through St. James's to the park and then up on to the Strand. He went into a chemist's shop and bought a small bottle of laudanum and, because it looked alarming on its own, a packet of blackcurrant pastilles in a pretty tin. He leaned against a shopfront, uncorked the bottle and sniffed the contents, which smelt of alcohol and cinnamon, then remembered the stuff had to be taken in water. There was a Lyon's Corner House nearby, so he went in there and asked for a pot of tea and a glass of water to go with it. Experimentally he added just the recommended number of drops to the water and knocked them back.

It tasted bitter, rather unpleasant, but it was only right that death should. Given time and the right space in which to do it—a quiet corner of a park, perhaps—he could imagine tipping in the whole bottle and gulping it down. How much worse would it taste? And did it matter, since he'd be dying by then?

A current of warmth began to surge through him to the top of his head, and suddenly everything seemed to slow down, the bustle of horses and buses in the street, the chatter of people and clatter of china and cutlery at the tables around him. It seemed as though all the joints in his body relaxed, every ache, even the memory of how an ache felt, lifted away. He could quite easily have laid his head on the table before him and fallen asleep.

Then he noticed a crowd on the pavement opposite. They were milling around the window displays of a place that clearly had been a shop but now, instead of a shopkeeper's name, announced CANADIAN EMIGRATION in large letters. Curious, doing his best not to slur his words, he paid for the tea, left the laudanum bottle behind, merely smiling at the nippy who called after him holding it up, and crossed the Strand for a closer look.

It took him a while to press through the crowd. There was a model of a farm—a pretty wooden house with a veranda and gingham curtains—surrounded by an ingeniously simulated field of golden wheat, and above it an announcement he could not quite believe, of free land. One hundred and sixty acres could be had, it said, for nothing but three years' partial residency on them and what sounded like minimal work.

He read all he could of both window displays—the second had a similar announcement above a model train encircling a placid herd of identical cows—then pushed inside, queued to speak to a clerk and was sent away with a brightly colored leaflet about homesteading in the *Last Best West*. It gave advice about shipping lines that sailed to Halifax from Liverpool and a list of outfitters who could equip him for the adventure. One of these was at the other end of the Strand, near the Savoy, as was an agency for the shipping lines.

The outfitter, already used to such enquiries, handed him a list that was remarkably like those he and Jack had to tick off when packing for school. *Dress suit*, he read. *Best tweed suit. Tennis suit. One cloth suit of "leather suiting" and extra trousers for same. Three suits hard in wear. Cord trousers two pair. Ulster coat. Pea jacket. Mackintosh. Dressing gown (useful as extra warm garment in extremis). Flannel shirts twelve. White shirts two. Flannel pajamas four. Winter and summer drawers—four pair apiece. Four vests. Twenty-four pair socks. Six collars. A cholera belt. An India rubber bath. Portmanteau for cabin. White cravats and cuffs. Cardigan. Two jerseys (Guernsey knit for endurance). Twelve pocket handkerchiefs. Six Turkish towels. Waterproof sheet (large and of best quality). Pair large blankets. Rug. Six pair dress gloves. Three pair hedging and ditching gloves. Two pair Canada mittens. A housewife with buttons, needles etc. including saddlery needles and waxed thread. One pair boots. One pair high boots. Dress shoes. Unnailed shoes. Slippers. Ambulance braces. Helmet of Jaeger wool.*

He had absolutely no idea how Canadian mittens might differ from the English variety and was faintly alarmed at the prospect of a cholera belt, whatever that might be, but reading the list evoked the adventure pleasantly even before it was under way.

Had Winnie known the ugly truth, he could have backed away from her, weighed down by shame. He could not quite believe that, made worldly by the theater and Notty, Pattie had forborne to tell her. Winnie had a quality to her, however, that made people withhold bad news. She had a family reputation for sensitivity, so *Don't tell Winnie* or *Whatever will Winnie say?* were common refrains.

When he returned that afternoon, having booked as modest a berth as he could countenance and arranged for his strange kit to be sent on to await him at Liverpool in a new steamer trunk, and then called back at the Canadian Emigration office because he had thought of numerous questions to ask them, he thought it best to tell her exactly what he was about.

She had been laconic, even softly mocking, over breakfast, but, faced with a firm arrangement and dates and a ticket, she was distraught. "It's all my fault," she kept saying. "I've driven you away. I've not loved you as I should."

"You've loved me as best as you could, which was better than I deserved," he said, and applied soothing variants of the phrase until the noise she was making brought in Mrs. Wells and he was obliged to tell the whole story again.

He might have expected mother to react like daughter, but her response was rather sturdier. "Well I think that's rather splendid," she said. "Living among all these petticoats is no place for a man, and out there you'll be able to make something of yourself. You might even find gold. Or oil! And you can shoot us all fur coats!"

"Mother, I'll be planting wheat," he explained, "and maybe oats. I'll be farming."

But she still thought it was splendid and in turn helped break the news to little Phyllis—a thing he had been dreading—saying that Daddy was going off to the Americas to join the cowboys.

Phyllis was too young to have a sense of distance or time. Her parents were either with her or not, attention was either granted her or not. The idea of her father as a cowboy made her laugh, especially as her nursery maid had recently taught her that cows said moo, but at bedtime she was seized by a terrible panic and clung to him wailing that he was not to go. So of course he lied to her, saying he'd soon be back and that she was to be good for Mummy and not make a fuss. And his words left a painful lump, like an overlarge mouthful of apple, in his throat.

Over supper, the younger sisters were drily satirical. "But Harry, you *can't* be a farmer!" The idea clearly struck them as absurd.

"I don't see why not," he said. "I love horses. Jack's a vet now. Why shouldn't I be a farmer?"

"It'll be such hard work, won't it?" Winnie asked, as though the idea had only just occurred to her.

"Yes. At first. It'll take some getting used to. And the weather. Out there, the winters are terrific."

"But there are wolves, aren't there?" Kitty said. "And bears!"

"Don't frighten Winnie," their mother said.

"Not in the prairies. The man in the emigration office said the main problem would be rabbits—which one can always eat—and coyotes, which are only really a pest if you keep hens or sheep."

"Could we please just talk about something other than Canada?" Winnie asked, quietly but firmly, and they all remembered she was about to become a grass widow and ate on in silence.

At bedtime she came across to his room and lay on his bed, leaning against the footboard opposite him. "I can't possibly sleep," she said. "Not yet. I'm so sorry. It never even occurred to me to ask, but...do you want me to come with you?"

"Heavens, no," he insisted. "I mean, of course I'd love your company, but it's going to be tough at first, at least until I

have somewhere to live. I'll be roughing it. Sleeping in a tent.
But...maybe you could join me after a while. Once I've a little
house with a...a garden and a veranda and a cozy stove. First
thing I'll do is plant some roses."

"You'll write?"

"Of course, silly. Try stopping me."

"I'll write every day. I warn you now."

"Just send me Phyllie's pictures from time to time with little
bulletins on the back. *New teeth coming through. Made dress
for Clara Butt. Pattie to be duchess after all.* That kind of
thing."

"Oh don't be light-hearted. That makes it worse."

"Sorry." He tentatively held her small slippered feet, which
were resting on the pillow by his side. "To be honest, given, you
know, how things were when we...I didn't think you'd care
that much."

"Of course I care. No wife wants to be on her own."

"You won't be on your own. Not in this house."

She sighed at that, trying not to laugh, and fell to twining her
dressing gown ribbon about her fingers. It was an extremely
fetching dressing gown, of striking severity, made of oyster
satin with a dark blue trim. She was sure to have made it herself, and all at once he felt how wasted she was on him, that
she was really rather magnificent.

She stayed in his bed that night and every night until he left,
not expecting him to make love to her and not clinging to him
as Phyllis had done, but pressing close against him, as if for
simple warmth and reassurance. He was disgusted at himself
that he could sleep at all, for her tender touch made him feel
like a murderer, but he was grateful for it too and slept soundly.

Once he had reassured her that she and Phyllis would be provided for financially, whatever success or failure he made in the

far West, they avoided the topic of his imminent departure by common, tacit consent. Instead, the two of them made his remaining days a sort of holiday, although the spring was proving late, wet and cold. They took Phyllis to the zoo, where he hid his alarm at being reminded just how large grizzly bears were, and to Kew Gardens, and impulsively took a chilly, eccentric day trip back to Herne Bay to walk beside the sea and eat overcooked sole in a deserted hotel dining room, where Winnie suddenly touched the back of his hand and murmured, "I feel I'm sending you off to war."

Nobody came with him to St. Pancras to see him off. Instead, Winnie and Phyllis saw him as far as Strawberry Hill's little station. There Phyllis picked up on the atmosphere, and cried so hard that conversation became impossible and husband and wife were able to part in laughter.

Chapter Eleven

He had already communicated the official version of his departure to Jack, and Jack had sent back a telegram saying, *Blimey,
Governor. Stay night before. Will see you off L'pool.*

He thought about dodging this kindness, if only out of cowardice, knowing it would be even harder to lie to Jack than to
Winnie, easier simply to slip out of the country like a felon.
Then he thought of all the times he had put himself out for his
brother as they were growing up and realized that those small
sacrifices had been a kind of burden on Jack. Traveling from
Chester to Liverpool docks and waving off his boat, and being
made in the process a party if not to his disgrace, then to its
codified implication, would be a liberation for Jack. It would
complete the process of maturing and severance that moving
away, marriage and fatherhood had begun in him.

On the long journey to Crewe, Harry read, until he could
recite passages by heart, the booklet he had bought from an
impromptu bookstall someone had set up near Canada House.
The Settler's Guide, it was called, *Or the Homesteader's Handy
Helper.* A fulsomely bearded farmer was pictured on the front,
under a large straw hat and with a pitchfork over one shoulder
and a hand jauntily on hip. He was worryingly uneven of gaze,
as though drunk or exhausted. Making repeated use of the
phrase *in actual bona fide residence*, the booklet seemed to
have been written for the dim-witted or for those with only a
frail grasp of English. *Write your name in full and plainly. As*

far as possible, confine each letter to one subject. One mealy-mouthed pronouncement in particular began to haunt him to the point where he wished he had not read it even once. *It happens not infrequently that a settler finds after a year or two's trial that he has unfortunately settled upon a piece of land which is not suitable for farming and out of which he cannot reasonably hope to make a living.* Since the promised virgin territory had been divided up into mathematically precise squares for settlement—and Harry had looked at one of the remarkably unrevealing domain lands maps in the emigration office—what was to stop him accidentally assigning himself land that was all rock or entirely under water? Such things could happen, the booklet blandly assured him; in so large a country, how could they not? But all he had to do in such an unhappy predicament was to file notice of abandonment and start the entire process afresh. He noted that the booklet had been published as long ago as 1894, fourteen years earlier. If this process had been in train so long already, surely all the best quarter-sections would have gone and only the bogs and rocks be left?

George spread out a map, which was seventy years old so did not show Saskatchewan or Manitoba—merely a sort of here-be-monsters void in between two relatively settled coasts—and declared she was really very envious of him and did he want a housekeeper, and Jack demanded to see the one-way boat ticket as proof they weren't being hoodwinked.

When George left them alone for a while after dinner, however, Jack asked more serious questions. What did Winnie think? Surely she didn't want him to leave her and Phyllis and would be coming out to join him? And surely the money situation wasn't so dire suddenly? And why now? Why not wait for the warmer weather and an easier crossing? And how on earth was Harry, who had never so much as weeded or tended a flower bed, going to plow a field?

Parrying the questions as best he could, Harry met gravity with gravity and said he now considered Jack in effect Phyllis's guardian and preserver of Winnie's best interests. He said he had transferred to Canada only such capital as he felt he'd need to set himself up until he could become self-sufficient, and had apprised both lawyer and broker of his change in circumstances and told them Jack was to be their contact regarding all his financial affairs in England until further notice.

That winded Jack. At last he asked, "Is everything with you and Winnie...you know?" to which Harry simply said,

"No. Not really."

At which point George came back in to see what was keeping them and rescued the conversation.

Traveling to Liverpool the next day, Jack was careful, talking only of immediate concerns, what they could see from the train windows, the absurdity of Harry's having to take evening dress for the boat, which he would surely not be needing on the prairies. Playing the man of science, he teased Harry about his cholera belt, asking how on earth such a thing was supposed to work. As a parting gift, he handed over a wooden campaign mirror. "George said you're bound to grow a wild beard out there, like everyone else, but we Canes can't have standards slipping too far, now, can we?"

The little object, with its tiny folding shelf, felt as poignantly useless as the leather prayer book his favorite housemaid had given him when first leaving him on his own at school. Standing on the dockside, shaking Jack's hand for as long as he could, with the black, cliff-like bulk of the ship looming beside them, the image of a forbidding future, he felt wretchedly alone. If anything, the feeling was worse because he was thirty now, not five, so not an obvious object of anyone's pity.

As he presented himself and ascertained that his steamer trunk had indeed arrived and been taken to his cabin, he was formally entered on the ship's passenger list. "How many of us are there?" he asked.

"Five hundred and eleven, sir," he was told. "If no one gets cold feet."

"So many?"

"Well some of you have more room than others, sir."

Feeling a pang of guilt, Harry moved on through the barrier and looked about him. He was pleased to see several families, wives looking anxiously about, children fascinated by the business of the wharves. And the languages were an amazing mixture. He heard Irish and Scottish accents as well as English and what he guessed was a Canadian one, but there were also people speaking some sort of Slavic language, and German, and another tongue, at once musical and liquid, which baffled him.

"Excuse me," he asked. "But what are they speaking?"

"Welsh," he was told. "They've given up on Patagonia and are trying their luck in Canada instead. No land for sheep, mind you. Not with all those bears and wolves."

As people began to board, he saw that most were entering by a lower gangplank. None of the family groups seemed to be climbing to his deck. He reflected that had he been buying berths for a wife and several children as well as himself, he too would have economized. His cabin was no great stateroom, far from it, but it had its own minute bathroom and a porthole, at least, and access to a deck for fresh air and exercise.

He discovered at dinner that the majority of passengers on his level were young, male and upper class in ways that reminded him of the worst aspects of his schooldays. They had declared themselves by heartying around on deck, some already quite drunk. Their rowdy good cheer discomfited him, the more so as he saw the few women in evidence flinch from it. At dinner he found himself seated amongst them and felt guilt by association, as they teased the waiters and cracked jokes about seasickness and dubious meat presented as veal cutlets.

I'm not with them, he wanted to assure the waiter and sommelier. *I'm not like them in the least.*

They weren't so bad once they drew him into conversation, merely young and untested. By chance, those nearest him were all third sons.

"There's the heir and the spare and the heiress-beware," one said. "And most of us are the heiress-beware."

While it was possible their parents had packed them off to the Canadian West on the off chance they might actually make fortunes out there, or at least become respectable landowners like their older brothers, most seemed to regard it as a lark. His neighbors laughed when he confessed to being a little apprehensive about the realities of farming, and said they planned to go fishing instead and that apparently the shooting was excellent—wild duck on every puddle.

"But what about meeting the conditions for claiming your land after the three years?" Harry asked one.

"Oh," he said airily, "the Troll's taking care of all that. Good old Troll. No sense of humor but he takes care of everything, what?" He gestured vaguely toward the other end of the long table, to where two ladies, who were either missionaries or in deep mourning, were taking an early leave as the ocean's swell began to rattle cutlery and glass. Harry could see nobody remotely troll-like.

The conversation then descended into a shouty competition

for other rhymes with *heir* and *spare*. *Mama's despair* was popular and *grizzly bear* was riotously received. The boat gave a lurch toward the bows that sent a decanter crashing to the deck, and soon after that, one young man was violently sick, with no warning, into his neighbor's lap.

Never having sailed further than across the English Channel on calm summer days, Harry assumed he would prove as weak as his fellow men and had prepared for the worst, packing a powdered preparation said to be good against *mal de mer* and armed by George with a box of strong ginger biscuits she claimed had helped her with morning sickness.

The movement of the ocean was dramatic, its effects often noisy and frightening, sending objects and people toppling. When darkness and the lack of horizon made it hard for the brain to make sense of the violent sensations it was receiving, he convinced himself the boat was going to be broken into pieces. Waves seemed regularly to smash against his porthole—which he only had the folly to open once—so the fear and discomfort suffered by passengers on the lower decks did not bear imagining. And yet, to his surprise, he suffered no sickness. All around him passengers retreated to their cabins where, when the noises of ship and sea allowed, they could be heard groaning and worse. Presumably the crew all had their sea legs, but they too seemed less in evidence for a day or two, as though taking discreet advantage of the prostration of the passengers. On his deck, at least, they ministered to the sick, and he saw them bundling soiled sheets into sailcloth bags or mopping a corridor floor where someone had failed to reach a sink or bucket in time.

The restaurant was deserted. Only in the nearby bar could two or three fleeting revenants be spotted on occasion, wordlessly dosing themselves with Scotch or brandy, each in their own unsociable corner. For the most part, though, it was like walking through a ghost ship, its dimly lit saloons unoccupied, its occupants encountered only as muffled sighs or whimpers.

Harry took possibly dangerous constitutionals around the deck, putting his new waterproof coat to the test as he clung to this railing or that, gasping at the wind and marveling that the ship could safely slam into such walls of gray water. He borrowed books from the library and played rounds of patience. He picked out tunes on the piano but found that made him both self-conscious and powerfully homesick. He wrote letters, mad, passionate, excoriating letters to Winnie and Browning, to Robert and Jack, which he crumpled and threw off the deck into the hungry brine. He took lunch in his cabin, thinking that would cause less bother, but felt the need to dress in the evening and go to dinner, if only to lend some sense of closure to an odd day.

There was one other man sufficiently well to have an appetite for solids: a tall, strikingly handsome individual with the bearing of a school bully and short, thick hair so white-blond he might almost have been an albino. The first time he sat at one of the small tables sensibly laid around the perimeter of the room, where there were plenty of handholds for both waiter and diner to seize. On that occasion they did no more than bow to one another. The night after that, however, again coming in after Harry and seeing him dining in solitary state, he approached his table.

"May I?" he asked.

"Please do," Harry said. "I've spoken to no one but myself and the crew all day."

"The only two real men on the deck, eh?"

"Well...I don't know about that. I was quite surprised to be so unaffected."

"Perhaps you have seafaring in your lineage?" His accent

was curious, neither English nor Canadian. "Munck," he said, holding out a hand. "Troels Munck."

"Ah!" said Harry before he could stop himself.

Munck held Harry's hand and gaze slightly too long for comfort. His grip was firm. "They call me the Troll," he said.

"English schoolboy humor. They're very young. Munck I can guess at, but Troels? Was there a St. Troels?"

"I doubt it. It means Thor's Spear. My parents are proud nationalists."

"You're Danish."

"Well done."

"Hardly an educated guess. I went by your hair color."

"Ah."

Harry saw that he was vain and, after they had been served mulligatawny soup and a glass of sherry each, decided to please him further. "You have no accent," he lied. "At least, you don't sound Scandinavian."

"We moved to Halifax when I was a boy, then to Toronto. It's a wonder I don't sound Irish."

They were of an age, Harry guessed, though the other man's bulk and air of steely assurance made him seem the older. Harry was fascinated by the size of his hands, which seemed out of proportion, and the fastidious way he ate every morsel before him, wiping his soup bowl so clean with pieces of bread that it shone in the swaying lamplight.

Troels Munck noticed him watching. "I am not starving," he said. "Our mother used to beat us if we wasted food, and old habits die deep."

"Hard." Harry could not stop himself. "We tend to say they die hard."

He stuttered on *die*. There was a pause, as the waiter cleared away the soup. Harry feared it signified offense.

"Of course," Munck said eventually. "Alliteration is a very Nordic habit. I should have remembered." He murmured a few vigorously rhythmic lines of what was presumably Danish poetry, then smiled at Harry in a way that once again put him in mind of school and dangerous prefects. "So are you also coming to Canada to seek your fortune?" he asked after their glasses had been refilled.

"Oh no," Harry confessed. "Not really. I'm to try my hand at farming—taking on a homestead—but I doubt it will make my fortune."

"You don't...if you don't mind my saying...you don't look like a farmer."

"Not yet. I dare say that will come."

"You have never farmed before?"

"No. I've been reading a book my brother gave me. *Elementary Agriculture and Animal Husbandry*, which seems about my level." He laughed.

Troels Munck, however, became extremely serious. "Please take my advice," he said. "Learn to farm first. How to handle animals, how to plow, how to make hay and stack corn. There is an abundance of land but very many people with no idea what they are doing on it. The posters lie; the wheat does not grow itself."

"Well, I know that—"

"And the winters and the isolation will be harder than anything you have experienced in your soft English countryside."

"I'm a Londoner, actually."

"All the more reason! Ah. Beef. I like beef very much."

Munck gave his full, painstaking attention to the meat and vegetables set before them, breaking off only to look across the little table at Harry, almost boyishly, as if for reassurance.

"The sea air makes one hungry," Harry said, and his

solicitude felt like a flirtation. He was suddenly conscious of the spectacle they must present to the waiter: two men eating and drinking together at an isolated table for two, like a grotesquely mismatched courting couple.

He stifled the idea as it formed, but not swiftly enough to stop it triggering the absurd and painful notion of Browning. Of Browning on the boat with him, perhaps in an adjoining cabin; of Browning traveling to Canada to start a new life alongside his. By a kind of emotional convulsion, he sought to muffle these thoughts by recalling his blurted declaration of love and Browning's harsh dismissal of it.

He ate his overcooked beef and sipped his unpleasantly cold claret, but the loneliness left in the wake of the swift succession of thoughts was so keen he felt it must show in his face like the rouge casually retained on a chorus boy's cheek after a show.

Munck met Harry's eyes and raised his glass, with a half-smile. "You're not stupid," he said. "Are you? Not like those English puppies, so sick in their bunks."

"I hope not," Harry said, stirred, despite himself, that they were now somehow complicit. "They are like puppies, aren't they?"

"Barely house-trained...So you're a man about town. Why homesteading? Why such a drastic change? Are you in disgrace? Did you murder someone? Should I be locking my door?" Again that tempting, dangerous sense of mutual understanding. Those blue eyes glittering with cunning.

"Nothing so exciting." Harry kept his voice measured. *I must get used to this*, he thought. *I must rehearse.* "If you must know, my business affairs took an unexpected turn. The best way of supporting my wife and child was to leave them to live off what I have left while I live simply and alone in order to earn more."

Munck's face registered surprise.

"Does that strike you as odd?" Harry asked.

"You being married?" Munck said. He shook his head. "It's understood."

Waving aside the waiter's offer of puddings, he divined correctly that what they both wanted was a little cheese to help down the remains of the wine. The cheese, unlike the claret, was at the perfect temperature and proved to be the first delicious thing Harry had eaten on board, apart from the honey at breakfast.

"What about you?" Harry asked.

"Am I 'broke'?"

"Are you married?"

"No." Munck looked momentarily sulky, like a boy deprived of a treat. "I was crazily in love when I was a student, in love like a fool, and it spoiled me for marriage."

"Didn't she love you back?"

"Her family thought I was the wrong nationality. And that I was common." His frankness laid the ugly little truth on the table between them, where he seemed to regard it a moment before sweeping it aside with a gesture of distaste. "So now I travel from here to there, helping foolish young men to part with their money."

"Are you willfully deceiving them, the English puppies?"

Munck smiled.

"No need. They are rich and stupid, determined to have fun and impervious to inconvenient truth. No. I help them. I book their tickets on the boat as I shall for the train, for which the shipping line lets me travel for a fraction of the usual cost. I shall find their homesteads for them, somewhere they can waste their time hunting and drinking. I'll order them wooden houses to live in, and hired hands, glad of the money, to build those

houses and fulfill their cultivation quotas so they get their land
after three years. If they freeze to death or abandon their land, I
shall see that I acquire it at a knockdown price. No deceit necessary. *Skål!*"

"Cheers."

They took a turn around the deck before retiring. The plunging and rising of the boat was as dramatic as ever. Or was it the
water that rose and plunged? It had become impossible to tell.
The wind was powerful, drawing great washes of spray across
them, but the clouds had briefly cleared so there was a moon
lighting a path to the rocking horizon. Harry held on with both
hands to a rail—it felt greasy in the wet—and looked at the
stars until he was dizzy.

Munck was perhaps a little drunk. He clapped a heavy hand
on Harry's shoulder to shout in his ear that this was nothing, that to see the night sky in the Canadian West would be
like seeing stars for the first time. Then he insisted on shaking
Harry's hand again, saying, "I don't care that it's not correct or
whatever. You can call me Troels. I hate my surname. But that
means I have to call you Harry."

"Done," said Harry, and then laughed because Troels did
sound awfully like Trolls, at least when an Englishman attempted to say it.

Then Troels marched them as near the bows as the deserted
deck would take them, exclaiming that it was better than the
Test Your Sea Legs ride at a funfair and laughing as the plunging of the ship briefly took the deck from under their feet.

For the first time Harry felt sick, not with seasickness but
with fear.

It would be so easy to plunge over the rail into the salty
abyss and for nobody to know. And this new would-be friend
seemed as out of control as the ocean around him and might

even tumble alongside him. It would be terrifying, of course, but matters would rapidly be taken out of Harry's control. He would change his mind, as so many suicides surely did, as he was launched out into the void and the black waters rushed up to slap him in the face, but what did that matter once it was too late?

He took his leave, his lips accidentally brushing Munck's ear as he was obliged to shout over the noise of sea and wind, squawking lifeboat fastenings and clanking cargo.

"I thought you were a man!" Munck laughed, trying to hold him back, which made Harry all the more desperate to be safely inside. Munck's mocking laughter followed him as he lurched his way up the deck from handhold to slippery handhold. When he finally arrived at a hatch and let himself in, far wetter than he had realized, he turned to see the Dane's white-blond hair seeming to flare in the darkness as he continued to take his violent pleasure.

That night Harry suffered dreams in which Troels Munck murdered Browning with his huge bare hands. This was frightening in itself but became all the more disturbing for the mounting understanding that he did so under Harry's instruction, leaving Harry obliged to kill for him in turn.

BETHEL

I write to introduce to your professional notice
the Rev. Mr. Outram who I regret to say is a
sexual pervert or invert. He has been in danger
in England & I hear he has been in Vancouver
in danger. I feel the only way is for someone to
get a medical hold on him & if possible get
him into some retreat for treatment &
observation.

Dr. George Henry Savage to Henry Stearns
of the Hartford Retreat, 1902

Chapter Twelve

Harry walked the trails in the woods, trying to do as Gideon advised and not dwell on the memories their session had begun to dredge up but simply to be *open* and *neutral*.

"Think of the memories as pus; once it comes to the surface, you wipe it away. Or better yet, as mud; brought out into the air, it dries in the sun and then crumbles to dust."

It was good to be outside again, to feel the sun on his face and hear birdsong. Birds in woods sounded so different from birds on the prairie. There were far more of them, for one thing, and their song seemed to come from all around, as in a cathedral. He watched ground squirrels furiously chase one another around a fallen tree. The view across the valley, when the trees parted to grant him one, was like a young girl's watercolor in the simplicity of its unmixed, banded elements: meadow, river, forest, mountain, sky. It was early June, he guessed, though in fact he had no idea, not having a calendar and not having thought to ask. Everywhere he saw yellow lady slipper orchids in bloom, and he passed several tangles of a pretty clematis that reminded him of one in Mrs. Wells's garden at Ma Touraine. Here and there between the pines grew a small silver-leafed shrub he recognized from somewhere. From before the asylum. It had a yellow flower with a powerfully sweet scent out of all proportion to its tiny size. He forgot its name. Plant names had never been his department.

The view was miraculous, a vision of heaven, as he had

thought on waking, but it was also oppressive in its foreshort-
ening of the horizon. Only when he had climbed right through
the woods to a treeless, rocky ridge where the view opened out
on every side was there relief to his prairie-molded mind.

"Wolf willow," he said to himself, abruptly remembering
the name, and with it, the scene glimpsed through a prairie
cabin's bedroom window when he had been recovering from
fever. Cree women sitting in a row at the table on the cabin's
veranda, polishing and drilling through the seeds of its bitter
berries for use as beads. For the second time since arriving,
he heard a train approach and tracked its smoke as its great
length crossed the far side of the valley from west to east.
Its whistle sounded and he experienced the same sensation of
dread it had caused him that morning.

He was still in the woods when the gong rang for lunch
and he was obliged to run. He arrived in the dining room
red-faced and breathless, to find everyone sitting already and
staring at him.

"Ah! There he is!" Mabel exclaimed.

"We thought you'd run away," Bruno added.

Abashed at the thought of having been the subject of the
group's conversation, and finding his head too full of thoughts
and fears to talk, he glanced around for an empty chair and
impulsively turned away from the main table to where the
handsome Cree woman was sitting in the same isolated spot
she had occupied at breakfast, by one of the windows.

"May I join you?" he asked. "Oh. I do apologize."

She had just taken a mouthful so couldn't answer him, but
glanced rapidly over to the others, anticipating disapproval.
Then she gave an apologetic little wave of her napkin and gestured toward the empty chair, so he set down his plate and sat.
He filled both their water glasses from the jug, knowing how

easy it was to choke when suddenly expected to speak while eating.

"It's all right," he said quietly. "You needn't talk. My head's so full of things after my first session this morning, I'm not sure I could get my words out in the right order."

She mimed her thanks, took a sip of water and dabbed at her lips with the napkin. Aged no more than twenty-five at most, she had the strong brows and dramatic cheek-bones of many of her sisters: a face from a museum. He was amused to notice that although her dress—a midnight-blue thing with lace at the neck and cuffs—was much like any white woman of fashion might wear, the beads around her neck were not jewels but seeds threaded on a sturdy piece of wire.

She noticed him looking at them and instinctively touched them with thin, brown fingers.

"Wolf willow," he said. "I was enjoying the delicious scent of it on the hillside just now." To his surprise, he saw, as the beads came free of her lace jabot, that a small ebony crucifix hung from them. "I'm Harry," he said. "Sorry. Having said I'd leave you in peace, I don't seem to be able to stop talking!"

She held out a hand so hesitantly that he realized she sat on her own not simply because the white residents wouldn't have her with them but because company frightened her.

"Ursula," she said, and even though she spoke very softly, her voice cracked.

There was a titter from one of the men at the main table, and Harry suddenly realized they had all been watching since he'd scandalized them by sitting to dine with a redskin. He must have frowned when he looked their way, for they promptly turned back to eating and chatting. Facing Ursula again, he saw she wasn't a woman at all but a man in woman's clothing.

Her hand was large, but he found that the way she had

presented it made him shake it gently. He was angry on her behalf with whoever had tittered, and felt that he too was being
tested. Her effort to be female was so complete, so intense, that
he found he still thought of her as a woman, and felt accord-
ingly protective and solicitous.

"How did you manage?" she asked quietly. "In your first
session?"

Her accent was not exactly English, but neither was it Cree;
she spoke as one who had been rigorously educated.

"It was...strange. I had no idea what to expect. It was so
different from...where I've been."

"We've all been somewhere bad before this," she said.
"Now you're relaxing finally, you'll find you need to sleep a
lot. Just give in to it. The dreams need to come out. Do you
have chores yet?"

"No."

She looked out of the window and smiled drily. "You will.
We all get chores. I think those are our real cure, and not
what goes on in our sessions. Some work in the garden. Some
cook. Billy and his friend Kenneth care for the sheep. Bruno
has been redecorating a bedroom with murals—she's a gifted
artist. Samuel," she discreetly indicated the black man at the
other isolated table, "is tidying the grass and hedges. Mabel is
cataloguing the books."

She continued to talk very softly, almost in an undertone, as
though afraid that if she spoke up, her manly voice would burst
through like muscles through a bodice.

"Do you have a chore?" Harry asked her, and this time her
smile had a trace of bitterness.

"I'm the unpaid housekeeper. Some of us chore more than
others."

Lunch was a faintly punitive cheese and parsnip tart with

beans and boiled potatoes. They ate in silence for a while listening to a funny story one of the men at the main table was telling. Evidently its climax was slightly improper, for he dropped his voice to a barely audible level and, having strained forward to hear his final sentences, Mabel laughed and flapped her napkin at him while Bruno looked uncomfortably elsewhere.

Harry was given no chores that day. Possibly, as a new arrival, he was being allowed time to settle in. Feeling guilt that he had nothing to do, he approached Samuel, who was clipping a hedge. "Could I help?" he asked. "I farm at home. I'm quite capable." But Samuel only smiled, as though the idea were absurd and Harry plainly of no practical use to anyone. So, thus kindly dismissed, Harry retreated to the wicker chair outside his cabin. Unable to keep awake, he retreated yet further to lie on his bed. There, as Ursula had said he would, he fell into a deep but mercifully dreamless sleep, in which birdsong, the occasional bleating of a sheep and the clicking of Samuel's shears reached but did not wake him.

When he opened his eyes again, the light was no longer on his open doorway and Gideon Ormshaw was standing at the foot of his bed in his dazzling shirtsleeves, looking at him with those beseeching seal eyes of his.

"Sorry," Harry said, sitting up.

"Whatever for? You're bound to be tired. I doubt you slept properly or relaxed for a moment in all your months at Essondale."

"Funnily enough, I can't remember," Harry said. "At least, I prefer not to. Are you going to make me?"

"Only if it comes to seem relevant."

Harry sat up further, rubbed his eyes and stood. The cabin

felt very small with two of them in it. He walked outside so
that Gideon would follow him, but felt afresh the ambiguity of
the situation. This was the doctor's home and yet they were not
quite guests; a host would not enter one's room without knocking. It was supposedly a place of healing and yet one felt it was
not wholly merciful; one might be turned away, one was constantly being watched and assessed.

"You seem uneasy," Gideon said.

"I am always uneasy when I'm unoccupied. It's funny. I was
raised to idleness, but now, if my hands are idle, I worry. And
also..."

"What's troubling you?" Gideon gently touched Harry on
the arm. "You can speak freely here."

Harry looked down to the brown river. "I feel you are exper-
imenting on us, or with us," he said.

"I am. Of course I am. I trained up in its systems, but one of
the many points on which I disagree with psychiatric medicine
is its confidence that it knows what it is doing."

"Doesn't it?"

"No." Gideon sat on a bench and Harry sat beside him.
"Places like Essondale exist because we don't know what else
to do with people who threaten themselves or who frighten
us by hearing voices or talking to people who aren't there.
We have sought to catalogue all the ills of the mind, giving
them tidy Latin names and subdivisions—dementia praecox
and hebephrenic schizophrenia—like so many strange flowers
in a sinister corner of a garden, but really they're of no more
use than the fanciful names of the constellations. As for treatments, we pretend we know what we're doing, using darkness
or continuous baths or cold wraps or sedatives, but strictly
speaking, it is all experimental and every unfortunate inmate
of a place like Essondale is a sad hybrid of untried prisoner

and guinea pig." He sighed, turned, smiled, and patted Harry's knee. "Sorry, Harry. You got me preaching."

"Did you come to give me a chore?"

Gideon pulled a wry face at that. "Not exactly. At least, I hope it won't *feel* like a chore. I'd like you to continue something you've already started."

"Sleeping?"

"Talking to Ursula!" Gideon exclaimed, apparently impervious to irony. "More importantly, letting her talk to you. Until you so startled the others by sitting with her at lunch today, she had spoken to nobody."

Harry pictured Ursula alone at her small table, picking at her food, heard again her painfully shy shred of a voice.

"You call her she," he observed.

"Yes. But I take my cue from her clothes."

"Was Ursula in...that other place too?"

"Only briefly. You won't have seen any Indian patients because, naturally, they're kept in a separate section. I was lucky to find her there before the flu epidemic wiped that section out. Before that, she was in one of the Indian boarding schools. Where, of course, she was obliged to live as a boy. I've asked her to fetch us provisions tomorrow. I thought you could accompany her, help carry things."

"Of course."

"You're sure?"

"Absolutely."

"Good. Thank you, Harry. And, er, don't feel you have to report back everything she says. The important thing is that she's opening up at last."

Harry nodded, and Gideon smiled before leaving him on the bench and turning back to the house. Harry watched him breaking off to talk briefly with Samuel and then being accosted by the giggler from breakfast whose name he found it quite impossible to remember.

Harry tried to imagine Gideon without the drooping mustache. The lips it concealed were full, rather girlish, perhaps. It was easy to imagine the good doctor an adored child, praised and indulged so as to give him his placid air of entitlement. They had, none of them, Harry suspected, asked to be there, grateful though they were. They were his human toys, taken from the dirty box on a whim, and could be thrust back into darkness and neglect just as casually if they somehow failed to interest or satisfy.

Ursula arrived a little late at her separate supper table, having had some business with the servants, by which time Harry had been claimed by the Giggler and his friends with the worrying insistence that he was *not to be a stranger* to them. Happily Mabel came to the rescue, never one to listen when she could talk, and he found himself drawn instead into a pleasantly impersonal conversation with Bruno about horses and the sad fates of the ones shipped out to the war. When Ursula came in, she caught his eye and gently inclined her head in greeting.

After supper, they crossed to the library so that Gideon could read to them, a regular occurrence apparently, but not an obligatory one, for Samuel and both the Giggler's friends absented themselves.

"I want to read you all a recent short article by Edward Carpenter. Mr. Carpenter's socialist outlook might not be to all your tastes, but I believe you would find him sympathetic in other ways. You may remember I read you a piece of his on the inequality inherent in marriage."

Gideon made a little bow, cleared his throat, smoothed a page of the booklet before him, and looked around their little gathering quite as though he were about to read them "The Elves and the Shoemaker" or "The Three Billy Goats Gruff."

"*A curious and interesting subject*," he began, "*is the connection of the Uranian temperament with prophetic gifts and divination.*"

It was a fascinating article about the tradition common to so many ancient and enduring cultures, including the Inuit and North American Indian tribes, in which certain boys and girls adopted the characteristics of the opposite sex and were elected as shamans or priests. It leapt back and forth in time, from the Sioux to the Assyrians, to mistranslated references to temple prostitutes and attendants on Ashtaroth or Astarte in the Old Testament and Herodotus. Oddly, it said nothing of the continuing practice among Christian priests of hiding their legs and gender in robes in order to impart mysteries.

Harry stole glances at Ursula as the reading progressed. Characteristically, she had chosen a hard, upright chair rather than sit with the rest of them, who had sunk into armchairs or shared sofas. She was listening intently but was quick to leave at the end, and he caught the disappointed look Gideon cast toward her as she slipped out. Harry chose not to linger either; he was overwhelmed by sleepiness again, and the Giggler had been inspired by the reading to whip out a pack of Tarot cards and proposed to read everyone's future, the kind of thing that made Harry nervous.

A man stood before him in bright moonlight. They were outside the little Bethel cabin, which was how Harry knew this was a dream, but the image was as clear as in real life and the threat as intense. He was a big man, a giant almost, blocking Harry's view of the moon. Harry knew him at once by his distinctive meaty smell and the mocking tone of his voice. He leaned in closer and said something so repellent that Harry let fly a punch to his jaw that sent him sprawling.

He landed heavily, knocking his head on something as he went down. Seeing him spread-eagled there, briefly vulnerable in the moonlight, stirred lust as well as fear, which made the fear worse.

Harry knew the only hope was to drag him to the river before he regained consciousness. He seized him by his boots and began to tug him over the grass, but, of course, the boots came off in his hands. So he took him by the feet, having feverishly tugged off his socks for a better grip, and carried on toward the river, even though he knew it was hopeless. The feet, big and bony and hot, felt impossibly intimate in his grasp and the body heavier and heavier.

Then, for a second, he knew the man was no longer unconscious but was watching him, smiling at his pathetic efforts before going on the attack. The feet lashed out, as fierce as fists, and soon Harry was sprawled on his back, winded, and the giant was straddling him, pinning his wrists with one hand and gripping his neck with the other. He bent to sniff him, his nose grazing his cheek and the side of his neck.

"When I've killed you," he said, almost tenderly, "I'll fuck you, real hard, for old times' sake. And then I'm going to fuck your wife and kill her and then, I reckon, I'll fuck your little girl."

He woke shouting, to find he was in a muck sweat with the top sheet somehow twisted crazily about him. Moths fluttered around his still-lit lamp. He remade the bed, climbed back into it, established that the dream had been just that and turned the lamp out. But now he couldn't sleep because a tremendous wind had blown up out of nowhere and was causing his loose screen door to tap with maddening irregularity. He slipped out of bed again and opened the inner door so as to fix the screen door back against the outer wall of the cabin.

The wind had made the night magical. There were stars, but the air was full of the sound of rattling leaves. Moonlight picked out the river's stealthy motion. He watched for a while, reminding himself that he must go for a bath in the morning. There were quaint ladies' and gentlemen's bath houses built beside the river, and he had heard the Giggler say that someone lit the stoves at dawn so the water was always beautifully hot by about nine.

Then he saw a door open. It was the one to Samuel's cabin— the last in the crescent of them laid out on the gentle slope down to the river. He stepped back into his doorway and watched as Gideon came out, returned a lingering embrace to the black man half in shadow, then padded away across the grass toward the house. Samuel emerged fully into the moonlight. He wore only pajama trousers, with a blanket over his bare shoulders. As Harry watched, he lit a cigarette and enjoyed a lingering smoke, leaning against his cabin wall.

MOOSE JAW

A subject like this is generally held to be an
unspeakable one, as it would soil both him
who talks of it and those who listen.

George Drysdale, *Elements of Social Science
and Natural Religion*

Chapter Thirteen

He saw little of Troels for what remained of the voyage and only found out later he was spending time on the next deck down from theirs, where he had business with several of the migrant families Harry had glimpsed on the quay in Liverpool. The weather and seas grew calmer—or perhaps they were all acclimatized finally—and their fellow passengers began to gather for meals again. Harry found himself taken up by the ladies in black, respectable Torontonians who were indeed in mourning, having returned to England to bury a father. They had recruited a card-playing parson and needed Harry to make up a four for bridge.

When Troels reappeared, he was once again in the thick of the only slightly chastened English puppies. He caught Harry's eye, even raised an unsmiling glass to him, but Harry began to wonder if he was regretting his boisterous friendliness of the night they dined *à deux*. Then Troels found him in the crowds on the deck, when they finally came in sight of land again.

Had Harry considered, he wondered, the suggestion of learning farming skills for a few months or a year even, before taking up his homestead? When Harry said that he had indeed and that it seemed eminently sensible, Troels said that in that case a plan had taken shape. En route to the prairies—ahead of the puppies, who were to linger in Toronto, wasting their allowances—he planned to visit a cousin by marriage, who, having only daughters, always needed a hired hand on his farm.

"You don't wish to see Toronto, do you?" he asked with an off-putting air, and Harry, whose conversations with the card ladies had made him want to see Toronto very much, lied and said certainly not, he was keen to save his money and be on his way.

Which was how, within a day of their landing in Halifax, he came to be boarding a train with a one-way ticket to a place called Moose Jaw.

The train was a shock. The card-playing daughters had declared it *marvelous* but had never actually ridden it and, he suspected, valued it as much for its symbolic value. The train was colonization, civilization even, embodied in steel, timber and two steam-belching locomotive monsters. It needed two of these, Troels assured him, not only because of its great size and weight but because of the distinct possibility that not all the snow in their path would have thawed yet.

There was a large first-class section but Troels vetoed this at the ticket office, saying it was for rich tourists and fools and that they would be better off merely visiting it for meals. Instead they were housed in one of a long, long sequence of carriages apparently adapted with the express purpose of settling the western prairies as cheaply and swiftly as possible. The seats were wooden, as unyielding as any church pew. Beds folded down like so many outsized tea trays from cupboards ingeniously cut in the ceiling. These beds were almost immediately taken up, either in simple preference to the wooden seats, because men and women were exhausted after sleepless nights in even greater discomfort below decks, or for fear that, with such a crowd on board the train, there would not be enough berths available come sundown.

At either end of each long carriage was a stove. These stoves never went out and were rarely without some passenger frying chunks of fatty sausage on them or cuts of other, equally anonymous meat. The air was thick with the scents not just of cooking, but of dirty clothing, alcohol, tobacco and under-washed person. They had been told to stow all luggage, clearly labeled, in the luggage vans, but inevitably there were things people were too nervous to part with, so there were bundles and boxes in every direction, clutched in laps or used as foot-stools or even pillows.

Schooled in conformity, and flustered by Troels' impatient efficiency, Harry had stowed everything except his passport, money and the agriculture manual. He had read the last through once already and now, mistrustful of its confident sim-plicity of tone, began reading it again, alert to crucial detail he felt sure he must have missed first time through. His attention strayed repeatedly. There was a constant hum of conversation around them, much of it in languages he did not know, which made it no more distracting than birdsong, but his eyes were drawn to people.

More specifically, they were drawn to relationships. The ma-jority of their fellow passengers were men between twenty and forty, some of them clearly traveling with a brother or father, but there were some women with children too, and these wives and grandmothers were the focal points of small, ordinary family dramas—the telling of stories, the soothing of anxiety, the imparting of wisdom, food or punishment—which seemed to Harry heightened in their significance for being surrounded by so much undiluted masculine harshness. He was not the only man watching these scenes with a kind of hunger. When a wizened old Welsh woman sang a lullaby to her grandchil-dren, the whole carriage was briefly hushed and there was such an audible sigh of appreciation when she had done that she laughed, self-conscious suddenly, and did not sing again.

Troels did not read and paid little attention to the men and women around them. Sprawled directly across from Harry, who had let him face the direction of travel because he said he felt uneasy when facing "the wrong way," he ate up the passing landscape with his eyes as though willing it to move by more swiftly. He was a tour guide of no charm and few words. Where the pattern of dark forest and eerie lake gave way to human habitation, he would rouse Harry from his reading or reverie, knocking a knee against his and pointing out, with a faintly admonitory air, a place name or some dry detail in the way a man stored his straw or stacked his logs.

Harry tried watching the passing landscape too, felt he should as he had been lucky enough to secure a seat by the window and to have a measure of control over precious drafts of fresh air. Once they had left the bustle and dirt of Halifax behind them, however, he began to be overwhelmed by the lack of variety in the outlook of forest, lake and yet more forest, and the sense it gave of just how enormous and underinhabited his new country was.

He was not alone in this response. People exclaimed in their various languages at the size of the trees, the depth of the forest, the beauty of the lakes, and shouted when they thought they saw a bear or a moose. But they grew quieter and quieter as it dawned on them, perhaps, how unlike this landscape was to the imagery of golden wheat fields that had been used to lure them there, and they began to fear that Canada was nothing but forest, forest, forest, lake, lake, lake. They passed a section of wood where sunlight seemed barely to reach through the trees, and the ticket inspector pointed out that the sound they took to be birdsong was the calling of frogs. As his words were relayed, translated into Russian, Welsh, French and German, the carriage fell briefly silent and something like dread seemed to steal among them until an oblivious card-player broke the tension by laughing in triumph.

Though unused to the continent's great distances, Harry was also aware that it would take them Canadian days, not mere English hours, to reach Moose Jaw, and that he needed to slow himself down, dull his senses a little and numb his anticipation in order not to find the monotony of the journey insufferable.

Periodically he and Troels would leave their seats—Troels securing their places by wielding stern-sounding Russian against the Ukrainians around them—and make the long journey through several carriages identical to their own, though each was colonized by slightly different racial groupings, to the relative magnificence and luxury of first class and the dining car. There they lingered as long as the harassed waiters permitted, even though the indifferent food served in high style put Harry in mind of condemned men and their last wishes. Beer was a shilling a bottle and he allowed himself two with each meal, one for thirst—because he did not care to drink the water on board—and one to help him doze when they returned to their hard seats.

With each passing meal, he became more and more conscious of his increasingly grubby, unshaved appearance. Harry had never been a dandy, but he had always been clean. He was mortified, on their second visit to the dining car, to find that his own fingers left an unpalatable gray streak on the white linen.

Come sundown, there were not nearly enough fold-down beds to go round. There were several children—who presumably had been counted by the ticket office as riding on adult laps—whose parents early on tucked them into beds, from which no adult had the heart to eject them later. Muttering that the next night they would insist on their rights, Troels commandeered their corner of the carriage and established a "bed" on the floor between their seats, which he carpeted with their coats.

"If we lie like spoons in a drawer, it will work," he said.

It was a coffin-like space and their feet and ankles stretched out into the passageway, where a careless passer-by might have trodden or tripped on them. Harry lay down stiffly, hesitant about being quite so close to his traveling companion.

"On your side," Troels commanded, "so we fit."

Harry rolled on to his side, facing away under the line of wooden seats.

"There," Troels said, as someone dimmed the already dim carriage lights and a child began to whimper, and he threw his left arm heavily across Harry, pulling their bodies closer together. "Now we fit."

"Good night," Harry told him.

"Sleep now." Almost at once, Troels' breathing slowed and he fell asleep.

Harry remained awake, gaining an unlooked-for comfort from the weight of the big man's arm around his chest but troubled by the tickling of his breath on the back of his neck and the knowledge that he was, in effect, sitting on Troels's lap in a public space.

Chapter Fourteen

The farmer for whom Harry was to work was a Dane who had elected to move north from the American Mid-west in search of cheaper land and better prospects when his older brother inherited the family farm in Wisconsin. His wife was a second cousin of Troels, and relied on him to bring her news of their wider family when he passed through, and rare treats such as European magazines and catalogues.

Troels found hired hands for her husband and for several farmers across the region. Inexperienced newcomers like Harry were ideal, he said, because they knew nothing and were keen to learn, so did as they were told without showing too much initiative. Initiative could be irritating to a farmer who liked things always done in a certain way. Troels did not hide the fact that this was a business transaction, for which his kinsman would pay.

Harry didn't mind in the least. He saw the sense in learning farm techniques from an experienced farmer and hoped that the family connection, and being introduced as a sort of friend, might prevent his being too harshly exploited. Troels had warned him his accommodation would be basic and away from the main house.

Farmer Jørgensen had three daughters and no sons and, like all such farmers, was terrified that one of his daughters would be seduced by a penniless hired hand. Unless, of course, that hired hand proved to be a thoroughly good farmer, in which case he would become a useful son-in-law with prospects and no longer have to be paid a wage.

Troels was not a man who liked waiting and had planned that they would go directly to the Jørgensens on arriving at Moose Jaw. An accumulation of small delays, however, meant that they arrived far too late for that and had to arrange for a night in town.

Moose Jaw was far more developed than its age had led Harry to expect. It already boasted some large brick buildings—a school, a hospital, some hotels and a post office—and the station where they arrived would not have disgraced a small city back home. The buildings' size and confidence only emphasized the raw, provisional nature of their surroundings, however: wooden shop-fronts, more like fairground stalls than real buildings, streets of churned mud and worse, and everywhere vacant building plots carefully outlined with posts and wires but boasting as yet nothing but spring weeds. There was a certain bustle, the tinny sound of a pianola from inside a pub, but there seemed to be no more women in evidence than had been on the train or boat. Harry had not appreciated until now how much hats and dresses adorned a scene.

They passed across the street from the Dominion Lands Office, and it was dispiriting to see a cluster of men around its window, much like the one he had seen all those weeks ago on the Strand.

The hotels and inns were inexplicably busy, and there were no free beds at the City Hotel or the next place they tried. Finally they found one free room at the Maple Leaf. After days of not washing and having no privacy, Harry would have cherished a hot bath, a shave and a few hours of solitude in a quiet bed, and would gladly have paid whatever price was asked for them. He enjoyed a peaceful bath and shave, at least, across the corridor, lingering in the soothing gray soup until it began to turn cold. And while Troels took his turn, he lay on the half of the bed he had instinctively claimed, eyes closed, attempting to make out the words of an unfamiliar song some man was singing in a bar across the way, trying not to acknowledge the panic that had been stealing up on him ever since they disembarked from the boat.

They had brought only minimal luggage with them; most of it they had left in the care of the station for collecting the next day. Trained at boarding school to snatch what privacy he could, Harry had been scrupulous in taking from his bag only the articles he needed, and had replaced most of them tidily afterward so as not to make a small room feel smaller still.

Troels had been under no such constraint, but seemed actively to use his belongings to make his mark upon the place and lay claim to more than a fair fifty percent of its charmless yardage. Not only were his clothes scattered across floor and bed and shabby bureau, but the savory, slightly meaty scent of him, not unpleasing but insistent, seemed to have permeated the room while Harry was in the bath. It felt like Troels's room, into which Harry was intruding, an effect redoubled when Troels strode back in, humming, wearing only a towel, which he immediately tossed aside. He appeared to feel no embarrassment whatsoever at his prodigious nakedness, cheerfully chatting while he selected clean clothes from his exploded Gladstone bag.

They should eat steak, he said, almost certainly, since that was the best thing Moose Jaw had to offer, and with local beer, since whatever wine was on offer would be filthy and expensive. Then they should find women.

Harry reminded him he was a married man, but Troels waved aside his objection. Why had he gone to the trouble of shaving in a town full of unkempt beards? he asked in a bullying tone. Who else was he hoping to impress? Harry began to speak quietly about the maintenance of standards but let the matter slide. Troels, he was coming to understand, was a natural bully, and a man who often said things purely to goad a reaction from others but cared not a fig if one made no answer.

That their own hotel had already stopped serving food when they came down was something of a relief; the boiled cabbage smell in its hall and the purse-lipped little notices about noise, water usage and "visitors" pinned to the back of almost every door did not inspire confidence that it was a place that understood pleasure. Instead, they found a noisy tavern—the one where a heavily bearded tenor was still singing sentimental songs—and were served steaks with fried onion and fried potato. There was far more meat than Harry could eat, but he knew he could count on Troels to finish it for him.

As they drank one beer after another, Troels made him talk about Winnie. Hoping that drink and conversation might postpone indefinitely the threat of *women*, Harry made himself sadder and sadder evoking Winnie's quiet charms, her prettiness, her sly wit, her kindness as a mother and ingenuity with a needle and a bolt of silk. Troels seemed so keen to hear more about her that Harry began to fear the insanely confident Dane would no sooner have settled him as a hired hand than he'd be sailing back to Twickenham to woo her for himself.

Then Harry began the story of Pattie's adventures on the stage, which led someone who had overheard to exclaim that her picture was on display. There was an incongruous screen, a thing that belonged in a boudoir, not a bar, which was presumably used to cut down the drafts on bitter nights in winter. It had been painstakingly papered over with pictures cut from some London magazine, all of them of actresses or noted society beauties, Gaiety Girls being prominent among them. The eavesdropper, who was plainly drunk, insisted on dragging the screen across to them, spreading the word as he did so, so that a small crowd of inquisitive, burly men arrived at the table with him.

"So?" Troels asked. "Which one is she?"

And there, thank God, she was, unmistakably voluptuous in a cluster of coyly draped flower maidens, smiling with her mouth slightly open, her creamy, almost muscular shoulders breaking free of a gauzy wrap.

"Can she sing?" Troels asked.

"She can hold a tune," Harry conceded. "But it's not a voice to fill a theater."

"Does it matter?" someone else laughed. "She can fill a dress!"

"She have a feller?"

"She...she has an admirer," Harry told them, and thought, with nostalgic affection, of Notty and his habitual expression of mild bafflement. "A minor aristocrat." He stuttered slightly on the M.

"Oh," someone else said, mimicking the accent Harry never thought of himself as having. "Only a m-m-minor one! Dear me!"

"He gonna marry her?" another asked.

"I...I doubt it," Harry said, with a pang at his disloyalty, and bit his tongue rather than mention gold watches and villas in Pangbourne.

The men then fell to assessing the girls glued to the screen—their hair, teeth, breasts and, in the saucier pictures, legs—in a way that made Harry think of his father roughly tugging apart a horse's velvety lips to examine its teeth.

Troels slipped away during the discussion, which made Harry realize how dependent he had already become on his insistent control. Were the other man to have melted away into the night, it would have been days before Harry regained the ability to make decisions for himself.

"Time to go," Troels now called, across the men's banter.

"We need to pay," Harry told him, standing.

"It's done," Troels said, and headed out, giving no option but to follow.

The night air was sharp and soberingly clean after the fug indoors, and reminded Harry he wanted sleep, not women, but Munck had done his research and paced ahead.

"They're nice girls," he said. "Friendly. Irish. Recommended," and he turned down a side street that was abruptly residential. There were low wooden houses, some with small verandas or large porches, where log piles seemed to take precedence over rocking chairs. A dog barked. Most houses were already in darkness. In the window of the one Troels approached was a lamp with a pink glass shade, an ugly thing like some fleshy orchid in a winter garden.

Troels knocked on the door. Harry hung back.

"I really think..." he began at last, but the door opened and a motherly woman in an approximation of evening dress waved them in. She did not introduce herself or ask their names, used, perhaps, to visitors who spoke little English. She gestured to them to sit on chairs that were lined along one wall, as if in a dentist's waiting room, tossed a log into a pot-bellied stove, then settled across from them in an armchair, where she opened a novel, licked her finger and turned a page.

A baby cried nearby, then fell silent with disturbing abruptness.

Troels was far too tall for his chair, which squeaked beneath him as he tapped a foot impatiently. When a door opened and a man came out buttoning his shirt, Troels fairly jumped to his feet, but the woman flapped her hand to make him sit again and it occurred to Harry that perhaps it was she, not the visitors, who had no English. The other man let himself out and walked away, whistling the same song Harry had heard from their bedroom earlier. Troels sighed so heavily Harry felt it through the floorboards.

Then one of the inner doors flew open again, the woman nodded, and Troels sprang up and went through it. Before his silhouette quite blocked the doorway, Harry saw past him to where a skinny girl, little more than Kitty or May's age, it seemed to him, was arranging herself on a bed improvised from packing cases. She turned toward the door a face devoid of expression.

As soon as Troels had closed the door behind him, Harry seized his opportunity to escape, taking his leave of the reading woman with a stammered apology as he fumbled some coins into a little brass saucer apparently set out for the purpose. Retracing his steps to the hotel, thanking his stars he had pocketed their key before Troels had, he found he was in a kind of terror, so walked slowly to the end of the main street and back again until his heart had stilled.

He fell asleep within minutes of climbing into their creaking bed. When he woke, in darkness, it was to a commotion he realized was Troels dropping on to the mattress beside him.

"You left early," Troels said, putting out the light.

"Yes. My heart wasn't in it," Harry told him.

"You did well. She was too thin and, I think, diseased."

"Ah."

"I left too. Sleep now."

Harry had observed on the train that Troels was a man seemingly capable of sleeping by effort of will. "Sleep now," he would say, and he slept. Far from slipping back to sleep himself, Harry was now utterly alert, roused by the consciousness that he was sharing a bed with a man so big he had to hook an arm over the bed's edge to stop himself rolling against him. Exhaustion overcame him eventually, but he seemed to lie there, wakeful, for an hour, smelling the mix of sweat, steak and soap that radiated off Troels' skin, aware of his every breath and shift of posture.

Light was filtering through scrappy curtains into the room when he next opened his eyes.

Trying to move slightly, he found that Troels had flung an arm across him and had pushed a thigh so firmly against one of his own that it was possible to tell that, even had he come to bed in his long johns, he was no longer wearing them.

Assuming it was a mistake born of sleep that would mortify Troels when he woke, Harry hooked his arm over the mattress edge and made an effort to haul himself slowly free. He had thought the other man was fast asleep because his breathing was so heavy, so jumped when Troels held him all the harder and said clearly,

"No you don't."

The pleasures he had tasted in bed with Browning had been deep and sometimes bruising, but never violent. What Munck proceeded to do to him was savage and degrading, without affection or even curiosity. The pain was so intense that he felt torn open. When Munck suddenly thrust into him, the burning sensation was so intolerable, he cried out, at which Munck slapped a gagging palm across his mouth so that he had to fight for breath. He bit in response, which only saw his mouth clamped the harder and the assault intensify, as though Munck found invitation less exciting than resistance. In the confusion of extreme pain, fear and being only half awake, Harry believed he was about to be murdered. The ordeal was all the more horrible for his treacherous body gaining an animal satisfaction from it, which Munck could not fail to notice.

But then, with a few final thrusts and a furious Danish curse, it was over.

Munck rolled off him and got out of the bed. Harry made himself turn toward him; if he was to die, he would look his killer in the eyes at least. But Munck barely glanced at him as he snorted, "Huh! Too tight! You'll be better at it next time," and tugged a towel about himself before slouching across the landing to wash.

Which was when Harry saw the red streaks where Munck had been wiping himself on the bed sheet as he spoke.

They snatched a breakfast so greasy Harry had to fight the urge to vomit rather than swallow, and paid a carter to fetch Harry's luggage and drive them out of town to the Jørgensen farm. Munck behaved as though nothing out of the ordinary had passed between them.

Harry could not play the game of normality. Indeed he found he could barely speak. Munck showed no concern at this, merely a passing petulance, like a boy's toward a defective toy.

"Your friend doesn't talk much," the carter observed at one point. "He's not simple, is he? Old Man Jørgensen won't like that."

"He's homesick," Munck said, whereupon the two of them laughed.

And Harry should have felt homesick, crossing this cold prairie that meant nothing to him, apprehensive at the thought of his ever more forbidding-sounding new employer, and angry at the carter's impudence, but all he felt, apart from a shaming soreness whenever the cart's wheels crossed a rut in the muddy track, was a numb acceptance that a few hours had seen him become of no account. He stared at fields where there were still traces of morning frost, at the myriad small, bird-haunted ponds, at barns that looked quite unlike barns at home in either shape or color, at tracts of uncultivated wilderness in between, and at tiny sod houses seemingly sprung from the tidy plots around them, registering what he was seeing yet feeling no more than if his head had been a camera or his eyes cold chips of mirror.

The road they were on barely resembled a road, much less a major one, which the carter assured them it was. The Jørgensen farm lay down an even less convincing narrow track to one side. The track was rough but the fields to either side were neatly fenced with posts and wire, the deep ditches at their edges still nearly filled with the waters of the spring thaw. The first acres they passed were all plowed.

"What does he grow?" Harry asked, his words emerging as a kind of croak.

"He speaks!" the carter laughed.

"Wheat, of course," Munck said. "Some oats too, probably, for his horses."

"And the hired hand's porridge," the carter added, and they both laughed at him again.

As they progressed, the plowed fields gave way to similarly fenced and ditched pasture on which cattle grazed. The land was bowling-green flat, broken only by the fences, and equally tidy lines of willows and some hazel-like tree planted to yield shade and shelter. Even on this calm spring day, the breeze seemed constant.

Harry had plenty of time to take in the farmhouse and its barns, which lay at the end of the long, straight approach, all of them wooden, all painted the same distinctive brick red with white trim. The inhabitants had plenty of warning, too. A group of white-aproned women appeared on the veranda, a large, black-coated dog galloped out from one of the barns to escort the cart in, barking all the way, and by the time they had drawn up, a weather-beaten, unsmiling man in a tweed suit and felt hat had emerged from one of the barns. Harry remembered he was here to be hired for work, so made an effort to look less pathetic than he felt; though had the man—Jørgensen, he assumed—drawn himself up, shaken his head and sent him back to Moose Jaw, he would not have been entirely sorry.

Then Munck raised his hat and shouted out some greeting in Danish and was recognized, and at once their onlookers were all smiles and hurried forward. Munck jumped down to shake hands with Jørgensen and be embraced by his kinswomen. Harry held out his hand and saw, from Jørgensen's glance at it and momentary hesitation, that he was no longer this man's equal.

"Harry Cane," he said, introducing himself.

Jørgensen laughed drily. "Hurricane? We'll have to call you Windy!" unwittingly hitting on the nickname Harry had suffered as a frightened boy in flannel shorts. Jack had been nicknamed Sugar, a neat illustration of the greater affection he had always inspired.

"Can you farm, Windy?"

"Not yet," Harry said, "but I'm keen to learn. I know about horses," he added, spotting two carthorses and a pair of handsome bays that were watching from a paddock beside the house, apparently suspicious of the carter's nag.

"You ride?"

"Yes."

"Good. Last man we had was a *kryster*—terrified of them."

Jørgensen explained the terms of Harry's employment,

which, as in an old fairy tale, was to be for a year and a day. He would have full board and lodging and every Sunday off.

"You look a little fancy for a hired hand. Do you have any rougher clothes?" he asked, adding, when Harry hesitated, "Overalls and boots we can find you, but I'll take the cost off your first wages, all right?"

"All right," Harry said, and they each nodded, which seemed as binding as a handshake.

The talk of wages, the whole business of being, for the first time in his life, employed, was so novel as to feel virtually meaningless.

"Good," Jørgensen went on. "You'll meet the family over lunch. Let's settle you in. Where's your bag? Charlie?" he called to the carter. "Throw down Windy Cane's bag."

Then, of course, there was the sour little comedy of discovering that the new hired hand had no mere canvas bag of basics with him, but a gentleman's steamer trunk of solid leather embossed with his initials. As Harry helped the carter heave the great, very new-looking object down from the cart, the feminine chatter around Munck ceased and everyone turned to gawp.

After watching Harry pay the carter, Mr. Jørgensen seemed a little abashed at ushering such a piece of luggage into the small, low structure tacked on to the side of the house. "This was where I lived while I was building the place," he explained gruffly. "It's basic, but it'll have to do. Gets plenty cold in winter, but we'll find you some extra blankets for the bed then, and you'll get some heat through the wall as Esme's stove is just to the other side of it, and her bread oven. Privy's around the back. Water from the pump in the yard. The girls'll bring hot water for your bath on Saturday nights so you're clean for church. Kerosene for the lamp is down there. You're not a Catholic or a Jew?"

"No."

"Good. So you can worship with us. You known Troels long?"

"Er, no. Actually I only met him on the boat coming out."

"Good," Jørgensen said with a certain satisfaction, and Harry saw that Munck might be a cherished kinsman of the wife but was no favorite of the husband. "I'll leave you to settle in..." here he threw another glance at the huge, incongruous trunk, "then I'll fetch you for lunch before we put you to work, eh?"

The lean-to was not so bad. The narrow bed was firm, which Harry preferred. There were two wooden chairs and a table, a little shelf where he set a few books, and a jug and basin for daily washing. And the basic plank floor and spotty blue curtains prevented it feeling too agricultural. From the broom and dustpan hanging on the back of the door, he guessed he was expected to do his own cleaning. And it was private, his own small cell, with a narrow view across the paddock, where the horses were snorting in dismissal as the carter's nag left the scene.

Lunch was simple but delicious. A slice of ham with boiled vegetables, a piece of apple pie, a glass of cooler, clearer water than Harry had tasted since leaving England. He ate at the heavy old dining table with Munck and the Jørgensens, but, in a little touch of social demarcation, was allocated a hard chair where theirs were upholstered.

Mrs. Jørgensen bore the traces of the kind of delicate Nordic beauty that would never have lasted long without plentiful shade and city comforts to pamper it. She had a nervous smile, more like a twitch than a thing connected to actual feelings, and looked tired when not appearing apprehensive. The three Jørgensen daughters were very much their father's brood: big-boned, apple-cheeked, wholesome and plain, as savagely observant of their respective ages and positions as any farmyard hens. Their names, he learned, were Wilhelmine, Annemette and Gudrun, though they were usually known as Minnie, Annie and Goody. Minnie was humorless and bossy, Annie humorous but spiteful. Gudrun, the youngest, gave him a head-ducking smile when he was introduced, and he suspected she might prove his only ally.

The conversation at lunch was dominated by Munck and Mrs. Jørgensen, who spoke largely in Danish. The daughters spoke English, the older two with something of their mother's accent. Jørgensen said little beyond firing out an occasional question in either language, concentrating instead on his food.

Munck made no more attempt to include Harry in the conversation than he would have spoken to a parcel he had just delivered. Harry felt the wretched awkwardness of it all; it reminded him of how boys who had been friendly enough at school could become anything but when they rashly invited one to meet their families. And the lingering pain and shame from what had passed between them that morning made it worse.

He'd assumed that, after such a journey, Munck would be staying the night at least, and so, it seemed, had Mrs. Jørgensen. When her husband rose from the table saying, "Well, I'll set our visitor his afternoon's task, then drive Troels back to town," a startled, then angry exchange followed, from which it was a relief to escape to the fresher air outside.

Dismissing the altercation by simply walking away from it, Jørgensen joined him, suggested he leave his jacket and tie in his room, then equipped him with waders and a shovel and led him to one of the ditches alongside the farm's main track. He showed him how muck running off from track and field was blocking the water from flowing away to one of several big ponds, which he called sloughs, pronouncing it *sloo*. Harry was to wade in and dig the muck high on to the ditch's banks until the water ran freely again. That done, he was to repeat the task with every ditch in turn.

It was hard work but pleasantly thoughtless and, as the smelly water began to rush away between his legs, immensely satisfying, somewhere between building dams and making mud pies, two activities he had only ever watched in envy as a boy. His shirt was soon bathed in sweat and splashed with filth, his palms beginning to grow sore from the unwonted friction of the shovel handle on their soft skin.

He thought only of the job in hand and its repetitive rhythms, but hoped, if this were a test, that he was passing it. He was clearing his second ditch when Jørgensen drove Munck up the track beside him in a nimble little gig a fraction the size of the cart they had ridden out on that morning. Munck exchanged a quick word with Jørgensen, then jumped down.

He laughed at Harry's appearance. "Less the little gentleman now," he said.

Harry was too out of breath to do more than smile.

"Well, I shall see you in a year and a day, Windy. If the bears don't get you first."

"Yes," Harry said. "Thank you."

"And I'll find you a homestead in the meanwhile, yes?"

"Well... Why should you?"

Munck met his eye. "Because you interest me," he said seriously. "Be good. Don't forget me."

And laughing again at Harry's appearance, he jumped back up into the gig and the two men clattered off up the track, which was so long and straight that the gig had shrunk to the size of a toy before it disappeared from view entirely.

Chapter Fifteen

The ditch-digging he had done all afternoon until the light fled came to seem shockingly hard, and he had been spoken to little more at supper than he had been at lunch. Collapsed on to his bed for the first time, he thought he might weep, but was smothered in sleep too rapidly for that. Neither was there any emotional release in dreams, for he was too tired for dreaming.

As a rule, to lie in a strange room would have been to wake at restless intervals throughout the night, but he woke only when the cockerel crowed close by. He felt so stiff and unrefreshed, it was as though the night had mysteriously passed in seconds.

He washed and shaved in icy water, ate, worked and slept, and did so for barely varied days, dimly registering that his usually lively emotions had been numbed, as though by shock, and just as dimly aware that this was one of the mind's mysterious pieces of mercy. It was another mercy that the Jørgensens neither gave nor expected anything from him socially; he was an unregarded nothing.

There were times, many times at first, when Harry thought he had made a huge mistake. Quite unused to hard labor, for all that he was fit, his muscles and back never seemed to stop aching. His city-soft hands blistered and split so that he was obliged to bandage them every morning. When it was wet—and it rained so little that he would come in time to long for it—he found it impossible to dry his clothes out properly overnight. When the weather warmed up, he was no more comfortable, on account of the clouds of biting blackflies and mosquitoes that seemed to rise from the grass as he walked across it, and feasted maddeningly on any skin left bare, so he was obliged to labor in several layers and a hat, however hot it made him.

The work was repetitive and tended to consist of doing one thing all day, or for days on end, be it ditch-clearing, fence-mending or clearing ground. As the weather warmed and the Jørgensens' small herd could be turned out to pasture, Harry worked for days clearing their barns of the mixed straw and dung the animals had trodden down to the consistency of hard cheese over the winter, carting it out to the fields and there scattering the sticky clods by hand. And then there was ground clearance, the no less laborious process of ridding a sizable patch of land Jørgensen wanted brought under cultivation for the next season of its coarse prairie grass and larger stones. The stones almost defeated him. Few were small enough to lift free of the soil without some kind of lever. Once freed, they had to be rolled—he soon learned not to try lifting them—on to a stone-boat, a kind of flat sledge constructed for the purpose, which he would then harness with chains to one of the horses, to lug it slowly clear of the site and over to a slope where Jørgensen said Indians used to drive buffalo to slaughter them, and where Harry would now roll stone after stone.

But it was while engaged in this work, pestered by blackflies that were biting the tender skin on his eyelids to rawness, sweating so hard he had to tie a handkerchief around his brow beneath his hat to stop the sweat from blinding him, that he realized he was no longer resenting his labor but was strangely enjoying it.

He liked working with the horses, of course, though his

dealings were largely with the big black-and-tan plowing pair, not the handsome bays that pulled the family carts and gigs. Cleaning out their stables and giving them oats was the sleepy start to his days, usually performed before he was summoned in for breakfast. He was ashamed that, in a lifetime of riding, he had never fed, groomed or even put the bridle on the horses he rode, and grateful that he had watched grooms at work often enough to be able to pass muster the first time he took a curry comb to one of the big black-and-tans with Jørgensen watching.

There were chickens, which wandered freely around the yard and had been known to hop up the step into his room if he left the door open, and a farm cat, a stern yellow-eyed tom mysteriously called Mr. Schulz. Jørgensen's handsome flat-coated retriever was rarely more than a few yards from her master but occasionally came to watch Harry at work, scathingly immune to his friendly overtures. She grew less suspicious once Jørgensen, having decided, perhaps, that Harry wasn't as soft as his luggage might have suggested, began to give him jobs alongside him so that they worked as a team. Finally, after a long morning of watching them worm, debud and castrate some calves, the dog actually approached Harry with a tail wag and consented to being briefly petted.

"Hates that cousin of my wife's," Jørgensen explained. "Reckon she had you guilty by association..."

Jørgensen was a man of firm opinions and few words, and was not a seeker of confidences. Seemingly it was enough for him to have a hired hand who was reasonably fit and keen to learn. Harry's predecessor had not been a success. "Thought he knew how to do everything, so the *grødhoved* did it wrong half the time. I'd always rather you ask a thing than do it all wrong so it has to be done twice."

With no son to work alongside him, it must have been hard, Harry considered, to have to make do with a succession of unsatisfactory substitutes. The obvious solution would have been to find the perfect hired hand then have him woo one of the daughters...

The serious eldest, Minnie, was clearly marked by a lifetime of failing to impress her father. She looked after the geese and chickens and was an excellent shot, regularly bagging wild duck, of which there was a plentiful supply on the farm's sloughs. She also shot rabbit and the occasional hare. These she would pluck or skin herself in an efficient fury all the more self-righteous for being unapplauded and unregarded. Annie had made her realm the kitchen, which suited her as she was hot-tempered and cruel and food gave her an arena in which she could exert control and make her feelings abundantly clear by indirect means. Goody had the obliging sunny nature so often found in youngest siblings. Her sphere was the dairy, where she milked, churned butter and produced a bland, salty cheese.

Harry woke in quilty darkness in a thrashing panic because he thought he was wetting the bed, then realized that he was merely experiencing a forceful wet dream. He lay clutching a fist between his thighs as he joylessly spent himself, and remembered the dark violence of the dream that had woken him in such a state. As though thinking to leave it behind him with his seed on the sheets, he swung himself upright and stumbled from the bed, stubbing a toe on the heavy boots he had discarded as he undressed, and instinctively making for the door.

He opened it, welcoming the cold night air, and stared out at a landscape transformed. There were stars, a seamless spangled fishnet of them from horizon to horizon, coldly lighting the land and lending the farm buildings, outlined sharply against them, an eerie loveliness.

Harry looked on the scene and felt himself to be nothing, to be less than dirt. He felt a sense of self-disgust keener than the draft blowing in across his bare feet and sperm-splashed thighs, and knew Troels was not to blame. Troels had merely shown him what he was. And the feelings that shock had been mercifully holding in check were released in such a flood that he had to cover his mouth to stop himself crying aloud. He stood, leaning in the doorway, weeping, gasping, looking at the transfigured scene that was like a snowless Christmas card, until his feet hurt.

The next morning, his eyes were glued half shut with tears, and he had to bathe them open.

For all that he was given the least good cutlery and a hard chair at mealtimes, there was no question of his being left behind when the family attended church or went into town for provisions. He thought this a small kindness at first, until it occurred to him that he was still in effect a stranger to these people and therefore not trusted to be left alone with their house and possessions.

Jørgensen took the reins, of course, with his wife beside him, and the girls squeezed together on a little padded bench behind them. All four women were unanimous in their scorn of the social possibilities of Moose Jaw, full as it was of Norwegians, compared to Waverly, Wisconsin, which had offered reassuring touches of Danish culture; but Moose Jaw was all they had, so they got dressed up a little for trips into town, however mundane their errands, because as Goody repeatedly said, *you never knew.*

Harry's place was on the cart's rear, so he could prevent

anything from falling off and so anyone could see at a glance that he was of the household but not of the family. With a couple of burlap sacks folded up into a sort of cushion to guard against splinters, it was pleasant to sit dangling his legs and watching the landscape unroll behind him, emptying his thoughts, much as he did when working.

The journey to the little clapboard Lutheran church they attended or into town was the part he enjoyed. Once arrived at either destination, he felt at a loss, a prey to inquisitive stares and satirical comments only half understood. He had never felt especially manly. He had been raised to believe that what mattered was to be unmistakably a gentleman, and the very question of manliness had never much concerned him. Among these people, though, these tough, bearded men and their lean, travel-hardened women, he felt, for the first time in his life, unmanned or, even, less than human.

He encountered his first Indians on these trips. Their movements and access were strictly controlled, it seemed, so they were usually seen waiting outside buildings on ponies or on foot, or, on the rare occasions when a priest's missionary work had hit home, standing at the back of the church. Most had been encouraged on to reservations further afield, the girls told him, but evidently there were unofficial or "non-treaty" Indians left behind, possibly on an encampment some way outside the town. They came to Moose Jaw to find work or to trade.

Their presence made Mrs. Jørgensen exceedingly nervous on account of some terrible experience in her youth about which she would not be drawn. Obliged to pass an Indian on the street, she would encourage her daughters to hurry on ahead of her, as though the mere glance of a native man could sully them. The older two would make silly, untrue comments about how Indian men smelled bad and were usually drunk and stared at them. Goody, being younger and kinder, once rashly sprang to the Indians' defense, praising their women's skill at basketry and beading, but was shouted down by her sisters, who said she was a fool and that everyone knew Indian women were as drunk and hopeless as their men and little better than children in their lack of moral sense.

Harry was required to help load any bulky purchases from the dry goods store or agricultural depot, and then was at leisure while Jørgensen caught up with friends in the very bar where Harry had eaten supper on his first night, while his wife and daughters made their critical round of Moose Jaw's shops.

On this particular morning, he had no wish to revisit the bar and none to waste his money in shops, so he followed his usual habit of visiting the library—a puritanical approximation of his old Mayfair club—where he would read newspapers and write letters to Jack and Winnie, keeping an anxious eye on the clock so as to allow himself enough time to go to the post office.

Writing to Jack was easy: he kept his tone ironic and light and presented the facts as a kind of adventure, with himself as the unready, untrained hero, asking Jack questions about the care of horses and cattle. Writing to Winnie was much harder. His mind kept wandering back to the scene of his degradation. He was wary of sounding pathetic, but he found it hard to sustain the light, amusing tone he used with Jack. He described for her the unexpected beauties of the countryside, the surprising lack of birds, and how the flowers were like, and yet on closer inspection, exotically unlike, their English equivalents. He described his chilly little room, with its bed made of fruit crates that he had cunningly turned cavity outwards so as to create bookshelves and storage. And then, all at once, in the course of writing how he was sure she would soon be able to run up some curtains that kept out the night chills more effectively than the skinny piece of unlined spotted cotton with which his window was currently shielded, he began to miss her terribly.

His experiences with Browning and then Troels were enough to prove that the secret side to his nature would only lead to unhappiness, even disaster, if not kept in check by the love of a good woman. He didn't write any of that, naturally, but after asking her to pass on his best love to little Phyllis, he ended with a paragraph saying that it was clearly impossible just now and he knew she hadn't wanted to come with him initially, but later, when he was settled and had a house and land of his own, he truly believed she and Phyllis could be contented there with him. He assured her that having them join him eventually would make him happier than he could say.

He signed the letter with love and read it through swiftly, folded it around two clumsy drawings he had made of the house and the view from his open door, and sealed it before he could have second thoughts. He felt a shiver of fear at Robert's prohibition but waved it aside; if ever Winnie chose to join him, it would be her decision alone, made without consulting a brother who no longer lived under the same roof. Besides, Robert was pompous but not a tyrant, and his threats on that horrible night had quite possibly been a drunken bluff, counting on Harry's shame.

The post office was not far away, but he had to hurry there, having taken far longer over the two letters than he had intended. The Jørgensen women would have been there earlier; it was usually their first port of call. They were assiduous letter-writers, maintaining precious links with friends and relations left behind in Wisconsin and Denmark. They liked to take any mail they received to a Chinese restaurant they favored, to devour it at once along with tea and little dumplings. They would thereafter wring days of pleasure from the letters, even the displeasing ones, reading sections of them out for one another's horror or delight. It was a strange, self-exposing practice that made Harry tense to witness. Even had he been comfortable reading aloud, which he never had been, he would worry too much about the risk of inadvertently reading too far and exposing something private.

Jørgensen tended to leave the room during their recitals, so perhaps it made him uncomfortable too. He was not a letter-writer and confessed to Harry that his penmanship was poor, which Harry took to imply that his literacy was wanting. Certainly he was not a reader, and preferred to have one of the girls, Goody for preference, read to him of an evening.

The postmistress had a lively curiosity and, like many in her position, was attuned to niceties of rank. Harry's accent and, possibly, his lack of beard had aroused her curiosity the first time he came in to buy stamps, led there by serious Minnie. Firing off several quick questions he had been too startled to parry, she ascertained that he was the Jørgensens' latest hired hand, there to learn farming skills before setting up on his own somewhere. Evidently she knew, or had dealings with, the carter, because on Harry's second visit, she challengingly declared that she had heard all about his *magnificent luggage*. Since then, her manner of pointedly greeting him by name when he came in, granting him a rare *Mister*, although he was only a hired hand, hinted that, in intervals of tedium in her job, she had woven a romance from the little she knew of him.

Today was no exception, and she drew herself up behind her counter, saying, "Mr. Cane, what a pleasant surprise. What can I do for you today?" in a manner he felt sure was designed to alert others in the post office that this, right before them, was the very Mr. Steamer-Trunk Cane of whom she had been speaking earlier. He paid for two stamps to England and she took his letters off him then said, "I know how rarely you get in, so when the Jørgensen ladies were here earlier, I let them have your mail for handing on to you."

He hurried out, picturing spiteful Annie "accidentally" flicking open an envelope with her fingernails and reading out the contents to her horrified but fascinated sisters.

As it happened, he wasn't the last to arrive back at the cart. The Jørgensen women were all aboard, but Mr. Jørgensen was still in the bar.

"I'm worried he's gotten into one of his arguments," his wife said. "If you go in to look for him, it will remind him of the time."

So Harry found himself revisiting the bar after all. He half expected a waiter to accost him, saying, "You were here with that tall Dane that night," but of course nobody knew who he was. Jørgensen was indeed in an argument, something about fences and land rights, which he must have been losing, for he seemed to seize on Harry's appearance as an excuse to introduce him all round as *My man, Windy Cane, from London.*

Jørgensen's tipsiness, and his wife's teasing him for it and offering to shame him in public by taking the reins off him, led to a mood of hilarity, and they drove out of town with the girls laughing over something they had seen in the haberdasher's.

"Ooh, I almost forgot!" Goody reached into her bag. "Two letters for you, Mr. Cane," and they all laughed at her impersonation of the postmistress. She tossed the letters back to him and he had to scrabble for them to stop them blowing out of the cart.

"We're all rather envious," Minnie put in.

"Yes," Annie added. "Mother had none, so was all for reading yours instead, but Goody Two-Shoes forbade it."

Harry glanced at the precious envelopes. He recognized the

hands as Winnie's and Jack's, and registered a childish pang that each envelope was so very thin. He tried to make out the dates on their postmarks, but the road was rough and the jolting made the letters blur, and it was all he could do to keep his seat. He became aware that Annie was watching him, and the others less overtly so.

"Well?" she asked. "Naturally we're all agog."

"One's from my brother," he told her. "The other's from my wife. But I can't read them while we're in motion."

She turned back to face the front with a graceless shrug and he turned to face the road behind them, tucking the letters into his breast pocket, relishing the warming sense of a pleasure to be enjoyed at leisure. He would save them, he decided, until he was alone again after supper.

He was surprised to feel a sense of something akin to homecoming. While Minnie went to call the hens into their hutch, he helped Jørgensen and Goody unload the supplies, many of which were quite heavy. Annie and her mother hurried inside to make a start on supper, Annie scolding that it was certain the stew she had left to simmer on the stove back would be quite spoiled as the men had made them so very late. It gratified Harry to note that he could now shoulder a sack of flour or cattle cake without hesitation, and that Jørgensen assumed he could lift a thing rather than assuming he couldn't.

When he had stowed the last item, a heavy drum of molasses, he headed toward his room, thinking to wash his hands and face before supper, and found that Goody and her father were coming with him.

"Do you have a picture?" Jørgensen asked him, a little awkwardly. "Of your wife?"

"Of course," Harry said. "You'd like to see it?"

"Yes please," Goody said.

"As proof?"

"Troels never said," Goody told him, with a trace of apology.

Her father snorted. "Your mother's cousin says nothing unless it's to his own advantage."

Goody blushed prettily in the fading light, so that Harry guessed the poor girl nursed an impossible passion for her rough kinsman. For her sake he prayed it would go unnoticed and unrequited.

As he opened the door to his room and lit the lamp in there, he saw them look around at the small changes he had made and remembered with fresh amazement that it had once been Jørgensen's home.

"Clever," Jørgensen said briefly, gesturing with his empty pipe to where Harry had adapted the bed base by turning the crates to create shelves. "Never occurred to me to do that."

"Well you never had all those books to put in there, Pa," Goody told him, evidently itching to read the books' spines in the gloom.

If she hoped for racy novels, Harry reflected, she'd be sorely disappointed in *Animal Husbandry Made Simple* or *Agronomy for the Gentleman Amateur.* He reached to his bedside shelf and passed Jørgensen the little leather travel frame he kept there, holding the lamp so father and daughter could see.

Jørgensen's face softened. "How could you bear to leave her?" he asked.

"She's with her family," Harry said. "It's easier to make a start alone."

"But you'll send for her?" Goody asked. "And the dear little girl?"

"If they'll consent to come," Harry said. "They're used to city comforts."

"Might I know their names?"

Harry told her, and she sighed.

"Perhaps you'd let me stitch Phyllis a bookmark with her name and a little picture for you to send back with your next letter?"

"She's too young to read yet."

"At the rate I stitch, she'll be reading Dickens before it's ready for her," she told him with a laugh.

Annie's stew had begun to stick to the pot, then been angrily diluted with a slosh of water from the kettle and a pinch of salt, which had done little for its savor. The dark, dense rye bread served with it had its usual sour tang—for which Harry was, oddly, developing a taste—and, as ever, they drank only water, because the women of the family were all abstainers. But a cushion had been placed on Harry's chair—thin, but somehow representative of a change in attitude—and he began to be included in the family's conversation in small ways, asked to back one or another up in their arguments or to say what people in London thought of this or that.

When the meal was cleared away, he stood to retire to his room and Mrs. Jørgensen said, "Oh don't leave us just yet. It's so much warmer here. I want to hear about your brother. Is he married too?"

So Harry told her about Jack, always an easy subject of conversation: how they had been all in all to each other when they were growing up, how Jack had overtaken him in confidence and achievements at school, how Jack's courting of George (whose name amused them greatly) had naturally led to Harry's courting of her sister, and how Jack and George had effectively eloped with the family's blessing.

Told at the fireside, with the Jørgensen women variously knitting, darning and embroidering, and the master of the household smoking his pipe, it sounded like the stuff of fiction.

And as with any fiction, Harry edited as Mrs. Jørgensen's gentle interrogation nudged him onwards in the story. He omitted the salient details of the drama of Pattie. There were similarities enough—another houseful of daughters!—for the tale of Mrs. Wells to hold the sympathy of Mrs. Jørgensen. And when he reached the point where, giving them the received version, he lost his fortune, even Annie lowered her needles, having decided Frank was entirely to blame in the matter.

When Minnie chipped in to ask what was in the letters, her father said, "Allow the poor man some privacy, *kvinde*," and, standing to tap out his pipe in the stove, implied that the entertainment was at an end. When Harry stood too, to thank Mrs. Jørgensen and to bid them all good night, the response was casual—he was still only the hired hand, after all—but there was a response at least, and even a little smile from Goody. On previous nights, his leave-taking had been met with little more than silence.

Back in his room, lamp lit, pulling his overcoat back on against the night chill, he sat at the table by the lamp finally to enjoy the two letters. He read Jack's first, because he sensed it could be the least troubling. Jack had written as soon as he received Harry's note of the Jørgensens' address. He had never been one of life's letter-writers; in fact, he never wrote to anyone except Harry, and then only because Harry obliged him to by writing to him. (Having her mother's chatty fluency and ear for dialogue, George would be the household's letter-writer now.) With a pen in his hand, Jack became stilted as he never was in conversation. He had hated the letters they were obliged to write home once a week at school and had fought against it ever since. But precisely because of all this, his personality was forcefully there on the thin sheets of paper in Harry's hands.

(And yes, he had managed to express himself across three and a half sides in his pinched, scientist's scrawl.)

He dutifully commented on all Harry had told him of the journey, saying the fellow passengers sounded like sewers but that meeting the Danish Troll was evidently a spot of luck. He envied Harry the adventure of the long train journey (he loved trains, and had hopes of taking George on a railway holiday around Germany if ever the practice allowed him enough time off). He confessed he was relieved that Harry was taking time to learn about farming and the Canadian way of doing things rather than throwing himself directly into homesteading, and made a joke about not wishing to downplay his big brother's resourcefulness, etc. He had been asking around since Harry's departure, he said, and had heard *grim stories of chaps heading out into the Canadian wilds all gung-ho and coming a cropper.* He went on to write in some detail about challenges he had been facing at work, where he'd had to deal with a racehorse owner who insisted he knew more than any vet and wreaked havoc administering home-made cures that were quite possibly toxic, countering Jack's every protest with *well of course you would say that.* He rounded off with a maddeningly brief message that George and the children were all well and sent love, and that plans were afoot to bring *the Grass Widow and little Phil* on a visit to take their minds off absent friends.

Harry read the letter through again more slowly, made homesick by his brother's familiar slang and magnanimous, trusting outlook. He wished more than anything that Winnie might move to live alongside George, or even to share their household. Jack would never treat Phyllis as an object of obscure shame or refer to her, even out of her hearing, as *Poor Phyllis*, as he felt sure Robert and Frank and their wives would do.

He opened Winnie's letter. It smelled, as he knew it would, of lily of the valley. She had a trick, caught off one of their French governesses, of storing her writing paper in the same small drawer as her handkerchiefs, with several bars of Floris soap, so that both paper and linen would smell delicious and—indirectly—of her. Harry couldn't resist holding the neatly folded paper to his nose for a second or two to breathe it in. The scent was redolent not only of Winnie but of all the soft comforts he had left behind. The pieces of soap Annie sawed off a great block were harsh, orangey-pink things that smelled of nothing but puritanical cleanliness and conjured up nothing kinder than hospital.

My dear Harry, Winnie began. *I'm so glad finally to have an address I can write to, because I've been writing to you in my head so repeatedly it's hard to believe I haven't stamped and posted this already. And it will take such weeks to reach you, I expect. Oh dear.*

The thing is, Harry, that since you left us—which I quite understood you felt obliged to do—Tom Whitacre has taken to visiting again. You remember; I told you about him in Venice. I met him at a dinner party at Frank's and of course he asked lots of questions and soon found out about our marriage and you having gone to Canada. Mother saw no harm in inviting him to lunch, just like in the old days, now that I'm a respectable married lady and an old matron. (I worry that, since Pattie's adventures began, and Robert's and Frank's marriages, she has become far less strict in her supervision of the youngests. She's certainly less severe than she was when George and I were their age!) And of course we talked and talked and he charmed little Phyllis, or rather she charmed him (she is quite the charmer, darling!), and I found all my old feelings stirred up again.

Harry, I fought it all I could. I pretended to be ill or out

*when he called again (twice), but then he started to write to me
too. Well. The last thing you want is details that might wound
your pride still further. When you left, Harry, you did say you
wouldn't mind him visiting. You even started to say, until I
stopped you, that you thought it would be good for Phyllis to
have an "uncle" about the place.*

*I can hardly believe I am writing this. (This is a fair copy, as
you can imagine, after several I have scribbled on or cried over
or thrown in the fire.) You have been worked upon in no short
measure by us all, I feel, a thing my lawyer brothers would be
angry at my writing, but it is true and I love you too much to
be dishonest with you. I was persuaded that my heart would
mend and alter and it did for a while, Harry. The transfer of
my love would have been complete, I think, if only we could
have stayed at Herne Bay, where we were so happy and where
we were all in all to one another.*

There was a large gap between paragraphs, quite as though
the writer were taking a deep breath before feeling able to continue.

*If, for Phyllis's sake, if not for mine, you would consent to
my divorcing you on grounds of "desertion," Tom will meet all
the legal costs. He'd then be in a position to look after Phyllis and me so that we would, of course, no longer be adding to
your financial burdens. I will never let Phyllis forget who her
father is and will see that she is in regular touch with you as
soon as she is of an age to write.*

*In case you were wondering, the Whitacre department store
has been sold and taken on its new owner's name. Mother is
convinced that Tom is a reformed character. I am not a party to
the details but I believe he has given her some discreet financial
assistance, which the brothers know nothing about!*

I pray you will thrive out there, darling Harry, and that

you'll find the true, unstinting love you deserve, better than the sly half-measure you had from me. Winnie.

Harry had to read the letter through twice more, it was so far removed from the one he had expected. At first he felt sorrow at the rude demolition of his recent wholesome fantasy, then a flare of anger that his dashing—he felt sure Tom Whitacre was the sort of man thus described—rival should have made his approach to Winnie so soon after the field was left open to him. And indeed, at the convenient crumbling of Mother Wells's principles. But he couldn't help but see that her reversal of attitude was also rather comic, and rather than resentment of a wily manipulator looking to her own material comfort as well as those of her kinswomen, it stirred in him affection for a kindly pragmatist.

Physical exhaustion mastered a racing brain and he soon put out the lamp and slept, but when the cockerel's crowing woke him to a room already filled with light, he remembered her letter even before he saw it lying unfolded where he had dropped it.

He would not answer her directly, he decided. He did not want Whitacre to feel everything going too smoothly his way. But he would write in a day or so, apologizing for any awkwardness caused by his previous letter and giving her his blessing, just as he must swiftly write to Jack so that he and George should not be wounded at hearing the news second hand. If he withheld consent, he imagined it was only a matter of time before his consent would not be needed, since the desertion would have become a legal fact. Besides, he had no wish for anything to nudge Robert into making revelations that might overshadow Phyllis any more than a hopeless, absent father would already be doing.

He worked harder that week than he had since his arrival,

but did so with a kind of relish at being nothing more than a fit body in the service of a tidy aim. Spring was sufficiently upon them for it to be the week when Jørgensen taught him how to plow, first with the team of horses on land already worked, then, far more challengingly, with the oxen on land cleared but not yet broken. Plowing through centuries of roots left by scrub and tough prairie grass was like plowing wood, like some impossible task set the innocent hero of a fairy tale. Even with the strength of two oxen to assist him, his progress was as slow as forgetfulness, but Harry was light-headed with relief, absolved of responsibility and guilt, if not quite freed of nostalgia for a lost Eden of marriage and fatherhood.

Chapter Sixteen

The year and a day did not pass swiftly. Living what was in effect an antique existence on the farm, rising and retiring more or less with the sun, laboring six days in seven, the height of entertainment consisting of an occasional family visitor or borrowed novel—read with exceeding slowness because he would fall asleep after two or three pages—Harry felt his days pass at a fraction of the speed with which his calendar had unfurled in town. And yet, deprived of choice or variety, he was happy and healthy. He passed twelve months, through broiling summer, an astonishingly beautiful autumn and the shocking dry freeze of the long, long prairie winter, with only one negligible, three-day cold, if one discounted the odd attack of indigestion brought on by Annie's cooking.

The Jørgensens, who grew in kindness toward him while never quite abandoning the distance politic between employers and worker, were his chief entertainment, along with their melancholy dog and glowering cat. Mrs. Jørgensen took to doing his laundry along with that of the rest of the household, and at her prompting, Jørgensen advised him in the purchase of two sets of denim dungarees, which were infinitely easier to clean than the stiff wool suits sold him by the outfitters on the Strand.

Minnie, always grave to the point of rigor, surprised them all by marrying a rector from south of Moose Jaw she met at a combined church social that summer. He was reassuringly

middle-aged, but she became quite girlish as the wedding approached, despite Annie's efforts to make her fat. With Minnie
gone to a distant parish, not only did Harry graduate to an upholstered dining chair and better cutlery, but Annie underwent
a subtle alteration, her spite turning by degrees to wit, and in-
stances of kindness entering her behavior.

In one of the talks they often enjoyed while she worked
nearby, Goody astonished him by admitting that Minnie had
tormented Annie all their lives, physically when they were little,
and psychologically when they grew older. The parents had no
idea, apparently, and thought the sister's thriving in the other's
absence was yet more proof of her unpleasant nature.

The divorce proceeded in Harry's absence. He assumed Winnie would be married to Whitacre without delay but had no
way of knowing. She could hardly continue writing to him
once he had agreed to her terms; it would have made a nonsense of her desertion claim.

Then a letter came from Jack. *This is not going to be pleasant, old man,* he wrote. *Probably as hard for me to write as it
will be for you to read, but here goes. We had an unexpected
visit from Pattie last week. As you can imagine, she has become
so very sophisticated that poor George had rather given up on
her ever deigning to visit Chester and a house that might smell
of horse. Tears and lamentations and she was immediately clos-
eted with George while I was banished. Turns out Notty has
announced he can have no more to do with her since an unfortunate business involving you, old man, and an autograph
album and some pansy attempting blackmail. George relayed it
all, simply livid, couldn't believe Pattie had known about it and
kept it quiet for so long, though relieved, of course, that Robert
and Notty had seen that the police weren't involved.*

Pattie—who I gather can't quite bring herself to return that splendid gold watch—has retired from the stage forthwith and resolved to train as a nurse.

Naturally I don't believe a word of all this, Harry. It's simply too incredible and disgusting, and I think you're little short of heroic to have moved out there rather than involve the family in a scandal in trying to clear your name. But you must understand that now George is insisting I have nothing more to do with you, I have to knuckle under and do as the lady asks. She is my wife, old man, and pretty peppery when crossed. At least this way she can't complain if I continue to keep a weather eye on Little Phil for you.

Harry read the letter several times before burning it in the stove. He wrote several drafts of replies, now protesting, now beseeching, and burned those too. In the end he wrote a very short one simply acknowledging receipt, saying that it was plain that nothing he said would alter the painful position, and thanking Jack for his continued guardianship of Phyllis. Not surprisingly, his response went unanswered.

As summer turned to glorious autumn, Harry bought himself a gun and learned to shoot rabbit and duck, which Jørgensen showed him how to prepare for the kitchen, and his wife and Annie how to cook. He had worried that Jørgensen might renege on their handshake and ask him to move on with the coming of winter, not wanting an extra mouth to feed when there was less for a hired hand to do about the place, but his fears were groundless. Jørgensen still made good use of him every day. Until the snows came, there remained ditches to keep clear, fences to mend, and winter supplies to collect and store. And once snow lay thick around the place—shoulder deep or more where it blew into drifts—the animals still had to be fed and bedded in the barns, and ice melted for them so that they could drink. There was dung to be forked from the barns before it froze like rock, and logs to be piled for the kitchen stove. And of course there was always snow to shovel, snow of a texture and depth he would not have thought possible.

As for the cold, he had never experienced anything like it: a dry, iron clamp upon the land, like death itself, full of unexpected beauty, like the hard crystals that formed on the inside of the windows. The cold did something strange to the quality of sounds around the farm, deadening all background noise so that the smallest scratching or whisper was emphasized. It was easy to see how the unwary settler could die in such a scene, lulled into marveling at its deadly beauty even as his blood began to freeze. Just once Harry lingered outside as a blizzard got under way, amazed at the scale and savagery of it, but was furiously dragged indoors by Jørgensen and given a lecture about losing fingers and toes to frostbite and the impossibility of getting a doctor out until spring.

As winter progressed, he came to understand the hunger with which Goody had eyed his meager library when she first saw it. He had soon read everything he had with him, rereading much of it, and fell to trading books with the Jørgensens. With so little choice of entertainment and such long nights amid the stupefying silence and snow, far from any neighbors, the usual demarcations of books for women and books for men, books for children and books for their elders became irrelevant before the imperative of diversion. He read Jane Austen, which he had never thought to do before, and Lamb's *Tales from Shakespeare* and *Black Beauty* as well as Jack London, James Fenimore Cooper and Hans Christian Andersen. He even found himself, just like his employers, slowly turning the pages of the latest Eaton's catalogue, which displayed everything from wooden house kits (up to eight bedrooms large) to cream separators, from guns to underwear, the latter modeled by coyly simpering women. (Men's underwear, he noted, was listed but unmodeled, the men in the catalogues rarely appearing in anything less than evening dress.)

Winter had come on them suddenly, whereas spring arrived by slow, unconvincing degrees, far later than he'd have expected. What Jørgensen called chinooks, warm winds from the western mountains, arrived and began to shrink the snow into patches of dirty ice rather than melting the lot overnight the way warmer weather would have done at home. A thaw was announced with loud cracks around the place before it turned all Harry's laboriously cleared ditches to so many little canals. With the spring melt came a flurry of unexpected visitors, as neighboring households emerged from the long freeze like so many bears, hungry for news and less familiar faces and other people's baking. Mrs. Jørgensen cursed these visitors, who often arrived at the least convenient moment, when she had her hands full of chores or nothing but leftovers to set before them, but she welcomed them, too, being as hungry for faces and talk as anyone else.

Once the roads reopened, albeit with a few floods where sloughs had overflowed, the Jørgensens headed into town, trusting Harry with the guardianship of the place now they had passed a winter with him there. He was glad to be left behind—relishing having only the dog and horses for company as he set to work continuing to plow the patch of ground he had begun working over when the frosts arrived.

When they returned, shortly before dusk, Jørgensen's greeting was a little tense, even by his standards, and Harry wondered if the hoped-for lunch with Minnie and her husband had displeased in some way, or failed to materialize. The explanation emerged at supper. They had brought back quite a bundle of post, including a clutch of long-overdue Christmas cards, one of which was for Harry, clumsily painted by Phyllis. (This made him feel bad, as he had been taken by surprise by their long winter confinement so had been unable to send the child either card or present.) There were letters from their friends and relations and one brief one from Troels. And this was the source of Jørgensen's gloom, for Troels confirmed the date a year and a day since his departure when he would be coming with the carter to collect Harry, for whom he had identified a choice piece of land on a quarter-section two days' ride beyond the Battlefords, in northern Saskatchewan. He would bring another greenhorn to take Harry's place.

"You don't have to go with him," Jørgensen said. "I can't afford to pay you more than I do, but..."

"The man needs his dignity," Esme Jørgensen said, which earned what sounded like a Danish curse from her husband.

"She's right," he conceded later. "But you could find land on your own. You don't need his help. You're not a *grønskolling* any more."

"But he says he has the perfect place in view."

"Canada is big. There are many such places."

"Where are the Battlefords?" Harry asked, thinking they sounded charmingly like English villages in Sussex or Hampshire, and already knowing enough of Canada to understand they would almost certainly be nothing like.

Goody fetched the map of Canada from her father's desk and unfolded it on the cleared table. It was no use, however, because so much of the western prairie had still been "empty" at the time of its printing. But Annie had a map of the Canadian Pacific Railway system Troels had given her on his last visit, and after much poring over that with a magnifying glass, she found Fort Battleford. Another, lesser railway went on from there to stop at places called Unity, Vera, Winter, Yonker and Zumbro. "Troels says the sidings are named in alphabetical order because there's nothing else to call them in such a vast, empty space."

"It's miles away," Goody announced gloomily. "Miles and miles from civilization."

"Civilization will follow the railway," her father told her. "It just takes time."

Before he joined the women in retiring for the night, Jørgensen went outside with Harry on the pretext of checking the henhouse fence, as Harry had spotted a coyote prowling in the distance that afternoon. They talked in the codified language men used at such times. They spoke of oxen and horses, of the respective merits of log-built houses over lumber ones, of the need to sharpen the plowshares before Harry continued breaking ground in the morning. The unmistakable sense, however, was that Jørgensen would miss having him about the place and was wary of starting again with whoever Troels was bringing with him in exchange.

Chapter Seventeen

Troels arrived exactly when he said he would. "The Devil come to claim a soul," Jørgensen muttered as, alerted by the dog's barking, they gathered in the yard to watch his approach. The new apprentice looked little more than a schoolboy and made Harry feel gratifyingly labor-toughened by comparison, something Troels seemed to notice, for he grinned as he jumped down from the cart and shook Jørgensen and Harry's hands and said, "You made a man of him."

"Stay a few more months," Jørgensen growled under his breath, as Troels went on to embrace the women, "I might do the same for you."

Harry knew he didn't need to go with Troels. He knew he could find his own way to a piece of land and make an entirely independent start for himself. But in a country so vast, offering so many options, it was surely as well to exploit an informed traveler's recommendation.

"He'll take advantage of your trust," Jørgensen warned, but it was hard to see what advantage there could be for Troels in helping him. For obvious, unvoiceable reasons of his own, he would dearly have liked to see Troels on to the train in Moose Jaw and then go his own way. Unable to sleep because of a full moon, he had passed much of the night before Troels's return picturing scenes of trite but satisfactory revenge in which he did just that, or, better yet, contrived to leave him behind as the train pulled away, literally to leave him standing while he rode away to dizzying freedom and anonymity. And then he slept and had confusing, shaming dreams about welcoming his tormentor.

Troels was no sooner off the cart and standing before him again, unchanged except for a small scar on one temple, just as tall and remorseless as Harry remembered, than Harry found time spun savagely back and himself abruptly unmanned again. With Troels there, he felt his will and new skills ebb away and he was once again the English innocent who would go meekly where he was told, as though the man were his whip-clutching master and he his dog.

After a year of the modest, homely Jørgensens and their limited conversation, however, a year of dung and cows, of fence posts and ditches, Troels, with his height and worldliness and well-cut clothes and piercing stare, had all the glamour of a cruel god, and his smile, when he bestowed it, felt like sunshine after sodden February.

The new boy climbed down. He had only a small canvas rucksack for his belongings. "You travel lighter than I managed to," Harry told him, and the boy stared back rudely, saying nothing. Harry was surprised to find he could shrug and turn aside where he would once have felt bound to flounder on politely.

He returned to his room to finish packing. Half the possessions in his trunk had never left it. Now he found two neat piles of freshly laundered clothes into which Mrs. Jørgensen had discreetly added a few extra items her husband could spare. On the table was a stoneware jar of Annie's excellent cucumber pickle, which she had teased him was the very thing to make a diet of gopher palatable. Beside it lay a large handkerchief that Goody had been painstakingly hemming, night after night—he had not realized for him—and had embroidered on one corner with a blue silk H emerging from a clump of a flower he guessed was meant for a forget-me-not.

The evening was noisy. The catching-up on Danish family news, and the fact that his young replacement turned out to be a native Swede with little English, meant that Harry found himself linguistically excluded. The night that followed was much interrupted because the Swede, who claimed half Harry's little bed, was a snorer.

Jørgensen sent the greenhorn to work cutting up and splitting a pile of logs, then drove Harry and Troels and the famous trunk to the station in Moose Jaw. Having gravely led Harry to one side in the crowded ticket office, he handed him an envelope packed with his wages for the year: sixty dollars, to which he had added an extra twenty, "Because you proved better than most and didn't make fools of my girls." He advised him to bank most of it in Battleford once he had paid any fees at the Dominion Lands Office and bought lumber and a plow and horses. "You'll find there's not much call for cash. Men out there will prefer to trade: labor for tool hire, oats for fence posts and such. I've made you a list in there of what you need to get started. I've done this before. Troels never has. Remember that..."

Shaking Harry's hand and taking his leave, Jørgensen looked him full in the face for what felt like the first time in their acquaintance, watery eyes bright in his round, battered visage, and Harry had the uncomfortable sensation of being momentarily known for what he was.

On Troels's railway maps—he had one for each of the different companies they might travel with—the Battlefords did not seem so very far away. The map gave no sense of terrain or true distance, however, truncating a broad slice of the

continent to fit in all the stations in a convenient, compre-
hensible form. The Grand Trunk Pacific was the only service
between Moose Jaw and Regina. Then they picked up the
Canadian Northern as far as Saskatoon, where there was a
long enough delay to leave the train and find a hot meal. Then
they headed on via Clark's Crossing to Warman, where they
had to change and wait for another train west to Battleford
Junction, where they had yet another change, and a wait, for
the short ride into Battleford.

On account of the hard seats and the changes, with the
bother of extracting and reloading their luggage, the journey
seemed to take far longer than Harry's initial journey from Halifax had done a year before. Perhaps he was simply less patient
than he had been, and so conditioned by a year's outdoor labor
that sitting inside for so long had become less tolerable. The
rolling stock felt more basic, too, than even that crammed colo-
nial with its stoves and fold-down tea-tray beds.

Magnificently named, the Grand Trunk Pacific halted as often as any suburban service out of Waterloo, stopping at every
siding, as the humble stops for new settlements were called.
Compared to the railway *chateaux* at Regina and Saskatoon,
most offered little more in the way of a conventional station than a simple signposted platform across which a family's
worldly possessions might fairly conveniently be loaded from
crammed goods van to waiting ox cart.

Troels was either full of talk or eating. (He was slow to
share the picnic Mrs. Jørgensen had entrusted him with, although Harry was sure it was intended for them both.) Or else
he slept, leaning heavily against Harry's shoulder. His talk, as
ever, was scornful or self-aggrandizing stuff, and he showed no
great curiosity to hear about Harry's year, rightly assuming it
had been uneventful, and contenting himself with saying, only

half mockingly, at intervals, "So old Jørgensen made a man of you?" or "You didn't marry one of the daughters, then?"

Harry was curious to hear what had become of the English puppies from their boat. Most, as Troels had predicted, were having a high old time hunting, shooting, fishing and making no pretense of being there to farm. Some had evidently slipped beyond Troels's control (scornfully dismissive noises here); others had proved less happy. One had died in the winter, falling off his horse when drunk and freezing to death in a snowdrift, where he had not been found (and then half eaten) until the recent thaws. Another had surprised his fellows by setting out to homestead properly, to the extent of fencing his hundred and sixty acres within the year, then had been defeated by cold, drink and the lure of a low native woman.

"Which is how you, my friend, are about to come into a fine piece of land." The young Englishman in question was giving up—had been persuaded to give up—and was so short of money, having been cut off by his disgusted family on account of the Indian mistress, that he was prepared to file for abandonment if Harry would pay him for the cost of materials used for the fence. "Labor not included," Troels said with a chuckle.

Although many homesteaders had abandoned the attempt and fled south across the border to what they thought would be easier conditions in the American prairies, plenty were arriving to replace them, and, as always, the thaw would bring a rush of new entries. There were often ugly scenes in the long queues outside a Dominion Lands Office, as a man could sometimes wait all day without being seen, only to return the next day to find himself once again near the queue's end. And an entry had to be made in person. Proxies and agents were strictly unacceptable (here Troels pulled a face), so if a man were small or weak or easily jostled out of position, he could find himself beaten to the land he wanted. It was especially competitive for brothers, or for any group from the same Ukrainian village, say, who wanted adjoining properties. A story, possibly apocryphal, was circulating of a young man, little more than a boy, who repeatedly lost his place near the front of the queue until his five hulking brothers came along with him and bodily threw him over the heads of the competition the instant the office door opened.

When he finally arrived in North Battleford, Harry was overwhelmed with fatigue, although it was still barely five in the afternoon. Having ensured his trunk could be kept for him at the station, he found he could be decisive in his single-minded pursuit of sleep. He took a small bag of necessaries to the nearest hotel, where he made Troels laugh aloud at the firmness with which he requested a room to himself. They agreed to meet again at breakfast.

The room was tiny—a single-bedded cell where there was barely space for the washstand at the bed's end. He washed his face, gulped down two glasses of icy water—the Jørgensens' picnic had been full of salty cheese and pickles—and barely found the energy to strip to his undershirt and long johns before falling into bed. After a year of sleeping on thinly padded apple chests, it could have been a plump divan at the Ritz.

Used now to farming hours, he awoke at five before remembering where he was and relaxing a little. He retrieved the envelope of wages from his jacket pocket and teased out Jørgensen's note. *Shelter matters more than anything*, he read. *Even food. You need a bell tent, ideally one with a chimney flap, and a simple stove. Matches. Good knife. Fry-pan. Fork. (You can eat from the pan!) Remember to have the flue outside before you light up or you'll*...Here he had failed to spell *asphyxiate* a couple of times and had written *die* instead. *Don't*

*waste hours building a soddy unless the ground is very stony.
Get on and dig a cellar—good for storm shelter, fire protection
and storage—and build a lumber house right away if you can
afford it. Soddies are for peasants and you would not last a
month.*

From the train, Troels had pointed out newer sod houses
than the ones near Moose Jaw. Constructed of rectangular sods
packed together around a wood frame and, for the luckier, windows, they could be more or less sealed inside with layers of
paper and whitewash. They were snug enough to keep out the
wind and snow but were said to continue raining inside for
days after the weather outside had dried up.

While waiting for Troels to join him for breakfast, Harry took
advantage of being briefly near a post office to send Phyllis a picture postcard of a buffalo and some Indians. When he strode in,
Troels was in an ebullient good humor and soon let slip that he
had found a woman the night before. "Blonde, German, built
like a feather bed and very fond of her job." She had left him
with a great hunger for chops and egg and, it seemed, a rapac-
ity for the morning's fierce business. "We must catch our prey
promptly, even if we have to drag him out of bed," he said. "A
weakling like that may have made the same promise to others."

"What about the...his Indian woman? What if he's married
her?"

"He's weak and lazy but he's not a complete idiot. Yes,"
Troels went on eagerly to their waiter, "more coffee. More! We
must get him to the Land Office before he changes his mind,
Harry, and make sure that you are absolutely the next person
to go in after him."

"Troels?"

"Harry?" The Dane turned on him an expression at once patient and mocking, as he gulped his coffee.

The dining room had filled rapidly with other guests, all men, and become correspondingly noisy. Harry wondered how many of them were about the same business as he, were in fact his rivals.

"Why are you doing all this for me?" he asked.

"Because I like you and believe in you."

"Forgive me for being indelicate, but...do you look for some kind of payment? A percentage of the sale, perhaps?"

"Oh. That. That I will have from Varcoe when you pay him for his fencing. Most of the money will be mine."

"Ah." Still Harry didn't understand. "But if the land is so good, why not take it for yourself?"

"I'm not a farmer, Harry. I'm a businessman. Yes, yes, sleeping under the incredible stars, hunting duck, riding across a prairie: all that is good, a kind of adventure, but the rest, putting up fences, breaking that impossible prairie ground day after day, watching wheat grow, watching it get eaten by bugs and gophers or flattened by rain or burned in a fire—*this* is not for me! But I can see that land, good land, is a good investment. When your three years are up and the land is yours—assuming you haven't blown your brains out or been frozen to death in your cabin or eaten by bears—if you decide it's not for you either, then you can sell it to me. How's that?"

"Agreed."

They shook hands across the little table.

"Maybe by then I'll be ready to settle down," Troels added, and laughed at the idea.

Varcoe was not living in a hotel, or a boarding house, or even in one of the little, low wooden houses beginning to cluster on building plots, but somewhere in the middle of a sea of mud, in an apparently unregulated district across the railway tracks, where scrawny children stared at them from the mouths of shacks and tents as they passed. Troels stopped at a wooden shed of a kind that back home might have been used to house a lawnmower, tennis things or a croquet set. A blackened tin chimney thrust out of what would have been a window at one end, the void about it plugged with bundled sacking. When Troels knocked on the door with his customary vigor, Harry thought instinctively of the tale of the three little pigs and the wolf.

The native woman who opened the door was surely a far cry from the salacious imaginings of Varcoe's English family. She was in a man's gabardine, fastened with a stout leather belt, and what might have been visible of her legs beneath a mud-spattered skirt were thoroughly hidden in no less dirty woolen socks. Only when she half turned to call out, "Varcoe? Men wants you," over her shoulder and revealed the astonishingly black hair hanging loose down her back and a generous glimpse of well-filled bodice where buttons were missing on her coat could he see how she might tempt a man. As they waited, she raked him with her gaze and he felt something of power coming off her.

Because of the way she had turned to call him, Harry had assumed Varcoe was in their little shed, possibly still in bed, so was surprised to see him approach from outside. His arms were full of waste wood: scraps of broken packing case and offcuts of lumber. Seeing Troels, he dropped the wood beside the door, brushed his hands clean on his jacket and told the woman, "I'm going with them."

She took his hat from a nail next to the door and handed it to him, an unsmiling echo of a loyal wife. She scorched Harry once more with her stare before turning back inside and shutting the door.

Introductions were made and hands shaken and Troels led the way impatiently to the Dominion Lands Office, where the day's queue had already formed.

"Remember," he said to Harry, "not a word about your business while we're waiting. There are bastards everywhere."

There was little danger of Varcoe chattering, except with fever. Twice on their way back into town he had been forced to a halt so as to give way to a racking cough that left spots of blood on his filthy handkerchief. From the little he let slip in nervy splatters of conversation as they walked, he had come to Canada after a brief, disastrous spell in his father's cavalry regiment. He was younger than Harry, possibly even younger than Jack, but he looked ten years older. From his accent, his thoughtless good manners, his guileless, happy surprise on hearing Harry speak, he might have been one of Troel's English puppies. Even were he cleaned up, however, given a trip to a Jermyn Street barber for a good haircut and to get rid of his uneven scarecrow beard, disease and hardship had wrought scarring changes in him. His polite phrases, the glimpses he gave of a sunnily untroubled Englishness, were the last twitches of a condemned limb. There was no risk of Harry falling into the clutches of a local woman, Indian or otherwise, or succumbing to the lure of alcohol or morphine, but he could not help look at the wreck of a man beside him as a terrible warning of what he too might become out here.

As though reading his thoughts, Varcoe suddenly clutched his arm. "I say, old man. Are you sure this is what you want?" he asked. "You don't exactly look the type."

"Perhaps I should grow a beard," Harry told him, instinctively joking out of discomfort. "I've been farming near Moose Jaw all year actually. I liked it."

"But not on your own, I'll bet. Gets pretty lonely out there."

"Oh, I expect I'll cope."

Varcoe was shaken by another fit of coughing, which caused the men around them to step aside, and before long he was going through the door ahead of Harry.

It was only as he was before the Dominion Lands agent himself, entering his claim on the acres for which Varcoe had just filed his deed of abandonment, that the rashness of what he was about—committing himself to three years on a hundred and sixty acres he had only seen on an entirely unhelpful map—was brought home to him. Most of the men who were entering claims would have spent days riding around, inspecting several possibilities before hurrying here to secure their considered choices. Or was that mistaken? Were there truly now so few good quarter-sections left, even in so vast a terrain, that he would have been insane to let this opportunity slip? Why else would there be such a crowd jostling for position outside? He pictured afresh the challenge in the native woman's inky stare. Would Troels take so much of the sum Harry paid for the fencing that what was left would barely keep her and Varcoe in food for the month? Should Harry not buy the man a train ticket to Halifax at least?

"Is there a problem?" The clerk at the desk brought him back to his senses.

Harry hastily apologized, and signed the next three years of his life away, receiving in exchange a precious slip of paper with the map co-ordinates of his new home: SW 23-43-25-W3. He shook hands with the clerk, who looked bewildered, so perhaps that wasn't quite the thing, and found himself back outside, where Troels congratulated him and swept him off to buy supplies.

Varcoe had disappeared. "I've paid him off," Troels explained airily. "You can pay me," he said. "He said to wish you good luck."

"Will he go home, do you think?" Harry asked.

Troels laughed but made no fuller answer.

Harry had a great pile of possessions waiting at the station, of course, but apart from the camp bed, rubber bath, gun, blankets and books, that was largely clothes. The forbiddingly named Winter, his new nearest neighborhood station, was fifteen stops away along the Grand Trunk Pacific line via Oban but would take two days to reach by horse and cart.

From Indian traders on the edge of town, he bought a pair of horses—not the speedy, half-wild stock he had glimpsed enviously at points on his journey, but sturdy sisters, more Suffolk Punch than thoroughbred. The Indians assured him they were already well broken to both cart and plough. As if to prove their point, they threw a second-hand cart into the deal. Smaller than most, but big enough for his needs. Thus equipped, slightly giddy at the sudden freedom to drive instead of walking, he took the cart to an all-purpose agricultural depot near the station where, mindful of Jørgensen's advice, he bought himself a tent big enough to shelter his trunk and camp bed and still leave him room to take a few steps. It had a flap expressly designed to take the little chimney of the stove he bought next. Excited from spending, after a year of punitive restraint, he bought tools: a scythe and whetstone, a mattock, a spade, a shovel, an ax and a simple walking plough as close in design as he could see to the one he had been using at Jørgensen's. Then, as Troels, grown bored, went off to buy them beer, bacon, bread and cheese, Harry bought a sack of oats for his horses and, all important, a water bottle. Then a frying pan, a sharp knife and, because, *pace* Jørgensen, he could not quite imagine himself reduced to eating off a knife blade, a bone-handled fork. And then, because eating from a frying pan would be too depressing and he might, who knew, have company occasionally, he bought a second fork and two white enameled tin plates and mugs to match.

"Care for a tablecloth with those?" the sales assistant asked and earned himself what Harry hoped was a most English look.

He remembered just in time to add a good length of rope, initially to lash down his ground sheet over his cartful of bounty, and to halter the horses; a hammer for the tent pegs, and two boxes of cartridges for his gun. By the time all this was loaded, Troels had returned with a better humor, and as excited by the buying of food as an overgrown boy heading on a picnic. He had consulted among locals, one of whom had scribbled out the directions to Winter on the brown paper the cheese was wrapped in.

BETHEL

From North to South the princes meet
To pay their homage at his feet.
While western empires own their Lord,
And savage tribes attend his Word.

Isaac Watts, "Jesus Shall Reign"

Chapter Eighteen

Harry slept at the slightest opportunity. It was as though his mind was in retreat, like a wounded or frightened animal, turning in upon itself rather than risking the exposure of whatever wounds it had sustained.

He was woken slowly by a gentle tapping. Still disoriented, he took a moment to recognize the young man at the door, dressed in a tasseled buckskin jacket, denims and a dark leather Stetson.

"Sorry to wake you," he said, doffing the hat. "It's time for your chore."

"You've changed," Harry said.

"Ursula doesn't go outside Bethel," the young man said with a wink.

"You make a fine boy."

"Thank you. I've had practice. Oh, and don't worry, I already signed you out on the register."

They headed up to the drive, where two plump dove-gray ponies and a cart were waiting. The ponies had been tethered ingeniously with ropes tied to heavy cookery weights.

"Clever idea," Harry said, as the young Cree scooped up the weights before springing nimbly up to the driving bench and taking the reins.

"It wouldn't work if they weren't this docile. I've never known a pair so placid."

"Must be the effect of watching the Athabasca all day,"

Harry said, climbing up beside him, and they laughed. It was disconcerting to feel a fluttering of desire for this man he had felt only respect for as a woman. "So if you're not Ursula, what should I call you?"

"What my father called me. I don't expect you to get your tongue around the Cree. In English it's Little Bear. I'm told Ursula means the same."

"It does."

Little Bear flicked the reins and the ponies raised their heads from the grass and shambled into motion. "The track from here to Hinton is pretty rough," Little Bear said, "so we'll have to go slowly. Which is fortunate, as these two don't know how to do anything else."

"That's fine," Harry told him. "I've no urgent business."

They set off beneath the trees and were soon on a muddy, heavily pitted track beside the river, which Harry imagined must become impassable in flood weather or deep snow.

Although he was now speaking out more than he did as Ursula, Little Bear was no more chatty. Harry decided to be honest with him.

"Gideon is very pleased you're talking to me," he said.

Little Bear met this with thoughtful silence but at last said, "Of course he is. He mistakes my silence for sadness. He thinks if I talk, I won't try to kill myself again. He believes talking cures everything."

"So your silence is shyness?"

"I think it's anger. He forgets English was forced on me when they tore me from my parents."

"You speak it very well."

"I was a star pupil."

"As a boy."

"You heard."

"Was it so cruel?"

"Cruel schooling is the norm with the English," Little Bear reminded him. "So you might not have found it so. But we Cree love our children. We keep them close. Taking us away from our tribes and parents and forbidding us to speak or even think in Cree was only the beginning. You have to understand, as a *two-souls* I had a special position. I was being taught mysteries, things ordinary boys would never learn."

"A *two-souls* like . . . the people in Gideon's reading the other night?"

"The very same. I was special and my father was proud of me. But to the missionaries, I was an evil influence. I was fourteen, nearly fully grown, but to them I was an evil child. They cut my hair short and the evil they saw in me was beaten out day after day."

"Did you fight?"

Little Bear shrugged. "No. I was always quiet and good and a swift learner. And their Jesus was so kind, kinder than some of our spirits. He reached out to me and still hasn't let me go. For a meek, mild dead man, he has a tenacious grip!"

"Then what happened?"

"My shaman had taught me better and earlier than the priest did, and I suffered . . . I suffered—what is it Gideon calls it?—a *paralyzing inner conflict.*"

Harry chuckled at this precise rendering of the good doctor's way of speaking.

"Is he helping you?"

"He lets me be myself. But only in limited ways. He bought me my two dresses."

"They're pretty."

"They're as much a disguise as any boarding school suit. And this jacket and hat he got me are no more than fancy dress."

"So why can't you go back to...to your people?"

"Even if I could find them, they wouldn't know me now. That's one of Gideon's wiser sayings, that most outcasts banish themselves."

"Do you think of yourself as an outcast?"

"Don't you, Harry? In any case, Jesus wouldn't let me go so easily."

"You know...Jesus was a good deal more revolutionary than the men who teach in his name. He never married. He was a friend to outcasts and non-believers. Nowhere in the Bible does he speak out against...living as you do."

"I know. I read all the Jesus bits. Which makes him all the harder to shake off."

"What about the others? Does Gideon help them?"

"Well, most are more residents than patients, I think. Their *cure* is to be able to take refuge from the world's disgust and punishments. Mabel tried to kill her husband."

"Really?"

"She didn't succeed, but her lawyer had her sent to an asylum rather than face trial. And here, she and Bruno can have their...There's a name for it." Little Bear thought a moment or two, then clicked his fingers. "Bostonian marriage."

He drove them on in silence and Harry chose to respect his privacy rather than grill him further. He admired the scenery, enjoyed watching the way Little Bear handled the lazy ponies.

When they arrived in Hinton, Little Bear stopped a discreet distance from the stores. "The quickest thing is for you to go inside with the list," he said, "while I wait out here with the cart. If I do it, I have to wait at the back door and they take too long to serve me."

"They don't like that you're an Indian?"

Little Bear laughed at him. "Oh you're so very English! No.

They don't like giving white man's food to Indians to handle. And then they really don't like that I speak like an Anglican priest. If him talk like this, him no thought uppity. But I can't play that game. You take the list and I'll do the carrying. Gideon has an account; just give the address as Bethel Ranch."

Harry took the drily vegetarian list into the small stores while Little Bear waited outside. He added a small box of matches to the shopping list because it felt odd having none rattling in his breast pocket and he hadn't liked to take the ones from his cabin. Knowing what small country communities were like, he prepared himself for the mention of Gideon and his ranch of peculiar people to earn him a comment or a sidelong glance, but there was nothing. Either the shopkeeper was waiting to gossip once he had left, or Bethel had succeeded in keeping the nature of sanctuary it provided a secret from its innocent neighbors.

As they called in at the post office to drop off and collect Bethel's mail, he fancied he and Little Bear received looks, not for where they were from but for the fact that they were an Englishman letting himself be driven about the place by a fancily dressed Cree who should, by rights, have been riding on the cart's rear with the groceries. The postmaster muttered something as he handed over the letters.

"I'm sorry," Harry said. "I didn't quite catch that."

"I said," the postmaster told him, "you have mighty queer taste in friends."

The remark left Harry shocked and angry, but he stumbled out in silence, cheeks burning, unable to muster a suitable retort. He said nothing of the exchange to his companion.

"You're having bad dreams still," Little Bear remarked a while after they had started back for home.

"Not especially," Harry said.

Little Bear laughed. "You don't have to lie to me. No. You are. You shout in your sleep."

"Really? I'm so sorry."

"*I'm so sorry.* So English! It doesn't bother me. I don't sleep much anyway. I like the night-time for walking about the place, which is how I hear you. Are you holding things back from Gideon?"

"Not that I know of."

Little Bear raised an eyebrow. He had a satirical, suggestive edge to his humor that Ursula lacked. "But?"

Harry smiled. "Now, now. Is that in the Bethel spirit of community openness and harmony?"

Little Bear shrugged. He flicked the ponies' reins smartly, setting all the tassels on his buckskin jacket in motion.

"I begin to feel he only wants to hear the things that will confirm his theories," Harry admitted.

"At least you feel he still hears you. Sometimes I talk and think he is completely deaf."

Little Bear pulled the ponies to a halt so they could watch a buzzard performing its mesmerizing wheels high above the treetops. "Did you fight in the war, Harry?"

"No," Harry admitted. "I was a bit old and I thought I was more use as a farmer."

"So the man you killed was here in Canada?"

Harry looked at him sharply, but Little Bear's expression as he nudged the ponies back into motion was as unreadable as ever.

"I'm so psychic, sometimes I frighten myself," Little Bear told him kindly.

Harry tried to focus on the scenery they were traveling through, the track, the bushes, the ponies' flicking ears, but saw again the broad shoulders and distinctive head. "He wanted to destroy everything. Everything I loved," he muttered.

"Just tell me, was he an evil man?"

Harry thought a while. "Evil like in a fairy tale," he said. "But fascinating too."

"Huh." Little Bear looked briefly at him and smiled faintly as if reading something in his face. "Bad men you want to kiss are the worst; he had only to use the right tone of voice and you offered your throat to the knife."

"That sort of thing, yes," Harry said, and cleared his throat, unnerved at the accuracy with which the young man beside him seemed able to read his darkest instincts.

WINTER

They were young and were certain they would
make good in God's open spaces, where a man
is a man.

Jennie Johnston, *A Glance Back*

Chapter Nineteen

While working for Jørgensen, in an area that wasn't exactly hilly, Harry had often heard people joking that the western prairies were so dull and flat that a man driving a cart there had to fight sleep because of the extreme monotony of the landscape, but could at least rest secure in the knowledge that if he did nod off, his horse would be equally bored and feel no temptation to leave the dead-straight track while its master slumbered.

Between Moose Jaw and Saskatoon, Harry had certainly seen stretches that seemed to bear out the jibe, but as he left the Battlefords behind and drove the laden cart along the almost deserted dirt road toward Cut Knife, he was pleased to see mature stands of trees and then even a hill or two. It wasn't exactly Derbyshire, he told himself, but neither was it Norfolk.

Compared to the area around the Jørgensens, however, it was astonishingly empty of people. He passed no more than four other carts on the road all day. Much of the land had not yet been cultivated, and he seemed to see more Indians—Cree, as he had just learned these were—than Europeans on his way. He was worried his new horses would become overly tired, having no idea how fit they were. He found a stream where they could have a long drink and a rest while he ate some lunch and drank a rashly celebratory bottle of warm beer. Safe from any man's satirical gaze, he spent some time talking to them and rubbing their faces and wondering what he should call them.

There was so little sign of life at Cut Knife, and he was so tired by then, that he nearly drove straight through it without noticing. At least Winter had a station. Cut Knife was no more than a few homesteads as yet, and certainly had no inn. The farmer he was sent to was chatty enough once he had gotten over his surprise at an unexpected visitor. He showed Harry where he could water his horses and secure them for the night, and suggested Harry sleep under his cart on the straw in his barn, saying there were thieving Indians about and that a fully laden cart was too much provocation for men with little to their name.

Cut Knife had only been settled four years before, he said, but they hoped to persuade the Grand Trunk Pacific to throw out a branch line to them from the Battlefords, if only to make shipping of grain and delivery of supplies less arduous. "And we have a hill nearby!" he laughed. "A regular hill." He described how it was where the Indians had murderously routed a revenge attack during the rebellion of the 1880s, defending their women and children from far greater government forces. White men were killed, he said, and added suggestively that one had been *mutilated*. Harry could tell from the detail of his narrative that he had enjoyed few opportunities to tell anyone the story since finding it out for himself on arrival.

The barn was bone dry, being almost brand new, and the straw fairly fresh. Harry furled himself in both his new blankets and bedded down, as suggested, beneath his cart, mounding up some straw beneath him as a kind of pillow. He had enjoyed softer beds, and warmer nights, but the smell of the straw seemed to act like a mild narcotic, and it felt somehow tremendously safe to have the big, warm, sighing bulk of his new horses close at hand.

He was up at dawn to feed and harness them. The farmer offered him a cup of tea and a slice of bread, as well as the use of his privy (of which he was proud, as it was as new a feature as the barn), then solemnly talked him through the actually very simple route to Winter before seeing him off the property.

The scene at Winter's tiny station when he finally reached it was like that at so many of the settler stations he had passed through on the way to the Battlefords. A little cluster of humanity—all men, of course—waiting to catch the next train or to do business with men getting off it. Troels strode out from their midst to greet him. He had spent another night with his German woman and was keen to share every lip-smacking detail.

As they turned north up what was evidently intended for Winter's chief street one day, humanity fell away again except for the evidence of an occasional shack, tent or soddy, or a distant glimpse of a farmer at work. Between Moose Jaw and Jørgensen's place the land had seemed entirely under cultivation already, whether for crops or as pasture. Here, as on much of the land Harry had driven the cart through that morning, the white man's incursion was still a fragile, piecemeal thing. Moose Jaw was a city by comparison, with hotels, a library, a choice of churches, a proud governmental hall, most of it built of brick. Even Battleford had enough brick buildings to lend it a convincing air of permanence. The few buildings they passed in Winter were wooden, built with whatever men could carry by cart from the train, presumably, and while many were in better repair than the pitiful structure where Varcoe was living with his woman, they were rarely much larger. Jørgensen's house was only built of

lumber but seemed palatial by comparison; it had two verandas, a second story, an attic and a cellar. But when Harry
commented on this, Troels pointed out that since settlement
in Winter was comparatively fresh, these were mainly places
where men lived alone, *batching it* in minimal space and comfort until such time as they could attract wives and acquire,
like Jørgensen, the trappings of domesticity.

The land rose steadily toward a distant ridge when all at once
Troels was jumping down from the cart. Using Harry's new
scythe, he stamped and sliced his way through thick grasses
and dazzling spring weeds to find a surveyor's post, off which
he read a number.

"Yes," he shouted. "I thought so. This is your new home!
The bastard lied about the fencing."

Wire fence heading off from a single post into the thick
prairie grass was what had alerted Troels to search for the surveyor's marker. But there was no equivalent fence along the
facing side of the property.

Having driven the cart a little way off the track, Harry tied
the horses to a tree beside a small slough so they could have
water. Troels and he then set about clearing ground for the tent,
one with the scythe, one with the shovel. It was slow work. The
grass was tough stuff, its closest English equivalent the sharp-
edged marram found on seaside dunes. Everywhere there were
sturdy clumps of weeds or small saplings that must have taken
root since Varcoe performed what little clearance he had managed during his stay.

As they worked, they came upon the sad wreck of Varcoe's
attempt at a shelter: a tangle of mismatched lumber and canvas
that must have given way under the weight of snow in the winter just past. Tugging the canvas aside and making a heap of the

lumber for firewood, Harry found a stash of perfectly good if slightly rusting tools including, most usefully, a post-hole auger, a small reparation for Varcoe's fraudulence over his fencing performance.

To his shame, Harry had never erected a tent before, not even in school, so was happy that Troels knew what he was about and took charge as they unrolled and set to pegging the baffling thing, telling Harry where to bang in pegs or secure poles. As they pulled the tent upright and he stepped inside, he felt a brief, boyish glee, which was swiftly followed by a species of panic at the realization that this frail structure and this alone was now his home.

As though sensing the faltering of his spirits, Troels insisted they get on with heaving the little stove into place and securing its tin flue through the opening in the tent roof, pulling tight the cunning corset of leather straps and canvas that closed the gap around it to hold out the worst of the weather. They shared a bottle of beer to slake their thirst after their labors and christen the new home, then Troels left Harry to pull his trunk and bags inside and begin unpacking, while he went off to discover the full extent of Varcoe's perfidy over the fencing.

Having assembled and made up his camp bed in one corner and arranged blankets for Troels and gathered a good heap of fairly dry wood for the stove, Harry left the tent—where the gloom and the strong smell of newly unrolled mackintosh was threatening to overpower him—and took his brand-new water bottle and whistling kettle in search of a stream where he could draw water fit to drink. He discovered one a little way up the slope, and tasted it gingerly at first, then eagerly when he found it sweet. (Jørgensen had told him horror stories of men settling on land that proved to have only alkali water on it.)

There were birds singing, more than he ever heard at

Moose Jaw. He made out the cool, deliberate notes he had already learned belonged to a chickadee. And there was an abundance of flowers. He made a note to send away for a botany book when he was next at a bookseller. That idea in turn brought home the realization that he had not seen what he thought of as a proper bookseller since leaving Moose Jaw, and that it might be months, years even, before he saw one again. Perhaps he could write to the one he used in London. He stood from filling his bottle and kettle and looked around him at prairie grass and saplings, at trees he would have to fell and boulders he would have to lever on to a stone-boat for the horses to pull out of the way—once, that was, he had a lever and a stone-boat.

Troels had been right, however. Harry looked about him with eyes taught by Jørgensen and saw that it was land with good potential, watered but not waterlogged, with a gentle southerly slope to part of it and even a small pillow of a wooded hill where he immediately knew he would build his house. At the same time, the gulf between the scene of fertile wilderness around him and the rolling wheat fields of the re- cruitment literature and railway posters hit him with a force that made him lean instinctively on a tree for support.

Just then he was surprised by the rattle of wheels and saw a white pony and trap coming along the track from the north. There was a slim woman at the reins, veiled against the dust. She raised a gloved hand in greeting as he emerged from the trees and, after a slight struggle, pulled her lively pony to a halt.

"Oh," she cried out as he approached. "I thought you were Mr. Varcoe come back at last. But you're not."

"No," he said. "Sorry. I'm Harry Cane. I just took over his, er..."

"He gave up?"

"Yes."

"Well, hello." She jumped easily from her little trap. "I was bringing him a couple of pies, but I'll give them to you instead."

"How very kind."

"You haven't tried my pastry yet..." She handed him two small, still warm pies, wrapped in a piece of brown paper. "My brother and I are your neighbors. The apple one has a little sugar on it so you'll know it from the rabbit."

"Where are you?" He looked around, seeing nothing but bluff, prairie, trees and more prairie.

"As the crow flies," she said, "we're there on the next little bulge you might come in time to call a hill." She pointed. "But the way to reach us is up this track, then turn in at the next gate on the left. Out here *neighbor* is a relative term, as you probably know. But that's where we are if you need anything. You'll need a fire ditch, by the way. Once the weather warms up in earnest. Around your tent, I mean. Just in case."

He glanced the way she was looking. "Ah," he said. "Thank you. We'll get on with that tomorrow. Or I will."

"It was a miracle we didn't get burned out last year, and we're overdue for a bad one. Are you here with your wife?"

"No. No. I'm...I'm not married." The sad little truth sounded brave in that setting. "I'm going to be on my own, but a friend's helping me get started. In fact it was he who picked out this plot for me."

Hearing Troels stamping back through the scrub and dropping off what sounded like an armful of logs, he called out, "We've a visitor! A lady. I'm so sorry, I don't know your name," he told her.

"Slaymaker," she said. "Petra Slaymaker," and to his surprise he saw she was looking past him with something like fear.

"Well, small world!" exclaimed Troels, brushing the strands of moss and grass off his hands and waistcoat.

"Mr. Munck," she said, and all warmth had left her voice. "Fancy that."

As Troels came to stand beside him, Harry smelled the musk of his sweat, and something else, something threatening, if threat had a smell. Miss Slaymaker had taken a step backward and now had a hand on her pony's bridle.

"What a delightful surprise," Troels said, and Harry knew at once that it was no surprise at all. "It's been months."

"Years," she corrected him. "We left Toronto four years ago. You look quite the man now."

"And you look as imperious as ever. Has some lucky man...?"

"I'm homesteading with Paul," she said.

"Is he managing?"

"He's thriving, thank you," she said briskly, turning her pony to face back the way she had come.

"Miss Slaymaker very kindly brought pies," Harry said, feeling he must say something, anything, to break the tension crackling between the two of them.

But she wasn't prepared to play the politeness game. "Are you in Winter for long?" she asked Troels.

"Just tonight," he said. "I have business to see to back East. Young Harry has to cope on his own, and is sure to do much better than Varcoe did. Poor Mr. Varcoe. But now that I know where you've been hiding, the prospect of coming back to check on his progress is suddenly much more attractive."

She tried to smile, but it looked more like a wince. "Good to meet you, Mr. Cane," she said stiffly.

All Harry could think to say was "Thank you for the pies," at which she gave a nervous laugh and took off up the track.

Troels, Harry saw, was staring after her, alert as a hound on a scent.

"Did she say where she and her brother are farming?" he asked.

"No," Harry lied.

In the tension of the minutes just past, he had held the rabbit pie so hard that its pastry had cracked, and dark gravy was leaking across his hands like blood.

Chapter Twenty

After helping to wolf the pies, Troels threw himself into digging a fire ditch round the little encampment with a single-mindedness that was unsettling to watch. He did not say he was upset, or what had upset him, but it was obvious. He said only, briefly, that he had known brother and sister when he was growing up in Toronto, and that they thought themselves better than their peers because their father was a doctor.

The ask-me-no-more tone in which he said this made it plain that there was more to the story than he was revealing, and Harry remembered their long-ago first conversation on the boat and guessed he had fallen for Miss Slaymaker—who had not struck him as remotely stuck-up, merely self-possessed—and been unable to countenance her rejection of him.

Troels dug as though proving himself and punishing Miss Slaymaker all at once. With sticks and twine they marked out the lines along which they would dig, and Harry worked one way, Troels the other, until they met at last on the other side of the rectangle, by which time night was falling and Troels was sweaty and in a better humor again.

Harry parried his teasing and set about lighting the stove to cook the sausages and onions they had brought with them. Then Troels produced a small bottle of whisky from his knapsack, splashed some into a mug for Harry, and they grew quietly merry, hunkered by the warmth of the stove, sitting side by side on the trunk in lieu of any other furniture.

Harry was immensely grateful to him for all he had done and, made stupid and sentimental by the whisky, could not help but imagine the two of them setting up some clumsy domestic arrangement there together. While Troels went outside to relieve himself, Harry bedded down in the blankets on the floor, leaving the bed for his visitor, who had, after all, labored hard on his behalf until well past sundown, whatever his obscure motive.

Troels returned, kicked off his boots, blew out the lantern and accepted the bed without demur. He fidgeted noisily for a while. Lent courage by darkness, Harry asked if he'd known all along that the Slaymakers held a nearby homestead when he had urged Harry to take this one on.

There was a pause and a heavy sigh, then Troels said that of course he'd noticed their name on the map, because it was such an unusual one, but that he had convinced himself it couldn't be the same people as the brother was such an unlikely farmer.

"Like me, you mean," Harry said quietly, at which Munck snorted.

There was silence for a while, broken only by the restful sound of a log settling in the stove, then Troels mumbled, "I'll come down there and join you, if you want."

His words were so indistinct that it took Harry a second or two to be sure he had heard them correctly. At once he thought back to the incident in the Moose Jaw hotel, to the pain of it, and the lasting humiliation. "I don't think that's such a good idea, really," he replied, louder than he had intended.

He had become, he decided, strong enough to fight Troels off, if necessary, and tensed himself in readiness. But no rejoinder followed and soon the other man was snoring, while Harry was left staringly awake, his limbs aching from desire as much as labor.

* * *

He woke to the babbling song of a skylark and a cold draft, to find the stove long out and the tent tied open. Troels was outside, standing on the cart to scan the distant view in the direction of the Slaymakers' place. All good humor gone, face puffy from sleep, he said simply that they must leave at once so he could catch a train east.

They rode on the cart in silence until they neared the little settlement at Winter, where a cluster of men and vehicles had already gathered in expectation of a train.

"I dare say I'll be back this way within the year," Troels said.

"Be sure to check on my progress," Harry told him, meeting sulks with bonhomie. "And give my best to the Jørgensens when you see them next."

Raising his hat to Troels as the train pulled out, he felt he had passed some trial.

In the weeks that followed, he lost all sense of days of the week. If the sun was up, he worked; if down, he slept. After twice mistakenly trying to buy supplies from Winter's still rudimentary dry goods store on a Sunday, he picked up a simple seed merchant's calendar, so he might cross off the days as they passed. Rather than be overwhelmed by the size and number of the tasks before him, he made lists and broke them down into further lists. Building winterproof shelter for both himself and the horses (whom he had mischievously christened Kitty and May, after Winnie's flighty youngest sisters) was clearly essential, but less urgent than clearing and plowing his first patch of ground so as to produce a wheat crop, however small. As for the fencing, it transpired that Varcoe had fenced off just one of the homestead's four half-mile sides. The side he had fenced was where the surveyors had left an optimistic road allowance on what was still untouched prairie. The side facing the road had yet to be done, and the other two he might slyly have been relying on neighboring farmers to deal with. And then, of course, he had lost heart or time or met his distracting woman. Harry found a great pile of fence posts dumped in the long grass, and after picking his way through on May, the calmer of the two horses, he discovered another load abandoned on a perfectly good cart, along with two rolls of wire and a big box of U staples, the box turned to pulp over the winter.

He established a routine whereby he began each day by augering then hammering in another five posts, stretching the wire between them before he harnessed the horses and set to clearing. Clearing, as he had learned at Jørgensen's, was slow work, best done methodically, felling useful trees first, using the horses to pull out such stumps as he couldn't burn, clearing scrub and the larger stones, and only then attempting to plow.

And in this place, attempting was the word. Plowing in England always looked such a smooth affair, the horses working in steady lines, guided by the plowman as the plow parted and folded back the ground in neat brown-black ridges like so many tidy pleats. Here, even more than on Jørgensen's land, the untouched ground was so thick with roots that even when a patch was sufficiently clear, one's progress remained agonizingly slow. He calculated that they walked a stately ten or twelve miles in a good day, which meant he had plowed a little less than an acre and a half. At the day's end, giving the horses their oats and looking about him, he tried to be glad at the ground he had thus covered and not to dwell on how long it would take one man and two horses to claim his quarter-section of a hundred and sixty acres. After dark, he would sharpen the plowshare as best he could with the whetstone, although once a week he had no option but to drive it in on the cart to be sharpened in Winter.

He had never appreciated until now the simple pleasure of food being cooked for one by someone else, whatever its quality. Following instructions on the tins of flour and oatmeal, he learned to make himself water porridge for breakfast and, in lieu of bread, a kind of rough stove-top substitute called bannock, which could be used to mop up meat juices or smeared with marmalade from another tin.

Taking pity on him, the clerk in the store taught him how to save money and time by slowly simmering up a mess of pork and dried beans with a few onions to produce a dish something like one he had tasted all too often at the Jørgensens'. Portions of this could be ladled out and reheated in the course of the week, or even eaten cold if he was too tired to wait for the stove to heat it.

His only conversations were with that store man, discounting the ones he had with the horses as they worked for him, and he made an effort not to seem too pathetically starved of human contact on his trips in for more bread or beans or salt pork.

The area he was clearing and plowing was hemmed in on all sides by small trees and prairie grass, so his views were minimal. But occasionally, on his dawn sessions working on the fence around the perimeter, he glimpsed another farmer, dark, bearded, walking behind a plow through land that had clearly been plowed for at least two seasons already. He raised a hand in greeting but the other man rarely waved back so perhaps had not seen him. As for Petra Slaymaker, he saw her just twice on his way to or from town. The first time she passed him at a trot, and made do with a brisk salute with her gloved hand in answer to his raising his hat. The second time she was in some difficulty with her pony and, knowing horses, he pulled up and jumped down to help her extract a sharp stone it had picked up in one hoof. She thanked him and asked how he did and whether he had heard from his friend Mr. Munck. He began to explain that Troels was not really a friend, but must have sounded half crazed with loneliness, for she seemed in a great anxiety to be off and he did not like to detain her.

He had sown his first few acres of wheat, which seemed a laughably small achievement, and had begun to clear a section on the rise of land where he imagined he might erect a little house, when he fell ill. Perhaps it was influenza caught from someone in Winter; perhaps he had poisoned himself with too large a pot of pork and beans kept too long at the back of the stove.

All he knew was that one fine morning he had barely eaten his porridge and started hammering in the first of the day's fence posts than he brought it all up again. He felt better after being sick, so after resting a few minutes and rinsing his mouth out from his water bottle, he returned to work. He managed to drive in a second post, but then all at once found his arms had no more strength in them, and he had to drop the sledgehammer again and lean against the nearest tree. Then he found he had to sit. He told himself it need not be for long. If he simply closed his eyes a little, the dizziness would surely pass.

After a while, he could not have said how long, he became aware that he was now lying down, staring up at the sky. He could feel moss and twigs against his ears and neck, and cold dew soaking into his trousers, and knew he should move, but the chill and damp were far outweighed by the great, soothing comfort of being horizontal and not having to stir. So he closed his eyes again.

He must have fallen unconscious, when something made him open his eyes again, the quality of light had changed, and the weather with it. The sky overhead was dark gray, where he had last seen it blue, and it was raining. He felt water sluicing down his neck and inside his shirt, felt the raindrops begin to fall as hard as hail on his face and hands. And yet still he couldn't find the strength to move, or the will. On the contrary, he almost relished the sensation of the water washing his face and the ground growing spongy beneath his fingers. He entertained a delicious fantasy that the ground would soon begin to absorb him if he only lay there still enough, that the sweet moss was beginning to embrace him and would shortly start to hide him from view.

He closed his eyes again. This was the stillest and most calm he had been in months, if one discounted the dead exhaustion of sleep.

"Hello? Are you all right? I've got your horse back for you. She was... Hello?"

He felt a hand, hot against his soaking chest, and opened his eyes again. It had stopped raining, although the plants and trees were still bright with it and the sodden ground seemed to be steaming.

A dark angel thinly disguised by a rough reddish beard was crouching over him, a hand on his heart. The angel smiled briefly. "You're not dead, then. Are you drunk?" Harry couldn't answer, but the man brought his face close to his and sniffed him. "No," he said. "Not drunk!" He sat back slightly and moved his hand from Harry's heart to his forehead, where it pushed back his hair and briefly sank on his brow. "You've a mighty fever. We need to get you home. The nearest doc's in Unity, but my sister's a nurse. This won't be very comfortable, but I'm going to put you on to your horse. Up you get now."

He caught Harry under his arms and hauled him into a sitting position against the tree again, so that Harry could see May standing calmly by, eating whatever grass was to hand. Then he heaved him upright so that, for want of strength, Harry fell close against him and was briefly aware of his relative warmth after the damp chill of the ground, and of a smell off him like spiced woodsmoke. Then the man was heaving him over his shoulder in a sort of fireman's lift, and, from there, across May's broad back.

To be slung, stomach down, over a horse's back was hardly easeful, but the warmth she gave off was comforting even in his stupor. Holding him firmly by the belt, the man hauled one of his legs up and over her. Harry was sure he would simply slide off head first, but as though sensing what was required of her, May left off eating and raised her head so that he could grip her mane on either side while his rescuer, after a couple of swearing failures, because she was tall and there was no mounting block handy in such a spot, managed to climb astride her too, by hauling on a low branch. Close behind him, thigh to thigh, and reaching round him for her reins with one hand, he held Harry firmly against him with his spare arm. After clicking his tongue to get May moving, he murmured, "Soon have you home," in a low, soothing tone that might have been addressed equally to mare or master.

The necessarily slow journey could have taken anything from half an hour to two. Harry had no sense of time passing, slipping in and out of consciousness as he was. More than once his rescuer brought both arms briefly around him to pass the reins from one hand to the other, murmuring that his arm was falling asleep. Riding bareback, they could move at no more than a walk. May's rather galumphing trot, which reminded Harry of an old insult of Jack's that a certain horse he had to treat in Chester was like a sofa with hooves, would have top-pled them both in no time.

At some point night fell and Harry woke to find his head flopped backward on the other man's shoulder, his view full of stars and the other's soft beard tickling his ear.

When he woke next, it was to see lanternlight and hear a woman's voice. A figure he soon realized was Petra Slaymaker was now leading May by the bridle. "I'd quite given you up for lost," she was saying to her brother. "I'd all but taken down the rifle to protect my honor." And she chuckled.

Shortly after that, they arrived at the Slaymakers' home-stead, where her brother lowered him back over May's neck. The sister held him in place while the brother dismounted, then the two of them unloaded him and carried him inside and laid him on a bed. He saw plank walls, framed pictures, and was aware of someone sliding off his boots and soaking outer clothes. A quilt was put over him, up to his chin, a real patch-work quilt smelling faintly of lavender and summertime. Petra Slaymaker held a bony hand against his head, then slipped a thermometer under his tongue. While she waited, she held his wrist and took his pulse, gazing intently at her pocket watch the while. She removed the thermometer, read it, then held a glass of water to his lips so he could drink.

"You've a high fever, Mr. Cane," she told him. "Paul will drive over at first light to fetch anything precious and your other horse. Sleep now. Rest."

Chapter Twenty-One

At the time, he could not have said how long the fever held him, but they told him afterward that he had been in danger and delirious for two days before it began to break. Day, night, heat and cold were all confused to him, and he was racked by dark dreams that blurred with waking fantasies in which he was being hunted by Troels Munck in league with his former brothers-in-law, hunted with dogs and guns across the empty landscape of Cut Knife, which at one time lay deep in moonlit snow, at another roasted in pitiless sun. So it was that his slow emergence from the fever, and growing understanding that he was not being hunted but cared for, was also the dawning of a friendship.

He had doubtless said much in his delirium, but the first words he consciously spoke from his sickbed were "You are very kind."

Petra Slaymaker was in the act of washing his face and arms with a flannel she had been dipping in a basin of hot soapy water. The soap smelled of cedar, or some such bracing wood, quite unlike the harsh stuff he had grown used to at the Jørgensens'. She paused in wringing out the flannel. "Oh," she said. "Welcome back. I'm not kind. Just ferociously practical. Can you hear this?" She clicked her fingers to one side of his head.

"Yes," he said.

"And this?" She did the same on the other side.

"Yes," he told her.

"Good," she said. "I've known fever like that leave a person deaf on one side. You were so hot that first night, I thought we'd need a priest! How do you feel?"

"Hungry!"

She laughed. "Thirsty, too, I bet."

"Yes."

"I'll bring you some broth."

"I should get up."

"Why? Do you need the pot? It's just here."

"No, but... There are things I should be doing."

"You'll be doing nothing for a while yet," she sighed. "You'll be far too weak."

"But..."

"Paul brought your other horse back here, and he loaded your things into your cart and drove that here with her. So even if they find your tent, nobody's making off with your treasures. You read?"

"Yes."

"We can trade books."

"Good. I'm a little bored of some of mine."

"I'll leave you to wash the rest of you, now that you can. And, er..." She glanced down at the chamber pot, over which a spotless piece of white cloth was draped. "Just don't try standing up yet. Or if you must, do it very slowly. You'll be dizzy. I won't be far away. This isn't a mansion."

"You gave up your room."

"Not me. I'm across the way. You're in my brother's bed. Paul's been bedding down on the couch."

"That's very kind of him."

"It is. He's tall as a pine."

When a woman was beautiful but did nothing to show her beauty off, or had no time for fashion or an elaborate coiffure,

Winnie would call her *fine*. Petra Slaymaker was fine. She had sky-blue eyes and good bone structure, wore her auburn hair tied back in a simple plait and was evidently an assiduous hat-wearer when the sun shone, for her delicate Scottish skin was almost unfreckled.

Left alone, Harry realized he was in another man's striped nightshirt—the brother's, presumably. He succeeded in swinging his legs out of the bed, but could only stand to use the chamber pot by clutching at the brass bedstead. His urine was alarmingly dark from dehydration. Lowering the pot without spilling the contents almost defeated him, and he had to sit on the bed's edge to wash his lower half. To climb back under the covers with skin that was no longer fever-sticky was a delicious sensation, and he had barely begun to look at the little room around him with fresh interest than he fell asleep again.

When he woke next, the brother was sitting beside the bed, eyes bright above his red-brown beard, wood chips in his slightly wild hair. "Brought you some broth," he said. "But I'm under strict instructions not to hand it over until you're sitting up and in no danger of scalding yourself."

A good, savory smell coiled up in the steam from the mug he was holding.

"Chicken?" Harry asked.

"Pigeon," he said. "Sit up."

Harry hauled himself upright against the pillows.

"I guess we never met properly," the brother said.

"You saved my life."

"Yes, but... I'm Paul Slaymaker. Petra's brother."

"How do you do? Harry Cane."

"Were you teased about that at school?"

"Of course. I was called Hurry and Windy. I... I don't know how to begin to—"

"Drink your broth. And there's a piece of bannock, if you've the teeth for it. A bit stale, I reckon."

"Thank you. I'm sure it's delicious."

"Ssh. Eat."

Harry had assumed Paul Slaymaker would leave him to eat, but the strange young man sat while he drank the broth and ate the rather dried-out piece of bannock, wrinkling his eyes in a smile whenever Harry caught his gaze.

"The children were staring in at your window earlier. You're an object of veneration," he said, as Harry was finishing.

"Your children?"

"No. Little Crees. There's a camp of non-treaty Cree a couple of miles away. Our little patch of wood has a significance for their women. Men in town wouldn't like our letting them, but…They often make the journey there and bring the younger children with them. Much against my better judgment, Petra is doing her best to teach the mothers to read and write. She's also studying to speak their language. She says it's harder than Ancient Greek. Horrifies the women at church, who probably have her down for a rebel and a witch. All done? Good." He took the mug and little plate. "Sleep now. I'm back to my plough. I'll be back at sunset and you can tell me all about yourself then. Assuming that what you said in your fever was just crazy dreams talking."

"Oh dear. Did I talk much?"

Paul Slaymaker stood. He was so tall, his hair seemed to brush the ceiling. He grinned down at Harry, teasing him. "Oh, not so very much. But you did hold my hand fiercely at one point and kiss it so hard I thought I'd have a bruise."

"Oh! Oh I'm so sorry."

"Don't be. Most flattering attention I've had since we left Toronto," he said. He had to stoop as he passed through the doorway.

* * *

At some point in the afternoon, Petra slipped in with a cup of tea and a ginger biscuit.

"Mr. Cane?"

"Oh please call me Harry," he told her.

She smiled to herself. "My father always said to treat patients with extra respect to compensate them for any loss of dignity caused by their afflictions."

"I believe I left all dignity behind in Halifax," he assured her.

"Harry, then. Might I ask you an impertinent question?"

"Of course."

She glanced out of the little window, her sharp attention momentarily snared by a bird swooping down from a tree. "I was simply wondering how you came to be friends with Mr. Munck."

"Oh but we're not really friends," he told her. "We met on the boat and he rather adopted me as a project or an experiment. He found me work on his cousin's farm near Moose Jaw all last year and he steered me out here because he knew a good quarter-section was mine for the taking if I moved swiftly. He frightens me rather. If I fail here the way poor Varcoe did, I think he'll swoop down and claim my soul, like Mephistopheles."

"So it's you, not he, who's the homesteader down there?"

"Yes."

"And you're not...close?"

"No."

His denial brought a pungent recollection of having his face pushed into a hotel mattress, but it was quite true, he reflected: he had not so much as a forwarding address for the man.

"I'm glad to hear it."

"He said you knew each other back in Toronto."

"Yes," she admitted, her lips tightening in distaste. "And I never thought to see him again."

"And you probably won't," he assured her. "He's constantly on the move. I expect spring has seen him sail back to England to shepherd out another clutch of trusting young puppies."

She looked confused.

"Rich young men," he explained, "looking for adventure."

"Remittance men?" she said with distaste.

"Is that what you call them?"

"When they live on money sent from home instead of by the sweat of their brow."

"Ah." She was looking severe, so he added, "I have some savings but I don't live off money from home."

She smiled a little at that and asked if it would trouble him if she practiced her piano.

They were Toronto born, to Scottish parents. Their father was a doctor, unworldly and impractical in his tireless devotion to the poor of Cabbagetown and the teeming slums peopled by settlers—many of them driven from the Highlands by landlords or from Ireland by hunger—who had neither the means nor the wits to move on into Canada's promising interior. The elder, with far more in common with their father than with their snobbish, dissatisfied mother, Petra had trained in all but a certificate as his nurse, but it was to his undisguised disappointment that Paul proved both squeamish and without scientific ability, interested more in Schiller than in test tubes. Their father died unfairly young, of cholera contracted from drinking tea with one grateful slum patient too many. Moving swiftly toward a second marriage to a wealthy Chicago meat merchant and city councilor she had met on a trip south of the border, their mother was keen to be rid of two hulking reminders that she was not quite as young as her hair color would have her fiancé believe.

She maneuvered for them to move to Edinburgh, where she had cousins who would take them in, but they rebelled, waving her off to her new life across the border and setting up house modestly together. Petra took in piano students, while her brother enrolled at the university, studying philosophy with a vague view of then training as a lawyer. But then some crisis had arisen, obliging them to move out to Winter and to make a dramatic new start.

Neither said as much. The subject was changed and a passage in their history skirted over, and Harry, with shameful secrets enough of his own, had no intention of pressing them for details or explanation.

It was a fine day, with a real hint of spring warmth to it. Drawn by laughter, after he had dressed, and stripped Paul's bed to air, Harry emerged on to the little veranda and was startled to find Petra at a table with three young Cree women. The women were working at copying letters with chalk on little home-made blackboards, while a crowd of children of different ages either hung around their necks or played back and forth between the nearby trees. The children hid when Harry appeared and the women looked wary until, in halting words of their own language, Petra reassured them. Then, as if to emphasize what she had said, she pointed at him and said in English, "Our friend Harry."

"Friend," the women repeated while Petra wrote the word down for them.

"Our friend. My friend. Your friend."

Chapter Twenty-Two

Inspired by the Slaymakers' example, Harry drew on his savings to order a house not unlike theirs from the Eaton's catalogue. It would not come intact, of course, but as a kit of preconstructed wooden panels, windows, doors, floorboards and roof shingles. It still took two men a week or three to hammer the thing together. Paul had hired a couple of railway workers to help build his, but he reassured Harry that it was still far quicker and easier than building a traditional log house, and the walls could be packed with wool for insulation and papered or painted to taste. It was also easily extended should one's needs expand.

While waiting for delivery, Harry allowed himself an hour a day to clear a site, choosing the high ground that would have a good view over his land and would not, he judged, be at risk of flooding in the spring thaw. Once he had cut down a few trees, he would be able to see one end of the Slaymaker place from one end of his, which would, he judged, be reassuring without feeling intrusive to either household. Petra joked that they could establish a signaling system with colored flags.

Reluctant to continue digging small holes in the ground any longer than he needed to, now that the season of biting flies was upon them, he dug himself a long, deep pit for a privy on the edge of the building plot—far enough away for hygiene but not too distant for battling to in deep snow. With Paul's help, he built a little pointed-roofed tarpaper shed over it and constructed a seat using the top of a broken-down deal table fallen off the back of some luckless immigrant family's cart. With a roof light for ventilation and an improvised bookshelf, it felt like a promise of civilization to come, even though it was some distance from his tent.

The time passed when he could sensibly plant any further wheat, but as his first tiny crop's shoots began to be distinguishable among the inevitable weeds sprouting alongside them, he maintained his punishing schedule of clearing, plowing and fencing off his territory. He was too tired of an evening to do much more than eat and sleep, but the Slaymakers sought him out occasionally for a trip to Winter for provisions, or to catch the train somewhere for a day out, or to join them for supper to stop him *going quite crazy*. And they all went to the nearest Anglican church on Sunday, even though it was a round trip of nearly two hours by cart. The Slaymakers were no more God-fearing than Harry was; they certainly weren't pious Lutherans like the Jørgensens, but went, he suspected, for the same reasons he did, for the reassurance and continuity represented by familiar words and well-known hymns, badly sung with no sturdier accompaniment than a wheezy little harmonium. And they went for the chance to meet people.

The Slaymakers were in many ways as self-contained and aloof as Harry was shy, and there was a tacit understanding between them never to linger much when the service ended or to commit too often to church socials or picnics at Manitou Lake. But, as Petra said, even in such a small and scattered community, it was better to be known a little than to be thought odd and avoided entirely.

Another reason they found for seeing him was books. Harry wrote to his bookseller in Piccadilly, where he had never thought to close his account, and ordered Petra a complete set of Dumas in translation and Paul a set of Dickens, to thank them for caring for him in his sickness when he would surely have died without their intervention. Once the books arrived, they lent him volumes as they finished them, and borrowed books of his in turn. The Dumas, especially, were so preposterously removed from the reality of their lives, with their silks and jewels, swordfights and conspiracies, that to read them was to be briefly transported, but they were fustian stuff for the most part, and he sensed from Petra's response to them that she would rather he had given her something less sedate. She retaliated with historical novels by William Kirby and John Richardson and with adventure fantasies by R. M. Ballantyne and the like, which made their prairie lives, with the Cree marginalized and faintly pathetic, and few encounters with wild animals larger than a coyote seem tame and unadventurous.

Since meeting Winnie, Harry had come to realize that he found the company of women easier than that of men. Or perhaps it was since his fateful involvement with Browning. Was it simply that women presented no danger of temptation? Whatever the reason, he found that Petra's initial guardedness with him rapidly gave way to a frank and easy friendship. She knew his partial history, that he had a wife who had divorced him for another man, and the sorrow of a daughter effectively lost to him, but she was without feminine guile or game-playing and seemed to accept with something approaching relief that he was not about to pay court to her. She felt uncomplicatedly like a sister to him, as George had done before her affection had turned to disgust.

Paul he found far harder to read. He was quite without that tiresome aggression or competitiveness that even casual male acquaintances seemed to feel bound to display and, compared to his more forceful sister, could keep his counsel to the point of seeming withdrawn. And yet he had a way of smiling that Harry felt sure might be satirical. He believed Paul thought him a citified fool. The more he thought this, the more foolishly he feared he talked in his presence.

Word reached him that his house, or the makings of it, had finally been deposited at Winter station. With even the larger of his two carts, it would take several journeys to gather every stack and bundle of the kit to the site. Several of the panels were heavy as well as cumbersome. He had to clear a way so that he could bring cart to plot without panels and posts snagging on branches, and then it took him a while to unload.

It looked very little like a house and every bit like a lumber yard where an explosive had been detonated. His initial resolve to be methodical and stack like with like had crumbled as the day wore on and he ran out of space to unload tidily. He was looking about him in the fading light, knowing he should stop and light the stove to heat up some unappetizing stew, when he heard laughter and turned to see the Slaymakers hurrying up from the track where they had just left their cart. They had been to the Battlefords on the train for the day, they told him, and called in to take him with them, but he must have been out fetching one of his loads. Petra insisted on giving him some cheese and a loaf of proper yeast bread—one of the great treats of such a trip—and began to rebuke him for thinking to take on such a big task unassisted, but Paul stopped her.

"Perhaps he'd rather do it on his own," he said. "I'm sure he's quite capable."

"I'm not," Harry told him cheerfully but said he didn't like to make any further calls on their good will.

"Oh stuff," Petra said. "You'll pay us back in kind some day, you'll see."

He admitted he had tried without success to find hired hands to help him and said the least he could do was pay Paul for his time, as he would have paid them, but he was overruled in that, too.

"You'll help me enough when our harvests are ready," Paul assured him. "And I promise not to pay you a bean!" Before they carried on for home, he showed Harry the pouch of precious instructions and plans tacked to the back of the door. "Campfire reading for you," he said. "For God's sake, keep it in your privy, or somewhere dry where the mice won't gnaw away something crucial...I lost a page of ours and had to improvise."

He arrived first thing the next morning with a gunny sack of tools, a ladder and a packed lunch, as he did every day, Sundays included, until the walls were up, the windows in and the doors hung. He helped Harry unroll and nail roofing felt in place but left him the tasks he could complete thereafter on his own: hammering down floorboards and fixing shingles and gutters.

Their conversation, such as it was, was almost entirely about the matter in hand—the bedding-in and assembling of the house's wooden frame, the raising and joining of its outer walls and inner tongue-and-groove partitions—yet Harry felt Paul's character steadily opening out to him and grew to appreciate his gruff commentary on what they were doing, his dry humor at Harry's expense, the way the softness of his gaze or kindness of his smile could make his pioneer's beard seem a mask or piece of disguise.

A more experienced man might have armed himself against such a thing, but Harry was not experienced. So he was charmed, drawn in, and before he realized quite what was happening, he found he was looking forward to Paul's company in a way Paul surely didn't intend, and finding small ways to delay his departure each day.

One morning dawned unexpectedly cold, and Paul arrived in a thick flannel overshirt, which he tossed aside as working warmed him up. Gathering up his things at the end of the day, Harry found the shirt and took it back to his tent with the tools, thinking to keep it from the dew. Lying on his camp bed after the evening's unvarying supper, however, to read by lamplight for a little, he became aware of the faint scent coming off it, Paul's scent of nutmeg and woodsmoke, and without thinking, he drew it to him as he never could the wearer, and pressed his face deep into its age-softened fabric.

It was a ridiculous thing: a schoolboy crush, grotesque in a grown man, which threatened to endanger a pair of friendships he was coming to hold dear. Waking to find the shirt draped across his pillow, he dressed quickly, washed and shaved in bitterly cold water as though it might instill upright sense into a softened nature, and took the shirt back to the emerging house while the kettle heated for his breakfast. He spent the day trying and failing to find his neighbor less appealing, looking in vain for whatever small, unflattering detail he might use to effect a cure.

Like the other women homesteaders, of whom there were still remarkably few, Petra's days were as full as any farmer's, and she had been obliged to master chores that in Toronto would have fallen to servants. So, like any farmer's wife, she maintained a clutch of chickens, milked a cow and had a pig to fatten, but she also had to clean the house, wash clothes and cook. She claimed to hate cooking with a passion, an attitude not helped by her having a natural talent for it. Since the nearest doctors were in Unity and Lashburn, her skills as a nurse, for which she would be paid as often as not in bags of flour or sugar, were often called for. All of which left little time for her particular inflammatory interest in bringing basic literacy to a handful of Cree women, and learning in turn from them both their language and the uses of local trees and herbs. Paul always said it was she, not he, who should have been enrolled at the university.

Still, she found occasion to drop in now and then on the building project, to see how the house was progressing and to hand over some reluctantly produced delight such as jam tarts or the bacon and egg pies that Paul teased would make them rich if only she would be serious and bake batches of thirty. That day she came in the afternoon bringing Harry a bottle of the pungent but effective fly oil the Cree women made, and a brace of muffins made from chokecherry, a fruit those same women had taught her to gather and preserve. There were several local berries, all of them prized, and he had yet to learn to tell them apart. She balanced on two floor trusses to admire the view Harry would eventually enjoy from the veranda, said she hoped Paul wasn't taking all the most satisfying jobs for himself, and pointed out that they would have to invite everyone from church to a housewarming picnic once the house was done.

"Really?" Harry asked, alarmed.

"People expect it," she said. "Normal people, that is. We've been to several since we arrived. You need never have them round again, but it satisfies everyone's curiosity and reassures them that you're no fancier or better off than they are, which people like. A good trick is to do it before you've moved in much furniture; if they can't sit, they won't linger so. You boys haven't forgotten we have to go to the bachelors' ball at the Haysoms' place tonight?"

Paul groaned.

"It's what the muffins are for really. You didn't tell him," she said, realizing.

"Forgot," Paul mumbled.

She flicked a stray nail her brother's way. "You don't have to come," she told Harry.

"Yes he does," Paul growled. "I'm not going alone."

"You won't be alone. You'll be with me, and I certainly can't go alone."

"Of course I'll come," Harry said. "You both make it sound so appealing."

"It won't be that bad, but you're both to dance with me at least once. Who knows? I might even land myself a rich husband and not just bruised toes."

Paul laughed slowly and sarcastically, which earned him another nail.

"I'll be off," she said. "Let you gentlemen resume your hammering."

Bachelors' balls, heartily supported by the churches, were designed to lure women into newly settled areas. Harry had heard the Jørgensen daughters talk of them with longing disguised as scorn, Moose Jaw being too established a place to need such crude affairs. Winter and the next stops along the alphabetical line, Yonker and Vera, were typical in having women still outnumbered by some twenty to one. And, of course, most of those women were only there because they were already somebody's wife. Such dances would normally be held in a church hall or large schoolroom, but Yonker, the nearest town to the Haysoms' place, was too new and underpopulated yet to possess either, so the Haysoms had mounted a broad awning on posts—a kind of marquee—on the side of their barn. Because the tracks were so dusty at that time of year, Petra had done as the other women did and traveled with her party dress in a bag so she could change on arrival. The band consisted of a fiddler, a banjo player and a man on a piano that sounded as though it had been jolted many miles on a cart to get there. Rather than have people raise a dust storm by dancing on earth that was powder dry, Haysom had gone to the trouble of constructing a dance floor. The planks nailed across a square framework produced a slightly bouncy and extremely noisy effect.

Dancing was already under way as they arrived, and Harry was startled to see, by the light of lanterns slung on poles around the dance floor's edge, men dancing with other men, not cheek to cheek admittedly, but holding hands.

While Petra hurried grim-faced to the farmhouse to change into something more feminine than her overalls, Paul turned to Harry and said, "Will you do me the honor?"

It took Harry a moment to understand him, and then, assuming he was joking, he just laughed and fetched them all drinks because the dusty journey had left him parched. When he returned from the bar, which had been set up at one side of the barn, he saw brother and sister dancing a waltz. They had no sooner finished than Petra was claimed for a polka by a short man who whirled her off as a boy might a beribboned tombola prize.

Paul found Harry and drank Petra's drink as well as his own. "Thirsty," he explained. "You'll have to rescue her or she'll be worn out."

The only woman not dancing was a white-haired matriarch, who had made someone bring her out a chair so she could

preside without participating. There were even children dancing, pigtails flying as they concentrated on the serious matter
of not being crushed by partners large as bears. And still,
throughout the little gathering, men were dancing with men.

Paul saw him watching.

"Strange sight," Harry said, feeling he must say something,
and worrying lest his stifled excitement was coming out as a
deep blush.

"Well, it's just numbers, if you think about it. If we all had to
wait for a woman to partner us, there'd be a big crowd watching and very few dancers, and the poor women would be worn
to a raveling and would have to stay until dawn to work their
way through everyone."

The polka finished and a Dashing White Sergeant was announced—a sensible choice, since it paired each woman with
two men. Petra hurried to their side, face flushed and eyes
bright.

"Rescue me," she hissed

"Would you like a drink?" Harry said. "Some fresh air? A
jelly?"

"I want to dance," she said. "With a couple of humans," and
she took their hands and led them both out so they could join
a set.

As they progressed around the crowded little dance floor,
they met and danced with several all-male trios, each of whom
gave a little cheer when they encountered Petra, as though cele-
brating her femininity, and Harry wondered how it must make
her feel.

When the dance finished and they had all clapped one another, Paul was claimed by a stately young woman from church
and Harry insisted Petra take a break for a drink. They stood to
one side, watching Paul become hopelessly muddled in a reel.

"It is hard," she admitted, "with so many male couples. Dresses give one a sort of signpost as to which shoulder to turn." In some remote communities, she had heard, where there were no women settlers at all yet, but where people could not forgo the pleasures of a dance, men who elected to dance as women would wear an apron or a knotted kerchief to facilitate tidy choreography.

As they watched, first one man, then another, both quite handsome, approached Petra to book her for the two next dances. She grinned at Harry. "I should have brought something to use as a dance card," she said.

"And there was I thinking you regarded this as a grim duty to be gotten through."

"Oh but I love dancing."

"I thought you scorned romance and the marriage market."

"This is quite unromantic," she reminded him. "It's good exercise and a great deal more amusing than baking muffins on a hot day. But yes, I suppose it's pleasant to be needed."

Her next partner was loitering, evidently anxious that Harry might be about to claim her. Harry took a turnaround in the dusk. For all the rusticity of the music and the even greater rusticity of the dancers' feet thumping in the improvised ballroom, there was a kind of charm to the scene, with the lanterns and brightly colored bunting rocking in the warm air sent up by the merrymakers. The big horizon, which could seem oppressive by day, took on a charm by night, and he had yet to cease marveling at the wonder of prairie starlight, undiluted by the man-made glare of town.

For a while he shamelessly held himself outside, enjoying the scents and darkness, but then he startled an old man making his way back from relieving himself behind a hedge and returned to the party. Suddenly unable to find a familiar face, he was assailed by shyness. Had he not been there with others, he would have left. Yet more revelers had arrived—he had heard their horses on the track minutes earlier—and he would not be missed. But then he spotted Petra, dancing with the second of her suitors, and soon saw Paul, watching him in turn from across the space. Paul stepped back into the crowd then shortly appeared at his elbow, gently nudging Harry to let him know he was there.

"She's enjoying herself," Harry said.

Paul watched too for a while. "Oh, she's hating every minute," he said. "A martyr to social duty and the tyranny of men, can't you tell?" He sipped his drink. "I'm so deeply in her debt that sometimes I..." He let his sentence drift. Such a low thing could not be heard above the din of dancing, but Harry could see from the slow rise and fall of his shoulders that he had let out one of his ursine sighs.

"You're in her debt?" he asked.

"She gave up everything to come with me," Paul explained. "I wouldn't have coped well without her. Well. I'd have managed..."

"But without thriving."

Paul smiled and nodded. The dance ended. Harry was just raising a hand to catch Petra's attention when the first of her two recent partners claimed her for a second dance. Seeing her glance around for him, Harry bent his knees slightly so as to be hidden from view behind her brother's bulk.

"Ever the gentleman," Paul said.

Harry laughed. "Hardly. My father dealt in horseshit."

The next dance started up. A slow waltz.

"Come, sir," Paul said, attempting an English accent. "I will be denied no longer." And before Harry could resist, he seized his hands and tugged him on to the dance floor. There were so many couples, most of them male and rather drunk, many of them taller, that Harry knew he wasn't conspicuous, but he felt as if there was a spotlight on them. "I hope you can dance backward," Paul said. "Because I have to lead."

"Oh. I was often the girl at school," Harry blurted.

"Indeed?"

"I mean..." But he couldn't explain that he meant in long-ago dance classes at his first boarding school, and besides, Paul wasn't interested. Harry stifled the urge to chat or laugh, in his nerves, and let Paul steer him in slow circles around the floor. He breathed in the scent of him, which brought back the night of his rescue in the rain. At times, there were so many people, so close about them, that Paul's big chest bumped into his or their thighs brushed. The music was hardly audible above the shuffling of boots, but was being supplemented by several people singing along to it as they circled. Petra was nowhere to be seen.

Cheeks burning, Harry fought the reflex to look into Paul's eyes and instead kept his gaze lowered as though monitoring the distance between them. When the dance finished, he made to step away, but Paul said, "Not so fast, coward," held his hand tight in his and, by wordless agreement, claimed another male partner on his other side for the Britannia Two-Step, another dance for circulating threesomes. Throughout the dance floor, women were taking the place usually danced by a man, with a man to either side of them. When they shortly passed by Petra, who now had two new partners to hand, brother and sister laughed as though showing off booty.

The dancing broke up for a pot-luck supper, after which Harry was careful to withdraw lest his inappropriate happiness be noticed by others. He took himself off to the Slaymakers' cart, and sat there enjoying the sound of horses snorting to one another in the semi-darkness and feeling his soaring spirits

sink back into something like realism. Paul was already dancing with one of the younger women, a bright-smiled, confident
thing with flaxen hair wound round her head like a victor's
wreath. Harry could not imagine such a man would be single
for long, especially one whose homestead was established and
who came ready domesticated by a pleasant, intelligent sister.

Chapter Twenty-Three

The next day was the last where he needed Paul's help on the house, and his neighbor seemed uncharacteristically quiet, sullen even, as they worked. Perhaps some girl at the dance had disappointed him, perhaps he was simply feeling the effects of too much beer, but it was the first time Harry had found his company oppressive. Here, at last, was the flaw he had sought in his attempts to cure himself, and it was with a guiltily light heart that he shook Paul's hand and thanked him as he saw him off at the afternoon's end. He made sure he repeated his insistence that Paul call on him for help in the coming harvest. Paul's response was something like a shrug, as though to imply he'd be of more help to Harry than the other way around.

The little exchange left a sourness, and he hid from the Slaymakers that Sunday when they came calling to drive him to church, and again when Petra rode by during the week with the eggs, butter and milk she had taken to trading with him for firewood.

He gained a rich satisfaction from finishing the house on his own and worked on it hard and fast, aware that his modest wheat crop was nearly ready for harvesting, just as Paul's was, and that he had a long list of other neglected farm tasks awaiting his attention. The finer points of the house's interior could wait, he calculated, for the short days of autumn, but it was with high spirits that he could finally take down his little tent and move the stove and his camp bed to their new home on higher, drier ground.

He could not hide indefinitely, and Petra found him easily enough one morning by following his fence and the sound of sledgehammer on post. He had barely greeted her when she started talking, lifting off her hat and fiddling nervously with its straps in a way that told him she had been rehearsing what to say as she walked.

"Whatever's wrong between you," she blurted, "I hope you sort it out soon, because there aren't enough people to go round for neighbors to fall out like this."

"We haven't fallen out," he protested.

"So why is he going around with a face like a bag of knives?"

"I don't know," Harry said, leaning the sledgehammer against his legs, and he saw she doubted him. She would make a most effective schoolmistress.

"And why've you been hiding from us?"

"I wasn't hiding," he said, filleting a lie with the truth. "I was busy."

"Ah," she said. "Well that's my mind set at rest." She turned abruptly to go, as though embarrassed, but then turned just as abruptly back to face him as though there were now a weight of words that could not go unaired. "It's the only way, apart from his coloring, in which he takes after our mother, unfortunately. He gets these...enthusiasms for people. Out of the blue. And then he goes too far."

"I'm sorry, Petra," Harry began. "I don't—"

She held up a hand for silence. Apparently if he started speaking, she would never haul the difficult words to the surface. "I was watching the other night," she said, "at that stupid bachelors' ball, and I worried it had started again and he'd..." She broke off, turning aside, turning back, refastening the bonnet ribbons she had nervously yanked loose. "Has it started again?" she demanded. "Am I going to have to...? I'm not sure I could face moving all over again."

"Why on earth should you?" He had never seen her upset like this. "Come where you can sit in the shade and I'll fetch you a glass of water."

"I don't need goddamned water. Don't be so English!"

"I'm sorry."

"No. I shouldn't. Forgive me."

"Petra!"

"I'll leave you to your work. Goodbye, Harry. I'm so sorry." She left, hurrying away, smacking grasses aside, and moments later he heard her urging on the pony she must have tethered to the fence.

He made a point of seeking Paul out that afternoon. He was as open and friendly as he knew how to be, reiterating his thanks for Paul's help with the house-building and asking his opinion about when the harvest should begin and whether he would do better to throw a housewarming now, or after the grain was in.

Paul seemed pleased to see him, showed no trace of the brooding he had displayed on their last day together. He patiently explained the harvest process. He had a binder, which needed one person to drive and one or two more to gather together the bound sheaves it left behind. They then had to rely on a continuation of the fine weather and wait for the fairly expensive and unpredictable services of a traveling team with a steam-powered separator.

"Thought I'd made you cross," he muttered just as Harry was leaving him.

"No? Why ever should that be?" Harry asked, and the matter was dropped.

* * *

Harry took Petra's sly advice and threw his housewarming before the little place was quite finished. Beer and lemonade were
easy—he had a delivery sent down the line from a place at
Unity—but he had worried about how to feed the guests until
she pointed out that everyone would assume him an incapable
bachelor and would bring pies and tarts for the spread. The vicar
made an announcement before the Sunday service. After the service several people asked for directions. And that was that.

Aside from his wedding reception, which arguably had been
Mrs. Wells's party and not his, it was the first party he had
ever thrown. People came, which surprised him, and asked a
lot of impertinent questions, which didn't. They enjoyed entering rooms and peering out of windows they would never enter
or peer out of again. They left behind a quantity of cheeses,
pickles and jams and even a side of bacon.

"There," Petra said, when they had waved off the last of
them. "Now they know you're just like them, with no more
mystery to you than anyone else, and you'll be left alone."

The house possessed no furniture yet except two hard chairs,
a table and a camp bed, but the array of jams and pickles on the
shelf and the bacon hanging from a hook made it look lived in.

Harvesting was parching, dusty work. Petra joined them, unrec-
ognizable in her denim overalls, thick gauntlets and a battered
broad-brimmed straw hat. They began the day merrily at first,
with quips and commentary, but the novelty soon wore off and
heat, flies and dust silenced them. Paul and two horses drove
the binder, which cut the wheat close to the ground and whose
clattering wheel, like a watermill's, ingeniously bound it into
small sheaves with a knot of twine. Harry and Petra fetched the

sheaves and stacked them together in regular stooks a few yards
apart to await the visit of the threshing team. Sometimes Paul
would wait for them, if he had twine to replace or needed to water the horses. More often they'd have to work hard to catch up
with his continued progress through the wheat. His team and
binder could only come within their own length of the fences,
so when he had done all he could in a field, Harry would then
walk around it cutting the fringes with a scythe, while Petra followed him painstakingly raking up and binding the wheat stalks
by hand, in the old, pre-mechanical manner. The two youngest
Jørgensen girls had done the same, and Harry was struck afresh
by how this work of scraping together, binding and stacking was
immeasurably dustier, scratchier and sweatier than Hogarth's
calm paintings made it look. On the Jørgensen farm they'd been
a team of six. Doing the same work with half the people felt
markedly less festive. As with any farming task, though, Harry
found the trick was not to look up at the enormity of the work
ahead, but simply to focus on the ground and task immediately
before him.

He had thought himself now reasonably strong and fit,
hardened by regular labor and long since recovered from the
effects of fever. Certainly his hands were well calloused after
his time at Moose Jaw. Harvesting involved repetitive bending
and lifting, however, of a sort hardly done through the rest of
the year, and the end of their first day saw him so stiff and
tired he found he could barely wind his alarm clock before
falling on to his bed. On the second day, he felt able to accept
Petra's invitation to join them for wordless stew before his
horses, no more lively than he, took him home. On the third,
when the sun was sinking and Petra had led the horses aside
for their evening oats and water, Paul turned to him as though
it were the most normal thing in the world, and they were not

all three dead on their feet with exhaustion, and mumbled, "Come for a swim?"

"I've no costume," he said.

"Well that hardly matters way out here," Petra said, and Paul added, "You're not in Kensington now."

"Are you coming too?" Harry asked her.

"Oh, I like my feet to touch the bottom," she said. "I've too active an imagination. At the worst moment I always think a pair of fairy hands is going to take a firm grip on my ankles. You boys have fun. I'll go in and be heating up more of the same."

On Harry's land the sloughs were broad but fairly shallow, ideal for the trout-like fish he was learning to catch, but on the Slaymakers' property there was one far deeper one, in the lee of the little wooded hillock of such significance to the Cree women. In fact it was the Cree children who had shown Paul how good this was for swimming in.

Harry was not a naturally good swimmer—a paddler, not a plunger—having quite missed out on whatever tuition others seemed to acquire in boyhood. He could swim a sort of breast-stroke he had taught himself from watching others and from reading a delightfully illustrated pamphlet, but never for long. That there should be any disparity in their techniques seemed not to have occurred to Paul, who marched down to the water and began stripping his clothes off in a way that left Harry short of breath, but the idea of total immersion after another day of broiling labor was as attractive as the near-perfect circle of water in its private fringe of green.

He began unlacing his boots, making an effort not to look at Paul, who he could tell from the articles tossed on the grass beside them was now quite naked.

"It'll be cold," Paul said. "Even in this weather, as it's deep and the sun hardly reaches it except around midday. The trick is not to paddle in but to jump. Like this."

Harry looked up from his unlacing just in time to see Paul's big body, arms comically tanned like evening gloves, as he guessed his own must be, flying through the air before crashing into the water. He hurried to undress too, wheat-numbed fingers fumbling with his shirt and trouser buttons.

Paul surfaced, hair and beard rendered sleek, swam a few strokes, then turned, treading water and watching. "Great to wash the dust off," he said.

Harry found he was hesitating to pull off his underwear.

"No mystery there," Paul called out. "We nursed you through a fever, remember!"

Feeling even more self-conscious now, Harry tugged the sweaty garment off and stepped into the water's edge. He flinched at the cold.

"No paddling!" Paul shouted. "Take a run-up and jump. You'll be fine."

Assailed by memories of countless sports-field humiliations around bigger, fitter boys, Harry took a few steps away, then ran toward the water and jumped. It felt even colder than he had expected, because his body was so hot from working in the unshadowed sun all day. The slough was very deep. He plunged so far in that he could look up and see Paul's slowly thrashing legs white against the water's green, and even so, Harry's toes made no contact with weeds or mud. He was gasping for air as he surfaced.

"So deep!" he exclaimed, and thinking he was struggling, Paul touched him on the shoulder, which made him more breathless yet. The pressure of his hand was warm in the water's spangled chill.

"The Cree children say it's bottomless. Are you all right?"

"Cold. Not sure how. Long I can. Stay in."

"You're too thin, man. Their mothers think swimming here aids fertility."

"You'd think it would have the opposite effect. Don't you find it terribly cold?"

"I'm an otter," Paul said with a grin, and letting go of Harry's shoulder, he struck out backward, briefly pressing the soles of both feet against Harry's chest to push off. He seemed to have shucked off a layer of maturity with his clothes.

For all that he was rapidly growing numb in his extremities, Harry felt relieved of constraint, as though the mysterious pool and the privacy offered by the trees and bushes around it had somehow transformed them into other men, in another, easier time. For a few seconds he felt able to hold Paul's gaze without shame as Paul drifted slowly backward, big legs lazily kicking at the water just enough to hold his body on the surface. Watching him in turn, Paul smiled like a small boy about to demonstrate a magic trick, then executed an athletic backward flip and disappeared into the depths.

There were too many reflections and floating leaves for Harry to see more than a couple of feet beneath the surface, so he was startled when Paul came up close behind him, tickling his back with his beard as he rose. Harry splashed around to look at him. Paul wasn't smiling now, but seemed grave.

"There's…" he said. "Let me just…" And he reached out to remove a strand of weed from Harry's hair. "You're really cold, aren't you?" he said.

Harry nodded, teeth chattering.

"I'll be out in a moment. The best place to dry off is that rock over there." Paul gestured toward a high outcrop catching the last of the sun, then dived again.

Harry churned his way to the water's muddy fringe and

clambered out. He held the dusty bundle of his discarded clothes in front of him and made his way around and up. After the cool softness of leaf mold, the stone was warm underfoot, giving back the heat it had absorbed through the day. He began to pull his undershorts back on, but realized he was still far too wet. Instead he sat, then tried lying back, using his clothes as a pillow, but felt self-conscious so turned around and lay on his belly. That way he could enjoy the sight of Paul swimming around the pool in a steady circle. He swam strongly, in a way Harry had never mastered. Harry marveled that he could find the energy necessary, then reflected with a touch of asperity, as many harvesters must, that Paul had been riding the binder all day, not ceaselessly cutting, bending and stacking in its dusty wake.

As if reading his mind, Paul chose that moment to roll over on to his back. By now Harry's head was over the edge of the rock and he had no time to withdraw it. Paul floated there, hair fanning in the water, and stared directly back at him. Then he turned again and swam decisively for shore. He bundled his clothes in turn but did not carry them prudishly before him as Harry had done.

Harry stayed as he was, facing down, but heard Paul drop his things and settle on the rock beside him. Paul nudged his shoulder with a cold, wet foot. "Warming up again?"

"Yup," Harry said, not liking to roll on to his back in case his pleasure in the moment had become too evident.

Paul sighed heavily. "We should get started on your wheat tomorrow," he said.

"What little the gophers have left of it," Harry said, but he did not want to be diverted into a talk about wheat yields and the threshing gang. Not yet. He half twisted around, propping himself on one elbow. Paul's hairy calves were inches from his face. "What did Petra mean?" he asked. As he said it, he

realized it would make no sense to Paul. Harry had been thinking so hard about the conversation with Petra that he had
momentarily forgotten Paul hadn't been a party to it.

"How do you mean?" The low sun was directly in Paul's
eyes and he was holding a hand across his face, so Harry
couldn't read his expression.

And now I wreck the friendship, Harry thought. "She said
you sometimes got enthusiasms for people and went too far.
What did she mean?"

Paul sighed again and, forgetting modesty, Harry turned
properly so he could see him. "She clearly regretted having spoken," he went on. "I probably shouldn't have—"

"She meant," Paul said, "I'm prone to doing things like this."
And watching Harry all the while, he deliberately kissed the
part of him closest to him, which happened to be Harry's toes.
Harry felt his beard and the extraordinary warmth of his lips.

"You'll get muddy," he murmured.

"Don't care," Paul rumbled and kissed again, the sole of
Harry's foot this time, gently at first and then, sensing Harry
encouraging him, more firmly, grasping his foot with both
hands. He stopped, lowered Harry's foot and gave a little
frown. Harry reached for him. And then Paul had come forward and was kissing him on the face and eyes and open
mouth, pinning him against the rock inches from its edge.

When they had done, seconds after, it seemed to Harry, he
felt Paul shaken by silent sobs in the half-light. He tasted his
tears.

They washed themselves quickly in the now black water and
then, of course, had to dress without drying. They walked to
the Slaymaker house in silence, bumping limbs as they went,
and when Petra waved them in, Harry's teeth were chattering
as much from elation as cold.

Chapter Twenty-Four

They cut and bound all of Harry's relatively small first wheat crop the next day, and were now utterly at the mercy of the threshing gang and how soon it would reach them. The previous year, Petra said, they had their first snowstorm the night before the gang came. The hope was that, with more homesteads established in the region, there would be extra gangs and a greater incentive for them not to leave the remoter areas until last.

Harry filled the interval by pressing on with clearing land, and being unable to plow up fields still covered in stooks, Paul helped him. Superficially the ground was baked hard by the summer, but its dryness made it that much lighter than the sodden soil of spring for the levering-out of large stones and the plow's slow progress, and the sight of his first stooks in the patch they had recently harvested was a powerful incentive.

The thing growing between them, which, with the superstition of new happiness, Harry hesitated to name, went undiscussed and barely acknowledged in a way that put him in mind of the pragmatic arrangements he had seen spring up at school. At the end of a day's labor, one or other of them would suggest a swim, and swim they did, the pleasure of it boosted by its teasing delay of what followed. Their embraces were often gentle, especially in passion's dying fall, but neither gave the gentleness words. The delight in all this was quite unlooked for. Harry had accepted that he was extraordinarily lucky even to have found friends in such a remote spot. His bitter experience with Hector Browning had taught him not to ask for what was not on offer. It was enough to catch Paul's eye occasionally, as they worked side by side, enough to enjoy the thing for as long as it lasted. He had noticed the way the few single women in their church looked at Paul and had seen his friendly responses to their attention; he doubted he would remain a bachelor for another harvest.

Then, one Sunday morning, Petra rode up alone. "He's gone down with a summer cold," she said. "Well, a late summer one, and people won't thank him for coughing and sneezing all over them at this time of year. How smart you look."

Harry glanced down at himself. "It's just my thicker suit," he said. "I thought there was a nip in the air."

"Fall comes so fast here," she said, and sat beside him on the bench he had set out on his veranda. "Shall we not go to church, for once? It's such a beautiful day and Joel Owen is not the most inspiring preacher."

"I need no tempting."

"Oh good." Warm from her ride, she unbuttoned her dark blue jacket and settled back, taking in the view. "If Hopeless Varcoe could see what you've done here, he'd be even more demoralized."

"I couldn't have done it without your help. Both of you."

"Oh...maybe not so fast. But you'd still have gotten there in the end."

"It's not mine quite yet."

"Two more years. At the rate you two have been clearing that ground, you'll have no trouble. Oh, I brought you eggs."

"Thanks."

"They're good layers. I was thinking you should build a little run here and a coop, then we could find you a pair so you could raise a clutch of your own."

"That would be nice."

As though unable to bear small talk a moment longer, she just came out with it. Pulling off her gloves, she said, "I saw you. Yesterday. By our slough. Wapun, one of the women, had lost her little boy and I came to look for him as he likes climbing the trees by the water."

"I..."

"I saw the two of you, I mean. You weren't swimming."

"Oh." Harry's head spun. He saw again Robert throwing the torn pages of an autograph book on the fire.

"I feel such a fool."

"Why?"

"Harry Cane, so help me God, if you tell a living soul, I'll take a rifle and shoot you in your sleep."

"Why would I tell?" He felt light-headed. In seconds, he had gone from almost bringing up his breakfast from fear to astonished relief. Could she really be so accepting?

"Just..." She smoothed her riding gloves together as though she would comfort them.

"What?"

"Perhaps not outdoors? Our land is tucked away, but the Cree children love that spot, and for all our fellow farmers would disapprove, we've never stopped them coming to it with their mothers."

"Of course."

"He's told you about Toronto, presumably? Why we left?"

"My dear Petra, he's told me not a thing."

She closed her eyes, whether to avoid the sun or his curious gaze, it was impossible to tell.

"He was at the university," she said, "the lucky boy, studying philosophy."

"You sound envious."

"I wanted to study far more than he did. I always had more application, but all I could learn was from books and from helping Father. I'd have studied anything if it got me out of the house, away from Mother's sarcasm and ladylike needling. Paul had been an odd boy growing up. Solitary, quiet, fond of reading. Mother was always on at him, saying he had no vim and no girl would ever give him a second glance because he never had his head out of a book long enough to notice what she was wearing. He didn't let her bother him the way I did. He's like a beast of burden—just lowers his head and bears it—whereas I always have to get mad and answer back."

"You had the vim."

"Quite. And gentlemen don't like ladies with vim."

"I do."

"You, Harry Cane, are a great comfort." She patted his arm absently, then stared out at his wheat stooks and the birds pecking around them as she remembered. "Out of the blue, he got a new friend. Another student. Edward Crosbie. Teddy. He was in a different faculty—studying law—but they sang in the same glee club. His father was a barrister and MP, probably still is, but Teddy insisted on living in digs like the other boys. He was at our house so often, he even got Mother's hopes up for me." She laughed shortly at the memory. "They were like reunited twins. Inseparable! I believe Paul would have changed faculties if he could, just to see more of him. It was all *Teddy this* and *Teddy that* and *Teddy says* and *Teddy and I*." She sighed. "As I hinted to you earlier, Paul gets these enthusiasms, and in this case, he had absolutely no sense that anyone might think their friendship odd or a little overheated. It was around this time that Mother failed to send us packing to Edinburgh, then headed off to her brave new life south of the border, so at least Teddy could visit Paul without her teasing and sniping."

"Did you like him?"

"If I'm honest...no. Not a great deal. There was always something a little febrile about him. And the family had so much money, he was spoiled, used to getting his way and having whatever he wanted. I worried he'd be a bad influence, put Paul off his studies or lead him into debt. But I wouldn't have wished..." She broke off. A bird was singing nearby. She smiled sadly. "The Dvorak bird. This one sings a bar out of the New World Symphony..." She glanced at Harry to see if he was still listening. "It was your Troels Munck who broke the news."

"He's not my—"

"You know what I mean. Munck wasn't a student, or not anymore. He'd had to drop out after one year for lack of funds, which left him bitter as hell. But he lived among them still, eaten up with envy, probably."

"Was he friends with Paul?"

"Not at all. But he met me at a concert when he was still a student and, well, it sounds vain and silly, but there's no other word for it, he pursued me through every channel he could think of."

"Flattering."

"Frightening, you mean. I got the impression he'd decided we were rich, which we weren't, but Mother was so very airs-and-graces with anyone she could impress, she'd possibly made him think she was an heiress or that Father had left us a big legacy. Whatever the case, he clearly felt that, as a doctor's family, we represented...I don't know what exactly. A cut above the merchants and trappers his parents mixed with? So he decided he wanted me, even though I certainly did not want him. I didn't want anybody, but especially not Troels Munck. And after two or three unendurable visits, he proposed.

"I said no, but he couldn't accept it. He went on and on. Cornered Paul. Even wrote to Mother, who of course was furious I'd mentioned nothing and thought I was lucky to receive a proposal at all. And he wrote to me. Sent flowers. Out-of-season fruit he couldn't afford. Poems he'd copied from God knew what dire miscellanies. So when he showed up that morning, on our doorstep, naturally I thought it was me he was after. I hid in my room and had Paul see him, but then I heard Paul shouting and came out. Teddy had taken poison."

"Was he dead?"

"No, thank God, or things would have been even worse. Munck had found him and saved his life. Unwelcome cause of eternal debt! He'd carried him bodily up the road to the infirmary, where they knew to make Teddy sick.

"When we got there, the father had all but stationed sentries at the bedside. Not only would he not let us see Teddy, but he wouldn't so much as acknowledge Paul. He took me aside and told me the whole sorry tale. He had found letters, passionate letters, love letters. He called them *unnatural communications*. They gave ample proof that the friendship had, how can I put it, progressed to the point of illegality. And the night before, he had confronted his son and told him it must cease, and that he was removing him from the university forthwith.

"We were to consider ourselves lucky. Had Teddy taken a more efficacious dose, had Munck not been alerted by hearing him fall off his chair . . . had Teddy died, Mr. Crosbie would have gone to the police with the letters. As it was, he was motivated only by shame and disgust, but he retained all the . . . persuasion in the matter. Paul was to quit Toronto, ideally quit the country, within the month, never to return, on pain of arrest."

"And you gave up everything."

"Oh, I gave up nothing," she insisted. "A handful of snot-nosed piano pupils, partial access to a society with which I had neither the funds nor the inclination to pass muster, and the un-wanted attentions of Troels Munck."

"He knew you were here. He stumbled on your surname in the Domain Lands Office when finding homesteads for his English puppies."

"I can't believe he'd still be interested."

"That's why he urged me out here," Harry told her.

"At least out here I can hold a rifle when I tell him his suit is conclusively rejected."

"Was there much talk?"

"A scandal, you mean? No. The wretched boy's father was true to his word, and he spirited Teddy away before we had be-gun selling the house and making the necessary reductions in our life. I still have childhood friends who write to me. Had there been 'talk,' at least one of them would have been honest enough to tell me. As it is, all they express is abiding astonish-ment at, and not a little envy of, my liberty."

Harry laughed. "The only sure and legal way of shaking him off is to take a husband."

Petra snorted. "Even if I were interested... You make it sound as simple a matter as picking out a candy from an elegant boxful. You saw the region's finest on offer at that bachelors' ball."

"Well..." he teased her. "There was the one with the barrel chest who offered you some chewing bacca. He'd keep you safe."

Chapter Twenty-Five

They were granted several weeks' fine weather, so the stooks were still dry when word reached them that the threshing team was only a day or two away, working its way from the homesteads of Vera to those at Winter.

With the tracks and farm access so basic compared to those on the Jørgensen farm, Harry had expected a far smaller, more elementary arrangement, so was surprised when the procession arrived. The traction engine was perhaps a little smaller than the one at Moose Jaw and was drawn by a team of four laboring horses rather than progressing under its own steam, but its great steel wheels seemed no less as they gouged their way through the Slaymaker turf. The water tank was towed behind it. Another team of horses pulled the separator—the all-important threshing machine—and the men not driving rode behind in a big wagon.

Certainly the process was as frenetic as he had experienced before, with the sooty-faced engineer a kind of shoveling, nut-tightening potentate amidst his court of laborers. These were a cheerful babel of nationalities, Harry discovered when they broke for lunch—Norwegians, Ukrainians, Irish, Scots and even Dutch—and all of them homesteaders earning cash to buy materials, grain or livestock for their own acres.

Their dedication made Harry feel guilty at his own good fortune, that he had sufficient money not to have to spend the winter in a tarpaper shack or leaking soddy, and enough set by that he could focus on doing his own work rather than another man's. He had overheard comments at the store soon after his arrival that made him realize he had to work extra hard to win local respect if he wasn't to be dismissed as little better than a remittance man.

While the engineer fired up the engine and worked up a head of steam, and his second-in-command positioned the thresh-ing machine far enough away that the huge canvas drive belts linking the two in a figure of eight were at precisely the right tension so the belts would neither overheat nor become danger-ously slack, the others labored along the nearest row of stooks, using forks to pitch the bales up to the luckless fellow on the wagon who had to race to catch and stack the things. When the wagon was full and the twin beasts of machinery set in roar-ing motion, one man continued as pitcher, tossing down bales from the wagon to a kind of table where two men with sharp knives cut their bindings and threw them into the thresher. Grain emerged from the separator by a chute at waist height, where other men queued to catch it in sacks that they had rapidly to tie with wire then heave on to a cart. The whirling canvas sails of the machine flung the straw high above it in a golden, sneeze-inducing torrent. It landed in a heap, which was periodically dragged aside to a bigger heap by a pair of horses harnessed to a big wooden rake. The grisly tales one heard of threshing injuries and deaths seemed no exaggeration when one saw this scene full of driving belts, flying steel wheels and exhausted men jumping here and there, half blinded by dust, laying about them with pitchforks.

Boys and girls from the Cree encampment watched for much of the day from the farm margins, drawn by the noise and ex-citement. Harry hoped they would have more sense than to come any closer.

With such a team of men at work, some might have been tempted to let them do everything, but on the basis that the threshers would work most efficiently if they could concentrate on the task in hand without having to move from the spot where they were established, relatively close to the house and to water for engine and horses alike, Paul and Harry took a cart off to the neighboring field and fetched the crop from there, breaking up the stooks to stack the cart as high as they dared before drawing it slowly back to the team, by which time they didn't have to wait long before there was another cart they could take off to fill.

As it was fine, and there was more room outside the house than in it, Petra served lunch on a table that was actually a barn door unhooked and propped up on empty fruit boxes. She had been baking in a bad-tempered frenzy all the previous day, and set out such a tremendous feast it was hard to believe it had all been produced by one reluctant cook on the one stove. There were roast chickens, broken into golden-skinned segments, jugs of onion gravy, mounds of the scones the Canadians called biscuits and which she improved with the addition of cheese and some thyme-like herb she gathered; then there were cauldrons of buttered potatoes, platters of roast ham and an array of home-made pickles. Harry was astonished, not only to see her single-handedly produce something like a Christmas lunch but to witness how complacently the team sat down to eat it. All of it. Petra meanwhile carried a laden tray down to the engineer's second-in-command, who had to keep the engine stoked, heating the water tank for the afternoon. By the time the deafening whistle shrieked to summon them all back to work, there was barely a biscuit or potato left, and only two slices of ham. And the team had devoured an array of lattice-topped fruit pies slathered with thick cream.

Harry complimented her on the cooking that the others had appeared to take for granted, and she sighed.

"The woman who leaves the threshers hungry or stints on their dessert is as far down the social scale as the one without a yard of flannel in the house when her baby comes!" She would, she assured him, be laying on exactly the same menu the next day, and then producing nothing but crackers and jam for a month.

The team slept out in an improvised tent slung between two carts. They all collapsed into bed soon after dusk. The engineer's deputy woke not long after three to light the fire, and roused them with the engine's brutal whistle shortly after five. Petra served them bacon, head cheese, sausage and boiled eggs (quicker to make in large numbers than fried ones), and Harry stumbled out to join Paul on a cart, feeling as though he had not slept at all. Paul was determined they could finish his fields before lunch so as to fit in the threshing of Harry's far smaller harvest that afternoon.

A sharp little wind had arisen overnight, with the sting that threatened colder weather. It raised a storm of blinding dust around the separator, fed by the muck and fragments blowing free as bales flew from fork to catcher, and soon all the men apart from the engineer, who was either superhuman in his powers of endurance or keen to maintain a distinction from the mere humans working under him, had masked their faces with grubby neckerchiefs, like so many rustic highwaymen. Grey clouds rolled across the sun and a scene that the day before had seemed the picture of summer industry, like an image off one of the Dominion Lands posters presenting the Western prairies as a place where wheaty plenty tumbled into the outstretched hand, was transformed into something quite the opposite, lent a hellish aspect by the flashing prongs of the workers' pitchforks.

Harry was traveling in and out of the scene with cartloads of wheat, and could not, in any case, have said with certainty how many men the engineer had working under him, but even masked in a spotted neckerchief, their unexpected visitor stood out, being a head taller than the rest.

He was standing on the top of the heap of unthreshed wheat bales. Seeing Harry as they pulled away with an empty cart for the final load before lunch, he raised an arm in greeting, but immediately turned aside to carry on stabbing the bales and hurling them at the luckless men on the separator, as though determined to trip them up in their work. It was so typical, Harry thought, so characteristically odd that Troels should throw himself into unpaid labor among men he had never met, compelled to impose himself and to prove himself their equal or better. He was like some relentless younger son in an old German tale, fighting everyone he met when he might simply have greeted them and passed by on the other side. It was a wonder he hadn't pushed the engineer aside to demonstrate a better method for winning the best performance from his machinery.

Harry nudged Paul as they drove out of the field, seizing as he always did now any licensed excuse to touch him. Paul glanced at him, sleepily flirtatious. His reddish hair and beard were so full of bits of straw, Harry longed to brush them with his fingers. "Troels Munck is back there," he told him.

"You don't say. Munck? What's he want? Come to see if you've taken to drink and a pipe-smoking squaw the way Varcoe did?" Paul chuckled to himself but did not seem remotely perturbed at the strangeness of Troels's having arrived unheralded. He was, his sister had pointed out, like a patient and accepting ox at times, not a man who would ever, like Harry, suffer a broken night imagining bad things that might never happen. Paul was given to welcoming life's blessings when they befell him, whereas Harry would fret about whether he deserved the bounty or would have to pay for it later. In their encounters, all of them taken now in the privacy of his house rather than up at the slough, Harry had said nothing of what Petra had confided in him. As their intimacy deepened, he was finding that he could talk to Paul less and less freely.

"Do you think he's come to see Petra?" he asked, before jumping down from the cart—it was his turn to pitch and Paul's to catch and stack.

"Do you?" Paul asked, and he smiled to himself. "She made it pretty clear that she didn't want any part of him, I reckon."

It amused Harry to compare Robert Wells with Paul, in this one regard. Paul was quietly amused by his sister's stubborn refusal to countenance the conventional romance of courtship—and the marital bondage that followed—and, if anything, seemed proud of her daring to be different. Faced with a similar rebellion against the accepted order of things in any of his sisters, Robert would have lectured and hectored them into submission.

Petra had been slaving again and had set out a great feast. She didn't recognize Troels at first, dusty as he was from the work and disguised by hat and neckerchief. And when she did, as he tossed his hat aside on to the grass, she wrapped her surprise in cordiality, hurrying to lay an extra place for him and asking if he was visiting the area long.

His response was oddly surly, sulky even. Far from seeming lovelorn, he barely glanced at her in greeting, said he was merely passing through on his way further west, and asked Harry to pass him the potatoes. She did not eat with the men in any case, claiming that cooking meat always dulled her appetite for it, and being kept busy ferrying pots and dishes and gravy jugs to and from the kitchen. From what she had said of their history, Harry assumed she would rather have her former suitor surly than cow-eyed.

The sulkiness was pointed, however, for Troels rapidly became the life and soul of the table, saying how far Paul had come from the head-in-book Toronto student he had known first, and teasing the threshing team that simply being paid didn't seem to make them work any faster. Hearing how Harry had already put up a little house like the Slaymakers,' with Paul's help, he said he would have to admire it another time, as he was due on an English homestead near Zumbro, the other side of Yonker. Another puppy made good, he said, with a wolfish grin at Harry.

When Petra set down slices of a pie made from one of the bilberry-like local fruits, Troels was no longer surly with her, and said that if it tasted half as good as it smelled, leaving them for a supper of burned bannock and undercooked jack rabbit was going to be hard indeed.

A big V-formation of geese was flying south high overhead, their honking a mournful warning of cold to come. As the team prepared to set off down the track to Harry's place, Paul settled up with the engineer and insisted Troels take something for his morning's work, but the Dane shrugged it off, almost offended.

"You paid me in ham," he said, patting his belly.

He shook hands with Harry and saw him up into the cart at the team's rear. "I'm glad it's going well for you," he said. "A little surprised, but glad." And he grinned again. "Varcoe never made it home, you know."

"Is he still in that shack in Battleford?"

"Dead and buried," Troels said, and raised his hat. "The fool was tubercular."

Chapter Twenty-Six

Harry's harvest was in tens of sacks rather than hundreds like Paul's, but it was no less satisfying to see it piling up in the lean-to stable he had constructed against the house and would use as a temporary granary until they could transport their grain to the station. By the time he was paying the engineer for the team's time and seeing them off, he was ready to fall asleep with his clothes on. Paul, evidently as tired as he was, bade him good night and drove away soon after the team had left.

Not daring to rest, for fear he might fall asleep in a chair, and worried that the weather was about to change for the worse, Harry worked on, shouldering the last twenty sacks of grain on to his cart and driving them up to the stable. The relative quiet, now that the relentless machinery had been silenced, felt like a blessing. The harsh crying of birds, marking out their territories or whatever they were doing, as the shadows lengthened, was now the only sound. The answering calls, from further off, emphasized the emptiness and breadth of the fields around him. More than the wild flowers, crocuses, roses, lupins and tiger lilies, which to his untutored gaze so often resembled English-garden equivalents, the songs of birds here were the daily reminder that he was living on a different continent. A mixed flock of them had descended on his field to feast on whatever spilled grain or unhomed insects they could find among the new stubble, but they rose up like so much wind-blown soot at the sound of a cantering horse.

Paul rode up, hatted and coated as though for a long ride in bad weather. Rain was beginning to spot the dry earth as Harry hurried out to him.

"He attacked Petra," Paul said, his voice tight. "I'm heading toward Zumbro. See if I can catch him or find where he was going next."

Harry saw he had his rifle slung in the scabbard below one side of his saddle. "What can you—" he started.

Paul cut him off. "She shouldn't be alone," was all he said and kicked his horse back the way he had come and down toward the railway road.

Kitty and May were both still fairly fresh. Threshing was harder on humans than it was on them. Harry quickly saddled up Kitty, who was marginally the quicker of the two, and rode her up the track. For use in broad daylight, or if one of them were walking after dark with a lantern, they had established a neighborly path that led more directly from one homestead to the other, but on a horse, and with little light, the public route was the safest, quickest way.

There was a lamp burning at one end of the house but the kitchen, the first room one came by, was dark. The few spots turned to rain in earnest as he pulled up, so he led Kitty into the stable and tied her up there. Petra's white pony snorted at her and stamped in her stall. Kitty merely sighed and resumed the supper Harry had interrupted.

Neither householder was in the habit of locking doors, Harry because he believed he had nothing of value in the house to steal, the Slaymakers because they said nobody was ever passing such a remote spot who wasn't a friend or trusted, at least. He wasn't even sure their door had a keyhole. So, out of force of habit, he turned the doorknob after knocking, and was surprised to find the door bolted against him.

He knocked again, worried now, and called out, "Petra?" Paul had said *attacked*. Perhaps her injuries were worse than he'd realized, and instead of cantering after her attacker, Paul should have gone for a doctor. Still, she had a well-stocked medicine chest and he could administer if she were sufficiently conscious to say what she needed. A window opened. Her bedroom window.

"I'm not injured, Harry." Her voice was strained and high. "You needn't have come."

"Petra, it's really quite wet."

She closed her window and he saw the dim glow of her lantern traveling past the intervening window and into the kitchen, where she pulled back the bolt. The wind was mounting, whipping straw fragments into a frenzy by his feet.

"Quickly," she said, and she closed the door behind him as soon as he was inside and shot the bolt afresh.

Seeing her made his heart race. She had a black eye, the lids so swollen they had closed. There was also a cut near her mouth.

"I fought back," she said. "With a broken plate."

"Good."

"He'll have quite a scar," she said.

"Good. Petra?"

"What am I thinking? Take off that coat. You're soaked through."

As she set down the lamp on the table and took his coat to hang where the warmth of the stove would dry it, he saw that the things from lunch were still all around the room, cleaned plates stacked for putting away, dirty crockery still awaiting attention. She had been interrupted in her work and been too hurt, or shocked, to return to it. Then he realized she was in her nightclothes and must be cold. She did not even have a shawl around her shoulders. As she turned from him to slide the kettle forward on the stove to heat, although he'd said he wanted nothing, he saw a long, dark stain on her dressing gown's rear, near the top of her legs.

"Petra, stop," he said. "Please. You should be in bed. You're bleeding."

"Oh. This again?" she asked, turning to pat at the cut by her mouth. "He bit me."

"Er. No. Lower down."

She didn't grasp his meaning immediately, then she gasped an apology and swept off back to her bedroom. She took the lamp with her, plunging him into darkness, but he had taught himself, back in his days at the Jørgensens', always to carry a matchbox in the relative dry of his inside breast pocket. He struck a match to find his bearings and, with a second, lit the handsome brass lamp that hung from a chain above the kitchen table. The kettle began to whistle, the whistle almost a shriek by the time he had found a dishcloth to cover its hot handle so he wasn't scalded in moving it to the back of the stove again. As the sound subsided, he heard a soft sob from Petra's room.

"Can I bring you anything?" he called out, cursing the lack of salient facts in a male education. "Some hot water? A towel?"

"No, no," she gasped. "I'll live, thank you. But don't go. Please don't go now you're here."

"I won't," he assured her, not quite touching the door to her room. "I'll be staying until Paul gets back."

She fell silent after that. He hoped she had done whatever needed to be done then taken to her bed and fallen asleep. She was evidently suffering from shock and needed complete rest.

Female hygiene was not quite a mystery to him; after being married and having lived for a while in a houseful of women, he knew about monthly bleeding and that rags were involved and bad temper and sometimes pain. Winnie, however, had drunk in her mother's philosophy that if women were to be delectable to men at all times, then there were things concerning which men were best left in ignorance.

Harry cleared the clean things off the draining rack, then plugged the sink, threw in a handful of soap flakes and emptied the kettle over them, refilled it and set it to boil again before he continued washing up the lunch things where Petra had left off. Washing of anything—oneself, clothes or crockery—was a long-winded task in a house where water had to be drawn from a well or, in Harry's case, a stream, then heated on a stove. At Harry's, where he had yet to incorporate such niceties as a sink or a drain, because the imperative of harvesting had called him away from indoor work, dirty water also had to be carried out and tipped away. Paul and Petra had only recently plumbed in a pump to fill an overhead tank, which—until everything froze, of course—then supplied well water to the deeper of two sinks. Once winter came and all the well water and streams froze for months, both households would be reduced to the hand-numbing tedium of fetching in snow to melt in a pot on the stove. For now, Harry worked as he had seen Petra do it, rinsing soap from each article in a chilly splash from the tap before setting it in the wooden rack to drain and dry.

In the mess on the table, he came upon a crescent of broken blue and white plate. It had what could have been gravy caked around one extremely sharp point. He rinsed it instinctively under the tap before tossing it into the bucket where they collected dry waste the hens and pig wouldn't eat.

Adding more hot water, and moving on to scrubbing pots

and pans, he thought back to lunch and how cheerful Munck
had been with them all. Had he come among them expressly
to do Petra violence, or had he simply been passing and then
seized on the opportunity fate and his hosts offered him? In-
sofar as Harry had felt any misgiving it had been that Munck
might once again pester her with his unwelcome love, nothing
more threatening.

"You don't have to do that." Her voice so startled him, he
dropped a pan lid with a splash into the soapy water. She had
dressed, cleaned up the cut by her mouth and tidied her hair
back from the wild state it had been in when she opened the
door. Apart from the black eye, she looked almost herself.

"I don't mind."

"But I do. Come and sit. I need a whisky and I never drink
alone." She fetched a bottle and two glasses. "It's only bourbon,
I'm afraid, not the real thing, but it will have to do." She poured
them each a splash of golden liquor and nudged his glass toward
him as he sat across from her. "I'm so sorry about earlier."

"Oh for heaven's sake."

"You must have thought me crazy."

"Not at all. I was worried, that's all. Are you sure you don't
want a doctor?"

"Quite, thank you. The eye will heal in time and so will the
bite mark. The memory will take a little longer. I'm going to
tell you, I'm afraid. I have to tell someone and it can't possibly
be Paul. Did he...did Paul have his gun with him?"

Harry nodded.

She exhaled fiercely. "Pray God he doesn't find him."

"Shouldn't I go to the police?"

"Dear, sweet man. You forget where we are. And even if
there were a mounted policeman to hand, or a whole posse of
them, what could they do?"

"Catch him?"

"And then what?" She started to pronounce a word she then found no power to say, so sighed and started afresh. "When a woman out here dares to accuse a man of...assaulting her person, she is nearly always disgraced by the process. While the man walks free to attack again."

"But why?"

She laughed bitterly. "Oh, so many reasons. Not the least of which is that the law is a blind woman and the judge usually an unloved old man. The lack of proof or witnesses. The embarrassment of the judge and jury. Her failure to scream loud enough to show she took no pleasure in the proceedings."

Only now did Harry understand that Munck's assault had not been limited to her face, and in his shame at his stupid innocence, he gulped his bourbon and had to suppress a choking fit.

"Sorry," she said. "It's pretty rough stuff, isn't it? Strictly for medicinal purposes. Like assault and battery." She sighed again. "Quite pointless! There was a horrible case only last year. An Irish girl on a homestead to the other side of the Battlefords attacked by her father's hired hand. He said she had encouraged him. She said she fought as hard as she could but that when she saw it was hopeless, she submitted, thinking to have the ordeal end the sooner. When the judge asked her why she hadn't screamed, she politely pointed out that screaming would have been useless since her father was away on business and the nearest people were some six miles away. Case dismissed with her name thoroughly blackened. I heard she was sent back to Ireland since no one here would marry her now." She met his eye. "Don't feel bad, Harry. Even if I'd been able to shriek loud enough for you all to hear me down at your place, the noise of the separator and the traction engine would have drowned me out. You wouldn't have heard even a gunshot."

He swallowed more burning liquor and, with it, the human urge to say something, anything, to offer specious comfort. He simply shook his head slowly and waited for her to continue.

She looked down at her lap and smoothed the fabric of her skirt. "It's funny," she said. "I've never had romantic dreams, even as a young girl. I think Mother was too efficacious an inoculation for that, as were the glimpses I had, through Father's patients, of the realities of what man could do to woman. But I was curious all the same, to hope I might...experience everything, in due course, some day, and with a man I respected. Now I feel a bit stupid, like a miser who has saved up a precious jewel in the dark only to have it stolen."

All animation went from her frame just then and he thought back to the day of his arrival at the Jørgensen farm, and how then, and for weeks afterward, Munck's assault had left him feeling dead on the inside.

"You're still you," he ventured. "He took nothing of wh...what makes you you." His stammer sounded doubly feeble in the silence of the room, and she did not honor his words with a reply.

"Tell me about your wife," she asked instead. "Winifred?"

"Winnie."

"Yes. Was she...when you married, was she...?"

"Yes," he said. "I rather wish she hadn't been. It somehow assumes the man knows what he is about."

"And you didn't."

"Pure as driven snow," he said.

At which she smiled.

"She was in love with someone else, though," he said. "A man they hadn't let her marry."

"So she didn't belong to you?"

"She never did. No."

"And did she know about...your...?"

"No. But back then, neither did I."

She widened her eyes slightly in surprise at that.

"Innocent, as I say," he added. "May I?"

She nodded, and he splashed a little more bourbon into both their glasses.

"May I ask one more question?" she asked.

"Of course," he told her, happy that her mind should think of other things rather than brooding on the attack.

She tapped her glass with her fingernails, shy of meeting his eye. "Is it...is it emotional or simply a physical need the two of you are answering?"

"When I'm with Paul?"

She nodded, glancing up and away.

"I suppose, in a different world," he began carefully, "if everyone felt differently, it would be both. When a thing has always been forbidden and must live in darkness and silence, it's hard to know how it might be, if allowed to thrive."

"I wonder," she said, "if everything were allowed, how many men would discover they were like you? I sometimes think most men dislike women intensely or resent them or something, and only marry them because that is what is expected, and because of children. And because no other option presents itself."

"Oh, but I like women very much!"

"Oh. Good. Only not...?"

"Not quite so much. No."

Paul returned, at once fired up from riding in the wet and dark and almost asleep on his feet from fatigue. There seemed, as always, an immediacy of understanding between brother and sister that left much unsaid.

"I thought you'd be in bed," he said.

"We were talking," she told him. "You're frozen. There's ham and pea soup. Let me heat some for you both. How far did you get?"

"Only halfway to Zumbro, then I realized I had no idea where I was going to go when I got there."

"So..."

"No. I shan't be arrested for murder just yet. But if he comes back..."

"I doubt he'd do that now," Harry ventured.

"If he comes back," she said, going over to the stove and sliding the pot of soup on to the heat, "you may carefully maim him for me. But now I'd like the matter laid to rest."

She had no appetite, but both men remembered they were extremely hungry and the simple meal that followed had a slightly hectic merriment to it from the strain of talking about anything but the outrage committed in that very room that afternoon. They talked of harvest yield, threatened bad weather and the need for Harry to build a proper, larger barn come the spring, and to set about, like them, laying down sufficient supplies for when the tracks and road became impassable with snow.

He had dreaded the coming of winter at Moose Jaw, partly because his little room was so cold, but mainly because the Jørgensens viewed it with such unremitting alarm as a season of death, danger and Nordic introspection. The Slaymakers, by contrast, seemed to regard it as children did Christmas, as a time of excitement and opportunity. She looked forward to being able to read in the daytime without guilt, and he could hardly wait to strap on his skis or to get out the little sleigh he

had spent much of the last winter restoring. Harry found their
attitudes infectious to the point where he almost looked forward to waking to find the windows crystalled over.

The rain had come again, so heavily it was drumming on
the roof, and they wouldn't hear of his riding home in it. Petra
found a pillow and quilt for him so he could sleep on the couch
where Paul had spent night after night when she was nursing
Harry through his fever. After months of being the only soul
in the house when he turned out the lamp, Harry liked hearing
the others pottering about the place as they settled, following
an unthinking routine in which she visited the privy before Paul
did and left him to put out the lamps. Tonight she had a request she didn't need to voice. "I'll bolt the door when I turn
in," Paul told her quietly. "Or Harry will."

Harry was the last to bed, as was only practical as both their
rooms opened on to his. He sprinted to and from the privy in
the pouring rain, then bolted the door behind him, removed his
jacket and boots, turned out the lamp and hunkered down on
the rather lumpy couch, pulling the quilt over him. He had not
long closed his eyes when a door opened. Even in stockinged
feet, the tread was so heavy he could tell it was Paul's.

"Thought you might be cold," Paul murmured, and draped
a heavy fur blanket on top of Harry's quilt.

Harry remembered it folded at the foot of the bed in Paul's
room. It was made of black bear pelt, barbarous, soft and
supremely warm. "Thanks," he said.

Rather than slipping immediately back to his room, however, Paul perched on the edge of the couch. Immediately Harry
was wide awake, mindful that Petra lay only feet from them
and was surely not sleeping. Half lying down beside him, Paul
reached for Harry's hand and drew his arm round him as
though to gain comfort from the awkward embrace. Harry

slipped his hand inside Paul's unbuttoned flannel nightshirt. Paul held its palm briefly against his breast so that Harry could feel the warm fur there, and the pounding heart. Then he took the hand in his and kissed it, just once and lingeringly, before standing with a sigh and padding back to his room.

For all its indirectness, for all that neither could see the other or look into his eyes, it felt like the most nakedly tender gesture that had yet passed between them.

Chapter Twenty-Seven

Petra abruptly ceased coming to church. The way Paul put it was "She has no stomach for it," and Harry knew from his own experience that she would be dreading eyes upon her, and anticipating judgment where there was only idle ignorance or bland curiosity.

Harry continued to go occasionally, even when Paul as well as Petra stopped. It was nothing much to do with God or Jesus. The building was scarcely conducive to uplift of the soul, being little more than a clapboard barn with a perfunctory bell tower at one end, and the vicar a sweaty-palmed misfit it was easy to imagine had been obliged to leave an English parish in a hurry. The comfort, a thing Harry could not have predicted, came from the sense of home and England that arose from the services, the flower arrangements on the windowsills, the sweet familiarity of the old text in the damp-spotted prayer books and the Union Jack that stood to one side of the altar.

Harry's most urgent task was the digging of a drain from the house so that he didn't have to carry waste water from his kitchen in a basin but could simply pull a plug in a sink. Then there were sacks of grain to transport to the depot at the station and winter supplies to be bought further afield, in places that deep snow would suddenly make feel unfeasibly far.

Petra arrived on her own one morning, as he was working on his kitchen. He had dug the drain and installed a sink and a pipe, and was now padding and caulking around where he had been forced to cut a hole in the wall where the pipe left the house.

She had an odd request. She wanted his company on a trip down to the nearest unofficial Cree campground. Their women visited her freely enough, but Paul disliked her going to their territory, and for all her rebellious bravado, she would have felt uncomfortable going there without a white man beside her.

The latest snowfall had not been too deep and the roads were still passable if one went slowly. Harry didn't want to cause trouble between brother and sister, however. "Does Paul...?" he began.

"He doesn't know I'm going," she admitted. "I let him think I was going to Vera with you."

"You were so sure of your power to persuade me."

"I can go to the camp on my own perfectly well."

In fact he knew from talking with Paul that he felt there was less to fear from the red men than the white women, and the damage their tongues and religious influence could do. The almost tribal mistrust of white settlers for Indians was repellent to him, but it was utterly ubiquitous and unchallenged.

"I wouldn't hear of it," he told her. "Stay here in the warm while I saddle up."

He pulled on his warmest outer layers, including the helmet of Jaeger wool obediently bought at the outfitters on the Strand, which was already proving so invaluable he seemed to wear it for months at a time, sometimes even in bed. Her need or wish was clearly urgent. She was a good horsewoman, the only woman he had seen locally who routinely took to the saddle rather than perching on a little, two-wheeled buggy, but there was a tension about her that made him worry about letting her set forth on her own.

There were two camps of non-treaty Cree who had lingered

in the area during the coming of the railway and the subsequent wave of European settlers, presumably banking on the railway bringing trading opportunities that would outweigh the seizure of lands. Chief Frencheater led one, on the east of the creek, Chief Whompom another, on the western side. The women and children so attached to the Slaymaker wood lived around Whompom. Rumors were rife as to how long these groups could stay, or indeed whether the mounted police would soon be called upon to evict them so the land they were on could be claimed for homesteading. Their traditional sources of food and income, through hunting and trapping or raising horses, must have been hard to pursue now that so much of their old territory had been fenced off.

As Harry and Petra made their way there, often letting their horses pick a route in single file where the snow had drifted across the road, Petra told him she believed the men were having to rely increasingly for income on the skills of the women in weaving blankets or making decorative leather goods and bead-work, all things that could be sold or at least traded in kind.

"We should both buy something if anyone suggests it," she said. "It's polite, they're hungry and you won't be sorry. They make some wonderful things. And don't expect many of the men to speak much English, especially not the older ones. I suspect it's a matter of pride as much as education."

On the still, wintry air, they smelled the camp before they saw it, woodsmoke and, mixed through it, a pungent scent of something cooking or being smoked. At first glance, the cluster of tepees seemed to Harry chaotic, but as they drew nearer, attracting a noisy crowd of children, who soon recognized Petra, he saw it was as orderly as any village built of stone, with smaller tents for domestic life and larger ones for communal activities. Even with snow on the ground, there were people at work outside, cleaning animal pelts that had been stretched on wooden frames, preparing meat for drying or mending carts. The white man's myth of pipe-smoking Indian indolence was dispelled at once by ubiquitous small sounds of industry. The contrast presented with the hovels where he had found Varcoe could not have been stronger.

Petra dismounted, so Harry did too, and she encouraged him to trust some boys to lead Kitty safely away to food and water. They were taken to pay their respects to Whompom. The chief and his sons had gone to check trap lines, they then learned, but his old squaw received them instead.

Harry said how do you do and doffed his hat and followed Petra's cue in sitting on a sort of skin cushion to which the old woman waved them. Petra stammered a few words in Cree, adding, "We've come to see Lily. Lily Thunder."

The old woman seemed to take this in, then pointed inquiringly at Harry.

"Oh," Petra said. "No. Just me."

At this the chief's wife called raucously for one of the children who had followed them to the mouth of the tepee, and dispatched her with what was clearly a command.

A long silence followed, broken only by the settling of logs on the fire in the tepee's middle; it seemed not to bother the old squaw a whit. She invited Harry, with a gesture, to share her pipe, but he declined with a smile, miming coughing, which she thought extremely amusing.

"Funny," she said to Petra, pointing at Harry. "Funny man."

"Yes," Petra said, glancing at him too. "Funny man. Oh. Here." She reached into her coat pocket and brought forth a jar of her pincherry jam and a napkinful of muffins. "For you and Chief Whompom," she said, and the old lady took them complacently and tucked them away on the ground to her side.

The little girl returned to the mouth of the tepee and announced that Lily would see them now. Released by the old woman, they followed the child through the camp. They received curious stares from all they passed, apart from the women who knew Petra, who greeted her warmly and reserved their curiosity for Harry.

"They're frightened that if they go to a reserve, their children will be taken from them," she muttered. "And their fears are well grounded."

Harry was interested in the Cree but made nervous too for the simple reason that he was not always sure if he was faced with a man or a woman. The men were beardless, and men and women alike wore their hair long. Over a certain age they were uniformly wrinkled, the women's features often just as powerful and craggily angular as the men's. To his untrained eye, the traditional clothes of one gender seemed confusingly like those of the other, a matter not helped by women electing to wear the most practical of Western garments, which were male, of course. Compared to Western women, for whom femininity often seemed a complex and time-consuming game they were obliged to play, Cree women struck him as unconstrained, as assertive, as powerful, even, as their menfolk. He was too shy to ask but suspected this was one of the things that had attracted Petra to their culture.

Lily Thunder's tepee was slightly set apart from the others and, unlike them, was positioned so that its opening faced away toward the creek and distant countryside, as though she acted as the encampment's sentinel. Taller than Harry, and athletic, with strong hands and a determined jaw, she looked as though she might have shot a bison or wrestled a young steer with equanimity, and yet she was hung around with feathered necklaces and had a small boy clinging to her leg.

"He's adorable," Petra said, ruffling his hair. "Is he yours?"

Lily Thunder laughed uproariously, showing gleaming teeth. "I look after him," she said in a guttural voice. "He loves his Lily, don't you, precious?"

The boy nodded and hid his face in her skirts.

Lily stopped smiling. "How can Lily help you?"

"Alawa said you could help me with...some medicine I need," Petra said.

"Come," Lily told her, but laid a firm hand on Harry's arm. "You," she said. "Handsome man. Wait out here."

Petra caught his eye to reassure him as she went inside. "Won't be long."

People evidently regarded Lily with some respect, for her taking Petra into her tepee seemed to grant permission to others to approach Harry. A man beckoned him over to admire some moccasins, and a woman tugged his sleeve to look at her jars of pungent bear and buffalo grease. He bought a prettily beaded pair of moccasins to post to Phyllis for Christmas. Although the season for pestilential blackfly had passed, he bought a bottle of the efficacious fly oil, too. As he was completing the purchase, people stepped back from him and he saw that Lily Thunder had come out into the snow to join him.

"I have questions," she told him gruffly.

"Yes?" He glanced over her shoulder, anxious for Petra.

"You the lady's husband?"

"No," he said.

"You her lover?"

"Certainly not. We are friends. Just friends."

"Friends." Lily seemed to chew the word over. "So you know about baby?" She saw at once from his reaction that he knew nothing.

"I must talk to her," he said. "Where is she?"

Again the restraining hand, this time against Harry's chest.
The other Cree had slipped well away; Lily seemed to hold a
sort of priestly power among them. He had the odd sensation
that she was reading his thoughts through touch, that her hand
told her more about him than her ears did.

"She by fire," she said at last. "Keeping warm. Thinking. She
must think first. Baby maybe angry and haunt her."

"She's...expecting a child?"

"Yes. Two months nearly. Father bad man, I think."

"Yes," he said.

"What she asks is against law. So she come to me, yes?"

"Probably."

"If you tell, I never see you. No one here see you."

He nodded. "Is it...dangerous?"

"Birth dangerous. Many things go wrong."

"What do you do to...to end the baby?"

"Easy. Herbs. Some good, some bad. Black cohosh. Blue cohosh. These good. Squaw mint not good. She be very sick and
dizzy. Heart go fast. She have to pretend to be ill some days."
Lily Thunder chuckled. "Not need to pretend—she feel so sick
from herbs."

"But it's dangerous?"

"Sometimes."

"People die? Women die?"

"With me, no. But when they take too much. Slowly and in
pain. Guts bad. But Lily will be careful."

"I must see her."

"You love her?" Again that strong hand spread against his
chest as though to read him.

"Yes, but... Yes. I love her very much."

Lily looked at the little moccasins he had bought for Phyllis.
She smiled broadly and stood aside to let him pass.

He found Petra hunched on a low carved stool before Lily Thunder's fire. There was a strong, sagey scent, not unpleasant but sharply evocative, perhaps from herbs or special bark cast on the embers. Lily had draped a striped blanket about Petra's shoulders before leaving her to her thoughts.

"You're not to go through with this," he told her.

"I must," Petra said.

"No. Marry me."

She gasped.

"Marry me. The child can be ours. I'll be its father."

"But you won't be."

"If I'm there, I'm the father."

"What if I don't want to marry?"

"The herbs are dangerous. She just admitted as much. We can marry quietly. In Battleford. I'd leave you alone afterward."

She smiled at the flames. "Love's young dream," she sighed. "And so convenient."

"Discuss it with Paul first."

"Oh, I imagine he'll be delighted."

"So don't," he said, irritated by her tone. "Take her herbs. Be sick. Kill the baby."

"It's not a baby. Not yet. It's just a . . . I'd be killing nothing."

"A what?"

"A threat," she said. "That's all it is." She nudged a stick back on to the fire with the toe of her boot. "A little wisp of thundercloud."

She seemed so relaxed, even drunk; he wondered if she had already been dosed with some narcotic brew the mannish witch had stewed for her. Then he noticed afresh the powerfully herbal fumes coming off the fire. He felt relaxed too, he realized, despite cold, wet feet and a racing heart. It was all so utterly simple. He would marry Petra and the three of them would farm together, alongside each other. With a child.

He found himself remembering Phyllis, the weight of her little hand in his as he stooped to let her walk alongside him by the river in Radnor Gardens, the sweet scent of her skin as he kissed her good night, her furious tears at Strawberry Hill station as he tried to say a meaningful goodbye.

He turned away to lift the cloth that hung across the tepee's opening and looked out. Lily Thunder was out there, watching and waiting. Petra's hand stole into his and squeezed.

"Are you sure?" she whispered. "Dear, sweet man. Are you quite sure?"

Chapter Twenty-Eight

Four years passed with a welcome day-to-day slowness that Harry felt might have continued forever. Just as he usually went to bed too tired in body for sleepless fretting over things that lay beyond his control, like weather or how they would cope with a failed harvest, so the three of them were little bothered by affairs beyond the boundaries of their adjoining farms. Harry had broken fifty-five acres in his first year and cropped five. In 1911, he broke fifty and cropped fifty-five. In 1912, he broke the last fifty-five and cropped a hundred and five and was able to enter his patent at the Dominion Lands Office in Battleford, with Paul and a second, newer neighbor as witnesses that he had done all this, fenced the perimeter and erected a stable, a barn and a dwelling. In 1913, he and Paul harvested to capacity.

And while Harry's place grew to look less and less like a rough-and-ready homestead and came to resemble first a proper farm and then even a home, with washing drying on lines slung between fruit trees, and chickens hunting grubs around a vegetable patch, so Winter grew from being a few sheds around a railway siding to a place that dared to call itself a town.

Harry and Petra were married after a Sunday service, with Paul as one witness and the vicar's mother as the other. Petra had grown fond of the house she shared with her brother, but Harry was legally required to reside at least part of the year on the land he was working to claim, so she joined him there. Besides, as she quietly pointed out, it was a house in which Munck had never set foot.

While so many homesteaders' quarters were still basic, and so many men lived and worked in an isolation that was potentially dangerous in winter, it was common enough for men to move in together for the iciest months, or to lock up their houses and take quarters together in town until the weather warmed. It saved on fuel and undoubtedly saved a few lives. So nobody thought it at all odd that Paul shut up house for the following winter and moved in with his sister and Harry.

Their practice through the winter, by which Paul would begin on the couch but pass at least a sequence of every night in Harry's bed, had set a pattern for the following spring, when Paul moved back to his own house. The two men would work independently through the day, but Paul would often join husband and wife for supper, and then Harry would "see him home" and not return to his own bed until the early hours. The arrangement was never discussed between the three of them, but it was plain to Harry that, though each was no less fond of the other, both siblings enjoyed their share of independence. Paul filled the conversational space left in Petra's wake with omnivorous reading. Petra, meanwhile, taught herself to shoot, and joked that Harry should never think of opening her bedroom door at night without knocking.

Petra's baby, their baby, was born the following June, after a labour long enough to allow Harry time to travel to Unity and back for Dr. Routledge. They called her Grace, after his mother. Although the assumption in a farming community was that every parent craved a son, Harry suspected that Petra was as relieved as he was; in a girl, any resemblance to the biological father would be less apparent.

Having complained roundly at the discomforts of pregnancy, especially with the onset of warmer weather and flies, Petra had given worrying signs that she might resent the baby as much as its gestation, and prove as little like other mothers as she resembled other wives. Motherhood answered some deep-seated need in her, however. She was unsentimental with the child, but fascinated by her, warmly patient with the incessant routines and repetitions of child-rearing and interested in every facet of Grace's emerging intellect and personality. She sent off for books on the latest pediatric theory and began to keep a journal in which she recorded her observations of the child's development.

Phyllis never thanked Harry for the moccasins, nor did she respond to the letters he still occasionally wrote her, so that he began to suspect they were destroyed before they could reach her. Vaccinated by this cruel loss of his first daughter, he approached fatherhood the second time round with a certain reserve. He did not consciously harden his heart, but he loved with hands metaphorically behind his back.

The unforeseen response was Paul's. Though appreciative of the way the marriage shielded Petra, he kept brooding about the idea that she was having Munck's child. "What if he comes to claim it?" he asked Harry as they lay together. "What if it looks like him and hates us on sight?" He was thus completely unready for the gust of love that swept over him when the baby, wrapped in a shawl, was first put in his arms. And if she looked like anyone, as her face began to uncrumple and fill out, it was him; she had a sternness about her when she was concentrating that was remarkably like his, and when she began to laugh, toward the end of her first year, it was with a childish version of his slow rumble of a chuckle.

He was incapable of passing her without touching her head

or sweeping her up, and the adoration was mutual. As soon as she was old enough to appreciate them, he was forever bringing her things: a flower, a feather, a peg doll or a toy boat carved with his penknife. And when she was teething or fretful, Paul could soothe her as neither parent could, simply by holding her against his chest and murmuring. Before she could quite say his name, she called him Papa, which amused Petra no end.

The circumstances of this second fatherhood were entirely different from Harry's first. The first time, he had not been working. Now, he did almost nothing but work, and when he came in at night, Grace was often asleep. His snatched lunchtimes, along with Sundays, were his main time for seeing the child. Phyllis had been guarded by a nursery maid and then her mother, whereas Grace had only Petra, who was always happy to hand her over, if only to admire her from the other side of the table. Both the house in Herne Bay and Ma Touraine had boasted nurseries—airy rooms far distant by design, where the less palatable aspects of babies and infants, along with their noise when unhappy, were kept far from scenes of adult seren- ity. In a wooden house, however sturdily built, there was no such luxurious dividing-up of living space. One was either in bed or not. Internal walls of wooden panels nailed on either side of a frame, even when the frame was stuffed to cut down on drafts, did little to dampen the cries or happy shouts only two rooms away.

They were none of them especially hungry for news, even Harry, who while still in England had maintained a daily rou- tine involving newsprint. Newspapers came their way very occasionally, usually days old, left behind in some hotel bar or station waiting room by a recent arrival. News of another kind arrived by letter, although Paul rarely had the time or in- clination to write to anyone, so received little mail, and Harry's correspondents had both forsaken him. Petra maintained several correspondences with former school friends, although the change in her circumstances had opened a gulf between them. On getting married and preparing to become a mother, she joked that finally she had news that the simpletons could understand, and sure enough, a little rush of parcels ensued, wedding presents and then items for the baby's layette, most of them far too fine for a child on a dusty prairie farmstead.

As a Londoner, Harry had marveled that there could be country dwellers so parochial they cared about nothing beyond their farm gates, but now he came to understand perfectly that local news, picked up after church or in the dry goods store or on the railway platform, about whether a lumberyard was to open or a new poison for gophers had come on the market, was actually far more important than news from Toronto or London.

The coming of war changed that, even though war was declared in August, when harvest preparations were at their height. The news was sown swiftly, shaken from pulpits and scattered by posters and threshing gangs. The message from on high was confused. As a loyal dominion, Canada would, of course, support her mother country and send men, even if many of those men were not English by birth, but as her mother country's principal bread bowl, she was also pledged to send wheat. And wheat could not grow, harvest, thresh, bag and transport itself.

There was no question among them that Harry and Paul would stay to farm land that was just coming into its own rather than fight in a distant war that meant nothing to them. Besides, at thirty-nine and thirty-six, they considered themselves a little old for soldiers. They knew of other farms, with menfolk to spare, where younger sons had enlisted at once, happy to do their bit rather than continue as slaves to acres they would never own, but most farmers were staying put.

A notable exception was the remittance men, for whom the war came as an abrupt bugle call interrupting a carefree round of hunting, shooting and boyish play. Rumors were rife of them having ridden away leaving neglected land and houses packed with belongings ripe for thieving. A sadder rumor had it that they could not bear to abandon their fine hunting dogs to be taken on by Indians, who were said to be notoriously harsh toward their hounds, so they set up a macabre relay in which each shot his neighbor's dog before departing to fight for their county regiments at home. This might have been a final piece of satire at the ridiculous Englishmen's expense, but hunting dogs had certainly been abandoned. For a week or two their howls punctuated the night, markedly different from the wilder yelps and yodeling of the coyotes.

Paul took one on, a handsome pointer bitch called Bella, who showed up on his doorstep and refused to leave. She had clearly been a much-loved hunting companion, if not pet, for her trust and loyalty fixed on him the moment he read her name from her collar, and she took to following him everywhere, investigating the nearby ditches while he worked in a field but alert to his every gesture and swift to join him the moment he threatened to move on. Petra ribbed him that he now looked quite the English squire, but she liked the sense that they had acquired a family guardian. Grace was smitten with her rival for Paul's affections and had to be persuaded not to offer up the contents of her plate the moment Bella entered the kitchen.

The immediate problem presented on the farms by war was manpower. The threshing gangs had to be awaited with even greater patience than usual. So many of Canada's less rooted workers had enlisted with the Expeditionary Force, either from

patriotism or a sense of adventure, that many of the engineers
had trouble recruiting a team of eight and hanging on to them
for the full course of a harvest season. Men in the prairies ar-
gued that *farm or fight* presented two equally noble options,
but for the moment at least, exchanging dungarees for khaki
seemed the more heroic one.

Harry had heard nothing from Jack in years now. He had written to him when he arrived in Winter, writing to their lawyers
too, as it seemed only responsible to keep them informed. The
lawyers drily acknowledged receipt, but from Jack there came
nothing. The continuing silence was hurtful, but he strove to
understand it from Jack's viewpoint, bound round by a large
family to which Harry had become an unmentionable. He com-
forted himself that for someone as fundamentally fair-minded
as Jack was, the taking of sides could not have been easy, and,
for all the sorrow it caused him, decided it was kinder not to
heap coals on his head with further letters. He did not even
write about Petra or the birth of Grace, assuming such news
would only seem incendiary to his former in-laws.

News of the war stirred this all up again. Jack had enjoyed
every aspect of his time in the Harrow army corps, the marching, the uniform, the boot-polishing and gun drill. If he was
not at the front already, he would surely be on his way. He
would have signed up at once with the Cheshires. He might
even have been enlisted as a vet. The army used horses by the
thousand and would need specialists to care for them. Harry
could picture the eve-of-departure photograph George would
have boastingly circulated to her sisters: Jack looking splendid
in uniform, one reassuring hand on George's shoulder as she
perched bravely on a stool before him, somehow symbolic of
what he was fighting for.

* * *

It was a bitter October morning. The threshing gang had finally reached them, and there had been finger-numbing frost on the sheaves as they gathered them from the stooks to the roaring separator. It was Harry and Paul's second day of ferrying cotton sacks of grain from their farms to the agent at Winter station. There were plans afoot to build a grain elevator here—a high structure where grain could be loaded in bulk into silos and thence into waiting trucks for transport by rail. Loading it in sacks was unwieldy and time-consuming, and would soon be outdated.

Nevertheless, Harry enjoyed this work for the simple satisfaction of being handed a ticket after each load was weighed and then exchanging the tickets at the delivery's end for a check that could be cashed within the day or simply handed over at the store as credit against his account. It felt a part of the pleasing process of preparing for winter. Petra said it was the only time of year she noticed him humming songs to himself.

"Your father's like a squirrel laying in hazelnuts," she told Grace.

A train was in, filled with boys and men heading off to war and fluttering with suddenly ubiquitous flags. Wrapped against the cold, families had gathered to wave, or, less cheerfully, to see their own menfolk off. A boy with a cornet struck up a tune out of a carriage window, and a gang of people sang along to a song Harry had rapidly come to loathe.

> Come on Sandy, come on Jack.
> We'll guard your home till you get
> back!
> Down your tools, and leave your
> benches.
> Say goodbye to all the wenches.

In their midst an impromptu recruiting office had been set up. Two smart officers at a table hung with the sort of posters that, through post and railway, had spread across the country, like those flags, in a matter of days, and now fluttered on church noticeboards and at post office entrances. *Back him up! Your chums are fighting. Why aren't you?* Even the blameless Canadian beaver had been pressed into service to sell Victory Bonds with the slogan *Keep Canada Busy!*

King and country, like the peculiarly pro-empire version of God encountered every Sunday, were simply part of life's accepted fabric, like lawns and buttered toast. Since emigrating, Harry had come to see he had not a shred of patriotism in him, and the display of it in others brought on in him a hunted feeling. Luckily he was among kindred spirits. Paul said he felt more Canadian than Scottish or British, and Petra was disgusted by all wars and suspected the motives of those who waged them. She believed the key element to patriotism was display; that it was all about being *seen* to support a cause, being *seen* to wave a flag. But she had not, he noticed, said any of this outside the security of their two houses.

Harry turned away and heaved another sack on to his shoulder. He caught Paul's eye as they passed between cart and weighing machine. They had spent the entire night together, by an accident of exhaustion rather than romantic design, but waking to dawn light in Paul's room, with Bella curled up on their discarded work clothes, and to find Paul unguardedly tender while still half asleep, had transformed the day that followed and left Harry slow and stupid with love, not just for Paul, but for Petra and Grace, who were still sound asleep when he rode home and fired up the stove to make their porridge.

"Come on, lads! There's time before we leave. No one loves a coward." The voice was familiar, even if the accent had been modified to sound more Canadian.

Harry turned from loading his weighed sack into the truck to see that the taller and bigger of the two recruiting officers was Troels Munck. Paul had seen, too, and was already striding up the platform. "No!" Harry called out, and ran to catch up with him, grabbing his coat sleeve.

"Where does he get the nerve?" Paul growled. "I swear I'll break his face." He was so angry, he was shaking.

"He's not worth it," Harry said. "Maybe it's not even—"

"Oh, it's him. I'd know that smug fuck anywhere." The uncharacteristic profanity cut across the crowded platform like a whip-crack and earned them a glare from a coarse-featured woman wearing a Union Jack as a shawl.

The stationmaster's whistle had blown and the recruitment team were boarding the train when Paul shook free of Harry and ran after them. "Munck!" he shouted.

Scared that he was about to try jumping on to a moving train, Harry seized his shoulder. The larger recruiting officer turned on the top step as the train began to slide out past them. It was unmistakably Munck. He saw who had shouted, saw Harry with his hand on Paul's shoulder.

As his carriage pulled past, he smiled and mouthed *coward* through the open window.

A black mood descended on Paul that in a less complicated man one might have dismissed as a sulk. He was not a sulker, though, and people sulked when they didn't get their way or felt martyred or misunderstood. This was like a savage anger turned inward, to which he could not, would not give voice. When Harry tried to break through the storm cloud with calm reason, Paul merely said, "Stop it," not unpleasantly, but with a decisiveness Harry had learned to respect.

When they returned from unloading the day's final load, he did not come in for a minute or two, as he usually would, to see Grace and her mother, but simply whistled once to summon Bella.

Harry said nothing to Petra about their encounter with Munck, not wanting to upset her needlessly, and for the next two days, Paul kept entirely to himself, plowing the lightly frosted stubble and, Harry assumed, communing with his stormy thoughts.

The day after that, Harry loaded the last of his grain to take to the station. Petra had letters to post and needed to visit the store in any case to choose fabric for a new dress for Grace. He unloaded the grain first, so as to have the check to take to the store. Petra had decided Grace needed new boots as well before the weather broke, so the visit was not going to be a cheap one.

The post office formed part of the much-expanded general stores. The outbreak of war had made it more than ever a little forum for the passing-on of news and exchange of gossip, more so than the churchyard, where people could feel a little constrained by the nearby presence of a vicar. Petra had a certain standing locally, because of her usefulness as a nurse when there was not a doctor to be had, but the hospitality she had once shown the Cree women—even though both Frencheater and Whompom and their people had been moved on and their campgrounds staked out as homesteads now—left her marked out as not quite sound, not entirely patriotic.

"Of course no one says as much," she said, "not now I'm married and have a child, but they still use those euphemisms of me, I know. They call me *headstrong* or *eccentric*. And I'm sure Grace will soon be *Poor Grace Cane*, if she isn't already, as though I were letting her run barefoot and feeding her weeds and squirrel meat."

While Petra looked at the bolts of fabric, with Grace in closely critical attendance, Harry paid over his check for the grain and watched as the proprietor entered the amount in his ledger and locked the check in a drawer concealed beneath the counter.

"I've never seen a man leave with a parcel as fast as your brother-in-law did yesterday," the man said.

"Oh?" said Harry. Gossip made him uncomfortable, so he tried not to encourage it. He knew how much Paul, in particular, hated to be talked about by others.

"Mind you," the man went on in a sly undertone, "given how it was addressed, I'm not entirely surprised. Reckon I'd have run out the place too."

Harry saw that the discouragement had not worked and that he was now obliged to say something.

"So how was it addressed?" he asked.

The shopkeeper glanced at the other people there, with whom he had clearly been talking before Harry came in. "Oh, I couldn't possibly say," he said, taking in Grace and Petra's presence. "Not with women and children present."

"Why on earth did you bring it up, then?" Harry snapped, and immediately saw how his small show of anger had gratified the onlookers. Feeling himself redden, he turned aside to join Petra; then, when he saw that skulking at her elbow only gave an impression of impatience, he made his excuses and went to wait on the cart outside until she and Grace were done.

When Petra emerged with her purchases, she was in an indignant mood too, and Grace, who had a way of picking up on the spirits of those around her, was grizzling in a fashion certain to make her mother angrier still. "Small-minded petti-foggers," Petra muttered as she handed Grace up to Harry, then climbed up herself.

"What is it?" he asked.

"Oh, nothing really. I'm too thin-skinned. Grace, do be quiet. We're off now, see? Isn't that better?"

The sound of horses' hooves and forward motion of any kind had invariably served to soothe Grace as a baby, to the point where Petra had sometimes climbed into a saddle with her at dead of night in the hope of a little peace. But today the remedy had no effect and the child complained quietly but ceaselessly as Harry drove along the arrangement of huts, houses, mud, road and wooden sidewalks that everyone re-ferred to now with more optimism than irony as Main Street. The unsettling exchange with the storekeeper had stirred up a sense of dread, shame even, he had thought to have left behind. Grace's soft complaining, made worse by Petra's striving to ig-nore it so as to prove it ineffective, seemed to give his feelings desolate voice.

"I think we should call in on Paul," he said. "Or I could go on my own later, if you're getting cold."

"No," she said. "Let's. We can demand lunch or give him a slice of this pie. Are you worried? Grace, please be quiet. Shush, child!"

"Not especially," he lied. "Just... it's a bit odd not to have glimpsed him in two days." If only he had told her about the ugly scene at the station, she'd have understood his anxiety.

What if Paul had managed to injure himself sharpening the plowshare, or been badly kicked by one of the horses?

As they drew closer, he heard the dog barking and a whin-nying from Paul's horses, apparently all inside the stables. He began to wish he had dropped Petra and Grace off first. He found himself thinking of the boy back in Toronto, about whom Paul had never spoken, even in their quietest moments, the one who had tried to kill himself. He pictured Paul's heavy body turning slowly in the draft on a creaking rope, and his irrational sense of panic grew so strong that, climbing down to tie the horses to the veranda posts, he had to fight the urge to tell Petra to wait in the cart with the child.

He hurried ahead, which was the next best thing, rudely leaving her to manage the cumbersome business of clambering down herself while steadying a fractious four-year-old on the seat above her.

The door was unbolted, as he would expect. "Hello?" he called out, and knew at once there was nobody home. No swinging body. Not in the house, at least. The stove was cold.

He was about to hurry out to check in the stable and barn when he saw the parcel. It had been left on the otherwise empty table, as prominent, and meaningful, as a hastily penned note. It was small—a packet more than a parcel, really—and had been neatly torn open with a penknife along one side. Feathers, white feathers, were spilling out through the slit, and the clearly inked address label intended it for PAUL SLAYMAKER ESQ., COWARD AND BUGGER, WINTER, SASK.

He passed the packet to Petra as he hurried past her to the stables. Bella stopped barking as soon as he unbolted the door. She flew out and licked his hands frantically, then set off up the track toward the road. He called after her, yelled, but she gave only a rapid, questioning glare. He had not the understanding with dogs he had with horses, and knew he had no power to retain her. She would surely be following her master's trail into town until she lost it at the train tracks.

Chapter Twenty-Nine

They heard from Paul to say he was joining the Canadian Expeditionary Force marching out of Saskatoon. Petra warned Harry that her brother had always been an unreliable correspondent and it was best to prepare for silence rather than count on receiving even a letter a season. "He doesn't make small talk on paper any more than he does in person," she said. "He doesn't see the point in writing a letter just to be polite; if he thinks he has news, he'll set it down, otherwise he just lets time pass."

The first letter was written shortly after his arrival in France and was addressed to them both. It apologized for any lack of specificity but explained that letters were checked before being sent. It spoke mainly of his journey, his fear that their boat would be sunk during the crossing, his frustration at finally reaching London without being allowed time to see anything of it, the difficulty of sleeping, the itchiness of his uniform and his wish that in his haste he had thought to pack something, anything, even bloody Dumas, to read.

Barely six weeks after that, Petra received official communication that Paul was missing in action, and another month after that, they had his second letter, which he must have written shortly before the action in which he went missing. It was two letters, one for each of them. Harry's, sidestepping risk by addressing him simply as *My dear H*, was far shorter than the one to Petra, which was full of observation and narrative. It

was the first love letter Harry had ever received. It cut itself all
the deeper into his consciousness for being so spare and for arriving over a month into the horrible, suspended mourning of
knowing only that Paul was missing.

If you let me, Paul wrote, *and if I make it home, I want to
make old bones at your side. You have brought a happiness
I never thought to know. I don't have your picture (which is,
of course, a hint that I want one, and quickly!), but I don't
need one, for your face, like your voice and your touch, is
tucked away in my heart, from where I can summon it night or
day. Your photograph, like this poor writing paper, would soon
grow stained and crumpled from damp and much folding. But
the thought of you is indestructible and remains as fresh as on
the day I left you.*

Harry had managed to show little emotion since the official
notification arrived, wanting to spare Petra and Grace, but that
second letter sent him rushing out, hatless and coatless, into
the snow and thence to the stable. He did his weeping, as other
farmers had before him, to his horses, maintaining his compo-
sure with the women indoors but exposing his rawest emotions
to sensitive beasts who could only nuzzle his hand and search
his pockets for carrots by way of reply.

So yes, Harry and Petra had managed, spurred on by the merciful imperatives of land and animals, which must be tended
whatever one's desolation of heart. And Grace, whose keening
for her uncle's lost dog had been almost as hard to bear as
her frequent questions when Paul had first gone, helped them.
Like any child of a prairie farm, she performed simple chores
as soon as she could walk, feeding hens and gathering their
eggs in a basket when she was little over five, learning to milk
at six and to turn the heavy butter churn at seven. Inspired

by the sight of her mother cleaning out ditches and driving a plow, hair tied up off her face in a scarf, skirts abandoned for Paul's dungarees, she seemed to regard nothing as beyond her. There were plans afoot to open a school in Winter, now that the district had some fifteen children of school age, but finding the funds to build a schoolhouse and pay a teacher had proved less urgent than building a grain elevator. Meanwhile, Petra taught Grace at home and saw that she attended Sunday school, more to make some friends her own age than to gain any great knowledge of Bible stories.

From the day of Paul's departure, news from Europe became something urgently wished for, so they had a *Toronto World* posted out to them once a week. Lists were published of Canadian soldiers dead, missing, wounded or, very occasionally, taken prisoner. But just as everybody knew that letters could go astray or be lost altogether, so there seemed to be a shared understanding that, for all the patriotic sound and fury, the bureaucracy of the war was frequently clumsy and inept. They dreaded bad news, at first, dreaded it for two long years, then reached the point of simply needing to know.

Everything else was circumscribed—the respectable period for mourning a spouse or brother; the length after a death that a girl should wait before remarrying; the acceptable forms of words for offering sympathy; the degrees, to the last month and dress shade, by which widows could be inched back into the usual knocks and pleasures of society. But nothing dictated how long one should wait before giving up and mourning in the absence of a body or ashes or a telltale scrap of muddied uniform. Rules, which Petra so liked to kick against, at least in private, would in this instance have been a mercy.

Stranger than the simple envy of happier households to which a soldier had returned alive but merely injured was

Harry and Petra's unspeakable envy of the grieving, who had been given categorical proof and, however bleakly, released from intolerable suspense.

On a practical level, it was lucky that there was no farm bank account as such, nothing from which Petra might have been excluded. With the nearest bank so far away, Paul had fallen into the habit, as they all had, of keeping a stash of cash in a strongbox in the house and of making most of his grain checks over to his account at the store. The surplus, as she had been playing the role of farmer's wife, he had always handed over to Petra for banking, a habit he continued after her marriage, knowing her to be a trusty bookkeeper. Had he died, his one-page will, of which she found a copy in his kitchen dresser, made the property over to her as his next of kin.

They waited until the spring melt of 1918, however, before taking the symbolic step of removing a length of fence between the adjoining properties and fitting posts and a gate in its place.

Bellowed in newspaper headlines and rung out from clapboard church belfries, news of peace came swiftly, returning sons and daughters at a rather slower pace. That a lethal strain of flu had come back with them was such a bitter piece of news, on top of the disproportionate sacrifice the country had made, that it was as though some people could not digest or accept the truth of it. Some said that it was a last bit of Boche propaganda spread across the prairies by Hun sympathizers or Bolsheviks, perhaps from the interned Germans who had been released to work on farms when manpower became so short. Others, only marginally more rational, said that it was unpatriotic and cowardly to fuss about a thing like flu at a time when heroic children of empire were returning and needed to be celebrated and thanked.

Petra knew more about the flu, and sooner, than others in the district, because one of her friends, not quite lost to the conventions of home and family, had been volunteering as a nurse in an army hospital to the east and had seen wards and their staff decimated. Knowing of Petra's interest and basic nursing training, she sent her details of what to watch for. In the cities, people were taking precautions, apparently, wearing masks and, where possible, avoiding mass gatherings. Some even fled to the countryside. In the Battlefords and surrounding small towns, nobody seemed worried, as though the countryside and a farming life there were so healthy as to be proof against a mere fever.

After arguing with one of the church wardens, who had dismissed flu in her hearing as *no more than a bad head cold, provided you're man enough*, Petra insisted they stop going to church; missing a service of victory thanksgiving was, in any case, no great loss. When the threshing gang came to work on their harvest, she insisted Grace stay in the kitchen rather than help carry lunch to the table or clear away the men's plates. And when plans were announced for a grand Armistice parade in Unity, she insisted Grace stay home, even though all her friends were going.

Harry felt he must go.

"I don't suppose I can persuade you to wear a mask?" she said, and he saw she was only being slightly ironic.

"Would you rather I stayed here too?" he asked.

"No, no. You're right. One of us should be there for Paul. And your brother."

After years of wounding silence, Harry had received a no less woundingly uninformative photograph from Chester. Almost exactly like the one he had imagined George circulating at the war's outset, it showed Jack looking splendid, if older

and more tired, in uniform, with George in a chair before him
and an athletic daughter hanging off either arm. *Safely home!
Best, Jack* was all it said. He might have autographed another
ten identically.

So Harry promised he would shun sneezes and avoid handshakes, and if one were pressed upon him, he would wash
his hands in the hottest bearable water soon afterward. And
he promised to ride there rather than risk the potentially unhealthy confinement of a railway carriage full of people from
heaven knew where.

It was the first day off he had taken for months. The autumn
colors were already on the wane; leaves tugged from trees and
gathered into drifts by keen winds. As always, Kitty responded
as keenly as any dog to being taken anywhere but through familiar fields, and seemed to relish the relative ease of being
ridden rather than pulling a cart or plough.

Remembering the departing trains crammed with young men
off to fight, he had expected Unity's parade to be bigger. Of
course, it was only a parade of returned soldiers and nurses
from the districts around. There would be a much bigger one
in the Battlefords, and countless such parades from one coast
of the continent to the other, but still it was a shock to find so
many more men and women cheering and waving flags from
the pavement than were marching or being wheeled by nurses
down the main street. Their numbers were boosted by quasi-
military supporters from the area who had been too young to
fight—like boy scouts—or too old, like the veterans and marching bands who broke the marchers up to make their numbers
seem greater. It was impossible not to watch and think of the
hundreds, thousands, who had left forever. In Winter, Yonker
and Lashburn alone he knew of farms now without sons. He
found it impossible to cheer; indeed, the cheering of the crowd

became so oppressive that he felt obliged to move to its rear so he could watch it rather than feel a glaringly non-participatory part of it.

No one was allowed to sell liquor, of course, since Prohibition, but it was hard to believe the people around him had drunk nothing stronger than tea. One constantly heard rumors of stills hidden in barns. A theory had spread that the only sure prophylactic against infection from the advancing flu was to remain gently inebriated. It was said that Dr. Routledge had been approached so often already to supply alcohol for medicinal purposes, he had been driven to hang a framed notice in his front window telling patients not to bother asking since the answer, whatever their circumstances, would be no.

Harry felt and heard Munck before he saw him. A heavy arm dropped so suddenly across his shoulders that he flinched, thinking someone was pushing him aside.

"If it isn't my old friend Harry Cane. How are you, Windy?"

He must have come out of the shop at the side of whose doorway Harry had come to lean. He squeezed Harry's shoulder, pressing down ostensibly in affection but unpleasantly, too, to emphasize the difference in their heights and builds. Harry could smell brandy on his breath, and guessed there was a hip flask in one of his pockets.

This was the man who had raped Petra and almost certainly goaded Paul into enlisting so impulsively. What Harry wanted to do was cut him dead and walk away, to treat him as a nonperson, as he deserved, but Munck had him trapped and he did not want to give him the satisfaction of seeing him struggle.

He had heard it said by their usually ineffectual vicar at the first of several memorial services for the absent fallen that when a person died, the people who loved him best could unconsciously absorb the best aspects of his nature so that the timid became a little braver or the flippant a little less lightweight. "Death does not automatically confer nobility on the dying," he had said. "All too often there is no time for preparation or even dignity. But it can confer it on those they leave behind."

Harry realized he could remove himself from the moment, just as he had removed himself from the cheering, braying crowd. He could smell the brandy on Munck's hot breath and the distinctive salty musk that came off his big, warm body, and see how it was exerting an animal force over him, making him want to melt like some giddy flirt and lean into him, and he also understood that Paul had given him the calm strength to resist it.

"Hello, Troels," he said, his voice level, then remembered Munck as a puffed-up recruiting officer and took in the significance of the fact that he wasn't marching. He went quietly on the attack. "You're not in uniform," he said.

It worked. Munck withdrew his arm and shuffled into a sulky position, leaning against the shop window, hands thrust deep in his coat pockets.

"Shouldn't you be proudly marching?" Harry pursued. "After all you did?"

"They retired me early," Munck said. "On health grounds."

"Surely not. You're as strong as—"

"I had a fever," Munck cut in. And the rest of his explanation was a mumble beneath the blare of a passing band.

Anger boiled up in Harry like bile after too rich a meal. *Paul didn't need to go*, he wanted to tell him. *Farming was a protected, respected way to spend the war, and he was thirty-six. Even when they started conscripting, they didn't take them at that age. But you made him. Didn't you, bastard?* But he said nothing, merely turning away to watch a troop of boy scouts march past, young faces held high, bare legs gray and surely goose-bumped in the autumn chill. He turned back, stepped away from the doorway so that his back was to the parade. "So why are you here?" he asked.

Munck looked directly at him and Harry felt his new strength falter. "I like it here," Munck said. "Clean air. Good people. Productive land. Opportunity. And no fucking mud or blown-apart bodies." A violent spasm shook him, and Harry saw he was quite drunk. "You have no idea, Windy," he said. "I still have my legs, my arms, my face, my cock."

A woman passing heard him and clucked disapprovingly. Munck stared at her with such disgust that she froze for a moment as though he had physically restrained her, then she hurried on into the shop.

"I'm sorry about Paul," Munck added.

I will say nothing, Harry told himself. *Nothing about the packet, about what he knows and what he suspects. I will not give him the pleasure.* He sighed and adopted the cheery tone he despised in others. "Yes, well, the thing is never to abandon hope," he said.

The willed optimism of his words acted like some bleak enchanter's curse; whatever hope he had been nursing in secret from his braver, more realistic self fluttered and died. Paul was dead. Harry was sure of it now. He realized, watching the parade, that deep down he had known it for months. And with that knowledge he had taken on something of his lover's nature, not his courage or intelligence or impulsiveness, perhaps, but a little of his oak-like ability to endure.

"I imagine that sister of his will be moving back to civilization. If she hasn't already."

"Oh, Petra is still here," Harry told him. "We've been married for years." He saw from the fractional widening of Munck's eyes that he was both surprised and hurt. "Petra has been astonishing," he went on. "Quite the strongest and bravest woman I've ever known. She does pretty much all the work Paul did *and* manages to be a good mother to Grace."

"You have a child?"

"Yes, Grace. She's six." Harry suddenly wished she were there, flu or no flu, riding on his shoulders to see the parade. "Apple of my eye."

Munck made a snorting, dismissive sound. "So you're quite the big f-f-farmer now," he said. "Little Harry."

Chapter Thirty

It was dark when Harry rode up the track to the farm. Upset by all the parade had stirred up in him, he was left now angry, now triumphant, and always afraid, by the conversation with Munck. His mind kept returning to it, like fingers to an itchy scab. Chilled and tired from the ride, he wanted nothing so much as to eat an early supper, a bowl of hot soup or stew, before tumbling into bed. His heart sank when he saw that a visitor's horse was tied to the hitching post they'd recently set up.

Unfortunately it was a sociable time of year, after harvest and before the onset of snow, and the likelihood of acquaintances dropping in unannounced had increased with the ending of war and all the family news that generated. By the time he had rubbed Kitty down and given her food, he had resigned himself to playing host for a while, with the consolation that at least it would mean there would already be food on the table.

But then he recognized not the visitor's horse, but the saddle on it, fastened in place with one of the distinctively patterned girth straps that showed it had been hired from the livery stables near Winter station. This was a visitor who had come by train. He hurried up on to the veranda and in at the door to the brightly lit kitchen, barely able to hold back the name and the smile at his lips. *Paul!* he all but shouted. *Paul!*

He must have opened the door unusually roughly, for in the tableau before him, every face was turned toward him, startled.

Petra was sitting, as though against her will, in a chair where she never usually sat, Grace's chair. Her face was white with tension and fear. At one end of the table, in Harry's chair, an old carver he had found at a house sale in Lloydminster and of which he was particularly fond, sat Munck with a half-eaten plate of supper before him.

He had Grace on his lap.

They had all agreed how closely she resembled Paul, but seeing her face close to her natural father's, the likeness between them, with her white-blonde hair and commanding stare, was so strong that Harry understood that, for Munck, to look on her must have been like looking in a mirror.

"Harry. At last," Petra said. She sprang up, but Munck slammed the flat of his hand down on the table with such force that his water bounced and splashed. She shrank back down into her chair as if threatened with a whip, quite unlike herself, wary eyes on Munck and the way his other hand was spread around Grace's chest, pinning the child in place on his lap.

"Why, if it isn't happy Harry Cane," he said quietly.

"Hello, Troels," Harry said. "Twice in one day! What a surprise."

Seeing him, Grace began to cry, free at last to give voice to the tension that had been building up in the room.

"Hello, darling," he told her. "High time you were in bed. Better let Petra put Grace to bed," he said.

"Oh, but we were getting on so well. Like a burning house."

"Like a house on fire."

"I know what the bloody expression should be, Harry."

"It's long past her bedtime," Harry said. "Let her go. Then we can talk."

Munck stared at him. His eyes were swimming and he had brought the reek of forbidden alcohol into the house. He

A PLACE CALLED WINTER

slowly loosened his grip on Grace, who sprang off his lap like a frightened cat and ran across to Harry.

"There, there," he said, swinging her up into a hug. "I'm pleased to see you too. You missed the parade. You missed the trumpets and drums. But I can tell you all about them in the morning. She's very hot," he told Petra.

"She's been sitting too close to the stove," Petra said. "That's all." And it felt as though they were speaking in code.

"Go with your mother. There's a good girl."

She clung on tightly at first, but seemed to sense Petra leaving the table and drawing closer, at which she relaxed and he could pass her over. He merely met Petra's eyes as the child moved between them. He said nothing, but knew she had imagined this horrible scene so often on sleepless nights that she would already have rehearsed exactly what to do next.

They didn't visit the privy first, which would have been Grace's usual bedtime routine. Petra must have thought that leaving the house might be taken as a provocation. As soon as she shut Grace's bedroom door, there was a rumble of furniture moving and he guessed she had slid the chest of drawers or even the bed hard against it.

"Sit," Munck said, ignoring the sound.

"No," Harry told him. "You'll have to leave, Troels."

"You're turning me out?"

"You must know you're not welcome here."

"But we are like a family now." Munck inclined his head minutely toward the barricaded door. "Knowing your woman as well as I do..."

Harry stepped over to the outside door. His shotgun hung above it, high out of Grace's curious reach, but kept loaded. Petra knew how to use it and he could only imagine that Munck had caught her outside on arrival, or, worse, caught Grace.

"What? You're going to shoot me now?"

Ignoring him, Harry simply opened the door and held it open to the night. The waiting horse snorted, its breath misting the air. There was no cloud cover, and bright moonshine lit the slough nearest the house, which early autumn rains had already filled to its weedy margins.

To his surprise and relief, Munck had left the table and was clumsily pulling on his coat. Perhaps he would leave without fuss after all. He came out after Harry, and Harry closed the door to keep the warmth in.

"It's late," Munck said.

"I know. There'll be no train now until morning, but if you ride up to Paul's place, you can spend the night there. You'll find the house key on a hook on the back of the stable door. There should be hay and oats there still, for the horse. But in the morning, you must go and not come back."

"I don't see why I should go at all. I was explaining earlier, to your hospitable lady wife. You're going to sell me Paul's land, and at a knockdown price."

"It's not ours to sell. Paul will be back soon."

"Paul's not coming back."

"Why? What have you heard?"

"So sharp! What have I heard? Other than that he was shot for cowardice and that there's an MP in Toronto who'd see him hanged for buggery? Well, I've heard stories that, if I repeated them in the grain depot, where little Windy Cane is now such a respected grower that people are saying he'll be the next secretary of the Grain Growers' Local, or the post office, where people say Mr. Cane gets no mail at all from whatever family he had back home, but is always polite, such a gentleman...if I repeated those stories, I don't think it would take people long to make the connection between you and Mr. Slaymaker, how very helpful you are toward each other, how supportive, how very like brothers. Closer than brothers, in fact. And how your good lady wife is no wife at all but a...decoy for depravity."

"You know nothing."

"Are you denying it?" Munck read something in his face. "You'll be the one making a swift departure in the morning. Not me."

"What's to stop me telling people about you?"

"What about me?"

"What you d-d-d..."

"Spit it out, man."

"Did to me that time in Moose Jaw."

"You begged for it. You took advantage. Just as she did."

It was the mention of Petra that caused Harry to crack. Up to that point, Munck's threats and insinuations had only induced shame in him, and panic. Munck was standing only a little further away than would a dancing partner. With the instinct of a predator, he'd sensed the effect his proximity had on Harry so had moved closer, the better to loom over and demoralize him. Harry had never hit a man in anger in his life but had been obliged to take boxing lessons at school, horrible things on a square of bloodstained canvas, fenced in by yelling boys.

Now his fist flew out and struck Munck on the temple so hard, he felt he had broken every bone in his hand.

Munck staggered backward and tipped over the veranda rail. There was a cracking sound as he landed, then silence, not a curse, not a groan. Harry's only thought, overriding all sense, all the carefully inculcated morality of his youth, was that he had to kill him.

He jumped down. Munck was out cold. There was a lump hammer somewhere nearby. Grace had been using it to break nuts for her mother the previous afternoon. He had noticed it on the ground that morning and made a mental note that it should be tidied away. Finding it swiftly in the dark would be impossible. Instead, he seized Munck by his trouser bottoms and, hauling so that he thought his back would give out, began pulling him down to the nearby slough. If he could only get his head beneath the water, he could pin his arms behind his back and sit on him until the deed was done.

He glanced over his shoulder to judge the angle by which they were coming to the water. The easiest thing would be to stop a little short and then roll him. They were nearly there.

The kick to his ribs was so savage, he heard a distinct crack as it took his breath away. He was too winded to cry out. He felt freezing cold mud beneath his hair when he landed, so knew the water was close. Munck's weight settling heavily astride him winded him afresh before he could recover, and then Munck had both his hands pinned above his head beneath one of his fists, and had brought his face close, a bear sniffing meat.

It was a myth that grizzlies killed one with a blow of a paw or a bite to the neck or face; the truth was that they were interested in eating, not killing, so were known to waste no time in dining on one's liver.

Harry could see nothing of Munck against the moon except the outline of his big head with its short, thick fuzz of hair, but he could hear his furious breathing and smell the bootleg brandy on his breath and the heat of angry animal coming off him. His face was so close, his nose tip brushed the side of Harry's neck. Harry felt something hot dripping off him. He couldn't be weeping, and the night was too cold for sweat, so he must have cut his head when he fell.

"Harry Cane. Harry Cane," Munck murmured. "Little, *fierce* Harry Cane." His fingernails dug into the soft undersides of Harry's captured wrists. His other hand stroked the side of Harry's face, then his neck, then began to press against his Adam's apple in a way that would soon begin to hurt.

"When I've killed you," he said, "I'll fuck you again, real hard, for old times' sake. Then I'll fuck your wife and probably kill her because she's a handful, isn't she? She was so good last time. So grateful to have a proper man inside her for a change. And then I reckon I'll fuck your daughter."

He doesn't know, Harry thought. *He doesn't know Grace is his.* And the insane idea possessed him that if he could only impress on Munck that the frightened child in the back bedroom was blood of his blood and not Harry's at all, he might at least spare her.

But Munck mistook his struggle to speak for a struggle to break free, and started to strangle him. The terror of not being able to breathe was outweighed by the tearing pain of the fingers on his windpipe and Adam's apple. Munck was putting all his body weight behind it now. It felt as though something were breaking in there. Was there a bone to break—some sort of gristle?—or was the pipe like a length of hose? Petra would know.

But just as his thoughts were drifting and he began to lose consciousness, the agonizing pressure stopped and was replaced by a sense of being smothered and the painful pressure of something cold and metallic against his chin. He opened his eyes, to see nothing, for Munck was sprawled on top of him, and it was a belt buckle digging in so sharply.

With what remaining strength he could muster, he rolled Munck off him on to the grass and sat up gasping for air, one hand to his painfully bruised throat.

Had Munck suffered some sort of seizure? He was staring up at the moon. He groaned once, very softly.

"Munck!" Harry suspected a cruel feint, a cat briefly pretending to have been overcome by a mouse before resuming its torture and execution. He tapped him roughly on the thigh with the toe of his boot. "Munck!" he repeated, more roughly.

There was silence. The eyes had closed.

With no thought beyond his own survival, Harry seized Munck under the shoulders, crying out with the effort needed. He had to lean all his weight backward to tug the man into motion across the remaining five feet to the water's edge. Mud sucked at his boots then he felt the shock of icy water around his feet.

The eyes reopened and were staring up at him; moonlight caught their glitter. Munck let out a gentle whimper. "Harry?" he breathed. It sounded tender, as if doubt were entering his manner for the first time in their acquaintance.

Here Harry dropped him into the shallows. At first he held him under with his hands, one on either shoulder, arms held straight. Munck fought a little, kicking up with his legs, but he was at the wrong angle to make contact and only thrashed himself deeper under the surface. He gripped Harry's wrists furiously, glaring up at him through the water, but then he could hold his breath no longer and let it out in a last great bubbling convulsion that almost shook Harry free. His enraged grip became more like a firm hold, then a caress, and then his hands drifted free.

Still not trusting him, still disbelieving and afraid, Harry heaved first one then the other sodden boot free of the water to stand on his chest. He almost lost his balance as Munck's upper half sank deeper, so that Harry ended up with one foot pressing on his tormentor's face.

The night was still cloudless, and he could see every detail of Munck's long legs sprawled away from the slough and on to dry land. The silence was broken only by his own ragged breathing. His throat was so crushed, it hurt when he swallowed, as though he were swallowing sharp little bones. It even hurt like that when he breathed. At last, light-headed, he dared jump off the body and made a clumsy landing on grass. He pulled off his filthy boots and the soaking socks beneath them, then seized Munck's boots to tug them free. He felt a primitive need somehow to incapacitate the menacing body before him.

Munck's boots were a little too large but they were dry. He put them on and staggered back to the house. He tried to call out to Petra but found Munck's grip had all but killed his voice, and he produced only a silent yelp at the pain of the attempt.

He set his wet boots down beside the stove. Munck's had a far noisier tread for some reason, as though the wooden heels were hollow.

"Hello?" Petra was calling through the barricaded door. "Who's that?"

"It's me," he tried to say. "You're safe now."

Somehow she realized who it was, perhaps because he had knocked rather than thudded, perhaps because she had unconsciously learned to be reassured by the rhythm of his footfall around the house over the years. She dragged away the chest of drawers. He heard her gasp at the effort. Then she opened the door. It took her a moment to realize he couldn't speak, but when he gestured at his throat, there must have been marks there that explained, because she seemed to understand at once.

"Where is he?"

He led her to the door and pointed. She said nothing for a while, then asked simply, "Are you sure he's dead?"

Harry nodded and, leaning close to her ear, whispered, "I should ride into town, get word out."

"Who would you tell?" she asked. "And what would you tell them? He attacked us."

"No," he whispered, flinching at the pain. "I attacked him."

"You killed him in self-defense."

He was still too confused to think coherently, as though his ordeal had affected his wits. All he could feel was the hot blood dripping on to his neck and face as Munck closed in for the kill. His attempt to explain himself to Petra in throat-clawing whispers was cut short by a cry from Grace back in the bedroom.

"She's ill," Petra said, flatly. "It's flu."

"But how...?" he started stupidly, only she was running back to the bedroom.

Grace was barely recognizable from the pale-faced little girl who had clung to him earlier. She lay on the bed, blonde hair dark with sweat that shone on her chest and throat.

"Get cold water," Petra told him. "And a small towel we can dip in it."

Frightened, he did as she told him, pumping water into a big saucepan and fetching a towel from the neat pile in the linen cupboard.

"I'll ride for the doctor," he whispered.

"No," Petra insisted. "Even if you could find a doctor, we can't spread it any further. No one can visit and we can't leave. Not until it's over."

As ever, her resolution was absolute. He pulled up a stool on the other side of the bed and held Grace's burning hand while Petra repeatedly dipped and wrung out the towel and pressed it to the child's face and neck and brow.

She had witnessed such things often enough when acting as her father's nurse in the Toronto slums, but Harry had never watched such a fever at work. Nothing had prepared him for its violence and speed, for Grace's desperate whimpering and hand-clutching as she was racked by dry coughs that eventually left spatters of ruby lung blood on the sheets, or for the violent spasms that shook her as the flu cooked her brain before his powerless gaze. She lost consciousness in the small hours as the sun was coming up.

Her breathing had become so ragged and wild that its abrupt cessation made the room feel small and very quiet. He brought her hand to his lips as he had done times without number through the night, then reached out to lay it on her chest, where he pressed it once more with his.

Petra was simply frozen, staring at her. He reached up once more and gently closed the child's eyes, shocked at how hot her skin still felt.

"Could you open the window, Harry?" Petra asked at last.

"Of course," he said. He opened the little window and the room filled with dawn bird calls. Turning back, he found that Petra had climbed on to the bed and was clutching Grace against her as though force and need alone might bring her back.

"Harry," she said at last, half turning but still not meeting his eye. "Bury her while I'm asleep. I'm not sure I could bear to watch."

He dug two graves as deep as his strength would let him. The first was fifty yards or so from the house, where the soil was loose but unencumbered by tree roots. As he dug, he kept seeing Munck's bootless feet, pale in the corner of his vision. It was madness to think of the one death as retribution for the other. He could almost hear Petra scornfully dismissing the suggestion. But every time he glimpsed the feet in the grass, he remembered, and was afraid.

He wrapped Grace in a clean sheet and laid her in the bottom. Shoveling the earth back on top of her, he averted his eyes, but knew that the soft sound of clods falling on her would never leave him.

It somehow seemed fitting that Munck's grave should be off the property. He dug it to the side of the track that led to both farms, losing the energy to make it very deep. The sun was well up when he heaved Munck's big body up on to the back of the cart and took it out there to throw it in, and he realized that if anybody came by, he would look every inch the desperate murderer; he would look like what he had become.

He fashioned a rough cross from one piece of lumber nailed to another and pressed it into the disturbed soil above Grace, then, to allay his uneasiness, did the same for Munck. He could not bring himself to put a name on Grace's cross but he scratched Munck's name on his with his knife so that no one could accuse him of keeping the killing a secret.

BETHEL

Geese in flocks above you flying
Their direction know;
Brooks beneath the thin ice flowing
To their oceans go;
Coldest love will warm to action,
Walk then, come,
No longer numb,
Into your satisfaction.

W. H. Auden, "Underneath the Abject
Willow"

Chapter Thirty-One

Washing in the little riverside bathhouse before breakfast—a room far warmer than his cabin because of the stove heating river water for the bath—he couldn't help but watch the Athabasca's swirling currents furling by outside the small window and think with apprehension of what it would soon draw forth from him. He watched it again during an early breakfast, which he ate in companionable near silence with Ursula. It exerted a kind of magnetism on the eyes, as the sea might, but disturbingly so, for breaking waves at least held the gaze in one place, whereas a rushing river drew one's eyes forever to one side and out of the frame, as it were.

Before taking her place among the gentlemen of the chorus, as Harry had come to think of them, Mabel stood near Harry and Ursula for a minute, watching the river too, and seemed to have read his mind. "*Time like an ever rolling stream bears all its sons away,*" she sighed.

"What did you make of the reading last night?" he asked Ursula when Mabel, unable to draw him into conversation, had drifted back to her regular audience.

Ursula was in her black dress with the white cuffs and collar, which, with her cascade of long black hair, gave her the look of a tragic governess in a melodrama. She pulled a corner off her toast in a way that sharply recalled Winnie. "I hate that word," she said with surprising passion. "Berdache."

"I don't remember him using it."

"*A man dressed in women's clothes driven to the most servile and degrading duties,*" she quoted. "I looked it up just now. It's what the priest used to encourage the others to call me at school."

"Is it not a...Cree word?"

She smiled kindly. "I like it when you stammer," she said. "I like the way it makes you sound uncertain of yourself. Most men are so certain. No. No, it isn't," she answered him, glancing up as Bruno and Mabel began to leave the room and they all smiled at each other like two couples growing familiar through regular mealtimes in the same hotel. "It's Frenchified Arabic, I think. It means slave prostitute."

"Oh dear. What would you rather call it?"

She said something, in Plains Cree presumably, so softly he couldn't quite catch it, but it sounded like *ayarkwoo*. "Translation is impossible, since it could mean either both man and woman or neither man nor woman. Some of us call it *two-souls*. You are a two-souls, Harry."

"Me?"

"I knew it as soon as you first spoke to me."

Harry smiled in a way he hoped looked benign. "I can assure you I have never felt anything but entirely male or felt the slightest desire to wear a dress."

She merely raised her dark eyebrows slightly, and he remembered wrapping his legs around Paul's waist in the slough, and how it felt to be lifted and urgently turned by him on a bed. Meeting her eye, he had the uncanny sense that she had put the two images into his mind. "You can be two-soul on the inside," she breathed, as though imparting a secret charm. "You find women easier than men. To make friends with, I mean."

"Yes. I suppose."

"And they instinctively trust you because they sense the difference in you."

"Well I don't know about that."

"I know." It was a statement. She sighed. "It's a blessing and a curse. It can make you strong in here," she startled him by tapping her forefinger gently to the center of his forehead, "but it can leave you on the outside looking in. You watch so hard you forget to live. You chose the basket willow over the bow, but there's no rule to say you can't use both."

"I don't really follow," he said. His eyes strayed back to the vanishing waters.

As if reading his mind, she murmured, "Time for your session."

For several days, Gideon made no headway in his sessions with Harry. Something had changed. Had he been fanciful, Harry would have said it was quite as though Ursula had laid a protective spell about him. Harry found the river was just a river, at which he could stare, and stare, while listening to Gideon's soothing instructions with no effect.

"You're resisting me, Harry," Gideon said.

"Forgive me. I don't mean to," Harry told him. "Maybe it's all the rest and good sleep I've been getting."

Instead they talked, with no obvious attempt at hypnosis, about the distant past, his memories of his parents, his schooldays, Jack. Sensing it was the sort of thing Gideon wanted to hear, he talked in some detail about how very handsome Jack was, and about boarding school, about the abuses and devotions he witnessed between the older and younger boys at Harrow. And he told him about Hector Browning and the conflict between the guilty desires fostered by that liaison and his loving duties as a father and husband. Gideon tried to nudge him toward saying that he had written in the autograph book because he *wanted* to be found out and bring an end to the conflict, but Harry insisted that no, it had been an accident, a piece of stupidity, without which he believed the situation could have continued for years without alteration, a sort of parallel marriage like that between any husband and mistress.

He took on more chores, finally convincing Samuel to let him spend a day thinning trees and sawing up logs. Perhaps it was the physical fatigue brought on by this honest labor that made him suddenly open up.

When the last of his tale was done, Harry opened his eyes and saw not the kind, familiar walls of papered timber and the bearskin blanket he had retrieved from Paul's bed for comfort when Paul went off to fight, but a big window and a view over a fast-flowing river.

Perhaps it was the self-importance of any patient and Gideon actually remained clinically detached, but Harry thought the doctor seemed unsettled, frightened even, an apprentice whose spells were proving more powerful than expected. Gideon retreated from crouching beside him to sitting back in a chair between Harry and the view, as though to anchor him in the here and now. He reasserted his superiority through pity.

"You poor man," he murmured. "Poor, poor man. The epidemic reached Jasper too, of course. It followed the rail map across the continent, but we were spared out here. There were many deaths at the asylum. They had to dig a mass grave."

"I don't remember."

"I suspended my usual visits until it was clear the danger was over; I had to think of the safety of my community here."

"Of course."

"Your story is borne out by your admission notes from Essondale. They say you arrived with diminished speech ability, if not quite aphasia, and contusions on your throat suggestive of a strangulation attempt. It was assumed, however, that you had failed in an attempt to hang yourself."

Harry pictured his body creaking back and forth from a rope swung over a beam in his stable, his freed horses snorting uneasily outside the open door. It was entirely plausible. He frowned, looked at his hands, and noticed the marks of aging beginning to stain and crease them.

"Harry, how did you come to be on the train?" Gideon asked him.

"The train?"

"You were apprehended by the inspector on a train heading west from Winter."

Harry stared. He recalled the dread he felt whenever he heard a train's passage up the valley, but nothing beyond that. "I don't remember," he said.

"It's always hard to read between the lines in these curt little reports, but it mentioned *lewd behavior toward a group of returning soldiers*, and *uncontrollable weeping*. Is it possible you mistook a soldier for your Paul?"

Harry thought about Gideon's words as hard as he could, but they made no sense to him. Foreboding bubbled through him at the effort, so he said nothing, just looked back at the doctor's sad gaze. He was learning that disobedience could be misread as sorrow.

"Why would you have been on the train?"

"I've really no idea. I think I'd have returned Munck's horse to the livery stables. And that's near the station, but...I'm sorry to be so—"

"Might you have been going to the mounted police?"

"Possibly. But the obvious station for us would be Battleford or Lloydminster, and neither is due west from Winter."

"Don't worry, Harry. This isn't a police interview."

Chapter Thirty-Two

There was a small drama before lunch as Kenneth the Giggler left them. Perhaps it was not entirely surprising that he was collected by a buxom, respectable wife and a brace of shyly staring children. Bearing himself like a bank manager, suddenly, and giggling no longer, he introduced her to Gideon but not to the rest of them, who watched in friendly curiosity from the terrace.

"One wonders what his wife was told," Harry murmured to Bruno, of whose straightforwardness and lack of theatricality he had grown rather fond.

"*Nervous collapse due to exhaustion,*" she said drily. "That's the usual one."

Ursula caught his eye after lunch and asked if he wanted exercise as, having done her day's chores, she was hoping to go for a long walk in the woods. He agreed readily.

"You had a good morning," she observed. She looked a little drawn.

"Yes," he said. "And no. I'm seeing more clearly now, but it disturbs me that the memories are so sad and yet I don't seem to feel anything. It's as though they happened to someone else."

"Perhaps they did," she said, accepting the offer of his arm to climb over a log. "You have more than one soul, remember."

"Ah yes." He chuckled. "Silly of me to forget."

For some time they walked in companionate silence. He found it reminded him of Paul, with whom he could work or read without the lack of conversation feeling remotely awkward. And being reminded of Paul hurt, of course.

They reached the clearing in the woods he had visited before, but then Ursula led him confidently onwards. She paused now and then to examine a plant or to listen to a bird singing, quite as though they had messages for her. The further they walked from Bethel, the less she resembled the nun-like Ursula of mealtimes, so refined and modest. Nor was she like the young athlete who had so expertly driven the cart to town and back. Rather, she became an energized combination of the two: her true self, perhaps.

They came upon a clearing where a stream gurgled through a channel in the rock before plunging down the slope to the distant river. She stooped, scooped a little of the water and murmured appreciatively. "Sweet," she said. "Harry?"

"Yes?"

"I think I can help you, if you'll let me."

"Oh?"

"Trust me. I understand. Gideon has been leading you along a line—so very like a man; so methodical and tidy—but life isn't made of lines. He is like a traveler who looks left and right but doesn't think to look behind or above him. Men like that get eaten by cougars."

There was a little cave in the rock behind them, facing the view of distant mountains. Ursula walked cautiously to its entrance and sniffed the air there. She took a couple more steps into the darkness, still sniffing, then turned back to him. "Just checking," she said. "For animals."

"Bears?"

"Possibly. We passed some scat a while back but it wasn't fresh. I want us to be able to stay still safely for a while."

"What are you...?"

"Do you need to be back for any reason before supper?"

"No."

"Good. So. First we need a fire, because it's cold when you stop walking." She swiftly gathered dry kindling, bark strips and a few larger sticks. "I could do this the old Cree way," she said, "with two sticks and patience, but..."

"I picked these up in Hinton," he said with a smile, producing the matchbox from his inside pocket.

She smiled and took them off him. She flaked one of the sticks into a little heap with a very sharp little kitchen knife she produced from her reticule, lit the heap and, breathing steadily on it, added a few twigs then larger pieces of kindling as the fire grew.

"This is an old campground," she said. "Very, very old."

"There doesn't seem to be much room," he said. "Unless the cave is huge."

"Not for a tribe," she told him. "Just one or two people. People came here alone for a spirit quest."

"What's that?"

She stared at him in examining silence for a minute before answering. "We all have turning points in our lives, when we could go this way or do that, sit and weave the basket or go hunting with the bow and arrow. The spirits show you the way to go." She laughed suddenly. Not her usual feminine chuckle but a startlingly big, manly guffaw, a sound of triumph. "God forgive me," she said, "but it has been a *very* long time since I did this." She reached up to her neck and unfastened her long string of beads with the crucifix on it. She handed it to Harry. "Put this somewhere so He can't watch."

He slipped the necklace into his coat's inside pocket, where Jesus couldn't see her.

"Now," she told him, "you stay here and feed the fire and

think about who you love, while I do some foraging. I won't be long."

Bemused, he sat on the ground, cross-legged, while, clutching her knife, Ursula followed the stream over the edge of the ledge and down the hill. The fire was burning well now, and its warmth and cheerful crackle were welcome, for the spot was in shadow. He fed in a couple of sticks, looked up where the smoke now rose in a blue column, and watched a buzzard impersonate a child's kite, apparently riding the air currents for the uncomplicated pleasure of doing so. And then he made himself think about Paul.

He tried thinking about him not as a cruel memory would do it, reliving specific scenes, like waking beside him in the night, or swimming with him across the slough at evening. Instead he simply conjured up the pleasure of his physical presence, his kind brown eyes with the little lines about them, hinting at mischief, the small scar on the back of his left hand, the smell of him, bread-oven warm before waking, the breadth of his shoulders.

Oddly, he found that this conscious remembering did not make him sad but only—how to put it?—lambent with love. When Ursula returned, it was as though she saw this at once, for she reached out a quick bony hand to touch his cheek.

She had gathered a plant, some kind of flag or sedge, it seemed to him, though she called it something that sounded like *wickers*. Sitting across the fire from him, she trimmed it, throwing what she didn't need to sizzle in the flames. She retained the long, thin roots, which she had already rinsed quite clean in the stream. Using the knife, she cleaned off any fibrous hair and much of their skin, quite as though she were preparing salsify for the table. When she spoke, she was no longer Ursula but Little Bear. Grave. Manly.

"This is not the way," she said. "You should have been fasting for at least a day, and so should I. But it may be effective and the spirits won't mind."

"Is it poison?" he asked, a powerful recollection of Lily Thunder fed by the fire smoke. Lily, who he finally saw, hadn't been entirely female either.

"No," Ursula told him. "It does aid constipation, but for us, it will bring visions. Here." She passed him two lengths of root. "It's bitter," she warned him, "like ginger mixed with cinnamon, but you must keep chewing it, even if you can't swallow. You need the juice."

She raised a piece to her mouth and chewed on it, fast and hard, as a squirrel might. Then she tucked in a second piece. "God forgive me," she muttered.

"Ursula, please. Don't do this if it bothers you so."

The look she threw him was utterly serious. "I *must* do this," she said. "This is who I am. But what we do here, Harry, you will never speak of. Never."

Startled, Harry nodded.

"Good," she said. "Chew."

It *was* bitter, like biting directly into memory itself. It also rapidly had the odd effect of numbing his mouth, so that he became worried about accidentally biting his tongue. He certainly couldn't have spoken clearly, even if he swallowed first. Ursula dribbled slightly but did not seem to notice. She had shut her eyes and was rocking gently, crooning some Cree song under her breath. Thinking about Paul again, Harry swallowed the piece of root in his mouth and hurriedly pushed in the second, as though eager not to be left behind. He pictured the buttons on Paul's flannel shirts, and how the upper ones had a way of falling teasingly open on their own.

Unused to him sitting cross-legged, his knees were

complaining, so he uncrossed his legs, lay down on the rock, cushioning his head on his arm, and closed his eyes. Over the crackling fire, he could hear Little Bear and Ursula apparently in conversation. They were talking Cree. Quite suddenly she fell silent, then a man's voice, which sounded far older than hers, spoke to him from very close at hand.

"Three men," it said slowly, almost in his ear, and he felt a hot hand press hard against his heart. "Three men haunt you."

The ground seemed to sway rhythmically beneath him, inducing a momentary nausea, and Harry saw the inside of a railway carriage crowded with men. It was like being in a dream, only the physical details were a hundred times sharper. He could smell wet wool from soldiers' uniforms and the stale sweat off their shirts, and here and there as he moved through the unresisting crowd a sour-sweet gust of tobacco. The youth of the soldiers was astonishing. They were so much younger than the men he had seen waved off at Winter. Some were little more than schoolboys, with down, not bristles, on their jaws. And as they parted for him, he saw, to his amazement, Jack, lovely, handsome, perfect, sitting there in a captain's uniform, with his back to him, talking to Paul. He was sure it was Paul. They were talking happily, laughing.

Overjoyed, Harry plunged forward to meet them. He would sweep Jack into a tight embrace, understanding all, forgiving all as everyone cheered and clapped them on the backs. But just as he reached him, Jack turned and it wasn't Jack at all, and it wasn't Paul with him. Harry was driven forward by crazed momentum so seized the one who was nearly Jack anyway, hugging him tight, planting kisses in his dirty hair, then reaching out to grab the man who was nearly Paul. Which was when the other soldiers stopped being cheery and stared at him in disgusted silence. He tried to stammer out an apology before anyone hit him, but his mouth was full of swollen magic root and disobeyed him.

The train was passing through Unity and he saw himself through the window, slight and timid-looking, being pinned in place outside the shop by Munck. Handsome but really rather sad, Troels had been drinking brandy to overcome the shame of not being with the proper soldiers on the train, or in the parade. And looking from outside, as it were, Harry could understand how, for all his mockery and bullying, Munck saw in Harry things he wanted and could never have: Englishness, certainty of position, education in all the little things whose absence could make a man feel unacceptable. Troels, he now saw, wanted Harry's approval and affection but was not equipped to win them. Drawing closer, he could hear his drunken words.

"I had a fever, a bad one. It weakened my heart. They said I was more use recruiting than fighting; a mock soldier, a *toy*."

There was a gentle pressure on Harry's elbow. He turned away to see Little Bear in real Cree clothes, time-worn and authentic, with feathers on a necklace around his neck like the one Lily Thunder had worn. He lifted Munck's arm off Harry's shoulder, showing neither fear nor hesitation. Then he led Harry along the front of the shop and up an alleyway. At its end he pointed.

The wooden sidewalk ran out and they stepped off it on to a patch of rough ground, such as so often lay behind the buildings in small prairie settlements. All the building energy went into the fronts, into a line of stores and banks and hotels that would convey prosperity and stability to the new arrival, but beyond the facades, which often were just that—high structures like stage flats nailed on at the front of low tin sheds—this was what one found. Grass. Mud. A pile of lumber.

Perhaps wooden stakes optimistically marking the quadrants of a second street not yet built.

"Why?" Harry began, and found that Little Bear was no longer beside him.

The noise of the street had gone with him. The alley had gone. Harry turned back. An ox was lying off to one side, contentedly grazing whatever it could reach without moving. It was dark brown, with a black nose, its coat quite shaggy, suggesting it was shaped by life in a cold climate. Seeing Harry, it rose by lumbering degrees to its feet and tried to take a step toward him. But one of its front legs was wounded, snagged twice around with a piece of barbed wire. Harry felt no fear of it. In his experience, oxen were usually placid; it was cows that one had to approach with caution.

"Hey, boy," he murmured in the low tone he had learned from Jørgensen. "You're in trouble, aren't you?"

It collapsed heavily forward on to its injured leg, smothering the wire as its knees bent, then sank heavily down so that the wire must have been cutting into it in several places. As Harry came closer, he realized the beast had a ring through its nose. He took off his belt, slipped it through the ring as an improvised rope and gently pulled.

"Come on," he said. "Come on, boy. If you stand again, I can help you."

But the ox only pulled back on the belt, shaking its head from side to side and snorting snottily. Then it mooed at him, bellowed almost, only the sound wasn't the full-throated, belly-clenching cry he knew cattle could produce, but wretchedly muted.

He dropped the belt, crouched down close and reached out to touch the poor creature's noble face and run his fingers through the shock of black-brown hair between its massive felty ears.

"Come on, boy. Let me help you. Please," he repeated.

But all it did was moo sadly up at him.

He opened his eyes to see smoke rising from the dying embers that glowed just a couple of feet from his face. The Dvorak bird, or chickadee, or whatever it was called, sang so close at hand he fully expected to find it perching on his knee as he slowly sat up. As the confusion of visions left his head, he heard Petra's voice pointing the birds out to Grace.

"I miss you," she sang on the bird's three melancholy descending notes. "Hear that? I miss you. I miss you."

The sun was low in the sky. Very low. Could they have slept all this time and missed supper? After only a few weeks at Bethel, he was already sufficiently institutionalized by the place to suffer a flare of boarding school panic that he might have broken the rules. He stood, expecting to find Ursula lying on the other side of the fire, but there was no sign of her.

"Ursula?" he tried to call, only his mouth was still numb from the root and he could hardly form the sounds. "Little Bear?"

I miss you, sang the bird. *I miss you.*

She was only a short way back down the path up which they had climbed. At first glance he thought she was standing on a tree stump to see better into the tree above her, because she was suddenly several inches taller than him. Then he saw her turn slightly and realized she was suspended. She had strung herself up by the length of beads he had last seen as he slipped them safely into his coat pocket.

"Ursula!" he shouted and jumped to bear her up. However thick, the wire threading the beads and holding her up could only have been just strong enough to take her weight, for it broke the second he took the strain, and beads tumbled down into his face and all around him.

He lowered her to the ground, gasping. She normally wore the necklace as a double rope, and by using only one loop of this to hang herself, she had caused the second to pull tightly around her throat, where the beads and the crucifix cut so deeply into her skin that many remained stuck there, even now the wire was broken. Frantically he felt for the pulse in her neck, knocking beads free from her skin as he did so and making her bleed in several places.

"Ursula, can you hear me?"

She had stopped breathing. He parted her lips with his fingers and found she still had a chewed root of the plant in there. As he pulled that free, she coughed violently and rolled to one side to retch and sob.

"Why?" he asked her. She said something but he couldn't make it out. He brought his ear close to her mouth. "Why, Ursula?" he asked again.

"I don't want to go to Hell," she whispered.

"But you won't. Why should you? Hell was only made up to frighten us, like the monsters in a children's story."

"I'm a witch and a sodomite," she sighed. "I must burn."

"Don't be silly. Only frightened men say things like that. Jesus never did. Here. You need water."

He fetched her water from the stream in his cupped hands, spilling most of it on the way. She drank eagerly, cupping his hands in hers. Water splashed on to her dress. "More," she whispered. "Please." So he had to make several journeys. He drank himself as well. The root had left his mouth acrid and powder dry. When he brought the last handful to her, he found her scrabbling desperately in the grass in what little light remained.

"What?" he said, letting the handful of water fall. "Your necklace?"

The dinner gong sounded, far, far below in the valley.

"My cross," she said.

Gideon and the others were searching and calling as they arrived back at Bethel. Harry was carrying Ursula over his shoulder in a fireman's lift. She had walked at first, then grown faint. Luckily she was fairly light. It looked more dramatic than it was, but served at first to draw any anger away from Harry.

Gideon led the way to Ursula's cabin, opening the door so Harry could carry her all the way to her bed. She stirred as he laid her down, and looked from him to Gideon in the theatrical glow of Gideon's lamp. Gideon had seen the marks around her neck, Harry knew, but he merely asked if she wanted supper. She shook her head.

He turned gravely to Harry. "I will sit up with her," he said quietly, "but I must eat. And I'll need to get word to a colleague. Please wait here until I can come back with supper on a tray." He looked drawn, as well as peevish, and Harry felt a pang of remorse at having caused such worry.

While Gideon was gone, Harry turned back to the bed, drew Ursula's muddy boots off for her and pulled a blanket up over her. She touched a hand to his in thanks. "I'll fetch the cross for you tomorrow," he told her. "It'll be quite safe overnight, and easy to find with all those spilled beads to mark the spot."

"Thank you," she whispered and coughed again. The weals across her Adam's apple now looked livid and angry, fringed by clotting blood. "Did it help, at least?" she asked.

He nodded, returning the pressure on her hand, unable to put into words the thoughts the strange experience had suggested.

Gideon returned, and Harry was dismissed in such a frosty manner, he was almost surprised not to be sent to bed without any supper. Arriving so late at the meal, he was obliged to sit to one side, at the table where Ursula always put herself. People were courteous enough—Mabel made an aggressive fuss about making sure there were enough vegetables left for him—but there was pointed discretion where he had expected questions, and he received a distinct sense of a collective twitching-away of skirts from an incident best left unacknowledged.

It transpired that Kenneth the Giggler, however irritating, had functioned as a social catalyst. With him gone, they had become like any group of patients, ill assorted, ill indeed. Conversation was desultory, even from Mabel, and all pretense that a kind of house party was in progress evaporated. People left the table without waiting for others to finish, and before long, Harry found himself eating cheese and fruit at one table while Samuel munched mournfully at another, neither of them talking.

Gideon kept watch over Ursula all night. Harry knew this because he hardly slept and twice pulled on his coat over his pajamas to go outside to check. Both times the lamp was still burning and he could make out Gideon's distinctive profile as he read in an armchair in the golden wash of its light.

Sleep claimed him in earnest shortly before dawn, and he was woken by the breakfast gong and obliged to dress in a hurry. He ran over to the house, unshaven and feeling disreputable and grubby. Gideon must have been looking out for him, for he stepped out of his study as Harry came into the hall.

"Could I have a word?" he said.

"Of course." Harry stepped in past him and Gideon shut the door.

He looked more immaculate than ever, not like a man who had kept an all-night vigil. He was, Harry had come to believe, one of those formidable people—pillars of empire—who drew strength and purpose from self-sacrifice.

"Please sit," he said.

Harry sat. "How's Ursula?" he asked.

"Sedated. I've no option but to send him back to Essondale on the morning train. We don't have the facilities to keep him safe."

"But you can't! That's so cruel." Harry jumped up. "You're just punishing her for...And I promised to fetch her crucifix from where it fell."

"Sit down."

Harry sat.

"Fetching the crucifix won't be necessary. He'd not be allowed to keep it with him in any case. All potential weapons are removed on admission."

"Why are you calling her *he*?"

"I allowed him to live as he chose here so as to observe him while I tried to help him, but Essondale has sterner categories, of necessity."

"Must he go back?"

"What else would you suggest?"

Harry was about to suggest that Ursula might come to live beside him at Winter, as a nominal employee, a housekeeper even, but he sensed the idea would be unacceptable.

"You won't have been aware of it, but James, as he was christened, was released into my care under very strict conditions. He attempted to poison the priest in charge of his boarding school. Ordinarily he would have been tried, no question of it, but there was clamorous testimony from the other children that the priest had been regularly abusing his position of trust and...taking advantage of his charges in ways that would have caused a scandal had a court case been widely reported. There were ample grounds for treating James as not of sound mind, not least his recurrent religious mania and persistent compulsive transvestism. It's unfortunate, but I blame myself. I should not have pushed the two of you together so. While you were walking, did he try to feed you plants?"

Harry thought of Ursula's insistence on secrecy. "No," he said. "She only pointed them out to me."

"He was taken from his tribe when he was barely twelve. He'd not remember with any accuracy what little the shamans would have taught him by that age. I believe his version of shamanism is largely a self-aggrandizing fantasy. Your encouraging him to dabble in the teachings of his youth has dangerously broken his equilibrium."

"But I didn't en—"

"You didn't discourage him."

"No," Harry admitted. "I'm sorry. I was too interested."

Gideon let the apology rest in punitive silence.

"Will you be sending me back to Essondale too?" Harry dared ask at last.

"Certainly not. You are not ill, as I've said all along. At the risk of sounding brutal, you're a type I've encountered repeatedly, so you're of little clinical use to my researches here. You are traumatized, as I thought, and I believe you have the remedy in your own hands."

"I don't understand."

"I suggest you leave us today and go home. I'll be escorting James, who should see no more of you, but I'll have the carter come for you. That will get you to the station in plenty of time for the next eastbound train. You may keep the clothes you have been lent."

"That's very kind. I'll have them cleaned and sent back."

"There's really no need. You have no money with you, I take it?"

"None whatever."

Gideon passed him an envelope. "This should cover the cost of your ticket home and whatever sustenance you need en route. Goodbye, Harry. And good luck."

They both rose, and he shook Harry's hand.

Harry turned to go, then felt a sudden access of indignation.

"I think you should let Ursula come home with me to Winter. She has domestic skills, is an able housekeeper and clearly discreet. I could employ her safely and the farm is remote. No one would bother—"

Gideon held up a pale hand to silence him. "That's a ridiculous, unhealthy idea. I was naive to think my utopian experiments here could alter or disprove anything. I shall have no more Indian patients, and Samuel has agreed—with some alacrity, I might add—to take his meals in the kitchen from now on."

He dismissed Harry in the rudest way, by simply walking out of the room and leaving the door open as he went.

Harry ate a late, solitary breakfast. As he was finishing, the others gathered on the terrace to see Gideon and Ursula off. Harry went to the window, where he could peer over Bruno's tweedy shoulder. He saw Ursula shockingly transformed, not into dashing Little Bear with his tasseled jacket, but into a gaunt Essondale inmate. He had on a plain navy-blue drill suit with a collarless shirt, and black canvas shoes without laces, which appeared not to fit him. With what seemed like unnecessary cruelty, someone had cut his hair to collar length so that, instead of cascading down his back, it sprang out irregularly from his face, making him look the very type of lunacy.

Harry half raised a hand in readiness to wave, but the thin boy in the suit did not look up. As Gideon flicked the reins and drove away in the trap, Mabel called out, "Bye, Ursula dear!" and it sounded like mockery.

WINTER

Henry came from England to Moose Jaw, where he worked on a farm. He came in to the homestead in the autumn of 1908...He was secretary of the school, succeeding John Parker, a secretary of the Grain Growers' Local for several years...Has batched it all these years.

Jennie Johnston, on her former neighbor, Henry Cane, *A Glance Back*

"Bachelor" has the technical meaning of a man living by himself or with other men, with no woman in the house. A widower or grass-widower "batches," an unmarried man with a sister or housekeeper does not.

Elizabeth B. Mitchell, *In Western Canada Before The War: Impressions of Early 20th Century Prairie Communities*

Chapter Thirty-Three

Time and again the train passed small farmsteads that had all too obviously been abandoned, either because a homesteader had deserted the attempt to wring a living from the prairie or because the war had claimed him. For several hours of the journey, Harry was accompanied by a man who was some kind of demagogue or would-be politician, full of directionless anger and bewildering facts and figures. After such human losses as it had sustained, he said, Canada's economy would founder without a fresh burst of immigration. The whole glorious experiment could fail, he said, and the prairies go back to the Indian.

He said it as though it were the worst prospect imaginable for the territory.

Harry numbly wondered what he should do. After his nearly ten-month absence, his land and the Slaymakers' would be neglected. The harvest had been brought in before he left, at least, but the fields were all unplowed and unharrowed.

He was terribly concerned about the animals, and cursed the effect of powerful sedatives on his memory. Had he left the horses in livery all this time? If he had, they might have been sold or ridden into the ground. The hens, pig and cow would not have survived the winter, and he knew he must prepare himself for the grim task of dealing with their remains. But just possibly someone had called by when the worst of the epidemic had passed, some kind busybody from the church congregation, or even a friend of Grace.

In one of their soothingly factual mealtime conversations, Bruno had told him all she knew about what the flu had done, decimating households the war had already maimed. Especially damaging was the way it had not carried off the elderly, as flu usually did (Mrs. Wells had called it *spring's undertaker*), but had killed young adults, precisely the people on whom the burden of rebuilding the population rested.

He finally arrived in Winter faint from hunger, as the money Gideon had given him for the fare barely left enough over for a cup of tea. He determined to deal only with the immediate necessities. He needed money, provisions and a horse; he would settle back into the farm, discover the worst, and only then would he lay plans. His savings account, at least, would be intact, quietly accruing some paltry interest. He dreaded dealing with all that. Money was such a cold thing. The war and then the epidemic must have left countless legacies, little and less so, cold benisons falling on the numb and distraught, every bit as cruel as all those love letters overtaken by War Office telegrams.

Winter was never a large enough place to be called bustling, but it was still shocking to emerge from its station on a fine spring afternoon to see men and women going about their business on Main Street. He feared running into anyone he knew, feared their inevitable surprise or well-meant concern, feared the questions. *I have been ill.* He had rehearsed various responses in his head, but decided that was the best, because it was the truest.

He steeled himself going in to withdraw his first cash in months. The clerk was notoriously talkative, but there was a different, much younger one in position. He greeted Harry by name, although Harry didn't remember him, and issued his money with no inquisition other than an ordinary "How are you?" to which Harry answered with a rather tense "I haven't been well, but I'm better now. And you?"

Flu had cut the town's population in two, filleting out many in their twenties and thirties. The store had lost both its young proprietor and his hawkish wife. In their place, their son and daughter, both barely old enough to have left school, were scurrying earnestly around, watched over by their grandparents, who had come out from the east to supervise.

What hadn't changed was the little gaggle of people hanging around the post office counter in hope of "news." The place was surprisingly busy. Most people bought provisions in the morning, which was why, being shy, Harry had always favored doing it in the quiet of the afternoon. As he assembled his little heap at one end of the counter, asking the grandmother for things from the shelves behind her—bread, cheese, eggs, tins of corned beef, a packet of tea and one of coffee—there was a commotion outside. Someone had pulled up in a motor car. Everyone abandoned what they were doing and sped over to the window to look, except, apparently, for the grandmother and Harry.

"Noisy things," she told him. "It's just that flash insurance man. Now a tractor, like Mr. Slaymaker is said to be ordering, that makes sense." And she totted up in her head what Harry owed her.

He had never been terribly good at listening to the chat of strangers in public places, so took a moment or two to digest just what she had said. Something about a tractor...

"Mr. Slaymaker, you said?"

"Yes. Assuming I've got his name right. I'm still learning who everyone is here. The gentleman over there." She pointed with her pencil over Harry's shoulder.

Paul was standing among the cluster of people admiring the

car. Harry had to lean on a shelf of tinned fruit, feeling short of breath. It was definitely him, a little thinner, touches of gray in his beard and sideburns. He was holding a walking stick.

He sensed someone standing there, and turned.

"Harry?" he said. "Is that... is that you under there?"

They could only shake hands, of course, surrounded as they were, but Harry held on as long as he dared. Paul couldn't stop smiling, and Harry worried he must be looking half crazed in his turn.

"I'd given you up for dead," he told him.

"That's *my* line," said Paul. "Where...?"

"In a sanatorium. I've been ill. I've been near Jasper."

"But you're back."

"Yes. I just got in. That's why I look a bit..." He glanced down at his unseasonably warm coat and the ill-assorted borrowed clothes beneath it.

"You always were dapper," Paul teased.

"You're walking with a stick."

"Lurching, more like. I...I lost a foot."

"God!"

"I was lucky. The Huns had good surgeons. Eventually."

"You were a prisoner?"

Paul nodded.

"Why weren't we told?"

"I wrote. I wrote via the Red Cross."

Harry stood just outside the doorway, where there was a cooling breeze. He forgot all about his odd appearance and smelly clothes, and watched Paul post a letter and buy this and that. Seeing him perform such ordinary actions made Harry feel more than ever like a ghostly revenant in his old life. And when Paul returned to his side and muttered, "Drive you home?" he forced himself to sound neutrally polite, as a woman with a baby was standing directly beside them. "Yes please," he said.

The familiar cart was just outside. Paul's cart with the jaunty strip of red paint that Petra had applied when repairing its bench. The horse was new, but Harry could not believe he had walked right past the cart on his way in without noticing it. Paul stowed their purchases and climbed up nimbly enough, good foot first.

"You look like a hobo with that beard on you," he told Harry cheerfully. "People will say the English gent has finally gone native."

Although able to talk unreservedly at last, they were each, for their own reasons, beyond words as they drove out of town and up the familiar road toward their homes. The spring leaves and lush grass had a new-minted intensity to them. The chestnut coat and bouncing white mane of Paul's new horse shone in the sunlight, as though brushed by an attentive groom for just this moment. Paul pulled them to a halt at one point, jumped down, leaving his stick behind, and stooped to pick handfuls of newly opened Black-eyed Susan, the first Harry had seen that year. Climbing back up, he passed them to him, and Harry remembered that the cheerful yellow flower was one of Petra's favorites.

Paul drove to Harry's house first. For a while, Harry just sat there, looking at the place from the cart. The shutters were all fastened. More astonishing still, Kitty and May were grazing in the little paddock beside the stable, hens were clucking around the place and his fields seemed all to have been plowed, if not sown.

"I don't understand," he said. "I've been gone ten months."

"I can't have missed you by more than a week," Paul said quietly. "The earth on the grave was still fresh."

352

PATRICK GALE

Harry climbed down, still holding the flowers, and looked about him.

"The only casualty was the cow," Paul said, "and I reckon that was old age or grief."

He lost his footing for a moment when he climbed down, but Harry steadied him, feeling shy in the face of his unfamiliar disability. "Come," Harry said.

Paul watched as Harry knelt to arrange the flowers in a pickle jar set into the grave's now level, grassy surface. "I was all set to order a headstone for them," Paul told him. "By the time it's ready, the ground will be firm enough, I think. But now you're here..."

"We can choose one together," Harry finished. Standing again, slightly nudging Paul, who stood so close beside him, he looked at the crude wooden cross, pushed askew from a winter deep under snow and turning green now, and felt far removed from the man who had scratched two names on it before pushing it, sobbing, back into the mud.

"I wasn't in my right mind," he said quietly. "It must have been a horrible homecoming for you."

"My brain can't seem to accept it. In war, you see bodies all the time—naked, half flayed, burned, blown apart—to the point where they become meat. The frankness of it is...well, I mean, it means death is unremittingly a fact, ever before you. But this. I think if I'd seen their bodies, I would have accepted it more readily, because I'd have had to. Harry, can you bear to tell me?"

"Of course. Don't be silly."

"Just this once. So I know."

"Petra caught the flu nursing Grace." Instinctively Harry began to walk back to the cart, unsure this was a story he could tell standing at a graveside. "In the morning, her legs gave way when she tried to stand up.

"I nursed her exactly as I had seen her nurse Grace, bathing her with cold water I refreshed every twenty minutes, encouraging her to drink water, too, and catching it in a basin when she brought it back up again. She was formidably strong, and..."

He broke off. Paul had been leaning against the front of the cart, looking up at him, but now he climbed up to join him on the bench. He gently bumped his knee against Harry's. "Don't stop," he said. "Please."

Your speech is air-starved, Browning said again, *like a bird in a box. Breathe!*

Harry breathed, swallowed, breathed again. "She took two days to die," he said. "She really did battle with the fever. Grace lost consciousness hours before her little body gave out. Petra stayed conscious and coughed so hard and savagely. She was always so brave, Paul, but dear God, she was whimpering from the pain of it. When she finally slipped away, it was hard to say..." He stopped.

"Tell me," Paul said. "I need to know, man."

"It was hard to say if she had...drowned in blood or died from an overheated brain. The last bowl of water was scarlet. The bed looked like a murder scene."

Weeping freely as he had not done all winter, daring to hold Paul's hand between their thighs, Harry told him falteringly how he had stripped the mattress, rolled her to one side to get a towel beneath her, then washed her once more from head to toe, seeing her lovely, naked limbs for the first time in their marriage. He explained how he had then dug up Grace's body so as to bury her afresh, wrapped in her mother's arms in the one shroud.

For a while they simply sat on the cart, not speaking, just wiping their eyes, while the horse equably cropped the nearest greenery to hand, and birds called around them. *I miss you. I miss you.*

Petra, Harry saw, Petra and Grace, had, by their presence, made possible a fragile happiness that might now crumble from exposure, under the simple hopelessness of men without women. Petra gave permission and, indeed, a kind of blessing. Without her, what would they become? Two grouchy bachelor neighbors, a prey to every single-minded, organizing widow of the parish.

He must have sighed audibly, because Paul sat up, took the reins again and said, "Don't let's think about all that for now."

They drove on along the track linking the two properties. Harry jumped down at the boundary between the farms to open the gate that he and Petra had set up.

"Might as well leave that tied open," Paul said. "Now you're back..."

It was still broad daylight and there were a hundred tasks to do about the place, but they closed the door behind them and went without a word to Paul's bed. There they lay, fully clothed, boot rubbing boot, nose touching cheek, each seeking no warmer pleasure than the simple knowledge that the other was there, and holding him again.

Acknowledgments

This novel would not have happened without the lively anecdotes, evocative photograph collection and half-filled exercise book of memoirs passed down by my late maternal grandmother, Phyllis Betty Ennion, the little girl Harry left behind. I apologize to her and her daughters for my outrageously fictitious filling-in of blanks, and to the shades of the real life Wellses and Canes, whose dignity this novel has traduced.

Winter is a real place, though now an atmospheric ghost town. I am pleased to say that the acres Harry first plowed over a century ago are still under cultivation.

My heartfelt thanks to my editor, Imogen Taylor, and my agent, Caradoc King, for their invaluable support and expert judgment, and to my trusted readers, Penelope Hoare and Marina Endicott, for their keen honesty and shrewd suggestions.

Thanks to the late Paul Slaymaker and to Jørgen Troels Munk Levring for the use of their names—names loaned in support of the charities Diversity Role Models and The Kaleidoscope Trust respectively.

The research I conducted was partly funded by a grant from the Authors' Foundation and greatly assisted by the hospitable generosity of fellow novelists Marina Endicott and Barbara Gowdy. Along the journey from East to West, I was much helped by Toronto Public Library and the library of Toronto University, Steven Maynard, Neil Richards, Alan Miller, the

Canadian Lesbian and Gay Archives, North Battleford Library, and, unwittingly so, by Mary Luger, whose beautiful ranch near Hinton inspired the entirely fictitious Bethel.

A novel is no place for a scholarly bibliography, but these are just some of the books that inspired me and that might in turn interest this novel's readers:

James Gardiner, *Who's a Pretty Boy, Then? 150 Years of Gay Life in Pictures*

Sean Brady, *Masculinity and Male Homosexuality in Britain 1861–1913*

Matt Cook, *London and the Culture of Homosexuality 1885–1914*

Walter L. Williams, *The Spirit and the Flesh, Sexual Diversity in American Indian Culture*

Joel Braslow, *Mortal Ills and Bodily Cures*

Lesley Erickson, *Westward Bound, Sex, Violence, the Law and the Making of a Settler Society*

Adele Perry, *On the Edge of Empire, Gender, Race and the Making of British Columbia 1849–1871*

Jean Okimāsis, *Cree, Language of the Plains*

Heather Robertson, *Salt of the Earth, the Story of the Homesteaders in Western Canada*

Susan Jackel, ed., *A Flannel Shirt and Liberty, British Emigrant Gentlewomen in the Canadian West 1880–1914*

Reading Group Guide

A PLACE CALLED WINTER

The Inspiration for
A Place Called Winter

Several of my novels have grown out of real life experiences—
Rough Music was born of my turning forty, *The Whole Day
Through*, of watching my mother cope with widowhood and
her increasing loss of mobility—but this is the first of my novels
actively to take a real person as its starting point and take no
steps to disguise him. My mother's grandfather, Harry Cane,
was one of hundreds of young Englishmen who took up the extraordinary opportunity offered in the first decade of the last
century to claim 160 acres of free land in the Canadian prairies
in exchange for fencing it, living on it and bringing it into cultivation. The great homesteading adventure and the effect on it
of the Great War might have been a novel in itself, but what
fascinated me was that Harry left behind a wife and young
daughter in order to pursue it, and did not return to see that
daughter until the early 1950s. Why did he go? Why did he
leave them behind? And why, when he returned, as a prema-
turely old man, was my granny apparently so anxious to send
him back to Canada to die?

In a precious cargo of letters and papers I inherited inside
a chest of drawers, I found a little exercise book in which
my grandmother had begun to write her memoirs and immediately my interest was quickened further. For a start, the
family he and his brother married into was so colorful, not
least because one of his sisters-in-law went on the stage as a

Gaiety Girl. And then his wife was in love with another man, who her older brothers forbade her from marrying. And finally there was the unmistakable air of an issue fudged when my grandmother fleetingly described Harry leaving the country. She implied he was short of money thanks to some bad investments but there seemed to be more to the story than that. There was a cloud of disapproval hanging over him, of that particularly fascinating kind where details are too distasteful to be put into words. Poor Granny was effectively orphaned while still young, as her mother died of breast cancer and—since joining her father in Canada was apparently out of the question—she was raised by a host of uncles and aunts and almost certainly influenced by their views on her parents' sad story...And quite possibly, indeed almost certainly, there were details she was never told.

So what I set out to write was a version of Harry's story which respected the known facts, keeping real names, and houses and dates, but which satisfied my craving for an emotionally satisfactory answer to all the questions the material raised. In the process, inevitably, the novel moved further and further away from reality as I not only projected myself back into Harry's leisure-soft skin but became distracted by things I stumbled on in the course of my research, from all-male dances in lonely settlements to early psychiatric treatments and the linking among First Nation Canadian tribes of alternative sexuality to visionary powers.

A Place Called Winter is a departure for me, being historical and being told entirely from one man's viewpoint but I hope it will also be comfortingly familiar to readers of my other work in its portrayal of the daisy-chain of striking female characters who help Harry along his road to greater understanding. It was startling to be shown the beautiful finished cover which, in some ways, proclaims the book a Western. It is a Western, complete with terrifying villain and a hero forced to rely upon his own resources in a wide open landscape, but it's also a bittersweet, passionate love story and I hope there's enough of either in there to satisfy readers of either genre.

Q & A with Patrick Gale

You haven't written a historical novel for some time. Why did you decide to move away from the contemporary?

It sounds odd but I don't plan what I'm going to write in advance. I didn't decide, "Now for an historical novel!" Rather, I found myself more and more possessed by the material suggested by the fragments of my great-grandfather's story, and it so happened that the only way of telling the story that emerged was to set a novel in the early twentieth century. My approach to storytelling is so myopically focused on the psychology and emotional life of my characters that I was already nearly a third of the way through my first draft before I realized, with a curse, that I was going to have to deal in some way with the vast historical realities of the First World War and the Spanish Flu epidemic! In fact, many of my novels have large sections set in the past, because I have repeatedly been drawn to write about memory and its tricks; it's simply that I've never reached back as far as the Edwardian era before, only to the 1950s or 60s.

Your last three books are all set in Cornwall. Did you find it difficult writing about a country you didn't really know?

It was a huge challenge, and one I'm still not entirely sure I met successfully. (I've yet to come up with a firm identification for the bird I christened the Dvorak Bird on my travels.) Landscape is always important to me as a powerful ingredient in the shaping of character. That's perhaps why my first draft dwelt rather too lovingly on the London-based beginning of Harry's story, as a place I knew well was helping me decide who he was. I had to go out to Canada of course, as I wouldn't have dared write about it entirely from my imagination and Google. I retraced the real-life Harry's journey, with the one exception of using a jet plane where he made sea crossings. I traveled on the same railway lines and slept in log cabins in the landscapes I was writing about. I needed to see the skies he'd have seen, see the same flowers, hear the same bird calls. The one thing I didn't begin to experience was the extraordinary physical hardships he'd have put himself through, and I managed to catch only the very tail end of a prairie winter. Throughout the project my very handy get-out clause as a know-nothing Englishman was to write the story entirely from the perspective of a man as ignorant as myself.

Did you find that the novel being loosely based on a true family story hindered or helped the development of the narrative?

It hindered me at first. I was intimidated by the sheer cheek of what I was doing and by the instinct to tell the truth. But then, the more of my grandmother's letters I read and the more I compared the scant paragraphs of her memoirs with the historical studies I was reading for background, the more it seemed to me that she might have been no more possessed of the full facts than I was. When I set out to Canada the novel was only written as far as the point of Harry's own embarkation at Liverpool docks, and I promised myself that I would honor whatever facts about his Canadian life I managed to unearth. As it happened there were very few facts on offer beyond little glimpses of him in books of reminiscence to which his prairie neighbors had contributed; there was no unexpected second marriage, no trace of even an unofficial second family. So I was able to write a version of the events that can still sit alongside the official one handed down by my grandmother.

You write beautifully about places. Is it important to you to anchor a book in a real location?

Oh, always, even if the location I end by writing about is made up. I find places speak to me and suggest narrative developments all the time. This is possibly contributed to by the way in which my daily walks with our dogs form an intrinsic part of my day when I'm working on a novel. I walk through one landscape with my head still full of another, partly imaginary one, and the two seem to interact on each other usefully. I walked round and round Strawberry Grove, where my grandmother lived with her family as a child, trying to work out the view the Wellses would have enjoyed from their (now demolished) house on the riverside there. I got stung by the ferocious blackflies in Winter while taking (maddeningly indistinct) photographs of the farmland Harry first plowed out of untouched prairie, and I had a major plot revelation or two while staying in a cabin in the grounds of the ranch I would transform in my head into Bethel.

There's quite a sense of isolation in this novel: Harry is displaced, the country he moves to is newly colonized. Is alienation or isolation a key feature for you in your writing?

It's rare for my characters to be as isolated physically as Harry becomes. Repeatedly my subject has been the family, and I tend to write about people overcrowded by relatives rather than cut off from them. But I suppose a certain alienation has been a recurrent theme with me. Characters like Rachel, in *Notes from an Exhibition*, or Barnaby, in *A Perfectly Good Man*, are cut off from their loved ones by their peculiar drives and visions. In order to write novels I find I have to cut myself off and make myself view life a little askew, and I suspect that process may give rise to characters who are similarly cut adrift even within a crowded family or nosy village.

Sexuality is handled subtly and deftly in *A Place Called Winter*. Do you feel that gender and sexuality are central to the make-up of Harry and other characters in the book?

The great challenge in this novel was to write about sexuality while inhabiting the head of a man who realistically would not have had anything like the psycho-sexual vocabulary we take for granted now. He has to experience and feel things which repeatedly he cannot put into words, either because he lacks the words to describe them or because he knows those feelings to be entirely unacceptable, even criminal. At first my concern was all with Harry's own developing "deviant" sexuality but rapidly I realized that this is a man whose emotional education comes as much from the conversation and friendship of women as it does from the bodies of men. Even as his love for Paul is blooming, it is only with Paul's sister that he can even begin to discuss it; the thing is so fragile that, in Paul's company it has to remain instinctual, almost unacknowledged for fear it might otherwise crumble to dust. So then I realized that his story is unfolding at one of the most fascinating periods in the history of women and their self-knowledge, a period during which Western women, at least, move from something like servitude into something like self-determination. I liked the way the challenge of pioneer life highlights this. From what I read, the women who thrived on the Western frontiers at this time were super-women George

Bernard Shaw might have worshipped, not just talking independence, but living it too.

And then, of course, I stumbled on my research into the fascinating parallel world of the native North American two-souls, an inspiring, often tragic, story of the clash between brutally colonizing Christian patriarchy and a sexually ambiguous shamanistic culture. This is a story which goes right to the heart of feminism in much the way the story of early gay liberation is inseparable from the struggles of the Women's Movement.

You structure this book with a current story, framed by flashbacks to other episodes. How difficult was it to create a balance between the two different elements?

The story was always going to be episodic, just as Harry's own was, and I seized quickly on geography as a way of highlighting those episodes, taking Harry further and further west as he becomes more and more in touch with his true self. I always knew it was going to present a journey from scenes that might have come from an E. M. Forster comedy of manners where everything is suppressed, nothing spoken but what is socially acceptable, to somewhere reminiscent of E. Annie Proulx's Dakota wilds, as in *Brokeback Mountain*. The difficulty was that much of the novel moved incredibly slowly, first because Harry was being willfully blinkered and actively avoiding challenge or change, and then because the lives of men on remote farmsteads is necessarily repetitive and fairly uneventful. The first draft still had a bloody, dramatic climax which I knew would pay off for the reader who reached it, but it seemed to take an eternity to get there. The hope was that by taking the Bethel section of the narrative and using that as an episodic framing device to break up the earlier section, I would introduce a sense of threat and mystery that would drive the reader to keep going through all those scenes of fence-building or plowing!

Women are key in your writing. How important do they feel to you in relation to the way you create relationships and understanding between your characters?

I try to be gender-blind in my writing, not to let my maleness color the way I write about either men or women. I try simply to focus on psychology, on what makes people become the people they become or act the way they act. That means I write about women as often as I write about men, and children as often as I write about adults. However, I think there is something in the psychology of my particular sort of writing, something in the act of having to lose myself so completely in order to inhabit the mind of an imagined woman, that energizes me and causes my writing to take fire. Time and again the characters I have the greatest difficulty bringing alive are the male characters whose natures feel closest to my own. Just as often, if I find a narrative is stalling or simply failing to take off for me, the simplest way of invigorating it seems to be to find the female angle on it, to look at the story afresh through a woman's eyes. This may sound weird but actually it's pretty common among female writers; the history of crime writing, in particular, would be nothing without the contributions of women writers who discovered a particular imaginative liberty that came to them when they wrote themselves under the skin of men.

Patrick's great-grandfather
Harry Cane

About the Author

Patrick Gale was born on the Isle of Wight. He spent his infancy at Wandsworth Prison, which his father governed, then grew up in Winchester before going to Oxford University. He now lives on a farm near Land's End. One of the UK's best-loved novelists, his most recent works are *A Perfectly Good Man*, *The Whole Day Through*, and *Notes from an Exhibition*.